The Hunt for Satoshi

Arlo Fox

Old Town Books

Book Cover by Deb Thompson debthompsondesign.com

Contents

Chapter One

Tuesday January 11 2022

Manhattan

Ellen Kelly straightened her neck and felt the vertebrae pop as her phone dropped to the desk. Her fingers ached from sixteen hours of continuous note taking. Outside her fourth-floor window the Chrysler Building pointed a bright shining finger into the January night. Inside there was nothing but an unmade bed, a desk, a chair, her laptop, and clothes she'd left lying on the floor.

Basic, but perfect. Nobody but Hosein knew she was here. Next time someone asked her advice on going into hiding, she'd tell them to do it right in the middle of Manhattan, where you can have pizza ordered to your room anytime at all.

Her stomach gurgled at the thought. Why not celebrate with a jumbo pizza for one? Her work here was done, and she was tired of microwaving tv dinners from the D'Agostino on the corner.

All that remained was to get her colleague over so they could join up the pieces together. She smiled in triumph. Hosein teased her for being a fresh Harvard journalism grad while he had thirty years of battle scars from the trenches, but it was she who'd found the missing link.

A whistleblower from Cheyenne, Wyoming, where a local skirmish in the national battle over regulating the crypto industry was being fought. Wyoming felt a world away, yet this connection brought it all home. Hosein had already linked election fraud in Atlanta and Salt Lake City: a third example made it a provable conspiracy.

Big money fixed elections in the dark. They were going to turn on the light.

She stood up and did some stretches while she waited for food. Two weeks spent in this room, zero contact with her colleagues in the newsroom. No exercise, no friends. No contact with Hannah, even though they'd only been dating six months and there was no reason to assume Hannah would hang around. Two missed routine calls to Dad, who would definitely have noticed. The only conversation for a fortnight was with sources, and Hosein.

Two weeks fuelled by the lurking paranoia that they might not get to the bottom of the story after all, and she'd just be another frustrated journo who wanted to break a big story but couldn't get it past the fact checkers.

It *had* all been worth it. They had their story, and it would set the internet alight. This time justice would frustrate big money. It didn't happen often.

Her thoughts slid into other channels. The Beyonce tickets she'd scored for Hannah. If that didn't make her stay they were doomed anyway. Her sister, who hadn't been kind when she said she wouldn't be able to come to her nephew's fourth birthday party with no excuse better than "work". This could be her victory lap. Ellen would turn up in Summit, New Jersey with the biggest battery-operated dinosaur toy FAO Schwarz would sell her. All hail the conquering hero. Ellen grinned through the exhaustion. No greater praise-hog than an aunt and journo who hasn't had a win in a while.

The intercom buzzed.

"Pizza."

She hadn't had time or inclination to butter up the doorman, and he repaid her with monosyllables.

"Send him up."

What would Hosein think? Absolute discretion, he'd argued for, but then he was an extremist. Speak to no-one - that's what he'd say. It was hard to know who he hated more, the government of his home country, or sloppy work habits amongst collaborators.

She'd hadn't let anyone up to the door since moving in here. One time couldn't hurt. If residents at Dumont Plaza couldn't have take-out delivered to their rooms, most of them would starve.

Two confident raps on the door.

"Delivery for room 42."

The voice was pure South, a rarity in the most diverse city in the United States. Ellen opened the door to see a man with bright blue eyes in an NYU hoodie holding a pizza box in both hands. His smile was so wide his cheekbones pointed like icebergs. Oh no! With the excitement and the exhaustion she'd forgotten the basics. Tipping.

"I'm sorry," she said. "I don't have cash on me."

"No problem, ma'am," he said, the soul of politeness. "You can leave a good review instead if you enjoy your dinner."

"You're sweet," she said, reaching for the box. "Where's that accent from...Louisiana?"

"Not bad," he said. "I'm from Arkansas."

"Oh yeah?" she said. "I was once in Little Rock for a week, covering a story."

"You're a journalist? I did not know they made them so pretty."

Ellen stiffened.

"I'm sorry, Ma'am," he said, "Didn't mean to be too personal."

"Don't worry about it," she said, annoyed. When your only interpersonal contact of the day is with the pizza delivery guy, it's a shame for it to be spoiled.

"One moment, Ma'am, it might spill," he said, reaching forward.

"What do you mean?" she asked, looking down at the pizza to see if there was a problem.

With a smooth, rapid motion he swung his right hand and slammed a syringe into her forearm, taking back the pizza box with his left. Ellen's eyes were already closing as she fell.

He stepped forward to catch her, stepping into the apartment, dropped the body, and kicked the door shut with his heel. The target lay at his feet, still breathing, but slowly, little bubbles of saliva appearing at the corners of her mouth. He stepped over her head, placed the pizza box on the floor, put a gloved hand under each armpit, and dragged her into the bathroom.

Her head bashed against the toilet bowl with a dull thud. Ellen's eyelids fluttered and she sounded like she needed to be sick. That was a positive sign. She might choke before her heart stopped.

He looked at himself in the mirror and did his selfie smile. He looked good.

He took the pizza to the desk and looked at the open laptop. The victim hadn't locked it, which would save time. The open document was full of names and numbers. His boss would recognise them all.

He took out his phone and pressed call.

"Job done."

He received brief instructions, and no thanks. No matter - he knew he'd done good. Now he was hungry.

He opened the pizza box and frowned. Why do women like pineapple on their pizzas? He could only eat as much as she would have. She was skinny. He swallowed a solitary slice, left the open pizza box on the desk, unplugged the laptop, and slipped it inside his coat.

Would anyone check for a missing laptop? No way. Single woman in anonymous apartment dies of fentanyl overdose - the cops would forget the case before the body was bagged up.

Check the bathroom. She'd already stopped breathing. Knew it.

He zipped up his hoodie, pulled down the top and let himself out. He checked the timer he'd set before knocking on the door: the whole thing had taken less than two minutes. Excellent.

Next stop: Chicago.

Chapter Two

Chicago

"Hey, stranger," said Millie, opening the apartment door.

"Daddy!" screamed Celia, running through her mom's legs and straight into him.

"Hello, ladies," said Rostam, scooping up his three-year-old in one arm while passing a brown bag to her mother. "Thursday night wiener delivery."

He picked Celia up in both hands and they rubbed noses.

"Daddy cold nose," she complained.

"You try buying hotdogs in Chicago this time of year," he said.

"You'd think she hadn't seen you in weeks," said Millie, smiling at the two of them, "and it's only ten hours since you dropped her at childcare."

Rostam leaned in and kissed Millie on the cheek. The warm fragrance of Chanel perfume and an apple shampoo enveloped him, just as it had when they lived under the same roof.

"The dog in the green wrapper is the veggie one," he said.

Celia was squirming too hard to keep hold. Rostam set her down and she ran back to the living room to throw herself in front of *Cocomelon*.

"She watches that at my place too," he said to Millie, following her to the breakfast bar kitchen while she put two hot-dogs on plates, and chopped up the half-size one for Celia.

"Drives me crazy," said Millie, "but can't get her to switch."

"I like it," he said. "Very Zen. I can tune out to the songs."

"Why doesn't that surprise me?" she said. "Pepsi Max in the icebox. And for Celia – oh, thanks."

Rostam was already filling a plastic cup with milk.

They carried trays into the living room and sat on cavernous, leather armchairs behind where their daughter lay happily on the carpet.

"How's work?" said Rostam, wiping off a smear of mustard from the corner of his mouth.

Millie hadn't taken her first bite yet. She was the only person Rostam had ever seen eat a hot dog with a knife and fork.

"I don't wanna jinx anything," she said, "but things are going well."

"Whoop whoop!" said Rostam. "You weren't happy when you first went back."

"Three months of maternity leave. Not enough time to wean a baby, but plenty for clients to start to forget you," she said. "All sorted now. My numbers are good. You remember Carmen?"

"How could I forget?" groaned Rostam.

"You know she's a bad enemy to have."

"I do."

"Just as good as an ally. She's got me in the mix for managing director next year."

Rostam swallowed his mouthful of hotdog. "Wow. You were talking about that way back on the training programme. If Carmen's behind you, it's a done deal."

Millie looked up from her plate, lips pursed, with an almost imperceptible shake of the head. Rostam knew that meant she was thinking about all the things that could go wrong.

"It looks good now, but things can always change."

Rostam knew better than to try to big up Millie to herself.

"Something funny," she continued. "They might put me in charge of crypto sales."

"You are kidding," he said. "You didn't put any of your Bitcoin-scepticism in writing?"

"Don't be smug," she said. "Things change, one of my accounts has become the biggest NFT player at the firm, and they want someone on our floor to be the champion for it. If it's going to be someone, why not me?"

"No better person," he said. "You know if there's anything I can do to help."

"No-one knows this space better than you.," she said.

"My lead won't last long. In a couple of years, they'll be teaching it at grad school."

Without looking behind her, Celia was doing a backwards bum shuffle towards him. Rostam used it as an excuse to wolf down the rest of his hot dog, pick up his daughter, and swing her onto his lap. He raised his eyebrows at Millie.

"Bitcoin expert, hot dog supplier, living, breathing cushion. Just call me the Swiss Army Ex."

It sounded smoother than he expected. Hope leaped in his chest. Might this be the night Millie would let him stay over?

The wrinkle on her forehead just above the bridge of her nose told him no.

"When are you going to junk the podcast and come back to work, Rostam?"

"You sound like Mom," he said.

"If you don't want your ex-wife and your Mom to scold you, you shouldn't do stupid shit," said Millie.

"Mommy!" said Celia, without looking away from the TV.

"Sorry, darling," said Millie.

"She never lets us get away with anything," said Rostam.

"Don't I know it," said Millie.

A moment passed, enough of one to remind them all how comfortable life can be, sitting together as a family, in front of the television.

"Audience numbers are up," said Rostam. "We're onto a conspiracy story which has legs. I can tell because the volume of unhinged incoming complaints is sky high. And bitcoin prices help, obviously. We're starting to make advertising dollars."

"Uh-huh," said Millie, sounding unconvinced.

"And that's not all the good news. James Hanratty called."

Milly wrinkled her nose. "The tech banker? Thought he'd quit."

"Gone solo. He's representing a West Coast venture capital firm looking to build an audio stable." He kept his voice calm. "The boss is in town and wants to meet."

"Anyone I know?" asked Millie, straightening in her chair.

"You know how secretive these guys can be," said Rostam. "Tomorrow afternoon. He's gonna send me details just before."

Millie slumped back into her chair with such force the sound of air leaving the leather cushions could be made out over the TV.

"Castles in the sky. FFS Rostam."

"Hey," he said, roused. "It's not as crazy as it sounds. People like to keep anonymous in the crypto space. Maybe it comes to nothing, but things are happening. I can feel it."

"You have a poor sense of probability for a math PhD," said Millie.

"And you have a stunning lack of optimism for a salesperson," he said.

Celia wriggled in his lap and Rostam shut his mouth. When would he learn? Everything with Millie was getting better, so long as he didn't waste time trying to persuade her he was better served running his own show than working in legacy finance. He'd be right when he'd been proved right.

"Just because you made money early in Bitcoin doesn't mean people will pay to hear you talk about it," said Millie.

"Do I ever say I told you so?" he asked. "All that time I was talking about the future of crypto, and nobody at Loeb was interested."

"To be fair," said Millie, "you never do."

"So cut me a break. At least until I find out about this investor."

Millie reached forward and put her hand on the back of his where it was clasped around Celia's tummy.

"You'll make it work, Rostam, one way or the other. I believe in you."

She smiled at him and he smiled back. It was progress of a sort, but didn't look like this would be the night they'd be reunited as a family. Maybe soon.

Chapter Three

La Jolla, San Diego

Theo McNamara opened his silver cigarette case and offered it to his guests, first the man, who showed his palm in polite refusal, and then the woman. She looked at her colleague and took one.

"I shouldn't really. It's been years."

She leaned forward to accept the flame from his solid gold Zippo, black hair shimmering with the waterfall elegance of an expensive haircut. Theo had an eye for differences. Few Columbia academics would choose that kind of personal styling, even if they could afford it after making rent. The fundraising staff knew it paid to stretch a little further.

He took a drag on his own cigarette and waited for the other side to speak. It was fun to make people work.

"This is a wonderful space," said the man, bald headed, eager, and so athletic he looked half-starved. He gestured to the view over the Pacific Ocean. "Do you entertain here?"

"I don't get many guests," said Theo. "But I have the same view from my office. We could go for a walk on the beach."

"I wish we could," said the woman, who'd been taking shallow drags on her cigarette, visibly trying not to cough. "This is heaven. When we get off the plane back East, we'll be dreaming of it."

"And we have to leave in five for our plane," said the man.

Theo smiled inwardly. Fancy them putting time pressure on themselves when they hadn't yet had the courage to ask for what they wanted.

"Mr McNamara," said the man, "or can I call you Theo?"

Theo looked at him.

"We know it's hard to make this kind of commitment, and we want you to know the President of the University would be happy to come out to discuss any extra details or questions you might have before making a decision."

The woman stubbed out her half-smoked cigarette and leaned in.

"We believe in honouring our major donors and what you have generously suggested is major. Isn't it, Donald?"

"It sure is," said Donald, seamlessly.

Theo wondered if they had practised this schtick.

"Would you maybe like to put your name on a fellowship?"

Theo smiled. "I'm happy to stay anonymous. The people that matter know where the money is coming from."

"Could we ask you," said Donald, looking at his colleague again, "just to confirm what we're talking about, so we know what to say to the President when we get back."

Enough was enough.

"Seventy-five million dollars for the computer science department. That's it."

Theo enjoyed the vicarious excitement in the room for a moment, and then was already bored.

"That really is very generous, Mr McNamara," said the woman. Julie? It didn't matter. "You're sure you don't want to have a building named?"

"No strings required," said Theo, looking at his watch. "Of course, I'll want input on the person chosen to run the department."

"Professor Skilles is a world renowned - ," began Donald.

"She's a good teacher, no question," said Theo. "Maybe the new boss will keep her on. It's up to him."

Theo stood up. "Have you organised transportation to the airport?"

The pair were only too keen to make their escape. This would make them heroes on their return home, Theo knew, to everyone apart from Professor Skilles and her team, who'd soon figure out they'd have to find somewhere else to teach.

His phone buzzed in his pocket. Without excusing himself, he walked into the next room, listened, and gave instructions.

In the antechamber Donald and Julie were caught between not wanting to miss their plane and the desire to make him sign something. Let them stew.

"I have business to attend to," he said. "Safe travels."

According to his doctor, Theo was supposed to take the stairs, but he indulged himself taking the glass walled elevator to his first-floor office. In truth, he only loved the view when he was on his own. The sun was falling towards the Pacific horizon. Two dots were fleeing the ocean. He had to squint to make them out.

Brown-billed pelicans?

The monitor on his desk flashed and dragged his attention back. Theo swore under his breath, lit another cigarette, and answered the call.

"I've been chasing you for hours," said the voice at the other end.

Theo left a pause. Cantillon was so used to being the boss, he had to be reminded of his place.

Cantillon's voice grew softer.

"I need to know, Theo - is this issue dealt with?"

"You can stay calm," said Theo. He took a long drag and enjoyed the silent anxiety at the other end of the line. "I just got the call. The Times will have nothing to print."

Cantillon exhaled loudly. "That's great. That's flipping great news. How did you do it? No. I don't need to know."

No, you don't, thought Theo, *but that doesn't mean you aren't involved.*

"Four weeks to go before the new SEC head is named. Do we have anything more to worry about?"

Theo considered telling Cantillon to stop causing trouble and just be a good boy. He checked himself. Cantillon and Loeb were a key part of the plan.

"There are three problems left," he said. "The story we stopped has a joint author. He won't be able to do anything now, but we can't leave him free indefinitely. There's a pair of podcast bros making a stink. And I've spoken to Tehran - Zadi has gone rogue."

Theo could sense Cantillon's agitation rising.

"I hate dealing with Iranians," said Cantillon. "What can we do?"

The birds were closer and more distinct. He'd been correct. Brown billed pelicans.

"I've got a plan," said Theo. "Take care of both problems at once. Leave it with me."

"Anything you need, just say," said Cantillon. "Once we get the appointment through, the sky's the limit."

"I know," said Theo, and cut the line.

He watched the pelicans approach while organizing events into sequence in his mind. It didn't do to be careless.

One pelican divebombed into the ocean, resurfaced, throwing its beak upwards while it swallowed. The other kept searching the waves, a reminder there were no time-outs on the ocean.

Trust the process, thought Theo. *Keep playing the game.*

He took out his cell and dialled back the last called number.

'Carl, you on your way to Chicago? Change of plan. Watching brief only. Make sure you know where Rostam James is. Don't let him see you. I'm coming over to handle it personally."

Theo could picture the frustration at the other end of the line. Men of action hate being told to wait.

"Don't worry," he said, "if things play out right, you'll get to finish the job in London."

He ended the call, stubbed out the cigarette, and sat back in his chair to review his notes. The sun set unnoticed on the pelicans while he examined his plan for flaws, like a jeweller analysing a gemstone he hoped to negotiate down on price. He'd got a long way following his own simple rules. *Find out your own weaknesses before your enemies do it for you.*

By the time he went to bed, Theo knew he'd thought it all through.

Chapter Four

Thursday January 13

Chicago

Rostam stood waiting for the green light to cross N Halstead. On the far side a homeless woman struggled up the frozen sidewalk. She could be any age over fifty, scaly grey hair piled on top of her head, like a pineapple made of dirty snow. She wore a purple sleeping bag as a cape.

As Rostam arrived on the far side, the entrance to Dick's an arm's reach away, a hunk of ice fell from the top of a building and smacked the homeless woman's shoulder with a dull, wet, threatening flump. She didn't make a sound, just brushed the freezing flak off with her mittened hand.

Some people get no luck, thought Rostam.

Two early drinkers barrelled out of the bar and passed her by on either side, their conversation unbroken. Rostam fished a twenty buck note out of his jeans pocket and offered it to her. Her gaze fixed first on the note, then travelled up his arm until she was staring directly at him. Her eyes were a watery blue, the colour leached away by loneliness and neglect.

"What's that for?" she asked.

"Coffee. A sandwich. Movie ticket. Whatever you like," he said.

"I didn't ask you for money."

Rostam was embarrassed, cold and in a hurry.

"I never said you did. I didn't mean to offend you. If you don't want it, I'll leave you alone." She kept looking at him. "Don't let my bad manners come between you and a hot drink."

She broke into a smile. The gaps between her teeth left her halfway between urchin and crone.

"I'll do you a favour and take it. Thank you, young man."

"Thanks for calling me young," said Rostam, with a warm sense of relief the interaction had turned out well. He pushed his way past a sticky, wooden door with heavy bars across the peephole window, and into the bar.

The room was half-full even though it was lunchtime, and the only food sold in Dick's was a pickled egg for 70 cents. The man he came to see sat at the far end of the bar with a metal bucket and an ashtray in front of him. It wasn't clear if he was staring at the bucket, or his own reflection in the filthy mirror behind the bar.

"Dread," said Rostam. "I can't believe I have to come here to see you." He settled into the empty seat and raised a finger for the barman. "Coffee. Black."

The barman was a museum piece almost as old as the bar itself: abrasive, slow and discourteous.

"That guy," complained Rostam. "How many times have I met you here? He doesn't recognise me yet."

"They hate tourists. You want recognition? Put in the hours."

Dread raised his beer bottle an inch from the bar top to salute Rostam in the mirror. Rostam nodded in return. It suited Dread to choose to look at his friends through a medium, even if it was only a dirty glass. Dread was heavy-set, white-skinned, and always wore a Grateful Dead tee-shirt as his first layer, whatever the weather.

"Been here all day?"

"Calm the cats, dude. I have standards. I wouldn't normally be down here until the middle of the PM. As it is, I found another connection between those appointments we fingered. Atlanta. Salt Lake City. Cheyenne. And guess what?"

Rostam took a sip of his coffee and waited.

"The winning candidates are all backed by the same SuperPAC."

Rostam nodded, excited despite himself.

"They're gonna have to go big on the regulator appointment in February. They fix the SEC, they've got the whole ballgame. I'll be watching."

"Hard evidence for the show?"

Dread grunted. Took a slug of Tecate from the bottle.

"Not yet, but I'll find it."

Rostam checked the time. Quarter of an hour left.

"I've been working this morning too. Listeners went over 200 thou for the last episode. Incoming is split - half on my crypto stuff, half on your conspirasphere."

Dread wasn't impressed. "Conspirasphere? Get out of it. This is the truth, buddy."

A smiling, high cheek boned tourist walked in and sat at the end of the bar, calling out a friendly general greeting in a strong Southern accent. Rostam was amused when the barman deliberately turned away from him to dry glasses.

"Remember I got a DM from an old Loeb contact last week?"

Dread shook his head slowly.

"You don't?" asked Rostam.

"I remember. I'm just saying now what I said then. Don't do it."

"What's the harm in hearing what he has to say?"

"We're only getting anywhere 'cos we're independent and call things as we see 'em. You want to work for the man, go back to Millie and Loeb."

Rostam looked at him, shocked.

"You're halfway right. Of course I want Millie back. She wants to see if this can pay. Not because she wants the money - she's making enough. She doesn't want Celia growing up with a chancer for a Dad."

"You ain't no chancer. What you are is confused. Nothing good is coming your way from the West Coast, man. Anyway, what you asking me for?"

"You're my brother from another mother, eccentricities notwithstanding. Doing you the courtesy of talking to you."

Dread turned slowly to his left until he was looking Rostam straight in the eye. His green eyes had the youthful glow of a man with a dream still alive, which offset yellow, irregular teeth, a patchy grey goatee and deepening fissures that spread from his eye sockets down into his cheeks.

"Say that again, Podcast King. Music to my ears."

Rostam chuckled. "Forget it. Now you know. They're picking me up in five. When I've heard what they have to say I'll call you."

Dread took a long pull from the Winston until it was almost at the filter, shook a fresh one out of the soft pack before him, and lit the new from the old. Rostam coughed.

"One day I'll talk you into quitting," he said, looking around the bar. The daytime crowd was older and male. The black man near the door was a permanent fixture, in a Guns n Roses black top-hat and horn-rimmed spectacles, smoking machine-rolled cigars. He was laughing at something the newcomer had said. Working joes and college kids wouldn't turn up until gone five. Most drinkers were on their own with cigarettes and beer for company. Two were on their phones, others had newspapers, and there was one old boy huddled over a massive paperback in the corner. *War and Peace,* Norton edition. It reminded Rostam not to take anything for granted.

"You got a shot? With Millie, I mean," growled Dread, once again facing his own reflection.

"I think so. It came as a shock to her, me walking out on legacy finance, but I really had no choice. Celia splits her time between us, happy as a clam. I don't think Millie lost her love for me, you know. She just forgot that she liked me for a while."

"She's a good woman, and I don't say that lightly," said Dread. "You wanna win her back, you got my blessing. Just don't sell our souls to the man while you're about it."

Rostam's phone buzzed on the counter with a no-caller ID SMS.

CAR OUTSIDE. JUMP IN AND I'LL SEE YOU IN FIFTEEN.

The warm feeling that came from discussing Millie and Celia gave way to excitement. Another look at the sullen set of Dread's profile turned that to anxiety. What could it hurt to hear what this West Coast guy had to say? Rostam finished his coffee, zipped up his coat, and headed out of the door.

Chapter Five

The shock of minus fifteen degree outside air still had the power to make Rostam gasp, even after five winters in the city. Industrial grade pebbles of salt spiked through his sneaker soles.

A matte black Toyota electric SUV was idling outside the saloon door. Hazard lights flashing, blacked out windows. Rostam looked up and down the street and rapped the passenger door window twice. His phone buzzed in his back pocket.

The message read *GET IN.*

Rostam opened the passenger door. There was nobody in the driver's seat. He peered into the back to make sure there was nobody hiding there. A man's voice spoke over the info system. It had a comforting, commanding tone, the generic sound of the voice that counted down satellite launches.

"Welcome, Rostam. Make yourself comfortable. You can sit front or back."

Static jammed Rostam's lower jaw. This didn't feel normal. It didn't feel safe. He slammed the door shut and stared at his own reflection in the black glass of the window, his breath turning cloudy in short bursts, showing his agitation. His phone buzzed again. This time he recognised the number.

SORRY I CAN'T BE THERE, ROSTAM. THE CAR WILL BRING YOU TO US. ENJOY THE RIDE. JAMES HANRATTY

The car must have cameras on him right now. How would he look - scared, cowardly, prudent? There's no reason to fear an autonomous car.

Rostam thought of Dread in the bar behind him. He couldn't walk back in there and say he'd decided against taking the meeting after all. He had his cell. Any problems and help was just a text away.

"Where is this meeting?" he demanded, as he clambered off the curb and onto the stitched leather backseat, denim jeans squeaking as he slid across to sit behind where the driver should have been.

"Thank you for joining us, Rostam."

The indicator switched sides and the car pulled away.

"Local law says you should wear a seatbelt in the back," continued the car, "but nobody can see through the glass. Please feel free to make up your own mind."

"Thanks very much," said Rostam, amused despite himself. "Any other life hacks for me?"

"I'm just a language learning model," said the car, "and I don't know you well enough yet to make suggestions."

"You're very modest for a clever machine," said Rostam. "Who programmed you?"

"So many coders were involved I can't name them all. It would be worse than Gwyneth Paltrow at the Oscars."

Rostam chuckled.

"Glad they gave you a sense of humour. Heading north?"

The car didn't respond. They were held at a red light. The windows, opaque from the outside, were super-normally clear from within. An antiquated station wagon pulled up to the left. Two kids who looked as though they might be unidentical twins in the back seat, one happily plugged into a tablet, the other crying and lurching forward. Mom was waving an open packet of chips behind her, while she kept her eye on the traffic light.

Normal life.

Millie and Celia were only a couple of miles away. He should be in a car with them, pacifying a harmlessly upset child with salty snacks. Instead, he was in the back of a driverless car, giggling at the jokes of a robot.

"What's your name?" he asked. "Don't give me some bull about calling you whatever I like."

"Thomas."

"Thanks, Tom. Are we heading to the Zoo?"

"I can take you to the Zoo after your meeting if you like. Stopping at Lake Shore Drive first."

Rostam rolled his shoulders.

"This feels weird."

"There are headphones in the seat rest. Put them on and things will feel more normal."

Rostam flipped the bird at the rear-view mirror.

Silence. Rostam began to feel he had been rude, which was ridiculous. The car was programmed to entertain him. He should be scared, being carried away by a strange car, but he felt fine. The car spoke again.

"Don't worry about hurting my feelings. If it is easier to vocalize than make gestures, please speak up."

"Get lost, Tom. Hate speech doesn't work when the other side gives you permission."

"Sorry."

"Oh my God!" Rostam smiled despite himself. "This is going to be hard work."

Traffic was now clear and they were heading uptown, Lake Michigan disappearing into the horizon to their right. Rostam took out his cell. No signal.

"Are you blocking my phone?"

"Security protocol. The car does it automatically."

"Turn it back on."

"I could, Rostam, but then what are you going to do, check last night's basketball scores? Enjoy the view."

"Is this James Hanratty's doing?"

"We want you to concentrate. Free your mind of the internet for a moment. Relax."

Rostam sat back and tried not to be angry. If finance hadn't come calling, he'd have his PhD in machine learning from Imperial by now. He didn't need to be told to clear his mind. What kind of surveillance would he be under at this minute? Video for sure. It wouldn't be hard to track his body temperature and heartbeat. No way for the car to read his mind, yet.

There were no moving boats on the Lake, just a handful of skiffs huddled together by a jetty, masts denuded of sails like fingers pointing at the blue iron sky, making everything feel colder. Rostam checked his Timex Ironman watch. 14:32. Chicago was busy at work.

"You taking me to Wisconsin?"

"We wouldn't do that to you, Rostam."

"Was that another joke?"

"If you like."

Indicators came on, signalling a right turn, and the car came off at an unsigned ramp, pulling up next to a boarded-up coffee and donut kiosk. Amongst the scattered assembly of benches and trash cans was a solitary man with a cigarette sticking out of his mouth, two steaming mugs of coffee before him. The car pulled into a parking spot looking out over the Lake. There was space for a dozen cars, every one empty. The doors clicked.

"I'm free to get out, huh?"

There was no reply.

"Now you give me the silent treatment."

Rostam kept his tone light but was angry. The AI must be programmed to keep passengers guessing: threat, joke, no reception, unlocked doors. *Don't get fooled into an emotional response.* But it was too late: he was relieved to be free. Rostam opened the door and stepped into the bitter Lakeside cold.

"Welcome, Rostam. I got you covered."

The smoking man was shouting, holding a purple cloth above his head. Rostam walked over and took it. It was too cold to play cute, and pulling on the snood was a release, escaping into the comfort of body warmth. Rostam was filled with instant, unwelcome gratitude. Was he being played? He looked around. No pedestrians to be seen. There was nobody to help him, but then he didn't know if he needed help.

"Is James Hanratty here?"

"James is in London. Just you and me. I want us to have the chance to get to know one another."

"Cute set up," said Rostam. "I'd expect you West Coast guys to prefer meeting inside. I don't even know the name of your firm. Why are we freezing by the Lake?"

The man laughed, as though this was a punchline. He was old, the corrugated skin of a dedicated smoker pulled tight over proud cheekbones, thick grey hair clipped a regulation inch from his scalp, deep suntan, and contrasting perfect white teeth.

"I believe in privacy," he said, "like you. There's nobody to spy on us out here." He raised his coffee cup to salute the Lake. "My name is Theo. Theo McNamara. I'm a big fan of the show. We all are."

"Who's we?"

"A collection of well-connected patriots and business associates. Smoke?"

Theo tapped a cigarette on his silver case and offered it. Rostam shook his head, zipped up, and thrust his hands deep into the hip pockets of his parka.

"What is it you like about the show?"

"We think the same way. Kill off legacy finance, set the world free with crypto."

Rostam took a sip of his coffee.

"How do you know we think the same?"

"We know a lot about you, Rostam. Math whiz. Iranian Mom. Left a glittering career in financial pattern recognition to do podcasts. Bitcoin single-digit millionaire. Loving father to Celia. Amicable ex-husband to Millie, even if she doesn't forgive you for quitting banking."

Rostam looked closely at the old man. His eyes were steel-blue and lent humour by a grin which showed the old man felt he held all the cards. If he was, as Hanratty claimed, a big venture capitalist, he probably did.

"You got my attention," said Rostam. "It's always good to meet a fan of the show. My understanding is you have a proposal for me."

"Sure. Sit down and we'll talk."

Rostam looked around. Nobody else was walking by the Lake. The sound of cars passing behind them on Lake Shore Drive blended with honking geese flying in a V overhead.

The old man sat down on a bench on the lake side of the green plastic table, attached to the floor by steel bolts. Perfect posture, looking straight before him. Rostam shrugged and swung his legs across the bench opposite.

"What are you looking for in life, Rostam?"

Rostam looked hard at the man across from him while the question revolved in his mind. The way it was asked said Theo was a man used to fixing other people's problems. Loeb wouldn't recommend someone who didn't have the financial firepower to do what he said. When he and Millie first met, they'd talked constantly of their hopes and dreams. Now was his chance to achieve them.

"I know two things for sure," said Rostam. "The legacy banking system has been screwing over the poor since before Jesus went to town on the moneylenders' tables. And big money keeps shifting the odds in its own favour. I want the show to help people understand this stuff."

"That's why you cashed in your chips at the bank and went solo?"

Rostam took time to think. This man knew a lot about him - but so what? Nothing wrong with proper due diligence.

"Call me a fool, but that's the truth. Two years into making the show listeners keep coming. I want to get it into other languages and out to the biggest audience we can find, without selling out to the big studios. Can you help?"

"We can help each other," said Theo. "We have a lot in common."

"Such as?" asked Rostam.

"When we came up the idea of crypto, it was about building a global community free from the tyranny of government oversight. Electronic communication has failed. It's the biggest tool the security services have ever had. We own too much bitcoin to let that happen again. That's why we're looking for a champion outside our organisation."

"People are catching on."

"Not as fast as we need to escape government control. The war has already started."

Theo's smile had vanished. Rostam wanted to get it back to talking about money.

"Look, Theo. I'm enjoying this conversation, but what is your proposal?

Theo nodded.

"Ok. Let's walk while we talk, shall we?"

The old man carefully unwrapped himself from the bench, the tails from his no-logo quilted black coat flapping behind him. Theo turned away from the car and led the way down to a chalk pathway carved alongside the lake, with a cycle path marked to keep pedestrians safe. His movements and voice seemed younger than his face.

"Turn around and look back at the city," said Theo. "What do you see?"

The sky was full of clouds heavy with moisture, trying to decide if they would drop rain or snow, but there was enough light to take in the Chicago skyline. Out of habit, Rostam clocked the Loeb tower where Millie would be at work.

"I see a great city."

"I see a lot of people working to put money in the pocket of the US Government. I know you like your history - I heard it on the podcast - but did you know this? It wasn't taxation without representation that caused the War of Independence. It was when the British Parliament passed the Currency Act of 1764. The moment the King decided he wouldn't let Americans have our own currency it was game over for the Old Empire."

Theo turned around and resumed the walk away from the car. A scattering of snow fell around them, and Rostam pulled the borrowed snood tight.

"You brought me here for a history lesson?" he said.

"It isn't the British we have to worry about this time," said Theo. "It's the US Government. There is a global conspiracy, and the folks in Washington aren't up to fighting it. Don't tell me you think they are."

Rostam snorted. "The Fed is clueless about crypto, sure. Beyond that what's your point?"

"Wake up, Rostam. When did crypto start?"

Rostam thought for a second. "Halloween, 2008. Satoshi's white paper."

"Crypto is building an alternative system to the dollar. And the dollar is this country's biggest weapon."

"Obama weaponized the dollar against Iran."

"Try not to take it personally, but yes, he did. We've got to stop governments using the financial system as a tool of oppression. Look at the Chinese."

"You don't know what you're talking about. The Chinese banned the use of bitcoin."

"They may not allow its use at home, but half the world's bitcoin are manufactured in China. Bitcoin's like fentanyl - they manufacture it in China to export to the USA and weaken us from the inside. North Korea does the same."

"What can we do about it?"

"You keep proselytizing on your show, we'll keep governments from interfering. We're going to make a big star out of you, Rostam, and as a mark of trust you're gonna help us."

Rostam chuckled, through his disappointment. The old man was just another crazy conspiracy theorist, even with good information.

"What do you think I'm gonna do for you?"

"I want you to join us. You can start by doing me a small service. My organisation has contacts with our peers around the world. One of the Iranians needs getting into line. We want you to fly to London and make contact with Bahman Zadi. Zadi's the main digital adviser to the Revolutionary Guards. His buddies all understand how crypto keeps their personal finances safe from the US government, but Zadi's trying to get the Supreme Leader to shut it down."

"Why should I chase him down for you? And why would he talk to me?"

Theo chuckled. "You're the perfect person. Zadi has contacts with the London Iranian diaspora. You have an in with them. I know he's been following your activities. And there's the connect with your Mom."

Rostam stiffened.

"You what?"

"Your mother and Zadi knew each other way back before she came over here. She hasn't told you?"

"The only things Mom likes talking about from Iran are her heroine Maryam Mirzakhani, and saffron rice recipes."

"Believe me, when Zadi finds out you're in town, he'll meet you. All you have to do is give him a message from us, and you'll be back home recording your next show. And you'll know you have our backing."

Rostam wanted to laugh, but nothing about Theo's body language suggested this wasn't serious.

"Ballpark?"

The old man's expression didn't change.

"Your show is weekly, right? I'll pay you a million per episode for six months. Or we can structure it with incentives around listeners. Or you keep producing the show on the zero budget you have right now and spend my dough building up a collection of shows around you. When it comes to podcasts, you're the boss."

Rostam thrust his hands in his pockets and took a deep breath through his nose. Twenty-six million dollars would change his life. Dread's bleak grin flashed before his eyes. What did he say about an offer that seemed too good to be true?

"Editorial independence comes first," said Rostam.

"No strings attached."

"Just make this trip for you, huh? I'll need to discuss it with my partner."

Theo tutted. He dropped his cigarette and ground it into the gravel with his heel.

"My turn to ask some questions."

When Theo started speaking again, his voice had lost the seductive tenor and turned harsh.

"Does your ex-wife need her career badly? Does your Mom want her paperwork at that Harlem high school gone over by immigration? Do you want to be free to take your lovely daughter for hot dogs?" He spoke slowly, and with each sentence a buzzing noise in Rostam's brain increased in volume, until he felt full of violence. Towards himself, or this old man, what difference?

"I've tried it the nice way, Rostam. Now we'll do it my way."

Fury rushed up from Rostam's stomach and flooded his brain. He took an involuntary step towards Theo, who shrugged gently. "You don't want to do that. You got choices here, and that would be a poor one. I've done you a favour offering you this opportunity."

"I don't need to ask you any questions. You can get lost. Tricking me out here and talking about my daughter."

Rostam turned around to walk back to the drive.

"You're a rational thinker - these are your choices. Do us this favour. You'll be back from London next week with a major financial backer and all the benefits that will bring. Or you can play prima donna and let the people you care about most suffer the consequences. You're a family man, Rostam - aren't you?"

Theo's voice had gone back to its initial timbre: light, detached, unthreatening. Rostam looked across again. Theo looked like an intellectual grandfather, or distinguished professor of some prestigious and obscure arts subject. It was impossible to reconcile the craziness of Theo's words with his appearance.

"There are a pair of fresh passports in the back of the car, along with a new phone and a selection of plastic. The passports will work, and so will the cards, once you've left the country. Call me when you decide. My number is the only one saved on your new phone."

"Good pitch, old man, but I'm outta here."

"Have it your way. Just remember this. Shut your mouth, open your eyes, and pay attention to what is going on. You don't believe me now - fine. You will soon. Call me when you feel like talking."

They were back at the parking lot and Theo opened the back door. The heat from the car was welcome to Rostam.

"You're staying here?" he asked.

"My ride is just pulling in."

Rostam looked over his shoulder as he slid into the back seat and saw an identical Toyota pull up. No driver was visible in that car either.

"Good luck, Rostam," said Theo as he closed the door.

"Where to?" asked the car.

"Um - take me home. Gramercy - "

"I know your address, Rostam."

"Of course you do."

Rostam looked out of the window as the Toyota performed an immaculate three-point turn. Theo was staring at him, a fresh cigarette burning between his lips. As Rostam's Toyota pulled out of the bay and onto the ramp back to Lake Shore Drive, he saw Theo raise a hand, as if in benediction.

Chapter Six

Theodore McNamara waited until Rostam's car had been sucked into the traffic heading south before getting into the backseat of his own vehicle. He unzipped his overcoat.

"Take the temperature down three degrees," he said. He couldn't allow the transition from the freezing outdoors to the warmth of the car to dull his mind.

"Call Cantillon."

He began to review the conversation with Rostam. The young man was spirited and idealistic. It was a long time since Theo had met anyone with sincere beliefs. Maybe there could be a use for him beyond London.

"Cantillon calling," said the warm, British, female voice of the vehicle's dashboard.

"How did it go, Theo?" Cantillon's voice began with the bark he used on his staff.

"Good afternoon to you too. You're calling from the office?" said Theo.

"Loeb won't run itself."

Theo raised his eyebrows. It was his belief that the current generation of chief executives were more showmen than decision makers, not as in his day, and Cantillon fit the type.

"Rostam James has been turned from a problem to an asset," said Theo. "I'm sending him to London. Good odds that Zadi will meet him, and that's two problems solved."

"You know Rostam worked here, right?" said Cantillon.

"I know all about him. What's your concern?"

"He's close to his ex-wife. God knows how. Neither of mine return my calls."

Theo left a silence.

"I don't like it," said Cantillon. "We're going to get rid of her."

"After London it won't matter."

"So, I can do it?"

Theo didn't reply immediately, gazing out to the horizon across the Lake. People like Cantillon had to be allowed to do things occasionally.

"Sure. We need Rostam to know he has no option but to deliver. Young men are stupid. It's why they make good soldiers, but it's also why they take silly risks. If he knows his daughter has nobody to provide for her but him, it'll focus his mind. You have it in hand?"

"It's done. What's our next step, Theo?"

"We already have someone in London. I'll send another to keep close tabs on Rostam. Our Middle Eastern partners will want to know how things are going."

"We can trust them to do the right thing?"

"We can trust them to look after their own self-interest, just like everybody else."

"We gotta stop Zadi before he makes a deal," said Cantillon. "From what I hear he has a line into Washington. And you say he still has the ear of the Supreme Leader in Tehran. He can't be allowed to continue."

Theo sighed loudly enough that Cantillon caught it over the phone line. Sometimes it was impossible to mask his frustration.

"Let's focus on what's under our control. Zadi's taken care of. You just make sure Rostam has no fall-back options."

Theo smiled to himself. He could visualize Cantillon's impotent rage as he had to swallow the rebuke.

"You got it, Theo. You see prices today? Up, up and away, baby."

McNamara grunted. The line went dead.

"Take me to the airport. And call Carl Force."

The car began to reverse, and the sound of a phone ringing came over the speakers.

"Boss," said Carl Force's voice, his Arkansas accent elongating the vowel.

"Carl, I expect Rostam to be on his way to London within a few hours. Certainly by the end of the day. I want you over there before he arrives."

"You've incentivised him, huh?"

"That's one way of putting it. He'll make contact with Ahmad Jamalzhad, his college buddy."

"I'm on it, boss. Saw him at a bar before he came to you. He won't remember me. You want me to let him know we're watching?"

"Wouldn't hurt. People behave differently under stress. Just remind him that while the leash is long, we can pull on it anytime. I'll tell him he should report to you when we speak later. He won't move until he realizes he has no choice."

"Should I be doing any more hunting while I'm there?"

Theo raised his eyebrows.

"If I wanted you to take the initiative, I'd say so."

"You got it, boss."

Theo sat back and gazed out of the window. It was easier to think while moving. He smiled to himself: of the three people he'd had to speak to this morning, he disliked Rostam James the least. Rostam would be wondering what he'd done to have his life so badly disturbed, but that's because he persisted with the illusion that people were free agents. That's not how society works. In the end, nobody is free, and only a very few even get a vote. Force knew it already, Cantillon thought he was one of the elect, and Rostam would find out for himself.

Theo shook a Marlboro free from his case and lit it, watching the flame from his Zippo lick the cigarette in the reflection of his window. Everything was under control, and he needed to concentrate to keep it that way.

Chapter Seven

Rostam didn't want to play more conversational games with the car. He felt like a blindfolded man holding two pieces of live electric cable, trying to guess if putting them together would empower him or blow him up.

Lead a stable of commentators. Validation. Expand the platform. That is a lot of money he's prepared to spend.

The pure oxygen of a potential big win reminded Rostam of his first successful trade, six months after graduating the trading programme. The vision dimmed as he thought of the catch. *An errand to London. Am I giving up independence, like Dread says? Become a tool of that guy. He wasn't threatening Millie and Mom, right?*

Rostam shook his head quickly from side to side. It was a trick his Mom had taught him when strong emotions clouded his judgement. Could he believe McNamara?

"You can make calls now," said the car. "Your own cell will work again."

Rostam scrambled his phone out of his pocket and fumbled it onto the floor. Adrenaline was getting to him. He hoped Tom wouldn't make a joke of his nerves. Anything he said in the car could be relayed back. A quick internet search showed Theo McNamara was the real deal. Major VC. Donor to half the Ivy League, and both political parties. Rostam encountered fantasists and fraudsters every day as he put together each episode, but this was different.

Rostam was in the back seat, sitting behind where the driver should have been. On the seat to his right was a black box, the size of an iPad. There was no writing on the package, which had the resonant deep velvet blackness of a Chanel package he had once bought Millie for a long-gone Valentine's Day. It hadn't been in the car previously. Someone must have put the box inside while he was walking by the Lake with Theo.

He picked up the box and gently shuffled off the lid. Rostam smiled at himself - he was instinctively treating it with the respect great expense confers on material objects. Inside he found a brand-new passport in an unfamiliar brown of the Islamic Republic of Iran. It had Rostam's photograph and date of birth. *If they're gonna fake my passport they could have improved on my photo*, thought Rostam. That wasn't the work of an amateur.

"Thanks, Tom," he said out loud. "I'm happy thinking my thoughts." His voice was steady. Good to show a good poker face.

There was little traffic and the car was already turning right by Belmont Harbor towards the tall block where Rostam and Millie each had apartments. The Toyota pulled up in the crescent outside the building devoted to Uber pick-up and drop-offs. The back door locks clicked upwards. Rostam reminded himself to try to appear cool.

"I'm free to go? Aren't you going to remind me to check to make sure I haven't left any belongings behind?"

The car remained silent.

"I liked you better when you were chatty, Tom. So long."

Rostam grabbed the black box and slid out of the car. From the outside it was just another SUV with blackened windows. Nothing remarkable for the casual observer to notice. The moment Rostam was clear of the car it indicated before pulling away and disappearing back around the corner toward the Lincoln Park Conservatory.

Rostam's cell buzzed in his trouser pocket. He walked inside his building to get out of the cold and nodded at George, the daytime doorman, without stopping for his usual brief exchange of news.

The elevator was already on the ground floor. Rostam punched the button for the 38th floor before opening messages.

Dread: *Tell me you didn't sell us down the river.*

Millie: *Good news?*

Rostam sat down at his desk. The view would have suited the old man. To Rostam's right Lake Michigan stretched away to infinity; to his left were the skyscrapers that are more impressive in Chicago than they are in New York, for want of competition. The view was as familiar to Rostam as the smell of his home: the aroma of last night's pepperoni pizza mixed with the apple wood of his favourite Jelly Roll strain.

Rostam fired up his home computer. He had configured the monitors to be as close to a professional workstation as possible, a wire steel framework like a collection of sheet music stands. He favoured one gigantic Samsung monitor with a quintet of smaller no-brand screens around it, so he could keep different work streams running simultaneously. It worked well for big sports nights too, a different March Madness game on each screen.

Often the subsidiary screens were filled with charts of different cryptos, bitcoin as a mainstream benchmark in the top right corner, with Ethereum, Tether, Dogecoin and Cardano in clockwise sequence. What was needed now was his main Bitcoin holding account, held on BTX, built up each month from his old banking paycheque and putting in as much of annual bonuses as Celia expenses would allow. This was the nest egg which allowed him the time and peace of mind to focus on the podcast.

If things worked out with Theo he could be back to building that up.

The cabbage patch doll Rostam hoped Celia would take to when she was older sat slumped on the windowsill looking out blankly. Normally Rostam projected kindness into the doll's outsized blue eyes but today they looked mischievous in an unkind, Puckish way. What was the right thing to do for Celia? He picked up his cell and called Millie.

Chapter Eight

Millie answered first ring. She spoke in the shouty whisper used at the bank for personal conversations. The etiquette was tortuous to understand but was employed universally. Everyone had personal conversations at work, but you had to pretend to be embarrassed because you should be working, not lollygagging.

When Millie and Rostam started the training programme on the same day, lesson one started with Loeb's famed business principles. Rostam's instinctive, back-of-the-bus reaction was to trash them one after the other. Millie had digested them whole and lived up to each one ever since.

"How was it?" said Millie.

"Interesting," said Rostam. "You wanna help me decide something?"

"Go."

"Theo McNamara. Look him up. One of those incredibly rich guys you've never heard of."

He could hear Millie tapping keys as he spoke.

"He knows everything about me," continued Rostam. "You. Celia. He knows stuff about Mom back in Iran she hasn't told me."

"Takes research seriously. That's good."

"Yeah, I guess. He wants me to fly to London to deliver a message."

"Why you?"

"He explained all that. Thinks I've got an in through Mom and the old LSE crew. The deal is, do this thing for him, back next week, we start building a whole stable of shows. Big chequebook. What do you think?"

He heard Millie do a sharp intake of breath and knew she was excited.

"Congratulations, Rostam! I knew it. Doesn't need thinking about. Get on that plane."

"You don't think it's strange?"

"Silicon Valley guys are weird. This is your opportunity. Don't screw it up."

"Is Celia at nursery?"

"Of course she is - it's Thursday morning."

"I'm going to pop in."

"No need. I'll take care of Celia. You can spend more time with her when you're back."

"Of course. You're right. You're generally right, Millie."

Rostam sighed.

"Now I'm really worried," said Millie. "What's worrying you?"

"I'm used to flying under the radar. Feel like I'm up in lights. Wish you were coming."

There was a pause at the other end of the phone.

"You do know we got divorced, right?"

It struck Rostam with force that had been a mistake.

"I know we are."

"You get out there and bring home what's yours."

"You got it."

Rostam's desire to add *I love you* was so strong he drew blood when he bit the end of his tongue. *At least I didn't swear*, he thought, while pressing the red button instead.

Dread could wait. Rostam didn't fancy being shouted down now the decision was made.

He speed-walked three blocks down to Celia's nursery. It was attached to a kindergarten. Ruinously expensive, but local and, just as important, recommended by Carmen, Millie's boss. It was lunchtime and there was a chance the infants had been allowed out to play. The fence was built to prevent pedestrians looking in, but Rostam could hear the kids playing on the far side. He leant his forehead against the wall and tried to pick out the sound of Celia's voice amongst the catcalling, random sounds and half-formed sentences produced by a morass of pre-schoolers. Would he be able to pick out her voice from a score of peers? Rostam wanted to believe he could but was too addicted to evidence based thinking to say so, even to himself.

After five minutes of standing there the warmth of feeling close to his daughter began to wane and was replaced by the deep sadness that extreme cold can bring. He kissed the unfeeling redbrick wall that separated him from his daughter and called the only number on his new phone.

"Theo? You have a deal."

McNamara didn't waste time sounding surprised.

"We have a plane waiting at CEX. The car will be with you in two."

Alright, thought Rostam. *Now I'm in it.*

Chapter Nine

Millie thought lack of protein was her biggest problem. Lunch at Loeb was, by convention, eaten at the desk, unless a client was involved. The canteen had changed menu, and the only non-meat options on the board were vegan. That sucked, for her.

"Being a vegetarian in the 2020s is as hard as being a liberal. Both sides squeezed against the middle," Millie told a fellow sufferer, raging at the lack of veggie options on the board.

Millie had almost reached her desk before she saw Jimbob hovering by her monitor, pacing and running his fingers through his two-inches-too-long floppy blonde fringe.

"Is this a new exercise routine?" she asked, with affection. "If you need the restroom, I can show you the way." Her assistant's good humour was often the only light moment in her working day, but there was no smile when he turned around.

"Millie, I got a call from Karen in Cantillon's office. You weren't answering your cell."

"We're not supposed to use cells in the office," said Millie, with the automatic show-no-weakness instinct of a born hall-monitor.

Jimbob leaned in and dropped his voice to the office secret volume. "Karen and I are pals, right?" Millie gazed at him. "Sorry. Whatever. She'd tell me what's going on if she could."

"So, what is going on?"

"That's the thing. She wouldn't say a word. Just that they need you up there like yesterday."

Millie got a small jolt of adrenaline that stopped her feeling hungry. Discipline must be maintained. "Don't over-react, Jimbob."

Jimbob whistled below his breath. "They don't call you the ice-queen for nothing." Millie started. "Ok boss, they don't call you that at all. Just trying to keep up."

Millie put her least-worst lunch choice curly kale and chickpea vegan wrap on her desk and headed for the elevator bank. Despite her pretence with Jimbob, she *was* worried. It was too soon for vetting on a promotion. Maybe this was a character test.

Lunch was a poor time to use the elevators. Private wealth, where Millie worked, was third floor, while the C-suite was on seventh. Millie had to let the first car go without her. She didn't want to arrive flustered in the Chief Execs office after squeezing into an already overcrowded elevator. The next one was only two-thirds full. Millie nodded at an acquaintance from compliance, standing rigid at the back, and hit seven. Every other rider got off at more junior floors.

Millie had only been up here once before with her training class, for a ceremonial shaking of hands with Cantillon. That trip taught her the value of internal real estate. Loeb made having an office special. On the trading floors everybody had to share. The C-Suite was different: even the assistants had their own glass cubicles appended to their bosses' rooms. When men – and they were still all men – got themselves one of these roles one of their rewards was the ability to choose their own office decor. With the exception of the Chief Risk Officer, who perhaps felt transparency came with the title and insisted on glass, the other permanent residents all elected for the rarest commodity of all in investment banking - privacy.

Cantillon, once a humble trader, had been Chief Exec for a dozen years. His office was twice the size of any of his fellow board members. Karen, his assistant, had floor space that could have accommodated six desks on Millie's floor. Jimbob had introduced Millie to Karen at the Christmas Party, after the two assistants had performed a karaoke of *Leader of the Pack*, but there was no greeting as Millie approached. Karen was standing in the corridor waiting. As soon as Millie was close, self-conscious about walking down the quiet corridor of power, Karen moved inside and knocked on her boss' door.

Millie's level of apprehension moved up a notch, but she was damned if she was going to show weakness in front of an assistant. Or even the big boss for that matter. She consciously drew back her shoulders and stood as straight as possible as she walked in.

"I'm told you want to - ," she began, before seeing that Cantillon was not the man behind the desk. In his place sat a slim, dark-haired man in his early forties whom she didn't know.

"My name is O'Dwyer," said the stranger. "We haven't met before, and I doubt we'll meet again. My role is corporate reputation and government relations. Heard of me?"

"I have not." Mille was pleased her voice was steady. She stared at him to establish eye contact, but he wouldn't meet her gaze.

"There hasn't been any reason that you should, until now. You do know that Loeb as a firm has strong relationships with the government of this country, and many others. That means we have to keep our own conduct at the highest level. We use a Pentagon-approved cyber security firm to screen electronic communications of all employees. Millie - you have been red-flagged. We'll do our own inquiry, but you won't be needed at the office. Security will take you back down to the third floor where you can collect your things."

Millie hated herself for the tears that had suddenly filled her vision and were threatening to run down her cheeks. Where was Cantillon? He wouldn't let this happen. He cultivated a paternal persona to Loeb employees, especially the ones who, like her, came up through the graduate programme.

"Why is there no-one from HR here? I shouldn't be hearing this on my own."

"There's nothing for anyone else to tell you. Frankly we're doing you a favour saying this much. Anyone else would be ejected from the premises with extreme prejudice."

"Sir - with due respect - I don't know what you're talking about," said Millie. The moisture in her eyes had evaporated, as though the rising tide of fury within her was raising her body temperature. "You pull me in here with no warning. Last I heard I was up for a promotion."

"This came out in screening," he said, now staring down at the knuckles of his hands, splayed out on the desk before him.

"You can't just - ," began Millie, before reflecting that they could do pretty much whatever they wanted. Her knowledge of employment law was close to zero, but not so close that she thought she'd outsmart Loeb HR on technicalities. O'Dwyer was on his feet and preparing to escort her down on the walk of shame back to her desk. Millie wasn't prepared to simply fold.

"Are you at least going to share your allegation with me? How can I defend myself against silence?"

"Be grateful you're hearing this from us and not the authorities," said O'Dwyer. Mille felt there was an unspoken *"you silly bitch"* at the end of the sentence, but also knew Loeb senior execs went through too much interpersonal training to let their prejudices show in a way that could come back at them.

O'Dwyer was now standing close enough she could see where flakes of the product he used to achieve a Gordon Gekko style slicked-back style stood out against blades of hair, indistinguishable from dandruff.

"There's no point arguing," he said in an attempt at speaking sotto-voce. "Let's go."

"Don't patronize me," snapped Millie. "Corporate reputation? Get a real job. In this industry you're either a producer or you're support staff."

Mille was staring at O'Dwyer, incredulous he had the authority to do this. She was now corporate detritus, to be swept up and stuck in the garbage compactor at the first opportunity.

Conflicting desires rolled about her brain, like different colour paints dumped together, waiting to see which shade would prove dominant. Might one of her clients have been up to no good without her knowledge? She had done nothing wrong.

A fissure opened in her mind. Who was Millie James if she wasn't an MD in Private Wealth at Loeb? She felt the bitterness every child knows when having been falsely accused, which never diminishes. There was no point in talking but she couldn't help herself.

"I guess this is how you guys work. Throw a bunch of confusion and hope your victims disappear before they work it out." Millie regretted saying it the moment it had left her mouth. Better to leave the room now before she said more she might regret. Instead, she turned around so that she could lead O'Dwyer out of the room, rather than the other way round.

The journey to the elevator bank felt like a perp walk. Executive assistants didn't hide their curiosity to see her escorted back. Now Millie felt grateful for the lunchtime rush below. Two people wandering the halls at this time of day would be less noticeable than at quieter periods. No sooner had she thought this then she found herself alone with O'Dwyer in the lift.

"What else do I need to know?" she asked.

"You'll hear from HR this afternoon. You are suspended with immediate effect, but you'll be paid your salary while the investigation runs its course."

"Big of you."

"We could be tougher. We don't often get calls like this."

O'Dwyer was looking at his shoes. The elevator arrived at the third floor and the area was full of professionals with their lunch bags. Millie looked through the double glass doors that led to her trading floor, where she knew the name of every person. More importantly, they all knew her.

"All I need from my desk is my purse and the photograph of my daughter. You can ask my assistant to bring them down to me along with my coat in the lobby. That's him - Jimbob with the blonde hair, standing talking to my neighbour with a worried look."

Mille wouldn't be the only victim. Poor Jimbob. She knew he liked working for her. This would come as a nasty shock. At least the drama of being associated with a scandal would be some compensation.

She got back in the lift and hit the button for the ground floor, leaving O'Dwyer outside. When she got there, she zapped her security card for the last time on the reflective black marble of the gates she'd been walking through for a decade. A wild desire to throw it at the security guards came over her, but she decided to bide her time and exchange it for her personal effects when O'Dwyer or Jimbob came down with them. She would go to pick up Celia early from nursery.

They were trying to take her career away. They weren't going to interfere with her daughter.

Chapter Ten

"Welcome Mr James," said a cheerful, dark-haired check-in woman, with a mole mostly concealed by foundation on her upper lip, as she returned Rostam's passport. "Your pilot has already refuelled and is ready. This way to security."

Rostam nodded in reply. It was going to take time to adjust to this kind of travel.

There were only a handful of people in the lobby of the private jet terminal, and nobody replaced the dark-haired woman when she came from behind the counter to walk Rostam across to security. The whole operation was more workaday than he expected: convenience over glamour.

"Do I still have to take off my shoes?" asked Rostam.

"'Fraid so. We're quicker than commercial, but just as safe."

Rostam put his coat and brown canvas carryon into a shallow moulded grey tray and his sneakers on the rollers of a small X-ray machine.

"That's great, sir. Now just walk yo'self through the scanner and we'll have you on your way," said a smiling, gum-chewing security officer, with smooth protruding cheeks and a PWK cap. Rostam thanked him and walked in, holding both hands above his head as the full body scanner swooshed around him. On the far side stood an enormous albino-pale man in a Homeland Security uniform. He carried the physique of a powerlifter and bored scowl of a frustrated bully.

"You can walk through now, sir," said the white-skinned giant. Rostam walked over to pick up his shoes and bag. "Mr James - we have a couple of questions for you. Come this way."

Rostam was aggravated.

"Can I put my shoes on?"

"It'll only take a minute."

The giant stood between Rostam and his luggage. The two men were the same height, but the guard must have one hundred pounds on Rostam. A hand came down on Rostam's shoulder.

"What the hell?" said Rostam, more surprised than angry. Nobody responded and before he knew it was too late to shout.

The hand belonged to another Homeland Security giant. Rostam found himself sandwiched between the two, walking at pace towards an unmarked door with a third uniformed man standing beside it.

Walking shoeless put Rostam at a disadvantage. He was unused to feeling short. Sticky linoleum sucked at his socks, while his minders wore rubber soled black lace up boots. Rostam looked over his shoulder for the smiling security guard but was already at the door. His three escorts came together in a phalanx behind him and pushed him through.

The moment he was through the door it slammed shut and the lights went out.

Rostam's arms were pinned to his side in a bear hug from behind. His legs were swept from under him, and he collapsed onto a hard, plastic seat. Hands pressed down on each shoulder. He opened his mouth to scream, only to have an outsized squash ball shoved past his teeth. He gagged, but couldn't expel air through his mouth. Acidic fluid turned on him, flushing nausea through his body. The rubber ball had straps attached, tied together behind his head. Rostam couldn't move his torso, so kicked out with his legs, but there was nothing to connect with in front of him.

Nobody spoke and Rostam's own breathing was too loud for him to make out other sounds. He tried to work out what was happening. It felt like the hands on each side belonged to different people. That meant one person either side, and the third behind him. There was no light in the room, so they must be well drilled.

Silence.

Rostam was convinced it was the giant albino who would be standing over him. The pressure on each shoulder was too great to think about trying to stand. He squeezed his eyes closed. Disembodied white ghouls populated the inside of his eyelids and screamed at him in three dimensions, like the time as a kid a cheap dentist put him under gas.

Rostam heard the flick of a switch and opened his eyes. The ghouls vanished, but the pressure on his shoulders stayed the same. Harsh, fluorescent light flickered on the ceiling. Footsteps approached from behind with the click-clack of leather-soled heels. The steps came close, and hands reached either side of Rostam's head.

"Let's give you some breathing room, shall we?" said a woman's voice, in a slow Tennessee twang, almost concealing a deep strain of hillbilly. "Open your jaws nice and wide. Don't want you to lose any teeth and spoil that pretty Persian smile."

Rostam did as he was asked. The twin relief of being able to see, and being able to properly fill his lungs, was overwhelming. He almost felt gratitude. He heard the woman drop his gag to the floor behind him. She picked up a plastic chair like his own and walked past him, swung the chair down, and sat across from him, folding one leg over the other.

"My name is Tina Waspell," she said. "I've been looking forward to this conversation more than you can imagine. Do I have your full attention?"

Rostam had allowed his head to drop towards the floor as he focussed on breathing. Now he looked up. Tina Waspell wore a checked print purple dress that fell halfway down her calves, held in place with a black leather belt around her midriff. The shoes he had heard paradiddling the floor were pumps, not high heels. Her coarse, straw-like hair, dyed brown with reddish tint, fell to her shoulders. She carried a leather purse on a strap, wore large-rimmed, brown-framed glasses, and a broad, thin-lipped smile. She could have been on her way to church.

"I don't have much of a choice," said Rostam.

Tina's smile broadened. "I guess not. I have questions for you, and then you can be on your way."

Rostam's fear was turning to anger.

"Who are you to ask me questions?"

The hands on either shoulder pressed down harder, and his ass slipped forward on the chair.

"Now boys," said Tina, "Rostam didn't mean to be rude."

He pushed himself back up, trying to look over his shoulder, but the man behind grabbed both sides of his face.

"Just look at me, Rostam. You're not about to bleat about your phone call, or MIRANDA, are you? I've higher expectations than that."

Rostam had no idea what to say, so focussed on trying to listen instead.

"We just want to know why you are flying to London today. Who's sending you, and what do they want?"

Rostam tried to think it through.

"If you had the right to question me," he said. "we'd be in a police station."

"That's not friendly. Let me ask you a different question. On your show you say - and I quote *- privacy in technology is necessary for freedom against government oppression and tyranny - if we want to regain personal freedom, we need anonymity."*

In Tina's Tennessee accent the word *an-on-ym-i-ty* stretched out like bubble-gum.

"You say privacy like it's a dirty word. I mean what I say," said Rostam.

"You want to keep secrets from the government that protects you," said Tina.

"The government works for us, not the other way around. Might seem different if you get a paycheck from Homeland Security."

Tina was no longer smiling. "You have a co-presenter on your show called Dread. Started talking about how libertarians are using crypto currencies to bring down the government. Are you in favour of that, Rostam?"

Tina spoke slowly, but she was still moving too fast for Rostam to process.

"Dread's a conspiracy guy. He's onto a story. That's what we do on the show."

"I suppose you do, at that." Tina reached into her handbag and brought out Rostam's bogus Iranian passport. "You wanna explain this?"

Rostam thought fast. "It isn't a crime to have dual identity in this country."

"But traveling under a false identity is." Tina gave Rostam time. "You know, Rostam, you're not the person we're after, interesting though you are. We want information on the man who sent you. Maybe we can even help. Give us a try."

Rostam stared at Tina, who held his gaze. She had the air of a strict but fair teacher dealing with a recalcitrant student. Did Rostam believe this woman could help him? He made up his mind.

"No thanks."

"It doesn't have to be like this," said Tina. "I'm here to help."

Rostam coughed. "What did Reagan say? Never trust someone who says they come from the government and they're here to help."

"I prefer to quote one of his predecessors. Ask not what your country can do for you -."

"But what you can do for your country." Rostam finished her sentence. "I don't believe you. You have no business holding me. If you had the authority you claim, you wouldn't need to ask me these questions. Let me go."

Tina smoothed her dress over her knee. "You're not the kind of man to underestimate a woman, are you?"

Rostam was considering his response when Tina raised her eyes to look above him.

"Go ahead, boys."

The unseen guard grabbed a handful of Rostam's hair and pulled it backwards. His chin jerked upwards, and he saw it was the albino who had been behind him. Rostam opened his mouth to shout, and the blonde giant forced the gag back between Rostam's teeth. He reached to one side and pulled a soft, black bag out with both hands, before pushing it over Rostam's head.

Total darkness.

Each leg was grasped and pulled from under him. One guard put a hand underneath each armpit, while the other two took a leg each. They marched quickly forward. It only took a couple of steps for

Rostam to give up the effort to make any sound. The grip on his legs was too strong for him to kick out, and his flailing arms made no connections.

The guards stopped marching and lifted him up. A crazy, pointless desire to give in and say anything they wanted came over him, but Rostam couldn't make a sound.

"One-two-three," said the albino's voice, and Rostam felt himself lifted, still horizontal, swung to one side, and dropped abruptly into freezing cold water. Strong, hostile hands pressed down on his chest and legs to stop him jack-knifing back out. One guard placed a hand over Rostam's face through the bag and pushed him down below the waterline.

Any thought but survival was extinguished. There wasn't time to fill his lungs through his nose. Every cell in his body had been revolting against the cold, but now there was no consciousness spare to waste on body temperature. The immediate primaeval panic of oxygen deprivation took over.

Rostam's mouth was clamped open, and water forced its way down his throat and into his lungs. He tried to shake off the force pressing down but couldn't move his head from side to side. A gigantic hand planted the heel of its thumb on his forehead while steel fingers stretched down to below his chin.

Pressure was relentless, the panic of breathlessness overwhelming. Rostam fought down the terror and let his body go limp. There was no strategy to it, just an acknowledgement he couldn't overpower the men who were drowning him. Then the hand over his face lifted away. Rostam lifted his head above the water. Some air reached his mouth around the rubber ball, but not enough. His nostrils sucked in whatever oxygen they could find. Rostam's eyes were open, but the sodden black cloth of the bag stuck to his eyeballs. He could see nothing.

Then the hand emerged from over his head and began to steadily, slowly, push his face back below the surface.

Every cell in Rostam's body wanted to scream out loud. It felt fundamentally wrong that hands were pushing him down, not helping him up. But somewhere he found the grit not to give these people the satisfaction of seeing him thrash about for survival. It made no sense for them to kill him.

Rostam used all his self-control to make his body go limp. From the lucky-dip treasure chest of memory came a recollection of ante-natal hypnotherapy classes he attended with Millie when they were expecting Celia. *Find your happy place* the over-priced and aggravatingly serene therapist had told her, over and over again. Millie's happy place then had been a beach in Thailand they visited together pre-baby. Rostam's vision now was of Celia's face, smiling with perfectly white milk teeth, and a snotty nose. He tried to focus on the memory of her twinkling grey eyes.

For a moment it worked, until blood flow roared in his ear canals, and his oxygen deprived lungs sent panic rampaging around his entire bodily economy. Celia's face began to disappear before his mind's eye, like a photograph held over a flame, a black tendril of smoke as the middle is carbonized before spreading to engulf the whole.

Then it was over.

The hand disappeared from his face and two arms hooked underneath his own to pull him upwards. Each leg was lifted back out of the water. Rostam could focus on nothing but getting air up his nostrils. His three pallbearers carried him to a plastic hard backed chair, plunked him down on it, pulled back his arms and wrapped his wrists together roughly with sticky tape. Rostam heard their footsteps marching away, so that he didn't know if he was in a room on his own or not. He didn't care. As his lungs began to forgive him, he became conscious of being intensely cold. His clothes stuck tight to his skin. Between breaths he could hear water dripping onto the cement floor. Already he was able to start to think again. He knew one thing for sure.

Whoever these people were, they didn't want him dead. Yet.

Chapter Eleven

"Mommy!" squealed Celia, all maroon coat, yellow rubber boots and black hair, as she squirmed in the arms of her preschool teacher. Millie had tried and failed not to be competitive about how pleased she was that *Mommy* had been her daughter's first word.

'Why can't we all be three years old," she thought, "when everything is fun?" Mille mocked herself: she hated taking instruction from anybody and had been the same throughout school. For a moment she was nervous that the teacher would ask why she was picking up her daughter early, as though news of her ejection from Loeb would have spread to everyone she encountered.

Get a grip Millie - not everyone's world is all about Loeb.

Seeing Celia was a tonic. And picking up her daughter from day-care was the first thing that felt normal since Jimbob told her she was expected up at the C-Suite, which had been two hours ago, when she was still employed. Celia was so excited to be back in her Mommy's arms Millie could almost forget what had just happened. The truth was that she was not going to get over this until she got answers. This would not be the end of her.

"Gad-um? Gad-um?" repeated Celia, as they began the three block walk back to their apartment.

"Sure thing, little britches."

Gad-um was Celia speak for ice-cream. Millie told herself that she didn't take her daughter for ice-cream every single time they walked back together, but she didn't interrogate her own claim. Millie's parents had been so lackadaisical about what was permitted and what wasn't during her own childhood it pushed her in a different direction. Celia was to have every opportunity - and that included treats - so long as she learned to work hard as well as play hard. Millie had always been jealous of Rostam's less conflicted response to his own childhood. He could be free and easy with Celia because he wasn't carrying the heavy emotional freight her counterculture upbringing had deposited on her back.

The ice-cream parlour was a throw-back: an Italian-American owned holdout, doubling as an espresso bar. It was almost painful to still be treated like the same person by Tony, the elderly proprietor of the store, who sincerely enjoyed flirting with infants as much as their mothers, when she felt her status - her identity - had been stripped from her.

"Everything ok, Mrs James? Not like you to skip coffee. Don't want to upset your digestion."

"Everything's fine, Tony." She wasn't going to pour out her troubles to this man, much as she liked him. In Millie's world, women took care of their own problems.

Millie wanted to get back to the apartment to regroup. It was only one more block to the apartment, but everything was under a destabilizing patina. It was the light, Millie decided. It would normally be dusk at this time of year when she picked Celia up at 5pm. In mid-afternoon the light was positively bright. Everything felt wrong.

They each had most of their scoop left to eat when they turned into the warm air of the lobby. Upstairs Celia was happy to be put in front of Disney+. Millie usually limited her screen time to under an hour, but this would be a bonanza day for television. She dumped most of her own uneaten ice cream in the trash and brought up Lisa Matsui's number.

"Lisa, before I start, do you have any idea about what happened to me today?" asked Millie.

"Not a clue."

Millie told her the story of her dismissal. Lisa listened intently, asking no questions until the tale was told.

"You were fired by O'Dwyer in Cantillon's office. That is unusual."

"Unusual how? In a way that helps us?"

"Not necessarily. Nobody from HR was there?"

"Nobody. Do you know this O'Dwyer?"

"No, but he checks out. He's on the Loeb website as head of government relations. It sounds like they were panicking. It was only a short time before this that Carmen was dangling a promotion in front of you?"

"Yeah."

"Carmen is connected at the firm. Makes me think something dramatic must have happened. Somebody must have got in touch with O'Dwyer, and he hit the panic button. Not Loeb's usual style at all. They're normally slick as you like when it comes to firing people."

Millie didn't speak.

"Sorry Millie. This must be a massive shock. I shouldn't go throwing words like that around."

"Nah. I'm a grown-up. They *have* fired me. I want to know why. I want someone to pay, and not just with money. And I want to be able to stay in the industry."

"If I know Loeb, they'll be burning down your reputation on the street. They've always been the same. When they want someone, nothing is too good for them. When they don't, things get nasty. My first job will be to stop that."

"And to find out what the hell has gone on here."

"Sure, sure. I'll do what I can. A lawyer doesn't prejudge but this is a wild accusation they've made."

"What's your gut - is there a way back for me? Can this just be a mistake?"

It was Lisa's turn to pause. Millie heard her inhale sharply and wondered if her friend was allowed to vape in the office. "Millie - I'm sorry to say I don't see a way back here. Nobody will be happier than me if we can hang these vandals for what they've done, but Cantillon is an old pro. If they've made a mistake we'll go for it, but that isn't my base case."

Millie winced.

"Ok. At least I know."

"Is there anything you can look into at your end? Any guesses at what is going on?".

"I'm gonna find out what's happened with Rostam. Maybe check in with his Mom in NYC."

"You do that, sister. Speak later."

Millie was about to wish Lisa good luck, but she had already hung up. For a woman who charged by the hour Lisa was parsimonious with her own time, and her clients' money.

Celia was entranced by Trolls singing a Lady Gaga song on Netflix. Millie went to sit next to her on the couch. It felt good to think about someone other than herself for a moment. Every few seconds the memory of her dismissal returned like a clump of malign hair in the sink. She wanted to talk to Rostam, but not until she knew what was happening. Hopefully he was having better luck on his trip.

Chapter Twelve

"Do you believe in second chances?" asked Tina Waspell.

Rostam shivered. He wanted to wrap his arms around himself for warmth, but the guards had taped his hands behind his back. At least they'd taken the bag off his head and slipped off the gag. He could see. He could breathe. He wasn't going to say thank-you for either.

"I do," Tina continued. "Let's start again."

"So, the face of evil looks like someone from the suburbs," said Rostam. "I didn't see that coming."

"Your judgment calls haven't been so hot lately all round, I'd say," said Tina, "but I don't want to rub your nose in it. Let's help each other."

Rostam lost his battle to stop his teeth chattering. Now it had oxygen, his body couldn't ignore the freezing cold.

"You want me to die of exposure before you get to the point?"

"Your clothes will be ready for you in just a minute."

"How about a towel as a down payment?"

Tina looked at him steadily, but without pity. Rostam held her gaze.

"Get pretty boy here a blanket now, will you?" said Tina over his head, without looking away. Moments later squeaking rubber soles approached from behind, and a large, coarse, blue blanket was thrown over Rostam's shoulders.

"Let's not go half-assed boys," said Tina. "Nobody can concentrate in soaking wet clothes. Take off his shirt and pants."

An enormous, starkly pale hand came over Rostam's shoulder, grabbed a handful of his shirt just next to his heart, and ripped it open. The discomfort of being manhandled was outweighed by the relief of having frozen wet cloth removed from his skin. Rostam heard the efficient, swooshing click of a blade emerging from the clasp of a switch knife. Rather than unwrap his hands, Rostam's sleeves were cut from his wrists.

The albino leaned over his prisoner's shoulder, untied his belt buckle and pulled the button fly of his black 501s all the way open. Rostam looked down at his exposed, soaked jockeys, and then back at Tina Waspell, who wore an expression of bemused tolerance. The giant knelt down at his side and neatly sliced a fresh seam down the top of the thighs of Rostam's jeans, down to his ankle. The two strips of wet denim fell to the cement floor with the dispirited crumbling slap of a wet flannel.

"Neat job," said Tina. "Delicate touch for a big guy, huh?"

The giant's knife had reached Rostam's right knee and paused, as though considering making a deeper incision. Rostam made an effort to keep looking at Tina. It wasn't obvious she had made any intervention, but the knife disappeared. Now Rostam was dressed only in socks, jockeys and a wrap of black tape. The giant's footsteps retreated out of the room behind Rostam.

"Hey," called Tina. "You left his blanket on the floor."

Footsteps got louder, Rostam's shoulders were draped with the blanket, and his shakes began to diminish. Tina continued to look at him with an exasperated gaze. From time to time, she shook her head slightly. Rostam almost persuaded himself that she tut-tutted at one point.

"What do you want from me, Ms Waspell? You're treating me like a terror suspect. If that's what you're shopping for, you have the wrong guy."

"You a money launderer, Rostam?"

"What? What makes you think so?"

"What's all this crypto bull crap if it isn't to escape paying taxes?"

Rostam laughed. It felt good, but he worried it might sound hysterical.

"What's so funny?" asked Tina.

"Is that what you think? That's one of the oldest charges in the book against crypto. Whatever else I am, I'm no money launderer. My tax returns are squeaky clean. What else you got?"

"Where are you heading?"

"London."

"What for?"

"I have someone I need to see."

"Pretty vague for a long trip. You going of your own volition?"

Rostam shook his head.

"This mystery figure have something on you? Those close to you?"

Rostam remained silent.

"Why don't you tell me everything? I might be able to help, and I don't see you've got any better options."

Rostam looked down at the floor and thought it through. Tina must be some kind of government employee, or she wouldn't be able to access this place. But Theo was offering serious money, as well as sounding like he had the potential to make threats. If this woman had something to charge him with, she'd have said so. He'd done nothing wrong and if she was really going to hurt him she'd have done it already. Still, he had to give her something.

"You know I do a podcast. I talk about crypto and what it can do to bring freedom to the world. I explode conspiracy theories because I like to do it, and it brings in listeners. We're doing good, I've got a new business partner, and we need to pay a quick visit to London." Rostam broke off and considered if there was anything else he should say. "I've broken no law and you've got no reason to hold me."

"You think you can handle this on your own?"

Rostam looked down at himself, still shivering, half-clothed, unable to stand up from the chair until he was untied.

"I guess that looks a stretch from here, but yes I do."

"Why the fake passport? You heading to Iran next?"

Rostam couldn't think of a good explanation.

"You could fill books with what I don't know about Iran, and they have. One day I might read one. The passport's just for kicks."

Tina stood up and walked around her chair, before resting both hands on its back. She stared at Rostam.

"You are keeping dangerous company. From now on, you're complicit in whatever happens. Blackmail is no excuse. Whatever he's offered you isn't worth it. Any excuse at all and I'll have you locked up, or my name ain't Tina Waspell."

Rostam doubted that was her name, but it made for a strong statement.

Tina Waspell seemed to make up her mind. "I'm gonna leave you now. You'll find your case and everything else in the room behind us. I've left my card inside your real passport. If you get smart enough to call me when you know more, you'll be doing yourself the biggest favour you've ever gotten."

Rostam watched her walk past him and slumped in the chair. There was muttering behind him, and the giant approached again.

"Stay," came a hissed instruction, and Rostam felt the tape that had pressured his hands together come apart. "Wait thirty seconds."

Footsteps receded and when Rostam turned around, he saw that the door had been closed noiselessly behind him. In a neat pile next to his suitcase were shoes, boxers, socks, a fresh pair of black jeans and a shirt. The pair of passports lay on top. Rostam ripped off his soaking cold socks and shorts and rubbed himself with the coarse blue blanket. At first, he couldn't feel the abrasive wool as the relief of dry heat overwhelmed all other impressions. The next day his body would be covered in tiny red welts, as though he'd rolled about on sandpaper. It felt good to dress again, and not to be under close personal inspection. Rostam didn't bother looking up at the ceiling - he assumed he had been on camera the whole time.

Behind the door was a simple box room. Signs announced that the next door led back to departures. There was no sign of a bath, or any obvious drops of water, though this had to be the room where he had been immersed. Whoever Waspell's crew might be, they were efficient workers who knew how to clean up after themselves. Rostam ran his hand through his hair, picked up his suitcase, and opened the final door.

Outside he could see the airport scanner, the affable guard with his PWK cap now being friendly to a family of three who looked like regular passengers. Was it possible that nobody else had noticed? All they would have seen was Rostam being taken into a back room by security, then security reappearing sometime later, and finally Rostam himself. The only change to an observer would be Rostam's hair style. Had he been back there five minutes, or five hours? Rostam had no way to check. He walked past the scanner and a harried young woman with a tablet cradled on her forearm spotted him and ran straight up.

"Mr James? Thank goodness you're here. I thought I'd lost you! Your plane is just this way sir."

Rostam followed the woman through the departure gate.

Chapter Thirteen

How many times had Millie said she wouldn't pick up her phone while spending time with Celia? She added another one to the list as she hit Rostam's number. Straight to voicemail. Of all days to go missing this was the worst. Most of Millie's friends - or good acquaintances anyway - all still worked at Loeb. She could hardly start comparing notes with a bunch of people for whom the news of her dismissal would be the major event of their day.

They'd have been told not to speak to her anyway.

Why hadn't that occurred to her before? Of course they wouldn't. As of lunchtime today Millie no longer had any friends at Loeb. This was no time for self-pity. She picked up her phone and made another call from lower down her speed dial.

Chapter Fourteen

Outside the terminal waited the strangest golf buggy Rostam had ever seen. The electric toy vehicle had a tall Perspex domed roof, like a secular Popemobile. The driver stood waiting next to it, a tall, skinny strawberry-blonde boy barely twenty years old. He'd made the error of using bum fluff to disguise a splattering of acne. In consequence his face looked like the surface of jam, left out of the icebox long enough to begin to sprout.

"Mr James, sir!" he shouted in a high treble. The young man grabbed Rostam's suitcase with his left hand and pressed a button on the remote control which had been concealed in his right, and a door-shaped slice of the Perspex roof suddenly folded down to the ground.

Rostam turned around to thank the woman who had brought him there, but she'd already disappeared back into the warmth of the terminal. Rostam climbed into the back seat of the covered buggy, while his driver stowed the suitcase in the passenger seat, before hurling himself behind the wheel.

"You sure picked a good day to fly, sir," said the driver, his good mood maintained in the oppressively hot interior of the car. "Nobody loves the City of Chicago more than me, sir, but it's hard to love it quite as much in January."

Rostam couldn't believe how quickly normality had resumed. He looked around to see if the albino guard was visible, and instinctively shivered as he remembered the icy water. But his chauffeur just carried on.

"We don't have far to go. Your plane is such a nifty little thing she can use the third runway. I'm gonna drive you past air traffic control and down to the hangers where the transatlantic jets park."

An enormous roaring overhead made it impossible to speak. Thirty seconds after peak volume overhead the kid still had to shout.

"We get military transport planes sometimes, sir. That's a C-130 Hercules. Supporting our boys overseas."

Rostam's ears were grateful the Hercules was heading into the distance. A moment later they had arrived.

The plane had a small retractable set of stairs already let down to the tarmac and a pilot on his way to welcome Rostam aboard, pulling on an aviator coat as he came down the stairs. Rostam put up his hand to stop him.

"It's ok. I can make my way up myself."

The cabin smelled the way sports supply shops had done in his infancy, redolent of fresh leather and lacquer. Rostam concentrated on the smell. Using his nostrils for information and sensation, rather than to preserve his life, as in the iced bath. He shut his eyes and had a sudden, alarming burst of vertigo, when his nose seemed to fill again with ice, his lungs only partially full and depleting fast. It felt as though the top of his head had greater density than the entirety of the rest of his body and threatened to fall backwards, taking him into an endless backward somersault through space. Rostam shook his head and opened his eyes. Now was not the time to give in to fear.

"My name is Andy," said the co-pilot, looking at him with concern. "Everything alright, sir?"

Rostam nodded, and strapped himself in. Even the seatbelt felt luxurious, like expensive linen with triple the thread count of what he was used to, and the tongue made a deep, satisfying clunk when it went into its buckle. Theo McNamara's group didn't scrimp on expenses.

As the pilots went through their checklist of buttons, switches and lights, Rostam took out his documents. Tina Waspell had chosen to leave her card in Rostam's Iranian passport, next to his familiar photograph and unfamiliar name, in an alphabet he couldn't read. The card was embossed with Homeland Security insignia, but no department. It didn't look fake to Rostam, but then neither did his fraudulent passport.

She did have a rank. SPECIAL COUNSEL TINA WASPELL 1 202 351 0650 was all it said. Washington area code. *Special Counsel.* The combination of Sunday School dress code and visible relish of absolute power was a terrifying combination.

Why did Tina Waspell want Theo McNamara? And which of the pair scared him more? Only McNamara was offering a path to what he wanted.

"We're cleared for take-off, Mr James. All set?" It was odd to hear this personalized address spoken directly to him, rather than over an intercom. Rostam gave the thumbs up sign. This was the first time he had had to start thinking about how he was going to track down Zadi.

G-force pressed him back into his seat as the small plane seemed to flip into turbo mode. There was no door separating the cockpit from the cabin. Rostam watched the red-and-white perforated metal buffer at the end of the runway grow from a spec into half of the view before George pulled on an elegant electronic control stick. All he could see over the pilots' heads now was dead air, full of soggy hail, lacking the oomph to transform into snow.

It was just as the plane emerged into late afternoon sunlight above the clouds that Rostam decided who to contact first in London. As the plane levelled out Andy clambered out of the co-pilot's chair and came back with a hesitant smile on his face.

"I was supposed to give you this when you came aboard," he said, pressing an invisible button flush to the walnut surface of the cabin to reveal a hidden cupboard next to Rostam's seat. He reached inside and brought out a MacBook. "You don't need a password or anything. They must think you're trustworthy."

Andy flashed a shy smile with this remark, which made Rostam wonder what the pilots would have been told about this trip. The minimum possible was a safe guess.

Rostam smiled at the idea that a character as secretive as Theo McNamara would depend on passwords. It was a certainty everything Rostam did online on the plane or his apartment in London would be visible to McNamara, but McNamara would know that himself. Trying to look up anything in secret there would be like a prisoner in maximum security trying to take a dump in private: simply cannot be done.

When he opened the laptop, a message appeared in block capitals on top of the generic Apple mountainous screensaver.

WELCOME ABOARD. PUT ON YOUR HEADPHONES.

Rostam reached into the wall space and found a pair of Sony over-ear headphones at the bottom. They had a jack attached to a wire, which initially surprised him, but then he reflected that it would be easier to insulate whatever the computer had to tell him from the pilots, should they fancy eavesdropping. The puffy leather around each earpiece felt reassuringly expensive, and shut out the rushing airplane white noise, so that for a moment Rostam was magicked away into his private space.

He closed his eyes and thoughts of Millie and Celia shot out of his unconscious like reincarnated metaverse avatars. Without thinking he slid the jack into the port on the side of the laptop and his reverie was interrupted by a man's voice speaking slowly, but with military precision. The accent was from the Deep South. The screen gradually changed to a series of swelling, shrinking and rotating shapes. The first was a donut. The second a sphere. Then a donut with a double hole.

"Welcome aboard, Rostam. You will land at Biggin Hill. You'll be met by a driver who will take you to your apartment on Albemarle St. It's a fancy address, just behind the Ritz Hotel."

Rostam shook his head. He knew all this.

"My name is Carl Force. The phone you were issued will have my details sent to you. Bahman Zadi will be in London on Saturday. Your way in is through the Iranian intellectual diaspora in London. Start with your old buddy Ahmad Jamalzhad - see if he can make the connection. Keep me updated at all times. I need to know where you go, who you see, what they say. When you have something, you want to say to Mr McNamara, you do it through me. Good luck."

Rostam took out the new cell and saw that a message had already arrived over the airplane WIFI. The contact had an image included - a thumbnail photograph taken from too many steps back of a pale skinned man with an angular face and short brown hair with an old-fashioned side-parting. He looked familiar.

The first thing to do on arrival in London would be to find a way to communicate that couldn't be monitored by Force. Clean electronics. If Theo McNamara and his organization were omnipotent he wouldn't have fallen into the arms of Tina Waspell and her crew. Then he needed to see Ahmad Jamalzhad. After that he'd decide what to do about Carl Force.

The southern voice over his headphones had stopped speaking, and the familiar noise cancelling silence was the first reassurance Rostam had enjoyed all day. He sat back in his chair and closed his eyes.

Chapter Fifteen

Friday January 14

London

Rostam came out of an electronic Aladdin's cave on Tottenham Court Road with a fresh laptop, burner phone, and a prepaid Visa card. The global green of Starbucks was visible a hundred yards north, just past the London Underground red-circle-and blue-band outside Goodge Street. Rostam needed to see if the new card worked and had to repress nerves as he waved it at the pay point, earning a dopamine hit when it read *APPROVED*. He took his macchiato to a corner circular table, covered in the previous customer's croissant flakes, next to a power socket.

As it turned out, his brand-new Razer Blade 17 came fully charged. Setting up a secure VPN over public WIFI took an hour, an extra double-shot macchiato, and more patience than Rostam thought he had in reserve. A lot of effort to send over the little he had on Theo McNamara and Tina Waspell to Dread.

Dread was the best digital detective Rostam knew. If he couldn't uncover Theo's game, nobody else would either. Rostam thought about sending Millie an update but decided not to worry her. He'd wait until he had good news.

Shaking his head, Rostam stripped the cellophane from the first Nokia box and fired it up. Ahmad's number was engraved on his memory. He'd be teaching at this time of day, but Rostam called all the same. Nobody answers the phone to unknown numbers. Rostam was reconciled to having to leave a series of voicemails until Ahmad would be forced to listen to one. He sat back and stared at the cafe ceiling in expectation of a long day of frustration, wondering how far his jet lagged soul had clambered up the trans-Atlantic umbilical cord to him in London.

Ahmad answered first ring.

"What now?" Ahmad's voice was resigned, more than angry, but anger wasn't far below the surface. It never was with Ahmad.

"We haven't spoken in months and that's how you greet me?"

"Who is this? I told you last time I've had enough - "

"Ahmad, this is Rostam."

"What the hell?"

The delight in Ahmad's voice reached out of the tinny Nokia head-piece and filled Rostam with joy. "Rostam, you slippery sod - what are you doing awake at this hour?"

"I'm in town, man. You at work?"

"You know me. Down the salt mines 9-5 24/7, innit bruv."

"Your students at Imperial know you speak like that?"

"What my students don't know would fill many shelves of the library. Don't spoil my day talking about them. When am I going to see you?"

"Would Dana mind if I come over?"

"Don't be ridiculous. She'll scalp me if you don't come round."

"When do you finish digging up salt?"

"For a special occasion, I can be home by four."

"Same address?"

"I couldn't afford to buy it in the first place, and you want me to move?"

"I haven't seen you yet and you're already complaining. See you at four."

Rostam checked his watch again and sighed. Time to do some preliminary research around Zadi while there was - probably - nobody watching, and then back to the Walpole apartment for a couple of hours sleep, before getting over to Brentford.

Chapter Sixteen

Chicago

Celia was still asleep on Friday morning when Millie sat down in front of her laptop. The girl was too small to remember that Thursday night was Dad night and hadn't minded swapping Werner Circle hot-dogs for pizza. Mother and daughter sang their way through *Frozen II* together. Each slice of pizza had Millie wondering how she would feel about not being able to pay for it, now she was unemployed. In the middle of the night that felt more like unemployable.

Millie had never considered herself lonely since the divorce. She had her daughter, her colleagues, college friends scattered around the major cities, a good relationship with Rostam, and an even closer one with Maryam, his Mom, in New York. But now, with Loeb blackening her name, and the open questions inevitable when someone of good standing is summarily fired, most of those relationships were history. Maryam was the only person she'd called.

She didn't like the idea of contacting old buddies just at the point she was on her ass. Alumni networks are for helping up those who are already helping themselves, not rescuing fallen comrades. Carmen owed her a conversation, but it was for her to offer, not Millie to demand, and Carmen was the definition of a company woman. This would be hard for her. Lisa Matsui was already hired. No point in hounding her before she had time to see what Loeb was going to offer. If they were going to offer anything.

Maryam had been brusque, compassionate, and to the point.

Get yourself out of that city and bring my granddaughter to New York. You need distance to give you perspective.

Millie's character was not to follow instructions, no matter how caring, but after a night of bad dreams, desperate three-in-the-morning reflections and no new ideas, a trip to the West Village looked like her least bad option.

Millie looked at her reflection in the black mirror of her laptop screen before logging on. Everyone said Celia had her eyes, and it was true: blue, large, and disarmingly innocent. Millie's rage now was like Celia's when she felt she was being punished for something that wasn't her fault. The horror of basic injustice - that feeling that *this shouldn't be happening to me - I don't deserve it - this isn't fair* - doesn't change much from infancy to adulthood.

Millie had spent summers helping build houses for Habitat for Humanity. She was a warrior for fairness, for equality of opportunity. O'Dwyer's accusations kept rolling round her head. He seemed to think she was some kind of traitor. He'd talked about getting a call. A call from whom? How could she defend herself against allegations as crazy as this? And how come Lisa seemed so pessimistic? Maybe that was just her natural under promise-and-overdeliver ethos.

Millie's workstation was in her spare room, to keep it safe from her daughter and to avoid having two screens on the go in the same space. The room was kept immaculate. Celia was discouraged from playing in here, and it had been a while since anyone had visited.

It wasn't yet six o'clock. There was no cloud cover and the lights of Chicago spread out to the dark horizon. Millie kept her apartment at a steady twenty-four degrees. The other side of her window would be minus fifteen.

For as long as she could remember, the first thing she'd log onto from home was Bloomberg. Before work email or checking the Wall St Journal she wanted to see what was happening in markets. But the Bloomberg licence was paid for by Loeb, so might be gone already. *It might run to the end of the month,* she thought, and placed the pad of her right thumb on the sensor.

The screen flashed into life, and Millie almost vomited onto her keyboard.

A PowerPoint slide filled the screen. A moving GIF of a figure dressed in a black burka, with a pair of bullet belts crossed from each shoulder, shaking an AK-47 held above the head in one hand.

MILLIE JAMES = JIHADI WHORE was the header.

But it wasn't the offensive message or crazy photograph that made her feel sick. It was the cursor. It was flashing. Someone had conjured up this obscenity right here. This wasn't some kind of prank message that had been sent to her computer.

Someone came in here and typed this at my desk.

Was Celia ok? Millie rushed across to the small chamber off her own room, the child's first bedroom of her own. She's only moved Celia there a couple of months previously. It was less than fifteen steps and seemed to take an hour to reach.

Her daughter lay in her infant sleeping bag, on her back, snoring gently, a picture of innocent beauty. Millie fought the desire to pick her up. It would be selfish - comfort for Mommy, not child.

Millie felt violated. Her home had been broken into. She ran to the apartment door and opened it, suddenly scared she might see a stranger in the hallway. The lock was undamaged. No sign of forced entry. There was no other door. Could they have come in the window?

Millie shut the door and walked around her living room, with floor to ceiling windows looking over the city. The windows could only open a couple of inches by design. It had always amused her in a dark way. This wasn't Las Vegas where an unlucky punter might decide to throw themselves out in despair.

There was no way in but the door, which meant they knew how to bypass the lock. Millie got on well with George on the front desk, but how well did she truly know him? Was he or his boss in on this? Or did these people know how to pick electronic locks? She wasn't sure which of those two possibilities scared her more.

Her world was no longer secure.

Millie found herself in the middle of her living room, looking to see if anything had been disturbed. She kept her home as neatly arranged as was possible with a three-year-old mobile unit of perpetual destruction on the premises. Nothing looked out of place.

What was there to steal? She scurried to the safe, recessed into a wall in the kitchen. She fumbled the combination once, twice. "Sharpen up, Millie. Get a grip on yourself," she said under her breath, subconsciously not wanting to swear loudly even with Celia asleep, and it helped. Millie slowed her breathing and opened the safe. Passports. Social security data. Birth certificates. Nothing out of place.

These animals just wanted to scare her? Well, they had succeeded.

Millie kept thinking.

What bugs might have been left? What other sick acts of vandalism had been perpetrated? Who do you call when someone has broken into your apartment, but nothing has been taken? She hadn't logged on after getting home with Celia the night before. She had had too much on her mind. Had O'Dwyer sent someone to do this, just as he was summoning Millie up to his office to fire her? Did Loeb have some kind of team who did this dirty work for them? Millie couldn't believe it - it felt so distant to her image of the firm. Was there any point in calling the cops? Millie dismissed the thought as soon as she had it. They wouldn't even visit for an accusation like this. She had a vision of a middle-aged, moustache-wearing Chicago cop telling her she didn't know how to take a joke.

At best she only had thirty minutes to think this through before the morning routine would kick in. She fought down something not very different from fear, and walked back into the spare room, where the figure in the burka was waiting for her, rifle waving above her head. No need to speculate about *whore* - that was just default sexist abuse. But why *jihadi?* It must relate to the accusations of disloyalty she received the day before.

Was there anything on her computer they would have stolen? Any old Loeb files? No - Millie kept everything confidential in the office. *Had kept*, she said to herself.

A connection clicked in her brain. *This must have something to do with Rostam. Has he been talking about Islam on his podcast?* She looked at the image again. *Is it something to do with Iran?* Millie had never been much interested in Islamic fundamentalism, either explanations for it or the constant rounds of anti-Muslim propaganda on the news networks. Nor had Rostam ever had anything to say about his mother's country. Even Maryam was quiet on the subject, outside of childhood memories. All the same, Millie didn't think the burka-wearer was Iranian. The black clothing was different somehow to the less elaborate version she sometimes saw on news clips from Tehran.

She picked up her cell. The last time she tried Rostam there had been no answer. WhatsApp said he hadn't been on since Thursday lunchtime. Things were moving too fast. Twenty-four hours ago she felt safe in her home and her work. It was twelve hours since it was only her home that was her fortress. Now she wasn't safe anywhere, in Chicago at least.

It was still only six o'clock, seven in New York. She hadn't wanted to run to her ex-mother-in-law yesterday when Maryam had offered. That was then. Things had changed.

What time did Maryam have to leave for school? Millie called and Maryam answered first ring.

"Jun-am. How are you doing?"

"You're wide awake early."

"I'm old. Drinking tea and looking forward to my subway ride to work. What's up?"

Millie told her what had happened.

"You need to get out of there. Come to New York."

Millie leaned forward to her keyboard and stopped.

"What's wrong?"

"I'm paranoid. If they broke into my apartment just to show they could, I must assume they're monitoring everything I do. Hang on."

Millie reached forward and pressed ESC to get rid of the appalling image in front of her, but nothing happened. She put her cell on speaker, dropped to all fours, crawled behind the workstation, and turned off the power. By the time she was back in her seat Maryam was talking again.

"There're seats on the 11.20 Southwestern. I'll buy tickets for you and Celia. Just take ID and pick them up at the airport."

"But - "

"Listen, whoever these people are, if they're bugging your phone, or your apartment, or can access airline booking software, they already know what you're doing. So what? If they wanted to physically harm you or Celia they had the opportunity. It's a mistake to underestimate your enemies, but don't turn them into God either. You've had a nasty shock and you're bringing your daughter for a rest with her grandma. Just pack whatever you need and jump in an Uber to the airport, ok?'

Millie felt tension draining out of her. It was a relief to speak to someone sensible who was on her side, when she didn't even know who was against her yet.

"Thanks, Maryam. I'll pay you back for the tickets."

"You bet your sweet ass you will, honey," cackled Maryam. There was no humour she loved more than American colloquialisms, which she normally got wrong.

"You nailed it. See you later."

"Travel safe and don't worry more than you have to. There's always a silver lining - this way I get to see my granddaughter."

Millie hung up and gazed out at the city lights, trying to unscramble her brain. It wouldn't be dawn in Chicago for another hour or more, and she was further away than that from being able to see the silver lining to her situation.

Chapter Seventeen

London

"What are you doing in Europe, you lunatic?" Ahmad flung his front door open and opened his arms wide to embrace Rostam.

"The Piccadilly Line isn't as miserable as I remember it," said Rostam.

"I remember Covid fondly. We moved from masks and social distancing to having our noses stuck in each other's armpits two-and-a-half seconds after restrictions ended. Tea?"

Before Rostam could answer there came the sound of squealing, as two tiny girls sprinted up the hallway from the kitchen he knew lay at the back of the house.

"Fatimeh. Esmeralda. Come to your Uncle Rostam."

But the girls had stopped short of their guest and instead were each hiding behind one of their father's legs.

"Good girls," said Ahmad, ruffling their glossy dark hair with a hand for each. "You keep this up. Don't go near strange men."

"Not even their father's best friends?" demanded Rostam in mock horror.

"The rest of my friends are open season. Just avoid this one."

Fatimeh, the older by barely a year, had already got over her embarrassment and grabbed Rostam by the hand.

"Come and see Mammy."

Esmeralda grabbed the other hand as they passed, and the two girls pulled Rostam into the kitchen.

Dana, a slender, white-skinned Irish woman, several inches taller than her Iranian husband, turned away from the stove and came over for a hug. Her hair smelled of shampoo and tomato sauce. The married couple made an aesthetic contrast: both slim and austerely attractive, Ahmad dark and of middle height, Dana tall and pale.

"You see what marriage has done for me?" said Dana. "That monster has me chained to the oven."

"Sure, he does," said Rostam. "I warned you about Iranian men and their habits."

"Bollocks," said Dana, with a wide smile. "Pure bollocks. You told me I was a lucky woman, and you weren't wrong."

Rostam gave her a kiss on the cheek. He knew Ahmad did most of the cooking. Somehow as a household the Jamalzhads managed the impossible juggling of both parents working full time while staying involved with their six- and five-year-old daughters. On nights when he couldn't sleep Rostam couldn't help contrasting that achievement with his divorce from Millie.

"And how are Millie and Celia?" asked Dana over her shoulder as she went back to the pasta sauce.

"Fighting fit. Millie's going great guns at Loeb. Wouldn't be surprised if she made managing director this year. And you know Celia. That girl is a force for good."

"I follow her progress on Facebook assiduously. Put your name in the pot?" Dana pointed at the saucepan on the hob.

"I'm grand, thank you. Jet lag plays havoc with my digestion."

"Keep digestive issues to yourself, granddad."

The kitchen felt full, with Rostam standing next to their circular wooden table while Fatimeh and Esmeralda ran round and round him, touching his legs on each rotation as though he were a lucky charm, while Dana stood on wooden spoon duty at the stove and Ahmad leaned on the door jamb, smiling benevolently at his family and best friend.

Rostam looked over, caught his eye and jerked his head towards the back of the house, where Ahmad and Dana shared a study.

"Girls, stay with Mammy for now. Daddy and Rostam need to have a little chat."

There was an obligatory wail from the children which lasted no longer than the time it took Dana to offer them a chance to take turns stirring the pot with her wooden spoon. It was only a couple of steps to the study. Ahmad let Rostam through first, right hand pressed to his own chest in classical Iranian hospitality, and closed the door quietly behind them.

"So, what's up?"

"You know what I said about not thinking I'd ever suffer from paranoia?" asked Rostam.

"Uh-huh."

"Well, as it turns out, they really are out to get me."

Ahmad chuckled and threw himself onto an agglomeration of beanbags by French windows, which looked onto the rapidly darkening tiny square of decking which constituted a back garden in West London. Rostam sat at the computer desk by the door.

"How come I get the ergonomic desk chair, when you're the poor bastard with a bad back?" asked Rostam.

"You're in the working chair, I'm on the listening beanbag. Tell me what's going on."

Rostam sat back and sighed before answering. "It all happened so fast. This is Friday evening, right? Not even lunchtime back home."

Ahmad nodded but said nothing. He was a great listener. This had been the root of their relationship, Rostam expounding plans for world domination, Ahmad taking them in, and pointing out their flaws.

"All those years of thinking the system was out to get me. Well, it wasn't all a waste of time. Got me into crypto early." Rostam was suddenly exhausted. The smells of supper cooking and sounds of the girls playing in the kitchen next door, his old friend sitting on the study floor as though they were students again, a domestic environment where people liked him. It was very hard to reconcile with Theo McNamara by Lake Michigan; Tina and her frozen bath in darkness at the airport; the brand-new private jet; the antiseptic luxury of Walpole Apartments. "I could fall asleep right now."

"Why don't you?"

"No time. You'll understand when I tell you." Rostam was reluctant to bring his drama into his friend's life, so delayed. "C'mon Ahmad - give me a bit of real life. How are things with you?"

"I'm doing great. Got tenure last summer. Machine learning is the hot area at Imperial - they love me. You know how it works. The bean counters measure academic success by how many students you can attract, and right now my seminars are full. Of course, that means I don't get any real work done, but that's the curse of the employed academic."

"Better to be a useful member of society than a mathematician stuck in a garret, scribbling formulae on the walls."

Ahmad laughed. "That ship has sailed, my friend. Two daughters to feed. I don't think Dana wants a third graffiti-artist in the house. The girls have that job down. Now, your turn."

Rostam tried to decide where to start and found words splurging from him.

"Turns out broadcasting comes with fringe benefits. You know you're doing well when you start getting death threats more days than you don't."

Ahmad gave what Rostam knew to be a typical Iranian shrug to indicate being both mystified and amused by the randomness of the universe, all at the same time.

"Crazies aren't the only listeners. I've been found by West Coast venture capital."

"The holy grail," murmured Ahmad.

"They flew me here private. I'm stashed in some grace-and-favour apartment behind the Ritz Hotel."

"I'm trying to work out if I should feel sorry for you, or just jealous."

"They want me to deliver a message to an Iranian boss. Bahman Zadi. He's connected with the academics here."

Rostam stopped speaking. A day later, and a continent away, he was struggling to process what had happened. Ahmad didn't hurry him. Rostam looked at the bookshelf and noticed two copies of *Gödel, Escher, Bach.* He looked back at Ahmad.

"Can you help me?"

Ahmad's eyes widened in shock. Rostam rushed on.

"They gave me a file on Zadi but it read like something from a whack-job Wikipedia. These guys think he is Iran's head of crypto. Early sixties. Smart cookie. Farzanegan School, Sharif, then a year at MIT. Popular guy. Not obviously religious at that time, but not a drinker."

"That doesn't mean he's religious. I'm not a drinker either."

"And you're a pagan. I know. We are talking about an Iranian math guy after all. I'm the only one of us who likes to have fun. Zadi went back to Iran to do his military service, even though he was doing well enough at school to stay in the States. He disappeared for a few years. This is McNamara's hypothesis: Zadi is working with the Russians, Chinese, and the smart guys in the crypto room to build an alternative to the US dollar. Nobody knows better than us how Obama and Trump weaponised the dollar system. Zadi made his bones helping the big wheels in the guards to start moving the money they've stolen into bitcoin. Now he's helping to effect oil sales through sanctions in crypto too. If these guys are correct, the Chinese have been paying for Iranian oil in bitcoin for the past six months."

"You want me involved in all this?"

"Of course not. But do you know someone who can put us together? I'm desperate here. It was an offer that came alongside a threat. I don't want to go back with nothing."

"What kind of threat?"

"Theo knew too much about my family life."

Ahmad slowly inhaled and exhaled through his nose while maintaining eye contact with Rostam. It was a familiar sight from long hours of discussion in the past. Other people had Rodin's statue as their image of The Thinker. Rostam had this picture of Ahmad: knees up, sunken cheeks tightly covered in a clipped black beard, long narrow nose, deep dark eyes, and hair that had already receded almost to the top of his head.

"You and Millie still talk. What does she think?"

"Millie's right behind it. I'll be honest - if I pull this off, it wouldn't hurt my chances with her. I didn't get a chance to see Celia, though I did pop by her kindergarten, like a deadbeat dad."

"Deadbeat dads are dads that don't care. That's not you," said Ahmad in an absent tone that told Rostam he was thinking about something else. "What do you want me to do?"

"Talk to your pals. People like that LSE Professor, Yazdi. Anyone else who likes hanging around with expat political types. Oh yeah, I forgot to mention. They've given me an Iranian passport."

Ahmad raised an index finger.

"Fake?"

Rostam nodded.

"Dump it. It can only help them monitor you - maybe report you when they run out of use. Funny they bothered with an Iranian one. You're the least Iranian Persian guy I've ever met."

"You're crazy if you think these people could care less."

"*Never underestimate the fear of the other*. One of Dana's favourite sayings."

"We should listen to her. Professors of anthropology know a lot of stuff we don't."

"Don't I know it, my friend."

Thudding feet came down the corridor and the girls barrelled into the room.

"Mummy said you'd pick us up," cried Fatimeh, running straight to Rostam.

"Did she? Someone's got to tackle you two little monsters!" he said, picking up Fatimeh under one arm, and a delighted Esmeralda with the other, before stamping around the office, huffing and puffing like a troll.

"Sorry, Rostam, you've got the girls all excited. What else can I say?" asked Dana from the doorway. "Hand them back to me and I'll stick them in the bath."

"Filthy creatures!" said Rostam. "Into the bath with you!" He set the girls down on their feet next to their mother. Both girls immediately jumped behind her legs, giggling with their hands over their mouths.

"You shouldn't be such a good troll," smiled Dana over her shoulder, as she ushered the girls away.

"Story of my life right now," said Rostam, settling back into the office chair. "In demand from all the wrong people."

Ahmad got up to close the door.

"This is something I'd normally run a mile from. You're sure?"

Seeing Ahmad take the situation seriously made Rostam wake up. Rostam smiled at his friend.

"I am. This could set me up for the next stage. And I'm also intrigued. Could they be right about this Zadi guy? I don't think the deep state - or whoever these people are - is entirely wrong to see crypto as an assault on the dollar system. The conspirasphere is full of people who think the NSA invented bitcoin. Half those lunatics seem to think Satoshi Nakamoto works out of the Pentagon."

"The guy that invented bitcoin? I thought he was US government too," Ahmad said, with a smile on his face.

"No way. Why would the State help create an alternative to their biggest weapon? They're not that smart. I've got my own theory and maybe this search will help. Anyway, you're the smartest Iranian I know in London."

Ahmad didn't respond.

"I suppose now you are a tenured Professor, flattery doesn't work the way it used to."

"I was just trying to remember how many other Iranians you know in town."

"None as clever as you, but they mostly tell better jokes."

Ahmad rocked onto his feet and stood up, sighing loudly. "I hope you do that too. Otherwise, it's just me."

"What?"

"Making an involuntary sound every time you stand up. My theory is it happens when you turn thirty or have your first child. One or the other."

"We're in the same club, man. Again."

"C'mon. Let's go upstairs. Bath time for the girls."

Chapter Eighteen

"You are going to keep yourself safe, now, aren't you?" said Dana, as Rostam left the Jamalzhads. "I'd feel better if you stayed with us."

"Don't make this any harder than it needs to be," said Rostam. "Me too, but you know how it is. People to avoid, puzzles to solve."

"You know your problem, Rostam? You'd sell your own mother for a clever quip."

"She's twice as smart and ten times as dangerous."

"Represent, sister! The Mammy's Union is strong." Dana punched Rostam smartly on the shoulder. "Seriously though, you ok?"

"Everything's under control. Ahmad is on my side. What could go wrong?"

Dana looked over her shoulder as Ahmad walked down the stairs and towards them.

"No comment. Just don't get him into trouble. He's been like an excited puppy ever since you called."

"Rostam wants to use me for my connections," said Ahmad, winking at his friend over Dana's shoulder.

"Just because it's funny doesn't mean it isn't true," said Rostam.

"Nothing's serious to you two, is it?" said Dana.

"Nothing's serious because everything is," said Rostam, kissing her goodbye. "Keep raging, Dana. It suits you."

"I'll make a couple of calls in the morning." said Ahmad.

"I owe you," said Rostam, and walked down the poorly lit terraced street towards the main road. He felt simultaneously better and worse. The temptation to accept Dana's offer and stay under the same roof as his friends and their children was huge, but it would feel like hiding, and might put the Jamalzhads at risk. You can't run away when you have a child of your own.

It was still raining but the clouds had done their worst. This late-night January drizzle had been what Rostam liked least about London when he lived there, but now carried the tinge of nostalgia which works alchemy on the past.

The Jamalzhads lived on a long street of near identical houses, each asserting its individuality in little paved front yards that ranged from immaculate plant beds to collections of scavenged bicycle parts, decomposing back to their constituent materials under the pressure of rain, rust and the kind of neglect which is slow murder.

Three young men in black puffa jackets similar to Rostam's own walked past him, leaving a pungent cloud of smoke behind them. Cannabis mixed with rolling tobacco. European style. Rostam found himself breathing it in through his nose. In his first weeks at Imperial finding tobacco in shared joints at parties had been part of the general culture shock. Now it had a nimbus of lost youth, like the drizzle.

Boston Manor station at midnight had more station staff than passengers. Partygoers were still in the city, not out here in a western suburb. A train back east arrived only a minute after Rostam arrived on the platform, and he had his choice of seats. He checked the Piccadilly Line map again to set his mental clock for 11 stops.

Rostam felt an overwhelming urge to close his eyes. With the instinct of an experienced urban traveller, he stuck his hands in the pockets of his coat, rechecked that the zip was up to the top to discourage casual pickpockets, drew his feet in below his knees so as not to sprawl across the aisle, and allowed his chin to drop to his chest. He was asleep before the train pulled into the next station.

The momentum of trains had a somnolent effect on Rostam even in the mornings back home. He frequently napped on the L. Even now, sleep starved and under huge pressure, he had no dreams. Which made it all the more surprising when he opened his eyes to check he hadn't missed his stop - no fear, they were about to pull into Earl's Court, and he had at least another ten minutes of rest ahead - only to find the person in the seat designated for vulnerable people by the door to his left was occupied by someone who was speaking to him.

"Evening, Rostam. What's the probability of bumping into you? A numbers guy such as yourself should be able to put a figure on it. 10,000 to 1?"

Rostam looked the speaker in the face. They had never met before, but Rostam recognised the Southern accent and dazzling smile. How had Carl Force found him?

Chapter Nineteen

"You guys really do go the extra mile, don't you? I was supposed to call you when the time came," said Rostam.

Force in person had the glossy skin and white teeth of a man who saw his appearance as a tax-deductible expense. His already wide smile broadened as he saw Rostam take him in, until his face seemed leporine: a long face with huge front teeth and sharp points at each cheekbone. He wore a black MA-1 airman's jacket and matching jeans, one leg folded across the other. The aftereffects of Rostam's brief nap gave Force's appearance an air of unreality. Rostam found his eyes rolling all the way down the newcomer's figure until he fixed on cherry Dr Marten boots, so highly polished they shone in the institutional light of a night-time underground carriage, with the raging ache of a tension headache.

"I expected you to call when you landed, buddy. Or when you checked into the apartment. Your file says nothing about you being a shy type."

The train pulled into Earl's Court station. Cold air washed into the carriage along with a lumpy torrent of new passengers. Friday night wastrels, spraying money around night-time London like water spluttering through a sieve. The empty seats past Rostam filled on either side of the aisle with chattering student nurses, eddies and swirls of drama, outrage and tears filling the air.

Opposite him slumped a drunk middle-aged man who'd wrung the last fun out of his soul years before, eyes flickering across young people with resentment that he wasn't one of them, never would be and, most likely, never had been. Rostam's gaze switched from the drunk back to Force's surprising boots, and then back to his wide open, ingenue blue ey es.

"That's because I'm not. I'm to call you in case of emergencies." Rostam shook his head. "The only emergency here is my lack of sleep."

"I understand completely." Force spoke with such sincerity it was almost believable. "We don't want you to feel under any pressure. Just want to make sure we know what's going on."

"You seem to know plenty."

Force rocked forward without unfolding his legs and tapped Rostam on his knee smartly twice.

"Don't be a tease, Rostam. We're here to help."

Rostam shivered when he remembered the last person to tell him that. He had never enjoyed invasions of his personal space. It would seem weak to complain, and disproportionate to tell Force to get lost. Anyway, he still wasn't wide awake.

The social rules that govern travelling on the underground Rostam remembered from student days didn't apply at midnight on weekends. Normally two strangers having a conversation would be remarkable, but other than the hilarity of the student nurses, who were heading to a gay nightclub in Charing Cross that Rostam was pleased to learn still existed, nobody seemed interested in the two Americans.

"Look, Rhett Butler, I've got my instructions. Why are you trailing me?"

Force's smile was unchanged. "I appreciate the compliment, but Rhett Butler was from South Carolina. I'm an Arkansas native."

"You Southerners all sound the same."

"Touché. I might struggle to distinguish *Noo Yoik* from *Chic-A-go* myself."

Rostam doubted that - Force looked like he had memorized Rostam's entire life story preparatory to this meeting.

"Whaddya think of the commercials they've got over here?" Force disengaged his blue eyes from Rostam and gestured towards the series of landscape layout commercials, above the horizontal map of the Piccadilly Line sketched along the top of the carriage. At one end was Huel, a dietary supplement. At the far end stood an impenetrably British advert for sofas. In the middle were a series of crypto ads. FTX exchange listed the lot by acronym: BTC, ETH, USDT, ADA, BNB, XRP. A service Rostam didn't recognise recommended Dogecoin. Gemini called users to its wallet.

"Just as big here as back home," continued Force.

"Crypto is a global marketplace."

"Don't know much about finance. Looking forward to learning from you."

"I'll tell you a secret," said Rostam, and looked across at the drunk opposite, who couldn't decide if he wanted to ogle partygoers or fall asleep. Force leaned in so close that if Rostam had been James Bond, he would have been able to identify the agent's brand of aftershave. Rostam waited until a web of drool hanging from the drunk's lower lip detached and splashed to the corrugated floor of the carriage.

"Nobody does," said Rostam eventually. He looked into Force's disarmingly blue eyes to see if could see blooms of anger. Rostam was disappointed.

"Good one, Rostam. Nobody knows anything about finance, eh? I guess that's why you majored in math instead of economics."

The train pulled into Knightsbridge where the bulk of the party crowd disembarked. It looked like an external power had forced a mass of mercury trails back together into a single ball, as the chaos of a score of drunks turned into a solid body and trooped up the platform together, their high-pitched chatter audible until the doors slid closed.

"That must be your crowd now you're divorced, huh? Out wild-cattin' again?"

Rostam was disgusted at the suggestion. The train was pulling into Hyde Park Corner and the drunk across the aisle shifted uncomfortably in his sleep. As doors began to open, he barked out a mostly liquid pool of vomit. Some splashed onto Carl's cherry red boots.

"That's my cue, Carl. Don't follow me. I'll call you, like the man says," said Rostam as he skipped across the spreading sick towards the door. Safely on the platform, he saw Force look both ways before pushing the drunk down onto the floor, before stamping on his hand repeatedly, teeth showing through a thin-lipped smile. The victim's body jack-knifed but Rostam couldn't hear his screams through the closed carriage doors. Rostam's imagination flicked back to Tina Waspell and her bullyboys.

That poor bastard won't get the use of his hand back. Is Force doing this for fun, or is he showing off for my benefit? Someone has to make these people accountable.

Force turned around and raised his index finger to his brow in Rostam's direction in a salute, before walking down to the next carriage, leaving his mess behind him.

Rostam negotiated the subway back to Piccadilly and the ten-minute walk to Walpole without his rage ebbing by a millimetre.

Chapter Twenty

Manhattan

Maryam couldn't contain her excitement. It was six months since she'd last seen her granddaughter, Celia.

"How was the journey, jun-am?" said Maryam.

Maryam came down to the street to find Millie standing outside her cab, Celia nuzzling into her shoulder, mismatched pair of wheeled suitcases and infant car-seat askew on the sidewalk of West 21st.

Maryam knocked on the window of the cab.

"Hey you, driver. You got three vulnerable females out here."

The driver tutted as he shambled out of the car.

"Get those bags inside, my friend," said the older woman, and he did as he was told.

"It's a relief to see one situation taken under control," said Millie. "Don't worry about Celia. She's just shy."

"The day I start worrying about how children react, call the undertaker," said her former mother-in-law. Millie leaned into Maryam's shoulder and breathed in her warmth, and the scent of lemons and sugar that emanated from her skin. "Too cold out here - tell me everything inside. You take the baby, I'll get the bags in the elevator."

The driver squeezed himself back behind the wheel and was lost into night-time traffic.

Before she could say a thing, Millie had been pushed inside the building and into the elevator.

"I used to enjoy traveling," she said to her former mother-in-law.

"Everything's harder with a child."

"It isn't that. Celia was a dream on the plane. Saved me from being lost in my own thoughts. Just feels like I'm escaping, you know?"

"No shame in that. Remember you're talking to an immigrant. To finish first, you must first finish. Sometimes that means an escape."

Maryam led the way down the corridor, herding suitcases before her like mechanical sheep.

"I've got rice - the little one needs to eat?"

"Yes please. She did her sleeping in the back of the cab."

Maryam rattled through the day's code on her combination lock and jammed Celia's little pink suitcase in the door to keep it ajar.

"Stick her in front of the idiot box and come talk to me in the kitchen."

Maryam was frying up saffron rice with handfuls of raisins and a squirt of honey when Millie joined her.

"Don't complain, Soccer Mom," said Maryam, waving the plastic honey bottle. "Sweetness is good for little ones."

"I'm complaining about nothing. You got enough for adults too? Didn't want to eat the slop on the plane," said Millie.

"Achievable goals. The secret to happiness. As it happens, I was expecting my journalist friend Hosein this evening, but he's gone silent on me. Not like him. What you kids call *getting ghosted*, am I right?"

Maryam ladled more rice into the pan.

"Ghosting is really just for dating. Heard from Rostam?"

"Not a peep. He probably thinks I'm still at that conference down in Florida."

"Wouldn't stop him calling."

Maryam shrugged.

"I didn't start putting things together until I saw that message this morning," continued Millie. "It has to be connected. He gets this exciting offer. I get fired. He disappears. Next thing I have to get out of town. I've been trying to work it out all day, but I've got washing machine head. You know?"

"I know, jun-am. Anything else out of the ordinary since this morning?"

"Nothing I noticed. Picked up the tickets the normal way. I mean, it's not like I know what to look for. I went through the apartment. Nothing else to see."

"Of course."

"I have a question for you though, Maryam."

"I'm listening."

"You're taking all this in your stride. How come you're not more surprised?"

"Pass me the bowls, will you? Just above your head there."

Millie found them.

"Just because I sound calm doesn't mean I'm not worried. There's no percentage in panic. You're doing good yourself. Things will become more clear than they are now."

"How do you know?"

"I don't know, but I have faith. Not in God, before you ask, though I'm not saying I don't believe. I put my faith in logic. There has to be a reason for what's happening, and once we find out what that is, we can do something about it. You want natural yogurt?"

Millie nodded. "Celia likes it too."

"Good girl. Did Cantillon's hatchet man say anything to you about Rostam?"

"Nothing. It was all on me."

"You been listening to the podcasts?"

"Nah - all that conspiracy stuff leaves me cold. Rostam keeps me up to speed with what he thinks about crypto. I don't have time for much else."

"And you're no financial criminal."

"I never even did a single trade in my personal account. Squeaky clean."

"You don't mind eating in front of the TV? I know your generation of parents have high standards."

Millie snorted and filled a plastic jug with water from the faucet. "I just pulled my three-year-old out of pre-school to run away from my problems. Some standards."

"Jun-am."

Maryam turned around in the galley kitchen, three bowls of rice balanced over a cat's cradle of outstretched fingers, blocking Millie in.

"Look at me."

The women were only centimetres apart, and Millie had to look down sharply to meet Maryam's gaze, but all the authority in the room rested with the older woman.

"My PhD supervisor taught me an important lesson. He wasn't much of a mathematician, to be fair, his best days were fifteen years before he heard of me, but he was no fool. You wanna hear it?"

"I have a choice?"

"*Don't beat yourself up*, he'd say, *you might bruise.*"

Millie nodded, conscious she was being schooled like one of Maryam's pupils, but enjoying the process.

"You've found yourself in a world full of dangers, none of it your doing. We've got all the enemies we need outside the camp, you hear me? Anytime you feel like blaming yourself, eat a cake, drink some tea, take up smoking, whatever you need to get over it. That's the last time I wanna hear self-pity coming outta your mouth."

Millie kept her gaze, but hoped she wouldn't be bullied into having to agree.

"Case closed. Let's feed that little Shaitoon."

Celia was stuck into a Barbie movie, cross-legged on the burgundy, beige and hazel Tabrizi rug, mouth open, shuffling from side to side on her backside in time with the dance on the screen.

"Flipping gender stereotype. Same as when I was a kid," said Millie, unable to stop herself.

"Boo sucks for you. I wish I'd had Barbie when I was a girl. Wish fulfilment is what grandkids are for."

Millie shrugged and conceded the point. "I need to get onto the head-hunter circuit and see what's out there. Don't wanna rush things with Loeb but my lawyer isn't hopeful. No time like the present."

"True enough in normal times. Maybe now we should wait."

"I don't just want to sit around waiting for Rostam to call. What's he gonna do about things anyway? Don't need some man to save us. Not even if he is your son, Maryam."

"I want to discuss it with Hosein. He'd normally be round tomorrow for backgammon."

"No problem. Celia and I can be out of your hair."

'Nah. I wanted you to stick around so we can all talk, but he's disappeared. Would be good to see if he has any an opinion. He's a smart man."

"Can't hurt."

"As you say." Maryam's attention moved to the screen. "Is that Barbie's fella, off talking to a different skinny blonde lady?"

"Ken!" shouted Celia.

"The dirty skank. Learn your lesson now little Celia. Pretty boys can't be trusted."

"Truth, sister," said Millie, leaning across and fist bumping her ex-mother-in-law.

"Barbie. It's a learning experience," said Maryam, not hiding that she was delighted with herself.

Chapter Twenty-One

Saturday January 15

London

The blinds remained undrawn, but January sun wasn't prepared to put enough effort into London to disturb anyone. Rostam padded over to a window looking down the length of Arlington St, leading to the Ritz on the corner of Piccadilly. There was only one taxi outside the hotel and no one on the pavements. This was no residential area, and tourists who had the determination to travel during a pandemic had better things to look at than the backstreets of St James's. At least it had stopped raining.

The penthouse had an elaborate Porsche-designed coffee maker on top of a wet bar so discreet it could easily have remained a secret. He swallowed the first double-strength espresso while waiting for the second, and took that through to the office on the other side of the apartment, looking west towards Knightsbridge. All Rostam could see was a haphazard collection of roofs, fire escapes, redundant TV aerials and chimneys. The property developers of Mayfair don't waste their focus on the view from above.

Now the blizzard of new information had been allowed to settle, he wanted to sort through it like a mathematician. He pulled the Razer towards him and downloaded graphics software from his Tor-encrypted DuckDuckGo browser. His abandoned PhD had been aimed at solving encryption problems by turning it into a geometry of surfaces problem, inspired by the foundations laid by his hero, Maryam Mirzakhani. The thesis would never be written, but the doodling of creating endless torus shapes to be set rotating on the screen stayed with him. When Rostam's mind went blank, it was to the vision of bulbous concave anatomically improbable shapes doing an infinite dance.

Millie had surprised him once at work in their shared office on a long ago Sunday afternoon. He had been gazing at his screensaver, feeling guilty about wasting time, and didn't realize he was under observation.

"Check out this painting," she said, leaning over his shoulder and typing *Matisse dancers* into Google. An oil painting of five human figures holding hands and dancing in a circle filled his central monitor. With a few tweaks he converted the immobile pixels into a rotating cartoon. He set himself the same task now. Walpole's WiFi was excellent, but accessing cyberspace through Tor slowed everything down, giving Rostam more time to think. He could see how the painting's figures and his toruses chimed with one another for Millie, though for him the human figure had none of the mathematical suggestiveness of his featureless, geometric shapes.

"Just imagine if each one had their own personality. Unique like a real person but blended into a single whole." He remembered stroking Millie's hands as they lay on his shoulders, and ending up in bed. The memory was agonisingly distant now: separated from Millie by a divorce certificate and the Atlantic Ocean, in his refurbished luxury prison at Walpole, rather than in the Manhattan sublet that was their first shared home on the graduate training programme at Loeb, on a mission that could realise his dreams, or destroy them. Had the memory of Millie come for a reason? His first torus, in the image of a doughnut with two holes, rotated before him on the screen. Not an image Millie would want associated with herself, too generous in its curves for her Peloton-era heavily aerobicized self-image.

Rostam fired up the MacBook and opened the preloaded Zadi file.

Theo McNamara's organization had plenty of information about Zadi but qualified it on nearly every page. There was even a colour code. Any text in black had more than one verification and could be taken as fact. Single source material was in red. Green was the colour for rumour and suggestion. Most of the document was green.

The Brits had sanctions on the IRGC, but Zadi wasn't officially on their payroll. According to McNamara's notes he had the unofficial title of General, and had served in every rank, and held an honorary role at Sharif University as a non-teaching professor of cryptography. His mugshot was different to the standard: a curly, black-and-grey hipster beard instead of the formal, clipped model preferred by the Hezbollah; wide, endearing smile; and top button of his shirt undone. He had the same dark complexion that Ahmad and Rostam shared, and his three-decade head start hadn't cost him his hair. Zadi was married, with a thirty-year-old daughter to whom he was said to be devoted. His wife was the daughter of a notorious Iranian judge of the revolutionary era, who had once sentenced hundreds of young demonstrators to death in a single group ruling. There were no photographs of the wife or daughter. Rostam shuddered at the memory of how much Theo knew about his own family.

Zadi had been a brilliant student, good enough to be sent to a school for the gifted at eleven. His own family was undistinguished.

Both parents had been teachers, which in Iran, as Rostam knew, meant they probably had to tutor through the evenings and weekends on top of their regular jobs, just to hang on among the reputable but impoverished middle class of Tehran. There was nothing in the file on the parents' political views.

Rostam found himself speculating over how they felt about their son. They would have been delighted when he got into Farzanegan school. Most academically ambitious Iranian parents would have wanted a star only-child like Bahman to establish himself abroad. Bahman performed brilliantly at MIT, coming in the top centile of his graduating classes. Some of his peers had gone on to become academics in the United States. More went to work on Wall St, and a greater number still went to the gold-paved roads of Seattle, San Francisco and Silicon Valley. McNamara's team thought he maintained contact with several of them, though this was a heavily green part of the file. That made sense. Anyone working in tech in the US communicating with someone connected to the IRGC would make efforts to stay as discreet as possible. That's what Rostam would do in their place.

Bahman Zadi had gone back to Iran instead, and even volunteered to do military service. There was a photograph of him in baggy green fatigues with a clunky rifle strapped across one shoulder, with the same beaming smile as his passport photograph, with each arm over the shoulder of an identically dressed friend. Bahman looked older than his friends but then he must have been - Rostam flicked back to the factual information right at the start - twenty-three when he did his military service, when most others were just eighteen. He would have been older, more experienced, and way smarter and better educated than pretty much anybody else he encountered in the Iranian military. Maybe this was part of the clue to his character, someone who was ambitious, canny enough to seek out an environment where he would shine, prepared to take an unconventional route to success.

His Nokia emitted an old-school ping. Only Ahmad had this number.

Result: Professor Yazdi is having a party this evening. We're invited: Dana says you can be my plus-one. Fair warning: I won't hold your hand and no goodbye kiss at midnight. Meet at Hampstead tube station at seven.

Rostam checked his watch. Five thirty. Time for a shower and not much else if he was going to be on time.

Chapter Twenty-Two

Persian pop music replaced ABBA as Rostam and Ahmad approached Professor Yazdi's front door.

"I've never got into this stuff. Mom didn't play it at home," said Rostam. "It was all Bach, Bird or Beatles growing up."

Ahmad laughed. "Don't blame your Mom for ignorance of your cultural roots. Googoosh and Anoushiravan are our Public Enemy and NWA. Now we've got Farzad Farzin and Sirvan Kosravi."

"Justin Timberlake and Bruno Mars?"

"Laugh it up. Those two make up for a lot of the ills Tehrangeles has done to Iranian culture abroad."

A young man in a dinner jacket opened the door and they were in.

The hallway was bigger than it had looked from the outside. Huge Persian carpets of brown, gold and green hung from white walls on either side and a bar had been introduced at the back of the room. The music was coming from a DJ standing uncomfortably at her single turntable in a corner, one hand to her right ear as she nodded along to the beat.

"She'd be more at home playing techno than P-pop," said Rostam.

Ahmad was too busy looking around for their host, his foot jiggling with social anxiety. The room was filled with small groups chatting quietly to one another.

“I introduce you as a cybersecurity guy, right?” said Ahmad.

The unease was catching. Rostam’s bluster was starting to wear thin. He needed Ahmad to believe in the illusion for it to work for himself. From just next to the bar a small, perfectly made-up Iranian woman waved at Ahmad. She wore a head of jet-black ringlets and a red dress whose lace fringe dragged along the floor.

“Professor Jamalzhad, this is an honour! And where is the lovely Dara?”

Even Ahmad had to bend deeply to accept the proffered air kisses.

“Hi, Camilla. Someone had to stay behind and mind the girls. I’ve brought my old friend Rostam instead. He’s visiting from the States. He’s in cybersecurity.”

“Salaam, Rostam. A new addition to our little circle. What a treat.”

"Thanks for having me," said Rostam, finding himself fixed into Camilla’s twinkling, mocking black eyes. It seemed that she was examining him through a comic lens, and he wasn’t sure he was getting a passing grade.

“Any friend of Ahmad’s is a friend of ours. Cyrus is always saying he’s the most respected Iranian professor in London.”

“Come on, Camilla,” said Ahmad. “I don’t even have proper tenure.”

“Nonsense,” said Camilla, managing to pat Ahmad on the arm without breaking eye contact with Rostam. “Do you know the rest of the gang?”

Ahmad looked around the room.

“I recognise one or two people.”

A burst of laughter as startling as a tray of dropped drinks shot out of the group to their right. Rostam looked across and saw the man leading the laugh was older and clean-shaved, with thick grey hair and matching lounge suit, well enough cut to make him look robust, rather than grossly fat. His audience were younger, two men and three women, all in their late twenties. Camilla grabbed Rostam by the arm and dragged him across the room.

"Let's start here, shall we?"

The older man was reaching the crescendo of an anecdote about how he had outsmarted a rival in a property purchase. Rostam couldn't tell if his audience were impressed, amused, or just intimidated. Camilla had enough experience as a hostess to let the dominant taleteller expunge his anecdote with a baritone bellow of laughter, swamping the accompanying glissando harmonies of his audience.

"Agha Farsian, I have two more disciples for you."

Farsian transformed his face from laughing jester to serious man of business, contracting his silvering monobrow above his prominent nose into the shape of a sail full of wind.

"Everyone here seems to be a medic or an academic," said Farsian with a practised rhythm that suggested this was neither the first nor last time he would produce this line. "Which flavour are you two?"

"This is Ahmad, the top mathematician in London, and Rostam, from America. Rostam is something important in cyberspace."

Rostam smiled and nodded as Camilla's introduction elicited a range of titters from the group. She rapidly went around the rest. Rostam registered professions: SHO, academic medical research, postdoc in physics. Farsian himself was some kind of auto-glass magnate. He carried himself with the authority of an emperor considering whether to admit two new supplicants to become courtiers. Ahmad, whose intellectual self-confidence vanished outside of the lecture hall or close family, was already nodding his head and smiling in an ingratiating fashion. Farsian had turned his attention to Rostam.

"What's your role in this mysterious cyber security of which we all keep getting reminded?" he asked. "Are you in charge of the coding, or something even more clever?"

It was time to have some fun.

"I started out in coding. You remember the malware attack of 2015, Mr Farsian?"

Farsian was nodding in agreement. He wasn't going to admit ignorance.

"Russian hackers sent malware down a Windows automatic update in Ukraine into a collection of multinationals networks. Collected hundreds of millions in ransoms - not that that was ever made public - and caused even more damage in terms of lost work and opportunity cost."

Farsian was still nodding. The attention of the group was now firmly on Rostam. He was amused at the mention of large sums of money elevated his status as a speaker. "I was involved in fixing that problem as a consultant. Saw where the big bucks were going to go so set up my own operation in the Midwest. Now we have three hundred coders and a handful of salespeople. Cyber security sells itself. Word of mouth mostly."

Now Rostam was the star of the group. Attention is a zero-sum game for men like Farsian.

"Would I have heard of your operation?" he asked.

"I doubt it. We have a lot of government business - they like us to keep a low profile. What about you? Any recommendations of where we could get good deals on new windscreens?"

The defeated look in Farsian's eyes told Rostam everything he needed to know. Game, set and match. Rostam avoided looking at

Ahmad, out of fear he might start to laugh. Just then an English accent interrupted from behind him.

"My glamorous hostess-with-the-mostest Camilla. Who are our new friends?"

The voice sounded like the toffs on Downton Abbey, which Rostam and Millie had binged on in a more innocent time.

"This is James Hanratty," said Camillia.

Chapter Twenty-Three

"Darling James," said Camillia, standing on tiptoe as Hanratty bowed down and kissed her cheeks three times: right cheek, left cheek, right cheek. Two of the junior doctors excused themselves and wandered off to join another group on the far side of the room, standing just by the elaborate carpet on the wall. Rostam concentrated on keeping his apprehension invisible as Camilla made the next round of introductions. Farsian looked relieved that the balance of power had once again been disturbed.

"And this is Rostam, a cyber security genius. Rostam, meet James, the most notorious flirt in North London."

"Only one of those reputations can be deserved," said Hanratty, shaking hands. "Good to meet you."

Rostam looked him in the eye and almost expected Hanratty to wink. His heart was racing, and it was all he could do to keep calm. Hanratty seemed prepared.

"I have so many questions about cyber security. Perhaps we could have a tete-a-tete?"

"You can tell me all about how to flirt in return," said Rostam, and was gratified to find the whole group laugh. Even Farsian had to concede.

"Can you spare Rostam, everyone?" said Hanratty. "Camilla, I'll show him some of the wonderful pictures you have upstairs."

Hanratty took Rostam by the arm before waiting for a response and walked him towards a wide staircase towards the back of the atrium.

"Do you believe in coincidence, Rostam?"

Rostam looked over his shoulder to see Ahmad inclining his head to hear another of Farsian's self-aggrandising stories. At least the car glass magnate would be pleased to see the last of him.

"Coincidence is just a word people use to describe events they consider improbable."

"Such a mathematical answer," said Hanratty, as they began climbing the stairs.

Rostam turned and checked there was no-one nearby. He grabbed Hanratty by the upper arm.

"What is going on?" hissed Rostam. "Why did Theo send me here if you are on the case?"

The sounds of the party downstairs were still loud but indistinct. There was another shift in music.

"I introduced you to Theo," said Hanratty. "Now there's someone else you should meet."

"I'm more interested in who you are."

"I'm a humble jobbing banker. We're not all free agents."

"You're here on Theo's behalf," said Rostam, releasing Hanratty's arm.

"As are you, dear boy. The moment of truth is here."

"What happens if I turn around and walk out?"

"You'd miss out on a big investment and the chance to go back to Millie a conquering hero."

Hanratty put his hands in his pockets and tilted his head back as though searching for an answer on the ceiling. Rostam could smell his aftershave. It felt unnecessarily personal. For a second, he wished Ahmad was with him, and then he dismissed the thought. Nothing dangerous was going to happen to him in Yazdi's house, but Ahmad was best out of it. Hanratty whistled three descending notes, taking Rostam by surprise.

"Try to relax, Rostam. You'll never know the whole picture, nobody ever does. But there's no way back to the shallow end for you, so you might as well listen. Go in there. Say what you have to say, get out, and I'll have you on your way back to Chicago tomorrow morning."

Rostam stared at him, sick of being manipulated. Without another word Hanratty turned around and led the way down the buffed decked corridor, their soles squeaking with every step over the sound of singing downstairs.

At the end of the corridor was a narrow staircase leading up, out of character with the rest of the house.

"This is the way to Dr Yazdi's study," said Hanratty, leading the way up.

The elaborate vaguely Islamic parquet flooring of the landing was here replaced by deep cream carpeting. Rostam instinctively worried he would leave dirty footprints behind him. At the top was a closed door.

"I'll leave you to it," said Hanratty.

He rapped his knuckles twice on the door. It was opened from within.

"Come in, Rostam," said a man's voice, speaking English with an American-tinged-with-Iranian accent.

Chapter Twenty-Four

The office was in a turret with windows all the way around.

"What do you think of the view, Rostam?" said Bahman Zadi, standing up from behind a heavy oak desk and walking over, right hand extended to shake. Rostam recognized him instantly. Zadi wore the same wide smile and greying hipster beard as in his mugshot from the file.

"Did you know Hampstead was this high up?"

The subtle charms of the dark expanse of the Heath lay north. Rostam's eyes were drawn to the glimmering spectacle of the city to the south: the 80s relic BT Tower garishly rotating, the London Eye surprisingly close, Canary Wharf winking in the East.

"I don't know how Dr Yazdi gets any work done. I find myself staring at the view. My name is Bahman, but you know that already. Our American friends will have briefed you, I'm sure."

The last thing Rostam expected to find inside was a charm offensive, but that is what he got. Bahman Zadi was short, with the erect posture and angular bone structure of an ascetic who kept time for exercise. His smile was almost shy, as if nervous Rostam wouldn't like him.

"Would you like tea? Dr Yazdi has kindly left fruit here. And we have *gaz* from Isfahan."

Zadi proffered a Perspex plate with nougat sweets on it.

"Are you *taaroffing* me?" asked Rostam.

"Ah, you know *taaroff*? I didn't think you knew any Farsi. *Bori-kalour*!"

"Mom is Iranian. Of course I know *taarof*. I don't know why Dr Yazdi has given the Revolutionary Guards access to his office. His lectures were always critical of your regime."

"You don't want tea then?"

Zadi's eyes were twinkling now. Rostam felt he was being rude. This was ridiculous. Anyway, he was thirsty.

"Tea never did anyone any harm."

Zadi walked into the corner of the room where a tarnished brass samovar was bubbling away.

"You'll take it the way we do back home?"

"When in North London do as the Iranians do."

"I knew you were funny from your podcasts," said Zadi. "It's better in person."

Rostam took the glass of tea offered and sat in front of the desk, looking to the dark side. His own reflection looked dimly back at him in the window until Zadi returned and replaced it. His host was in no hurry but drank his tea, the demure smile returning between each sip.

"So, Yazdi is one of yours?" asked Rostam.

"What do you mean by one of ours? If you mean an Iranian, yes of course. If you mean a patriot, also yes. If you mean, is he a spy, or a member of an official organization, or even does he agree unambiguously with the ideals of the Islamic Republic, then of course not.

You've heard Dr Yazdi lecture. He has complex and humane views on our country and its place in the world. I don't expect you to believe me but so do many people in my own organization, if not all. Come on, Rostam, you are a highly intelligent analyst in your heart. You know nothing is as simple as *us* against *them*."

"Tell it to the dual citizens you use as bargaining chips."

Rostam expected this to make Zadi explode. Instead, he retained the same, quizzical look in his eyes and a gentle smile on his lips.

"You're talking to me as though I was in charge of the world. Do you know who is in charge, Rostam? If you do, please tell me. Power isn't like a football match, where you pick the red team or the blue team. Professor Yazdi wants the best for himself, and his country, and his children, and all of that, just like everybody else. If you are on the outside posting ideas through a letterbox just hoping someone with power will read them, you're nowhere. So, Yazdi talks to us, just like I'm talking to you now."

"Did you agree to meet because you want to communicate with the people who sent me?"

"More because you are Maryam's son. How is your mother?"

"Teaching math in high school. Wondering what is going on. Would she be pleased if she knew we were meeting?"

"Probably not. She never liked politics. She'd tell us both to stick to numbers. Give her my best."

And the thing of it was - Rostam believed him. Zadi had the charisma of someone who has no reason to doubt themselves, underneath the humility of someone who wants to be liked. It made for a powerful combination.

"Do you know who I represent here?"

"I do. The question is, do you?"

Zadi abruptly released an incongruous, high pitched, child-like laugh, which he cut off abruptly.

"We don't have long, Rostam. You were sent here by Theo McNamara."

Rostam nodded.

"With a message?"

"He told me to say you shouldn't go it alone. He wants to talk to you."

Zadi contracted his eyebrows.

"He told you he was building a global alliance, I suppose?"

"Yes."

"The best liars are the ones who start with a truth. I'm going to tell you the facts as I know them, then you can decide."

Zadi took another sip of his tea before speaking.

"Where did the intellectual underpinnings of crypto come from?"

"Tim May. Eric Hughes. Nick Szazbo. Vernor Vinge. Seekers of freedom," said Rostam, becoming wrapped up in Zadi's story despite himself.

"Theo McNamara was a fellow traveller, once. Today Theo is ramping bitcoin and using the proceeds to buy influence. He's buying every local and national election he can. Next stop the new SEC chair in February."

"That's the story Dread has been following," said Rostam, mouth open.

"And you know why?" continued Zadi. "Theo doesn't want to eliminate government. He wants to be the next government."

Zadi picked up the Perspex plate.

"Are you sure you don't want some gaz?"

Rostam shook his head. Zadi took a piece of the roughly shaped oblong, pistachio-studded nougat from the plate, and delicately tore open its plastic wrapper. To Rostam's surprise he put the whole sweet in his mouth in one go and began chewing enthusiastically, taking a sip of tea to help with the process. Esfahani gaz was one of Rostam's Mom's favourites. It takes a long time to chew.

Yazdi had bookshelves running around the wall space, so the view beneath the 360-degree windows was as intriguing as outside. Rostam wasn't here to sightsee. He had to deliver his message and get out, but now Zadi had him gripped.

"Any fool can see that there are big international players in crypto," continued Zadi, "many of them enemies of the United States. McNamara has a dialogue with them, including the hardliners from my own country. They may have asked him to deal with me. Libertarians like Theo McNamara are as dangerous to your republic as religious extremists are to mine. They both need to be stopped."

"Why are you telling me?"

"There's only one way to stop McNamara now. Strike at the source of his power. Bitcoin itself."

Rostam laughed.

"Nobody can do that."

Zadi didn't smile in return.

"There is someone." Zadi paused. "Satoshi Nakamoto himself."

Rostam exploded in a snort of outrage.

"He's not a real person. He's most likely a Californian programmer - might not even be alive anymore."

"He *is* a real person. This is one of those examples of somebody who hides in plain sight. Satoshi exists, is alive and well, and lives in rural Honshu."

Rostam burst into laughter.

"How do you know?"

Zadi shrugged.

"Are you familiar with the Bitcoin 64?"

"Sure, the coders who helped Satoshi write the white paper."

"There is a Discord server with an elaborate puzzle made up of quotations in C++ from the original code in Satoshi's White Paper. They exchange messages there. We managed to figure out enough to leave a message ourselves. Nobody responded, but I think they might if you posted. You have a following in the crypto world, and you're not political. Everyone knows Satoshi hates governments."

Rostam thought it over. Whatever else Satoshi and his inner circle might be, they were people who loved a puzzle.

"Even if that is true, what do you want from him?"

"Nakamoto is a sincere person who wants the world to be a fairer place. He doesn't want his glorious creation to become yet another tool of American world domination. I want to talk to him, but it can only happen when he wants it to. He won't meet with someone who has been tainted by politics. But he might meet you."

Rostam stood up and walked over to the window overlooking the Heath, his reflection ratcheting towards him until his nose almost touched its mirror image.

"My priority is to get back to my family."

Zadi remained silent at the desk.

"Not everyone gets the opportunity to choose, you know," said Zadi. "I didn't get many choices myself."

"You're gonna tell me you'd rather have been a computer scientist at MIT?"

"Of course I would, but that wasn't my path. You think I wouldn't rather be solving problems and publishing papers? But you know how it is for talented people like us - the world won't leave us alone. The way I see this, it's a good outcome for you. You can't go back to your life in Chicago as things stand. You're under suspicion from the Americans."

"I have to get back there. My daughter lives in Chicago."

"So, you're going to have to give them something."

"You're not worried they'll try to snatch you while you're here? Or worse."

"What do you mean by worse?"

"Isn't it possible they're using me to locate you to take you out?"

Zadi stopped for a moment, then gave a shrug that reminded Rostam of Ahmad the night before.

"That could happen anytime. The British are lackeys to their American cousins, of course, but they don't want to be made to look stupid any more than anybody else does. They don't want extra-territorial executions or kidnappings on their soil. And I'm not known as a military general. There are no clips on YouTube of me in army fatigues carrying an automated weapon in Syria or Yemen."

"How do I know you're telling the truth about Theo?"

Rostam kept his excitement down. He stared through his own reflection through to the wilderness outside.

"Why do you think he was listening to your show? Because of your views on crypto? Of course not. You're sniffing out the connection between those election fixes. Theo and his friends are the connection. It's a matter of time before you can prove it. He is a traitor to the USA. He doesn't think he is, but high-minded traitors never do."

"I don't even know what that word means any more. This isn't World War Two."

"The courts know, and they'd find Theo guilty in a heartbeat. He and his network are deeply into bitcoin. They reached out to me eighteen months ago when they realised their SEC wasn't going to help. My personal opinion is that they think the American Deep State is poisoning their society, and that they're going to be submerged by the Chinese. They want to make sure they're the richest guys left standing when it happens. Whatever their motive, they want to build an alliance with Iran, and other countries. They figured I was their in, and I was happy to talk to them. Once I realized their interest was personal wealth and power, I cut contact. I'm not going to try to sell you on the story, Rostam, but I'm a man of peace. I want Iran back as part of the international community, and that means being friends with the Americans. Or at least not sworn enemies. And I don't see that happening while I'm in bed with people like Theo McNamara."

"So, you're not going to contact him. Do you think he expects you to?"

"I have my own theory. Just think about what I'm saying. Satoshi could give you the ammo you need to bring him down."

The temptation to talk to Satoshi Nakamoto was strong. How many times had he said online that crypto was the key to freedom? Nakamoto's White Paper was the closest thing to a Holy Book in Rostam's life.

"What makes you think Satoshi will speak to me? It's hardly as if you can bribe him."

"Money can do a lot, but power can do everything. He is - between us - also a vain man. I don't think the worship of a million teenage speculators does it for him. He wants to know that the people who understand the force he has unleashed on the world recognise him. Especially with the rest of the Silicon Valley aristocracy becoming more famous all the time."

"He should go on Saturday Night Live."

Rostam turned back from the window and saw Zadi was staring at him. For the first time the amused look left his clean shaven face and for a moment Rostam fancied he detected anger, or at least frustration. Zadi's voice didn't change in pace or volume. He was prepared to soak up as much as Rostam could throw at him.

"I agreed to meet you out of respect to your mother, and because I thought you were a serious person."

"I just want to get back Stateside. Job done."

Zadi sighed. "You really are an American. You still believe in fairy tales. Well, good luck to you. Ask Professor Yazdi to come to see me if he has time."

Chapter Twenty-Five

It came as a surprise to Rostam that the party downstairs was still going. He left Zadi at work at his borrowed desk with mixed emotions: the man was a mystery, but Rostam had liked him, and the opportunity to meet Satoshi Nakamoto seemed real.

The question everyone wanted answering. Why has he never monetized a single Bitcoin of his own?

At the bottom of the stairs, he bumped into Ahmad.

"Where have you been, man?" His friend was uncharacteristically excited. "You left that numpty Farsian in bits. Needed all of Yazdi's charm to get him back onside."

Rostam didn't immediately reply and could see Ahmad realized he had missed something.

"Did you make contact?" he whispered, looking quickly to each side.

Rostam nodded.

"And still alive. Before you mentioned it I'd almost forgotten to be scared. Thanks, man."

"What do they want?"

"He tried to recruit me. Claims he can introduce me to Satoshi."

Ahmad raised his eyebrows.

"You're not tempted?"

"Part tempted. Part pissed at these people pushing me around. He wants Dr Yazdi."

They found their host Yazdi bending over at the waist to kiss the hand of an older woman with the demeanour of a Russian princess, leaning on the arm of a handsome black man less than half her age.

"How can you stand this guy?" Rostam asked his friend. "He's no seeker for truth. He's a pole climber. Look at him."

"Don't be so harsh. It takes all sorts to make the world go round," said Ahmad. "Academia is a small world. I don't want to lose one of the few friends I have." He raised his voice. "Hey, Professor - I've brought one of your former students to pay homage."

Yazdi turned to them - a tall, spare man with a colossal nose. From the side it looked like nothing more than a bat in flight. Rostam had never liked him. It was Ahmad who was the fan.

"Always a pleasure to meet a student," said Yazdi.

"Ahmad's flattering me. I wasn't at LSE. I was doing postgrad math with him over at Imperial. We used to gate-crash your lectures."

"So more of a fan than a student?"

Yazdi laughed to show he was joking but Rostam didn't think he was. Ahmad was always too impressed by success, especially the academic kind. Rostam couldn't be bothered to keep playing cat-and-mouse.

"Your special guest wants to see you, Professor." Rostam tilted his head as though he could see through the ceiling to the office where Zadi was working.

"I see," said Yazdi. "Ahmad, would you like to join us?"

"Not especially," said Ahmad.

Rostam looked towards the heaving atrium, wondering if Hanratty was still circulating.

"What could go wrong? Come along, Ahmad," said Yazdi and, before Rostam knew what was happening, they were both gone.

Hanratty materialised over his shoulder.

"I'm just thinking of stepping outside for some herbal refreshment," said Hanratty, looking at his cell and then slipping it back into his inside pocket. "Care to join me?"

Rostam looked at him in surprise. The fact was he would like a puff, even if he had to put up with this idiot.

Hanratty and Rostam made their way through the crowd and grabbed their coats from the factotum at the door.

"You're still in your waxed jacket," said Rostam.

"It isn't just a costume so I can play the Englishman abroad you mean?" came the reply, with more self-awareness than Rostam had expected. "I'll tell you a secret. Two words. *Wool lining*." Hanratty pulled down the brass zipper and pulled the breast of his jacket open, like someone playing a trick. An inner lining of creamy wool was attached to the jacket.

They stepped out of the house.

"Let's cross the road," said Hanratty. "Nobody will cause a fuss, but I wouldn't want to embarrass our hosts. Camilla in particular."

At ten o'clock on a Saturday night there was plenty of traffic on East Heath Road. Hanratty waited until a black cab full of laughing women in party dresses passed before scurrying across. Rostam followed him, wondering why everything that had happened to him lately seemed to be dangerous.

On the far side James took a couple of steps off the sidewalk and into deep grass. From a side pocket of his jacket next to his rib cage he produced a conical joint, lit the twisted paper end with a silver lighter - Tottenham Hotspur's cockerel crest emblazoned on the side - and offered it to Rostam.

"There's nothing over here to impress someone from the States I'm afraid, but this won't disappoint."

Rostam took a deep puff, and then a second. "Tastes fresh enough. When it comes to weed, I'm happy to be like a philistine in an art gallery. Know what I mean?"

He passed the joint back to Hanratty.

"You mean you don't know much about it, but you know what you like?"

"That's about the size of it."

It felt oddly intimate to be standing here with Hanratty, half in the light of a busy road and half in the chiaroscuro of the Heath at night.

"Look, James, what's the story with you? You still haven't explained how - "

A flash of light crackled like electrical interference in the sky.

There was a crumpled boom from across the street, immediately followed by a crunching, metal-machine music of jammed gears and fractured masonry.

Both men spun around. It was Yazdi's house.

Purple-red flashed from the fire alarm box on the wall, and a piercing siren rang out. A pandemonium of human panic could be heard under the mechanical shriek.

"What was that?" exclaimed Rostam, feeling instantly foolish.

An unnatural surge of hot wind reached them, like the last licks of a wave at the feet of beach walkers. The air was full of particulates and smelled of burnt chemicals. People in party clothes began to stream out of the covered porch of the house across the street. Camilla ran out of the front door, shrieking a long, meaningless sound. Black smoke, irradiated by orange streetlights, poured upwards from the roof to join the night sky.

"I feared this might happen," said Hanratty. "You stay here."

Hanratty had dropped his smoke to the floor. He looked and sounded alert, and Rostam found the shock had wiped any cannabis confusion from his own mind. Hanratty sprinted across the road between a battered Morris Minor and a cherry red Ferrari, who beeped him with an infantile, screechy horn.

Rostam stared intently at the house. The cars in the driveway were all flashing lights. There was a cacophonous chorus of beeping horns. The roof looked off, as though it had fallen in at the back. The driveway was filling up with people. Some were running, all in the same direction back towards Hampstead Village. Nobody looked across the road. He couldn't see Ahmad. Was Ahmad still inside the house?

Rostam ran across the road, pushed his way through the crowd and approached the front door. Hanratty met him coming the other way, his face intent and serious.

"There's no good news here. We have to go."

Hanratty put his hand on Rostam's shoulder to turn him around. Rostam shrugged him off with intent.

"What about Ahmad?"

Hanratty pulled Rostam to him with surprising strength. "That sound was a bomb. It was at the back of the house. We have to leave. Now."

Rostam couldn't process this information at all.

"I'm not leaving without Ahmad. What about Zadi? That prick Yazdi?"

Hanratty grabbed him by the shoulder and attempted to pull him back towards the door. Rostam pushed him so hard the Englishman fell backwards, while Rostam ran into the living room. There was no visible sign of permanent damage, yet the air was filled with smoke, a corrupted distillation of July 4th fireworks.

The last guests and staff were pushing their way out. Rostam was the only person moving towards trouble, as he pinballed through them. He side-stepped a pair of middle-aged women in red and blue dresses on either side of an ancient man, a line of blood down one cheek, trying to catch the young and able-bodied.

Rostam ran up the wide staircase at the back of the atrium, looking for the site of the explosion, and found it at the top. Smartly shining decking was now scarred with debris. Papers, paperback books, two smouldering Persian cushions, one slipper, large shards of broken glass, coffee table askew on three legs, a laptop bent too far, screen hanging on by a solitary screw. Smoke and dust hung in a still, blanketed layer, and percolated upwards, so it was hard to see more than a meter ahead. Cracked walls. One handsome burgundy carpet wall-decoration now hung on by a single nail in one corner. Somehow that was the most obvious sign of disaster, until Rostam got towards the narrow staircase.

Above, a mass of shredded materials slanted down in a tangle where the ceiling should have been. Two bodies sprawled on the floor, one on top of the other, heads towards him.

Ahmad and Yazdi.

Ahmad was on top - he must have been closer to the narrow stairs. The blast would have hit him first.

Rostam fell to his knees and put his arms around his friend's chest, bringing him up for an embrace. Ahmad's flesh was clammy, heavy, inanimate. His eyes were tightly shut, as though he'd tried to shield them from the blast, and his mouth open, showing off perfect, white teeth. Rostam couldn't comprehend what had happened. *What a waste looking after those teeth all these years, and now wiped out for nothing.* Rostam's eyes clouded over. He started pumping Ahmad's chest, but there was no physical reaction. Beyond doubt, both men were dead.

Cold air blew down the staircase. The blast must have been in the turret room and taken off the roof. Everything was upside-down. Rostam wanted to cry, or scream, or hit someone, or give Ahmad the kiss-of-life.

There was no point to anything.

"Come on, Rostam. There's nothing we can do here. Let's go."

Hanratty had caught up with him and, this time, he didn't resist when the Englishman pulled him up.

"We should hurry."

Hanratty pushed Rostam in front of him and they made their way back down to the living room. He allowed Hanratty to pull him out the door. Hanratty turned right instead of left and marched him toward a turning.

"I've got a car close by. We don't want to be there when the police arrive. This affair will get messy fast."

Rostam's thoughts were revolving like dirty laundry in a machine filled with black dye. With each revolution they turned darker.

"You're prepared for this."

Hanratty snatched a look at him.

"You're suspicious - I understand. I am too. I don't know what just happened there but no, I'm not surprised. Zadi visiting London and appearing at a private house was always a risk. He thought London was safe enough. He was wrong. Just because I understand that doesn't mean I knew what was going to happen."

In front of them the lights flashed on a maroon Tesla X.

"Jump in."

"You made sure we were on the other side of the road when the bomb went off."

"Coincidence. Isn't that something you talk about on your show? The perils of narrativizing random occurrences."

Rostam got into the car and shut the door behind him. Now it was too quiet. He could hear Hanratty's breathing as he pressed the button to turn on the car. He wasn't going to get dragged into an epidemiological discussion of coincidence with one of his best friends dead behind him. For the first time he thought about who was going to tell Dana and the girls. Waves of sympathy, grief and fear coalesced and smashed down on him as one, leaving the impact of each emotion to run into the other. Then another wave followed of pure rage.

Ahmad was dead, and Theo McNamara was to blame.

Chapter Twenty-Six

Rostam watched unfamiliar neighbourhoods of North London wash over him. Golders Green. Hendon. Edgware. Ahmad's words rolled around his head on infinite repeat. *This is something I'd normally run a mile from*. Why had he taken Ahmad to that party? Why warn Zadi, and not his own best friend?

Rostam began to play the game of consequences. Would Zadi have been there if he hadn't asked Ahmad to set it up? Why did Ahmad go with Yazdi? Would Dana blame him? Whatever Dana said there was no way Rostam could absolve himself of guilt.

Hanratty drove steadily, keeping within the speed limit, and leaving Rostam to his thoughts. The tablet size dashboard monitor showed a teeming mass of incoming messages, but Hanratty kept his attention on the road. Eventually Rostam saw they were joining the M1 going north.

"Where are we going?"

"I have a house close to Bedford. Another thirty-five minutes. Less if we're lucky. Gives us a chance to plan next moves. Best not to get caught up in all that back there."

"Was Zadi killed?"

"I don't think so. I suspect he left shortly after you."

"Why did Theo do it?"

Hanratty kept watching the road ahead.

"We don't know who did it. There's no shortage of candidates. You can rule out the Brits. We don't have the gumption to assassinate foreign leaders these days. Israel will be happy to take the blame, without admitting anything. They won't mind people thinking they wanted to kill Zadi, but they'd be embarrassed to have slipped up. It could have been rival Iranians. Hell, it could have been the Saudis."

"Was it a coincidence you and I were outside when the bomb exploded?"

Hanratty looked over at him for the first time in the journey, lips pursed into a cynical smile.

"If I'd known a drone was going to hit the house, why would I have been in the neighbourhood at all?"

Rostam pondered this.

"Why did Zadi want to speak to a semi-Iranian like me?"

"Ah, you shouldn't say that. Don't throw away your heritage before you know what it's worth."

Rostam sank back and went back to staring out the window. Could he believe a word the Englishman said? It was hard to care more about that than his grief. He went back to mourning Ahmad in silence.

Hanratty pulled off the motorway. It was as abrupt a change as that of the Heath back in Hampstead to the City. There was no overhead lighting and few cars on the roads.

"Almost there," said Hanratty as he swung right at a T junction.

Within moments he was pulling off the road through large stone gateposts up a curved gravel drive to a large, white-painted house with red-tiled roof and shaggy lawn that disappeared off into the darkness beyond the Tesla's headlights. At the end of the drive stood a khaki

Land Rover Defender, sheltering an egg-shell blue antique Jaguar two-seater.

"Forgive an old man's self-indulgence," said Hanratty, pointing at the cars. "I like to think I save more emissions in this souped-up milk-float than I expel in those beauties."

"I couldn't care less about cars."

"Some of us boys like our toys," said Hanratty. "Come on. Let's get inside, have a hot drink, or a stiff one, and get our thinking caps on. I'm on my own this weekend. There'll be no-one to disturb us."

The air outside was clean, cold, and carried the scent of wet grass. It had stopped raining, but laggard drops were blown from leaves above onto Rostam's forehead. It was his first encounter with anything resembling nature since a walk with Celia through Lincoln Park six thousand miles, one week, and a lifetime before.

The darkness once the car was turned off was limpid, all embracing and comforting. For a moment Rostam allowed himself to imagine there was an escape from this. Then Hanratty unlocked his oak front door and turned on the porch lights, throwing him back into the real world. There was nowhere to hide from these problems, least of all this man's house.

"Make yourself at home in the kitchen. Caffeinated drinks are by the kettle. Spirits as well. I'm going to see what I can find out about what happened tonight."

Hanratty opened the door to the kitchen and then disappeared into what looked like a study behind. Rostam sat at the kitchen table to think things through. The spirits selection wouldn't have disgraced a boutique hotel. It wasn't in keeping with the feel of the place, which looked as much of a family home as Walpole Apartments was for temporary residents.

Rostam looked around for photographs but could see none. On the far side of the kitchen was a large refrigerator covered in souvenir magnets: Amsterdam, Bangkok, Berlin, Caracas, Fort William, Hanoi, Paris, Orlando, Newquay, Snowdonia. Rostam opened it to see what it would tell him, but the shelves were empty of anything bar two bottles of Puligny-Montrachet, an entire rack of San Pellegrino and a pair of whole lemons.

Rostam took out the Nokia and dialled Carl Force's number from memory. He picked up immediately.

"Force."

"What just happened?"

There was a pause. Rostam could imagine the hyper American trying to gather his thoughts in order.

"You're safe?"

"I'm not calling from beyond the grave. What do you mean?"

"I'm just pleased you're not dead. We know you were at the party."

"The party where you killed my friend?"

"Keep calm, Rostam. You don't know the big picture here. Don't assume you know the truth."

"Get your side of the street in order before handing out advice. I make contact, you use a drone and kill the wrong people. Incompetence and evil are a bad combination."

"You saw Zadi?"

"I saw him. He was upstairs in Yazdi's office. But I guess you knew that."

"What did he want?"

"Quit the questions. We both know you've used me to attempt an assassination. I'm not on your spy graduate trainee programme. I want to get back to my family."

"I thought you were divorced."

Rostam kicked at a skirting board in frustration.

"Get back to my daughter. But I've got things to do first. Just tell me what I have to worry about. Are the police looking for me? Can I fly? Am I safe back at the apartment?"

Force whistled under his breath.

"I don't see why not. Keep me up to speed with what you're up to. As long as you keep feeding back information I don't see any problems. The Brits don't know anything about you, and we know everything."

And that's how you like it, Rostam thought.

"Now you back off and let me follow my instincts," he said, after a long pause. "You only call me if there's anything I need to know."

"Gotcha," said Force, and hung up.

Rostam ran his hand through his hair and went over to pick out a coffee capsule. There was more thinking to be done.

Hanratty came in.

"You can stick to coffee if you like. I want something stronger. Still sure?"

"Knock yourself out, man."

Hanratty poured a large Johnnie Walker Blue into crystal glasses standing on a silver tray next to the rack of bottles, and then played with the tap.

Rostam didn't want to get dragged back into Hanratty's chatter.

"I should be in Brentford with Ahmad's wife and the girls. My God - she might not even know yet."

"Let's think this through. The news reports five casualties - two men and three women. Zadi was gone before the blast. As I suspected, seeing you was his priority. After that his team got him clear. Your biggest problem right now is the British authorities. You need to get out, and you can't go straight back to the States. Not until you know they're not looking for you."

Rostam could barely hear him over the buzz of grief and confusion in his mind.

"I need to call Dana."

"Do you really? The police will be there now. She may be a dear friend but it's her family who she'll need most. You feel responsible but you're not. You didn't plant the bomb. It would be selfish of you to go there now."

"You're an asshole. You know that, right?"

Hanratty sucked in his cheeks and straightened his posture.

"You're in a hell of a difficult position. You don't know who to trust. Fine. But I'm giving you sound advice here, and deep down you know I'm right."

Hanratty took a sip from his whisky. Rostam had already swallowed his maximum strength espresso.

Hanratty spoke in the measured, confidential tones of a headmaster advising a troublesome, talented pupil of his options. Rostam went through a series of emotions listening to him. There was an infantile desire to be told what to do and Hanratty's bearing and tone of voice made him a good choice. But Rostam's analytical brain told him this man was a manipulator, a polished liar. Now was not the time for a confrontation, sitting in what was so far as he knew Hanratty's home in the middle of nowhere.

"I'll sleep on it. I have someone I need to speak to first. I might step outside to make the call."

Chapter Twenty-Seven

The back door to the kitchen led through a porch filled with rubber boots, animal feeding bowls, and a long rack, divided between outdoor coats, and three separate collections of plastic bags from differently branded supermarkets. An old-fashioned brass key had been left in the lock of the outside door. The wind had dropped, and a full moon was visible between slow moving cloud cover beyond the trees at the back of the lawn.

Rostam walked onto the grass and up a slight incline. While still moving he manipulated his fingers in the now uncomfortable manner required to send text on the Nokia 6300 feature phone he'd found on the Tottenham Court Road.

WE NEED TO TALK

He had no way of knowing if Millie would be looking at her phone. It was almost midnight here which made it early evening in Chicago. On a Saturday evening she could be anywhere. The two of them often took Celia on excursions on weekend afternoons. The social whirl of the Midwest with an infant couldn't be much further removed from James Hanratty's enormous Bedfordshire garden, but Rostam fancied he could smell the pizza and hotdogs of home more strongly than the wet grass under his feet.

He kept walking until the incline levelled out and a copse of deciduous trees on rough ground replaced mown lawn. A bare winter's field was becoming visible in the moonlight when the familiar old-school Nokia ringtone made him start. The incoming number was an incomprehensible assembly of digits, letters, and punctuation marks.

"Hey, Millie. How'd you find an encryption device that quick?"

"I'm at your Mom's. She has a Tor browser set up on her home computer. Who knew?"

Rostam smiled in the lonely moonlight. He thought of his mom's rent-stabilized apartment on W 21st which was, as she liked to say, the one thing her husband had bequeathed her, other than Rostam himself. He wasn't at all surprised she had encryption software set up. It had always been one of her mathematical passions. He *was* surprised Millie was calling him from there.

"What are you doing in Manhattan?"

"Rostam, some things have happened."

Rostam felt a rough fist squeeze his heart.

"Is Celia ok?"

"Not Celia, thank God. Me. Two things, actually. I was fired on Thursday. I've got Lisa on the case."

"Oh Millie, I'm so sorry - "

She cut him off.

"The other thing is worse. Someone broke into the apartment while we were sleeping. We saw nothing till the next day. Your Mom told me to get Celia on a plane and come over."

The anger in Millie's voice acted as a catalyst to Rostam's volatile feelings. These people didn't care who they hurt.

"Any problems in New York?"

"We're here now. Wanna tell me what you think is really going on?"

Rostam thought for a moment. Thursday? The same day he met Theo McNamara. Millie fired and her apartment searched. Could that be a coincidence? After Ahmad's death he couldn't believe it was. He tensed. How much did Hanratty know?

"Where are you in the apartment?" he asked.

"Talking to you over headphones from Maryam's office in the spare bedroom. She's feeding Celia burnt rice and some chicken that's been on the stove since breakfast time."

A detonation of guilt exploded in Rostam's stomach and expelled all his breath. It took him a moment to answer. None of this would have happened if it weren't for him.

"I've dragged you into this, and it gets worse. I went to Ahmad and Dana's last night. Figured Ahmad might be able to help with this task I took. For money."

Rostam's voice choked, and he held the phone up in the air so Millie wouldn't hear it. He took a deep breath and resumed speaking into the microphone.

"He *did* help - we were at a party of a friend of his so I could deliver my message. I had the meeting. Just afterwards there was a drone attack. Ahmad and his friend were both killed."

Millie gasped.

"Oh my God. Ahmad. His girls must be toddlers now. And Dana."

Millie started to cry. Rostam kept quiet for a moment.

"It's terrible. I saw them all just last night. You've never seen a happier bunch than the Jamalzhads at home. I haven't even started to process it myself."

"Where are you now?"

"Hanratty's house. Your old Loeb buddy turns out to be Theo McNamara's stooge."

"What's his angle?"

"That's one of the things I haven't worked out yet. One of a lot of things."

Rostam paused.

"If I come home now, I've got no ammunition of my own. They can accuse me of being involved with the Iranians, or money laundering, or whatever they like. If I can't protect myself, I can't help you either. The guy I met told me I should go to Japan."

"What are you gonna find in Japan that makes a difference?"

"You wouldn't believe me if I told you."

"I've just lost my career and your best friend has been murdered. Surprise me."

"Maybe I can find Satoshi. The guy I met tonight gave me a lead."

Millie whistled - a low, husky, musical sound. Rostam had always found it sexy and realized that he still did.

"The Big Kahuna, huh? What do *you* think you'll get out of him? If it is a him."

"I want to bring him out of the shadows. What's going on here is a battle for crypto. But it isn't really about crypto. It is about who controls the dollar, or if it can replace the dollar. I'm just hoping I can get something over there to give me a weapon to fight back with."

"Have you got anyone to help you?"

"I put Dread on the case before I flew out here. Hanratty thinks I can't go home - the British police may be after me. I'm thinking Spider."

"Spider's a douchebag. Retired, right?"

"Not retired from moneymaking. Spider's a very rich man now. We speak all the time - or we did until everything went sideways last week. It's five days before the meeting with Nakamoto. How's Celia?"

"That girl is a force for good."

Millie's voice changed register. Celia had done that to her Mom ever since she was first born.

"You should have seen her on the plane. Stuck in cattle class. You know how people hate sitting with kids? By the time we got to LaGuardia anyone sat near us would have adopted her in a heartbeat. No questions asked."

"How long you gonna stay with Mom?"

"Not sure. She's happy to have us here. I don't have anything immediate to do at home. The first call was to Lisa Matsui. She's fighting to find out what there is to find out from Loeb. I don't fancy spending a lot of time answering questions from neighbours and Celia's friends about why I'm suddenly free during the daytime. There are worse places to hide than New York."

"I wish I was with you."

"You've got business to take care of first."

Rostam had kept absently moving forward through the English night while his mind was in the West Side. He reached the old red brick wall at the back of the garden and leaned against it.

"I can't come back from this with nothing."

"Is there anything I can do to help?"

"You could do worse than talk it through with Mom. Tell her the guy I met here was Bahman Zadi. I liked him, which sounds ridiculous but there you are. Both he and the Americans put a lot of stress on me having an Iranian mother. I think it's bullshit but you never know. She'll like to be asked anyway."

"Will do."

Rostam wanted to reach out and hug Millie through the ether, but they had reached the point in the conversation where the risk of saying things one shouldn't went up dramatically.

“Ok Millie. I’d better go. You take care of yourself. You’ve got a little girl and an old woman to look after too now you know.”

“We women can take care of ourselves. Do a better job of staying out of trouble.”

“I’ll call if I can, but even with Tor we better be careful. Whoever these creeps are, they’re watching us.”

Millie hung up. She had always been better at making a smart exit than him. Rostam slipped his Nokia into his back pocket and leaned on the brick wall, staring over the desolate moonlight fields down to a farmhouse just visible in the distance.

He had never felt so far from home.

Chapter Twenty-Eight

"Decision made?" asked Hanratty.

Rostam closed the kitchen door behind him. His coffee cup had disappeared and there were now two whisky glasses on the table, along with an ashtray with a partly smoked joint resting in it. The sweet aroma of cannabis smoke overlay the scents of garlic, coffee, and cleaning products.

Rostam couldn't believe Hanratty was an active part of any violent plot. All the same, the sooner he got away from him the better.

"Bali," said Rostam, taking off his coat and hanging it on the back of the chair. "No extradition treaty with the US. Probably not with the United Kingdom either."

"Okay." Hanratty saluted. "You'll have to go via one of the Middle Eastern hubs."

"I don't want to go anywhere near Iran."

Hanratty had his phone out of his pocket.

"I don't entirely blame you." He tapped away at the screen. "Singapore Airlines will take you via Changi. There's a flight at ten tomorrow morning. Only first class left available. What a shame."

"That's ok. I'll use the credit card Theo gave me to buy the ticket. Can you get me back to St James's? I left my kit there."

"We can make life a little easier than that. We don't have to leave here until six in the morning which gives you time to sleep. I'll send someone to get your stuff."

Rostam had had enough of being directed.

"I've had some country air and I'll rest on my flight. Lend me one of your vehicles and I'll get myself back to the apartment now."

Hanratty gave Rostam a small smile. Rostam realised everything the Englishman was saying could be misdirection.

He could just be waiting for instructions from McNamara. For all I know that psycho Carl Force could be on his way.

But when Hanratty spoke, he was calm, and didn't try to make Rostam stay.

"Take the Jaguar. Ask Farouk to park it in the underground car park he pretends isn't the main attraction of his street. And don't speed. There aren't many coppers left in this country but the ones with speed guns love to flag down a sports car. It's the closest uniformed petrolheads get to driving one."

Hanratty walked over to the back door where keys hung from a rack by a rackety antique dresser. He threw the key across the room to Rostam who caught it with a right hand trained by years of Sunday morning Junior League baseball. Even the key fob for this car was classic: heavy burgundy leather attached to a weighty embossed Jaguar head.

"You'll enjoy driving it. The tank's full. Be grateful - every time you step on the gas in that machine you spend a tenner."

There was a tone in Hanratty's voice which told Rostam that under his veneer of good behaviour the man was angry. Good.

"And don't forget to drive on the left-hand side."

"I guess there's no map function in a vintage car."

"The motorway will take you all the way back into West London. From there you'd better use your phone."

Hanratty walked him out the back way. Rain was falling and he cursed as drops hit his shirt. Rostam shivered in his borrowed coat. There was a sense of intimacy being alone with a stranger at his house and borrowing his car which Rostam deeply resented. He was frustrated his natural politeness wouldn't switch off.

"Thanks for the loan of the car."

Hanratty chuckled, despite beginning to shiver with cold.

"I have to suffer too."

Rostam nodded and dropped into the low-slung drivers' seat. The dashboard was walnut; instruments were all dials; and the seats were of cracked burgundy leather. He turned the antique spindly nickel key into the ignition and was rewarded by a deep growling from the engine. He flicked the right-hand wand and windscreen wipers came on.

"Lights are on the left. She's in good nick: you're not going to break down on the way. The radio's analogue but it works. You'll get the hang of it."

Rostam nodded and pulled the door shut. It was years since he'd driven a stick-shift automobile. He guessed that reverse would be hard on the left and felt absurdly gratified when the car edged backwards. He turned the wheel to go around the circular root towards the front gate and felt gravel scatter beneath the tyres. It was impossible to tell in the rear-view mirror if any had hit Hanratty. Rostam hoped so.

Chapter Twenty-Nine

Sunday January 16

Manhattan

Celia was playing with her grandmother. Maryam had produced an ancient Fisher Price abacus of coloured moulded plastic from the back of a closet crammed with Rostam's childhood. She sat cross legged across from the three-year-old shunting beads back and forwards, showing endless patience, as Celia fumbled numbers above ten. Millie knew Rostam's Mom for a short-tempered woman. Seeing Maryam teach reminded her it's only when you see someone at work you know their capabilities.

When did going to the store on my own become a treat? Millie asked herself as she softly clicked the apartment door behind her.

Millie needed time alone. Maryam was a good cook, but Millie had a secret: there was only so much Iranian food she could handle. The ten-minute walk to 7th Avenue would clear her mind, and the thought of fresh sushi and a berry smoothie as her reward didn't hurt.

Manhattan felt safer than Chicago, but the aftershock of her home invasion was ever-present, a blotch on her peace of mind whenever she closed her eyes. A week ago, she had been expecting a promotion, Rostam seemed ever-present and Ahmad was alive in London. The walk up 7th Ave against the traffic looked and felt familiar, but then so had Chicago, and it hadn't stopped an intruder breaking into her hom e.

The thought that any stranger could be an enemy was less frightening than the idea that she might know them already. Since her dismissal from Loeb Millie found herself assuming everyone was guilty until proven innocent.

It was almost lunchtime when she reached Wholefoods. She expected the store to be quiet, with no office business and general traffic low, but it was well populated with Manhattan shoppers, allergic to home cooking and telling themselves there were fewer calories in store-bought meals than delivered take-out. *Wholefoods, WholePayCheck* was what her friends called it. That was less amusing now she was out of work. It had only been three days, and Millie during the day Millie didn't feel it had really happened. At night things were worse.

The store was set up so that shoppers had to go past all the produce before they could buy take-home meals, and Millie took her time gazing at peppers, eggplant, zucchini and organic corn-on-the-cob, sprayed with droplets of moisture and under special lights, like clubbers heading for a night out, all primped, tweezed and painted to the max, no upgrade unticked. Millie had friends who professed to hate this kind of thing, all phony surfaces and no substance. She felt differently. Surfaces are important too. Often the first impression is through the eyes, and it changes how one feels about everything. More foolish to pretend it isn't important than to appreciate it.

The sushi counter stood on the first floor, next to hot sandwiches, and both had shoppers queued more than four deep. Millie checked her watch - she'd only been out ten minutes. No harm in doing some indoor window shopping, see if she could find anything as a gift for Maryam.

A store with twenty different kinds of olive oil has to have something she needs. What does she always use? Saffron! They'll probably sell me an organic version here.

Herbs and spices were racked at the far side of the first floor, passed benches full of snacking customers swapping gossip over coffee, or singletons brushing and prodding their devices, digital acupuncturists with invisible needles. It looked and sounded like normality, which was just what Millie needed.

She turned past the final carousel and found a whole aisle of herbs. She was just wondering how there could possibly be more than three different flavours of sumac when she heard a male voice.

"Hey, is that Millie James? It is, right! Remember me?"

Millie tensed as she turned to her right. She was looking at a lanky, sallow-faced white man around her own age, with slightly too-long dark hair and large, recessed eyes. He had a big smile on his face and radiated the sincerity of a door-to-door vacuum cleaner salesman.

"Manny Garvey. From Columbia. Applied econometrics."

Manny kept a couple of metres away, to demonstrate he was showing respect for personal boundaries. It seemed impossible, but his smile grew even wider.

"I'm sorry, but I don't recognise you," said Millie. "And I didn't take applied econometrics."

"Of course you didn't, but I remember you. Heard you're in Chicago now, working at Loeb. How's it going?"

Manny took a step towards her, and Millie became conscious that there was nobody else at this end of the store.

"Amazing selection of stuff they have, huh?" he said, oblivious to her anxiety. "What you looking for? I guess Iranian food needs lots of spices, huh?"

Manny, or whoever he really was, made a show of looking up the rows of produce.

"I'm not much of a chef myself, I'll be honest. More of a Dominos kinda-guy." He shrugged. "So shoot me! Simple pleasures."

Millie's found the presence of mind to take a deep breath and look around. The sound of chatter from the benches was still audible. A closed-circuit camera blinked red as it rotated at the end of the aisle. This man hadn't tried to touch her. She could always scream if she needed help.

Suddenly anger swamped fear, like a lioness leaping onto the back of a hyena.

"Who are you, Mister? We never knew one another at college."

Manny turned to her, fingers splayed out as he showed her his palms, arms straight down by his side, mouth open in a pantomime of shock.

"Why the hostility? I mean, I know chasing after the ones who got away is frowned on, but you're divorced from Rostam, right? No harm in a guy trying."

He brought his hands together, fingers steepled in a mockery of the namaste gesture Millie's yoga instructor liked to affect.

"Let's start again. Coffee?" he said, smiling.

"Quit the act. Who are you, and why are you threatening me?"

Now his hands had gone behind his back, and Manny inclined towards her. Millie was uncomfortably aware that he was a good foot taller than her, and looked like he had the wiry strength of a scaffolder.

"Okay, you got me. We weren't at college together. I was at Colombia though, just a couple of years behind you. Call me a cougar chaser, what can I say?"

That didn't deserve a response.

"We just want to talk," he continued. "We know you've spoken to Rostam. You did well to kick him to the curb. Don't let him drag you back into the shitstorm he's created. Last time I checked divorced couples don't owe each other any favours."

"You people got me fired, and chased me to a different city. What more do you want?"

"Hey, that was just Loeb panicking early. Nothing to do with us. You want, maybe we can talk to them. That sound good, Millie? We offered Rostam the chance to work with us, but he's gone rogue. You were always the shrewd one in that relationship."

Manny's smile was gone, replaced by an oleaginous veneer of concern, like a cosmetic surgeon pretending to be a medical professional, while silently calculating the size of his invoice.

"What's this *we* you're talking about? You're just some weirdo talking to me in the back of a grocery store."

"That isn't kind or nice. Weirdo? I'm in my Sunday best here. I wanna help you, Millie, and you have to realize you need the help. Unless you like kibitzing at your ex-mother-in-law's, that is, and I don't think you're that kind of woman." His tone of voice shifted. "How's Celia enjoying it in New York? Bit young for the shopping I guess. How many times can you take her on a carriage ride around Central Park before she starts to wonder what's she's doing here, you think?"

The mention of Celia helped Millie make up her mind.

"It's not easy, now you mention it. Small kids don't like change, you know?"

Manny's shoulder visibly dropped as he relaxed. Millie was pleased. He thought he'd talked her round.

"I bet. Kids like stability - I always said so," he said.

"Maybe we should grab coffee and talk," said Millie. "You can fill me in on what's really going on."

"I knew you'd get it, Millie. Let's go."

Millie raised her index finger, like a girl asking permission of the teacher.

"Could you do me a favour? We need saffron. It's on the top shelf. Bit high for a little woman like me."

Manny's smile was back. *Men never grow up. Thank God*, Millie thought to herself. Manny stepped right next to her and pointed towards the top shelf.

"This one? Twenty-five bucks for that? They must be kidding. Cocaine is cheaper per gram."

"So I'm told."

Manny was reaching up above his head, standing on tiptoes with a look of concentration, when Millie raised her right leg and brought her boot heel sharply down onto his left knee. She heard a sharp crack as he pitched into the bottles of spices and fell to the ground. As he fell, she moved around and kicked him hard between his splayed legs once, twice.

"You bitch," he said, but quietly, as though not wanting to be exposed.

"I'm not the one on my hands and knees," she said, turning around. He hadn't made much noise, but the falling jars had, smashing as they hit the ground. Store security was coming towards her, a squat, muscular older white man along with a large black woman, both in navy uniform. The man walked round towards the herb aisle. Millie stopped the woman.

"There's a man back there. He was sticking saffron in his pockets. When I challenged him, he attacked me."

"You ok, honey?"

"I'm fine. A little shook up."

"Stick around and help us file a police report?"

"I've gotta go, get back to my kid. You'll have it all on camera, right?"

"Should be. You take care of yo'self, honey. Keep out of the path of scumbags, you hear?"

"Will do."

Millie walked smartly down the escalator and out onto 7th, high on adrenaline. She tried to calibrate her emotions. Manny had done everything he could to let her know he knew all about her life, but he didn't seem to know what Rostam was doing. And how come he claimed to be separate from whatever was going on at Loeb? Whatever. Her dominant emotion was pleasure to have landed a punch on the opposition, whoever they were. One on the scoreboard for Millie James, which was better than a big, fat zero.

It was only when she turned onto W 21st she remembered she hadn't bought any food. The hell with it. The taste of victory would sweeten another portion of Persian rice.

Chapter Thirty

Tuesday January 18

Bali

Rostam felt numb until the plane landed at Densepar. Bali smelled different, musty and toasted, like perfume sprayed on cooling sweat. As he walked down the boarding stairs, hot sunshine on the back of his neck reminded him how far he was from home.

There would be nothing funny about an Indonesian jail cell if he got no further than passport control. If the British police had sent out some kind of international alert, now is the time they'd grab him.

Rostam walked up to the booth and presented his US passport. Of all the concerns that washed around his head in the twenty-four journey, being arrested at the border had not been one, but in this moment, it was an overwhelming fear. He smiled at the tiny, severe immigration official in white uniform and matching headscarf.

"Sunglasses off."

He complied and felt the woman's bright black eyes flickering between his photograph and face.

"Where are you staying in Bali?"

"With a friend."

The eyes were now trained on his own. It occurred to Rostam that this might not be a strong answer.

"When do you fly back to the States?"

"Next stop is Tokyo."

The official still had his passport in her hand and only now turned it over and pressed it face down onto a scanner. If Theo decided he had had what he needed from Rostam all he needed to do was attach a flag to the chip in the passport. Or had he got this wrong - was it possible Theo wasn't the problem? The longer this took, the faster his brain shifted through the gears of worry.

The officer picked up her phone and spat out a string of long sentences while continuing to stare directly at him. This was it. He was going to be arrested. Millie and Celia would be left alone. Rostam felt feverish with guilt.

"Thank you, Mr James. Have a good stay in Bali."

The hot gorge of panic in Rostam's brain was not immediately cooled by the return of his passport. He nodded in thanks and moved on, hoping his poker face had improved.

He walked through the baggage hall with the feeling of superiority of a traveller who only has carry-on luggage, and an enormous sense of relief. Beyond the automatic gates, into a scrum of Balinese awaiting their relatives, and the drivers holding electronic boards waiting to transfer international travellers to their hotels. He scarcely dared hope to see Spider here, and wasn't disappointed. None of his messages had been answered.

The heat outside swallowed him up, like he was charcoal tipped into an oven. Rostam slung his coat over his left shoulder, which left him no free hand to indicate to the swarm of shills shouting their offers at him that he wasn't interested. The chaos was an aural assault: voices, vehicle horns, aircraft noises from above, swooshing of electronic doors behind, slamming of trunks, the revving of scooter engines. The miaowing of cats, of which there was an epidemic in the airport.

He put down his bag to draw a line across his forehead and stop sweat pouring directly into his eyes, when one high pitched repeated horn honk became distinguished from the rest by repetition and pattern: Dah dah dah-daah daah da-dah de-dah de-dah. It was familiar. Of course it was: it was Darth Vader's march.

He looked up and there was Spider, one flip-flopped foot either side of a Vespa, with a Stars-and-Stripes full motorcycle helmet, visor pushed up, waving long arms at him.

"How Pale Face! Hop on. Me love you long time."

"You could have told me you've got the message, Spider," said Rostam. "You turned into even more of an asshole now you've emigrated?"

"What can I say? It's a crime to neglect one's talents," drawled his friend.

"What's with Old Glory on your helmet? Odd choice for a Calgary boy."

"Canada's full of communist pansies," said Spider, revving his engine like a teenager on a scrambler. "I'm sticking it to the man, man."

Rostam slung his left leg over the back seat and shoved his bag in between himself and the rider, resting his coat on top. He leaned forward and clasped each hand around Spider's rib cage. Even under extreme stress, seeing his old friend shifted his mood. Spider immediately twisted the throttle and the bike leaped forward.

"Calm down, Spider. You're gonna make me sea-sick."

"Don't be a pussy. You have been warned!"

Spider swooshed through haphazard taxicabs and zoomed up to security, playing chicken with the safety barrier. It shot up at the last moment, and they were away.

Chapter Thirty-One

It took twenty minutes to escape traffic around Denpasar Airport. Rostam spent them trying to retain his last Singapore Airlines meal. Spider's Vespa was more powerful than the scooters and tuk-tuks that ferried single riders, couples, and entire families around downtown Denpasar, and he wanted everyone to know it. Red lights were an invitation to accelerate. Squeezing past buses and trucks counted as double points. The invective Spider spat out at anyone who beeped their horns matched the notorious obscenity-poets of Wiener Circle back in Chicago.

"Sittin' pretty back there, sweetheart?" called out Spider after he abruptly pulled to the right, and headed up a steep narrow unmarked road, through dense trees of a deep lush green so rich Rostam felt chewing the raw leaves would improve his health.

"Since when did you care?"

Spider shrieked with gratified vanity and massaged the throttle ahead of a bump. Rostam's stomach disappeared beneath him. He shut his mouth in case of involuntary vomiting.

"Fat bastard. I flew over that without you," shouted Spider, with an exaggerated Albertan drawl.

Rostam stared at the back of Spider's neck to help settle himself. It had been a decade since the two of them met on the Loeb training programme. Rostam pulled out of his PhD and headed for the research department. Spider had somehow turned a philosophy major from Dartmouth into a prestigious job in proprietary trading.

Rostam fell under his spell immediately. Spider had an intuitive understanding of which senior people he could ruthlessly persecute, and which ones had to be charmed. It wasn't that he never got these judgements wrong, but he had no emotional engagement in any of it. One very late night, in Match Bar on Mercer St, Spider explained his rationale to Rostam and Millie, just before he disappeared back to the hotel room of a married managing director from Seoul, who had presented to their class on how to *always be closing* that afternoon.

"You've gotta know the rules. Not the rules the bosses tell you - they're just there to keep them above us forever. The rules that matter. We've chosen finance, kids...single mission - make money. Right now we've gotta do it for the handful of people above us who make decisions. Only about five of them at this firm. The rest is for the birds. So, stop taking the small shit seriously people and have some fun." Then he whispered in the ear of the forbiddingly stern and immaculately beautiful MD who had been phone-grazing in the adjacent seat.

Millie laughed watching the two of them leave, just before she stuck her tongue in Rostam's ear.

"He's funny and smart, but he means it. You can't trust someone like that."

Rostam had forgotten all about it as his heart did jumping-jacks of joy within his chest. Now it was a decade later, Millie and he had married, had Celia and divorced, and Spider was a retired prop trader and now full-time digital activist. They'd all been wearing suits back then. Now Spider was wearing a string vest, surfer shorts and flip flops. Somehow the costume change made no difference at all.

They swept past a road sign: SACRED MONKEY FOREST SANCTUARY.

"Hate that place," shouted Spider. "Brings tourists up here away from the beach. I'd have 'em kept there behind wire fences."

Rostam knew he meant tourists, rather than the monkeys.

Trees gave way to the high street of a small town. The scattering of Westerners on the sidewalks were not backpackers. They glowed with the studied shabby chic which only money and confidence bring.

"Ubud. Ugh-bud if you ask me."

Spider jerked his head almost all the way round so his passenger got the full benefit of the sick-making facial expression he pulled to enunciate *Ugh-bud*.

"Hipsterville Bali-style. No fear man, we're moving through."

An immaculately dressed white-skinned couple were stepping out of a silver air-conditioned Mercedes-Benz sedan just outside their hotel veranda. They made the mistake of getting on the driver's side, standing in the road while their bags were ferried inside. Spider dropped a shoulder and swept between the couple, skimming the man's hip and causing him to drop flat on his ass.

"Yee-haw!" yelled Spider into his slipstream, accelerating away from the melee behind them. "Welcome to Bali, suckers."

Rostam grabbed Spider closer to him, having to stretch to keep his suitcase flush between them. Ubud was already petering out, a Suzuki scooter dealership and an outdoor Pilates studio the last outposts, before green forest shot up on either side of the road, welcoming them into an oxygenated arboreal hug, and shielding them from the complaints of holidaymakers behind them.

Spider didn't slow down despite the absence of fresh targets, sweeping around each bend in the road as though he aspired to shaving their kneecaps on the rough, macadamised road surface. The engine began to keen in a higher pitch as the slope steepened. A three-wheeled flatbed mini-truck slingshot round a corner above and drove past them, the slipstream sucking gently on their skin. Rostam realized he'd pulled in his tummy in an infantile desire to reduce their breadth. Spider brayed a high-pitched laugh and turned an abrupt right into an unmarked driveway. He slalomed left, right, left again and pulled up outside a one-story glass and cedar wood building. A three-meter whipcord satellite aerial stood on the roof.

"Home base. You're not impressed?"

Rostam pushed his suitcase onto the ground and clambered off the scooter after it. He put his hands on his hips and pushed them forwards while pulling back his shoulders. The relief of being off the back of Spider's scooter was even greater than that from stretching.

"It's not bad for an apartment," said Rostam. "Nice view."

"Asshole."

"Don't be so needy."

Rostam walked up to the front door, made entirely of glass. He could see straight through the hall to the waterfall erupting out of the hillside behind. Extravagantly coloured songbirds looped in the bright sunshine, dashing through droplets flung furthest away from the rocks. Sunlight cut through cascading water, an endlessly changing rainbow-kaleidoscope.

"This is just the entry. Three extra floors down below."

Spider took off his helmet and stuck it in the plastic box at the rear of the Vespa. Rostam tossed over his pink helmet.

"Here's your Barbie-issue one back."

"Just because you wear a bitch's helmet ain't the reason you're a bitch, bitch," said Spider, as he walked over to look into his security camera.

The inside of the house was silent, immaculately clean and air-conditioned.

Spider pointed at the back wall.

"Reinforced Perspex. I figured I'd get sick of the sound of the waterfall eventually. Cost a bomb to keep the view and lose the sound."

An elevator door slid open automatically once Rostam closed the front door behind them. Down the steps was an open-plan floor. The entire wall to their right was glass, with the waterfall as a permanent light show. Facing it on the left-hand side was a projector monitor with a collection of LED screens protruding at erratic angles from black metal arms attached to the wall.

"My workstation," said Spider. "Spend a lot of time down here staring at the wall. Makes me laugh sometimes. I can see the world more clearly here from a bunker in the middle of the South Pacific than those Stall Street bastards."

Rostam didn't have to use much imagination to see Spider doing exactly that.

"Do you pour your own champagne and pat yourself on the back while you're at it?"

"I have people to do that for me," said Spider. "Staff is not a problem. Told 'em to clear out today in your honour. Thought you might like a little privacy while we catch up."

The next flight of stairs led to a wide wooden corridor with five doors leading off it.

"You're in this one."

Spider stared at a black mirrored panel next to the door at the waterfall end of the corridor. A numbered keypad sprung into life where his reflection had been. A rapid sequence of finger stabs followed.

"Your turn. Come and stare in here and you'll be set for this door and the front one."

"Fancy."

"Not really. Saves me having to issue you a plastic key card or any of that."

And means you'll know whenever I leave or enter my room or the house thought Rostam, as he self-consciously bent towards the screen to have his eyes decoded. After an uncomfortably silent thirty seconds or so there was a click and the door opened.

"Make yourself at home. Lunch down the next floor at midday. You're on local time now, right?"

"Sure."

Rostam shuffled into the room, suddenly feeling like a long-distance business traveller, rather than a renegade visiting an old friend. His room was austerely designed with the kind of minimalism that costs a fortune to mimic. The waterfall wall had drops of moisture splattered across it, though the main thrust of water must be a hundred meters away at least. Rostam walked up to the window and pressed his nose against it. A flock of tiny, fat bellied, long beaked songbirds played tag just before him, so that he felt he could reach out and stroke their orange tummies or purple wings. These birds didn't know that Millie had lost her job and was kibitzing with his Mom in downtown Manhattan; that Ahmad's corpse was now in a Metropolitan Police icebox; that Rostam wanted to crash the only system he believed in. They didn't know and didn't care. In the moment, Rostam envied them.

The bathroom felt suspended outside. It was alongside the waterfall wall, with another divider of Perspex alongside. To hell with it. There were no people visible. Rostam stripped off and prepared to use the toilet and shower in what felt like the open air, wondering what kind of exhibitionist puts their toilet next to a floor-to-ceiling window.

Clean, and dressed in fresh boxers, Rostam checked the time on his digital wristwatch. Eleven on Tuesday morning in Bali, which made it four in the morning in England. Eleven o'clock on Monday night in Manhattan. He pulled out his Nokia, wanting to call and saw he had no coverage. Rostam curled up on top of the industrial steel coloured bedspread and shut his eyes.

Chapter Thirty-Two

"Wakey wakey, hands off snakey."

Rostam opened his eyes. Spider was leaning over him, naked but for a sarong.

"Good morning to you too," said Rostam. "I sleep with my hands above the eiderdown, since you bring it up. New tattoos?"

'Hell yeah. New country, new life. It's hot all the time here. Your skin is your clothes."

Rostam swung his legs over the side of the bed. It wasn't comfortable to wake up being stared at in close range by anyone, even an old friend.

"Give us a twirl," said Rostam.

Spider was only too keen to comply. He stretched out his arms like da Vinci's Vitruvian man. His nipples were at Rostam's eye level. Across his chest was a landscape profile tattoo of a bulbous devil's face, large eyes filled in scarlet and marine, nostrils pushed together, as if painted by a Balinese Cubist, with prominent incisors square in the middle of a gaping mouth, like molars on the march, and curbed sabre teeth hooking both upwards and downwards from each corner of the mouth. The body was presented in a series of fractals stretching to the sides of Spider's rib cage, with green feathers, grey fish scales and moist, weeping blackened skin mashed together. Rostam could see Spider constraining his breath to facilitate the viewing. Only his sternum fluctuated at all to show he was still breathing.

"That might be the nastiest thing I have ever seen," said Rostam at last. "What is it?"

"My own personal demon. I started with Barong, chief demon of Bali. But he's not bad enough so I used a Fibonacci fractal sequence to fill in. Hurt like a mutha over the ribs. One of a kind, man. Like me."

Spider stayed still as a living statue. Rostam wondered if he was obliged to ask more questions. Then his host slowly rotated until Rostam was staring at his back.

The ink stretched from the tip of a dragon's tail on Spider's left hip, to an explosion of fire, which began at the mouth on his right shoulder blade and extended up over to his right bicep in one direction, and up the side of his neck in the other. The creature's body was twisted in multitudinous coils which filled up the whole of the back.

"Look closely."

As he spoke, Spider clenched the muscles of his extended arms and flexed his shoulder blades. The dragon's body shimmered and shifted as thought it was going to fly over to join the demon on the other side.

"That's Saramanak, queen of Indonesian dragons. You can see she's trying to climb over to scorch Spider's Demon. Just like the battle of the sexes. She'll never win. My demon is too strong."

Rostam rubbed his eyes. Was Spider for real?

"Dunno about the mythology, but it's a hell of a tattoo. When did you get into all that?"

"Living here opens your eyes. I finally realized I can be the man I was born to be. Spend more time in Bali, you'll see what I mean."

Spider stepped forward and walked back towards the bedroom door.

"You can turn off the light whenever you want." He pointed to a switch by the bed. "Press that and the window turns black."

"Oh. So I didn't need to take a shit in full view of the world."

"Don't sweat it. There's nobody watching. C'mon upstairs. Noodles if you want 'em. I've got stuff to show you."

"Five minutes."

Spider walked out of the room, and Rostam pulled on his jeans. His old friend had changed.

Chapter Thirty-Three

Spider was in the screen room. He was still in a sarong, sitting cross-legged on a rattan mat with no cushion, his crossed legs tanned so dark brown it camouflaged the thick black body hair which earned him his nickname. Incense candles burned at intervals around the room.

"Smells like you kicked over a bunch of perfume bottles in here."

"Back off," replied Spider absently, his attention jumping between screens. "My house, my rules. There's drinks and snacks in the corner. Your noodles went cold - maybe fruit is better."

It took Rostam a moment to spot a refrigerator recessed into the wall close to the waterfall window. He grabbed a Pepsi Max and plate of sliced fruit: mango, hairy rambutan, smelly durian and, thankfully, a banana. There was no Western furniture in the room, so he lowered himself onto a rattan mat next to his friend and tried to understand what his friend was looking at.

Spider offered no explanation of the different streams of text on each screen. Not all the language was in the Roman alphabet. Streams of Cyrillic and Arabic alphabets ran alongside with simultaneous translations. The largest screen was dominated by either Chinese or Japanese characters. It looked like a series of chat rooms. Rostam thought he recognised a couple of Discord conspiracy theory sites. Reddit featured in multiple languages.

Spider kept jumping between screens, sometimes typing in direct messages which usually, but not always, appeared on the public chat forums. The closer Rostam looked the more he realized he was being presented with a show. Experience told him the least effective way to find out what Spider was up to would be to ask him. Looking at the mostly inexplicable chat rooms became meditative. Rostam found himself thinking about Celia, and then Millie, and then Ahmad, and then Dana.

When Spider spoke it came as a surprise.

"What are you doing here, man? Don't get me wrong - it's a pleasure to see you."

On the journey over Rostam had felt a desire to share his dilemma with someone, anyone. An old friend like Spider would fit the bill. But now the opportunity was there he didn't know how to start.

"I'm in big trouble."

Spider waved his hand at the screens and they all turned off. He focussed all his attention on Rostam but said nothing.

"Have you ever heard of Theo McNamara?"

Spider shrugged.

"Can't remember. What's he done?"

Rostam had to force out the words as if they were too big for his vocal cords.

"He might have killed my best friend. Even if he hasn't, Ahmad's dead, and it's my fault."

Spider let the words hang between them.

"You better tell me the whole story."

When Rostam had got to the end, Spider stood up slowly and rolled his shoulders. Three times forward, three times back.

"First things first. We can find out if there's any search from the authorities going on. You're not the first Westerner to turn up here needing to know if people are looking for him."

Rostam opened his mouth but Spider shushed him.

"No disrespect to your late friend, but let's look at the positives. You haven't tried to hurt anyone. It makes absolutely no sense for anyone to wish you harm. You have no hard evidence this Theo was behind the attack. Meanwhile there may be an offer of meaningful financial backing for you. Right?"

Rostam shrugged.

"Hope is not a strategy, Spider."

"It isn't. But despair never helped anyone. Think positive. Worst case you're with me in Bali. Life's good here, especially for a single guy. Let me check out your situation and I'll show you."

"I'm not here to party."

"What do you want?"

Rostam wanted to slow things down.

"Some solid food, and your network password."

Spider yelped with amusement.

"That's it - the secret to happiness - achievable goals."

He reached behind one of the screens and tossed an iPhone across the room.

"Keep this by you. I've programmed my own code generator. Each one lasts 15 seconds. Food in the galley next to your room. See you in half an hour."

Chapter Thirty-Four

The kitchen galley on the lowest floor had everything one could need to cook, other than ingredients. An eight-hob oven; microwave; teppanyaki hot plate; deep fat fryer; two different rice cookers. There wasn't a splash of oil, thumbprint of fat or stray crumb to be found. Cupboards had nothing but crockery and cutlery - all with the density of the very expensive, and looking as though the only time they had been touched by human hand was when they came out of their boxes.

The icebox contained a jug of still water with half a lemon floating on top, one T-bone steak, a pound of butter and six eggs. It made Rostam pray for a packet of Cheerios and some cold milk.

He fried the steak in butter and added a couple of eggs while the meat was resting. There was nowhere to sit, so he ate standing at the counter in the kitchen, feeling like a solitary diner at some deserted stylish European railway station.

Back in his room he fired up the Razer Edge and connected to Spider's guest network on the third attempt. Fifteen seconds was just enough to type in eleven letters, digits and esoteric punctuation marks in order.

He sent a video link and hoped his friend would be online. Almost immediately a flashing icon appeared in the middle of his screen. One click on the icon and the entire laptop screen became a close-up of Dread's face.

'Wow, Dread. You in HD is something not even your mother needs to see.'

Dread took a long puff on his cigarette and blew smoke at the camera on his phone.

"We can't all trade on our looks."

"Are you calling me from Dick's?"

"Where else am I gonna be at two in the morning on a Monday?"

"What have you got?"

Dread took a pause to suck on his cigarette and adjust the sunglasses he wore inside after midnight.

"I heard what happened to your lady. Shame. She's an innocent bystander in this train wreck, but she was the connection. Theodore McNamara is in bed with the Loeb crowd. That's why they lashed out at Millie."

Rostam tensed his stomach muscles.

"You think McNamara tried to kill me too in London?"

"Only question is why you're still alive. There must be a reason. Where are you?"

"In Bali. With Spider. Waiting to see if it's safe for me to come home."

"If they're going to get you it won't be by the police."

"The authorities back home think I'm working with him already. Know anything about Tina Waspell?"

"Tell me."

Rostam told Dread what happened at Chicago Executive Airport.

"What do people think happened in Hampstead?"

"People assume the Israelis. Let me ask you this, Rostam. What if the reason your West Coast guy reached out is that he is the one behind these fixed elections? He'd need to shut that down. Acing you would be a short cut."

"You mean the whole thing is to silence us?"

"Once they get the SEC regulator they want, they're home and hosed. Gonna be feeling the pressure now. Couple of guys in Chicago start broadcasting their activities, not what they need. Look at you - on the run on the far side of the world. Meanwhile bitcoin prices keep climbing and their political strength grows."

Dread stopped speaking and gave Rostam time to think. It would explain everything.

"Zadi said much the same. But I just want to get back to Celia and Millie," said Rostam.

"What will you be coming back to if these people are doing what I think they're doing? They won't leave you alive and free if they know you've figured them out. We need a plan. Exposing them on the show won't be anywhere near enough. The truth isn't as loud as a lot of money. Think about it."

Dread disappeared from the screen. Dread seemed like the one person on whom he could rely and, as the silence of the house reasserted itself, Rostam found himself missing him. Even the songbirds flirting with the waterfall outside would make good company. He could see their beaks moving, but no sound made it through the glass.

The brief hope from Spider's talk had disappeared. Knocking down Theo's defences was impossible. Even if he did it, Tina Waspell would try to lock him as an accomplice. Neither option appealed.

Rostam remembered Zadi's crazy plan. Could it possibly work?

Rostam called up the site Zadi had suggested. It looked like the world's most complicated architectural model, a three-dimensional, higgledy-piggledy shape, an assortment of brightly coloured multifaceted geometrical shapes rotating, each with lines of text wrapped around them. He pressed on a purple tridecagon, and it enlarged to take up the whole screen. The text was C++ code. Rostam leaned in to concentrate.

Chapter Thirty-Five

Spider's voice came through hidden speakers in the room, jarring Rostam out of the zone.

"Good news, renegade. Nobody official is looking for you."

"That's the first good news I've had in a while."

"You're welcome. Come upstairs. We've got plans."

"I'm busy."

"We take the obligations of hospitality seriously here. Upstairs, now."

Rostam knew Spider would only keep bugging him if he didn't give in. When he reached the sitting room the sight that greeted him made him burst into laughter.

Spider was in yoga kit. As Rostam walked in, Spider raised one leg off the floor, and raised both hands above his head, until his palms met. He threw across a parcel of cotton clothes tied in a neat, tight bundle with a cream dressing-gown cord. Rostam caught it in his left hand.

"Neat. Let's go."

Outside the air felt thick and soupy, as though shortenings had been mixed into the atmosphere by a celestial baker.

"Almost thirty degrees and no sunshine. We're gonna get wet on the way. Sun'll burn it off later."

"Spider, what would you say to the idea that Satoshi Nakamoto is alive, and contactable?"

"I'd say, who cares, man? Bitcoin is decentralised. There's nobody in charge."

"I wonder what he or she would think about what people are doing with it?"

"Counting their million coins and happy knowing they've done the world the favour, I guess. Hang on."

They had only begun the descent on Spider's scooter back to Ubud when the clouds broke. Hot, large drops of rain fell so hard Rostam could barely distinguish one tree from the next. The outside world contracted to the confused prism of light that made it through the rain. Spider laughed and accelerated downhill.

Puddles formed instantly in the pockmarked road and rainwater soaked his boots. Spider swung across to the left-hand side of the road going around a tight corner, to overtake a tuk-tuk carrying a man, woman, and elementary school age girl with a long braid of black hair, peaked broad bamboo hat, and Grimes T-shirt. Rostam got a good look when Spider had to veer straight back across them as a taxicab shot up the hill, honking furiously. Rostam's knee clipped the father's on the tuk-tuk as they sneaked through.

Five minutes later Spider pulled into an unmarked gravel parking spot. A large copper drum hung from thick ropes attached to a huge wooden frame behind them.

"Best yoga studio on the island, and that's saying a lot. No sign 'cos they don't need to advertise. Get changed behind there and I'll see you up in the ring."

Behind there turned out to be a unisex changing room just off from the drum. Rostam stripped fast before anyone else turned up and unwrapped his clothes parcel. All it contained were a pair of pants and a short-sleeved shirt. Silk. White.

Rostam hadn't seen anyone arrive, but Spider was one of a small group in the dojo at the top of a small slope. He stood in the middle rank of yogis all facing away from the road. Most were female, though there was one older, bearded man in the back row. Rostam felt self-conscious walking across the long grass that grew on the slope, still soaking with rainwater and with occasional sharp edges that threatened to cut the soles of his bare feet.

There was a temptation to stay in the back row, but Spider turned around, caught his eye, and jerked his chin up in invitation.

"You know I've never done any yoga," Rostam whispered. "Apart from when Millie made me go to a pregnancy class. A nightmare. She never made me go again."

"Just breathe it out, man. This is vinyasa. All about movement and breathing. Open your mind and change forever."

Rostam looked at Spider's profile to check for signs of sarcasm, but his friend had his eyes closed, hands pressed together before him, taking an elaborately extended inhalation through his nose while bending down at the waist until his head was hanging close to his own knees. The thought of slipping a disc had scarcely run across the ticker tape inside Rostam's brain when the yoga teacher walked through the class from the back to take her position.

She was Western, tanned dark olive, tall and punitively thin, skin pulled tight back across her long nose and prominent cheekbones, as though she had a scrunchy clip at the back of her hair to maintain tautness. Silence radiated from her through the class. Rostam became conscious of the rustling of leaves in the breeze on the trees that surrounded the dojo. He could hear his own breath. The teacher said nothing while her glance caught each student. She nodded once at everyone. When her glance reached Rostam, he intuited an impersonal warmth in her glance and found himself smiling broadly as he returned her nod.

Once everyone had been greeted the teacher stood in silence, breathing. An unseen drummer bashed the huge gong behind them. Rostam felt the class falling into sync with the teacher, and he tried to do the same. After an interminable period of saluting the sun, she dropped onto her front and the class moved with her. Rostam's torture began.

Not a word was spoken for the duration of the class. Rostam did his best to emulate each movement but found it progressively more difficult to match intent to action, as the disparity between the shapes made by the teacher and her regular students and his own attempts became more clear. Occasional glimpses of Spider showed he was one of the more adept pupils. One position involved lying on his back and elevating the lower body vertically above, so that it felt all his weight lay on his neck.

Rostam gave it up as a bad job and sat cross legged while everyone else seemed perfectly happy. A stabbing empty feeling of failure disproportionate to the event swept through him. *This class is the least of my problems,* he thought, and at least that made him smile. His brain returned to the puzzle he'd left spinning on his laptop. He started it rotating in his mind, like a three-dimensional edifice put together in a haphazard mass of Lego blocks, trying to find the one piece which could be removed and let him inside.

At last, the teacher was standing again before them, palms placed together, and she did another sweep of the room, starting at the other side this time. When she saw Rostam sitting still, a small smile crept her lips. Then the gong was struck again, the spell was broken, and the silent yogis started speaking to one another in low tones, like normal people.

"Wow, man. You are terrible at this," said Spider, more loudly than strictly necessary.

"You didn't tell me I needed to go into training before coming along."

"Whatever. I don't care but you should. Hey - Lucy."

The teacher stepped over to them.

"Great class. Sorry about this no-hoper."

"Ignore David. Yoga is not a competitive sport," she said, extending a slim brown hand to shake. "Lucija."

"Hi Lucija. Rostam. I enjoyed that, but it's hard."

"That's because it's an advanced class. David should bring you to an introductory session. You did well to try to keep up."

Rostam couldn't quite place her accent, Americanised English but not from the States.

"You have a lovely speaking voice."

"Lucy's from Croatia." Spider stepped closer and put his right arm across Rostam's shoulders. "And she's agreed to come for dinner with us. Right, Lucy?"

"Sure. Mirna's staying with a friend.' She looked back at Rostam. "Mirna's my daughter."

"How old?"

"She's five. Good girl. A handful."

"I have a three-year-old daughter back home in Chicago. Celia."

Luciya's face broke into a smile but Spider shook his head.

"That's enough baby talk. Come on guys, we're in Bali, not kindergarten. Whaddya say we show Rostam here one of our sunsets?"

"Have we got time?" asked Luciya.

"You're with me now. Everything's taken care of."

Spider squeezed Rostam's shoulder and simultaneously leaned towards the Croatian. Rostam thought it a bit creepy.

"Lucy and I are talking about going into business together," he said to Rostam in a stage whisper.

Lucija frowned. "This is my place of work, David. We'll discuss that later."

Spider leered at her and reached across with his left hand to bump Rostam's shoulder twice.

"She's all business. Not just good looks and amazing yoga skills."

Now Rostam was embarrassed.

"Do I have time to get back into proper clothes? I feel like a fraud in this get-up."

"I've got a driver to get us to Keramas Beach. See you down the bottom."

Chapter Thirty-Six

There was no missing the car at the bottom of the hill. Spider, now in shorts, t-shirt and flip-flops, perched on the bonnet of a Hummer limousine, polished like a squat, three-dimensional black mirror. Rostam could see his own reflection growing as he approached.

"This is the fun-mobile for the evening, my friend," yelled Spider as he sprang off the bonnet. "Ketut's gonna drive us tonight. Say hi, Ketut."

Rostam peered in the passenger side window and saw a slight, older Balinese man raise a hand gingerly in greeting.

"It's not that I don't enjoy scaring the pants off you on the Vespa, but we've got company tonight."

"I'm busy, Spider. Any chance of an early night?"

"Rostam, you place yourself in my hands and stop worrying." Spider looked past Rostam. "Lucy, finally. Let's go!"

Rostam saw Lucija walking down past the gong. She'd changed into a mauve, floral-print long dress, and her black hair now fell half-way down her back. Her movements were fluid but measured, like a ballerina or athlete used to expressing themselves through motion. Rostam guessed she was closer to forty than thirty. Her confident, unostentatious maturity all the more striking set against Spider's locker-room demeanour. Luciya was austerely handsome rather than beautiful and, unless Rostam was very much mistaken, entirely out of Spider's league.

"We're travelling in *that?*" she asked, clearly amused.

"Nothing but the best," shouted Spider, and jumped into the front passenger seat. Rostam opened the rear door to let Lucija in first and then walked around to sit behind the driver.

"Step on it, Ketut. That sunset's not gonna watch itself."

Spider was fiddling with his cell while the car shot off downhill. Rostam saw another waterfall cascading beyond trees through his window when the car speakers disgorged a wall of drum'n'bass.

"Ganja Cru," Spider shouted over his shoulder. "Still love them just as much as back in the day."

Spider had knelt up on his seat and was nodding his head furiously to high bpm music. Rostam looked at Lucija, her lips curled upwards as she looked out of her window.

"Remember those rave nights in the East Village?" Spider was looking at Rostam.

"Sure," said Rostam, though they weren't especially important memories to him. Spider sensed it, and sank back into his seat to focus intensely on his cell. Rostam checked his watch. 6pm in Bali made it six in the morning in New York.

Air conditioning in the car was too cold. He cracked the window and the warm, wet, musty smells of the forest around them were sucked inside, clashing with the pimpmobile vibe and its urban soundtrack. Rostam sensed that Spider was putting on a show for which he was the target audience, but none of it worked. He'd rather be back at the house figuring out how to contact Satoshi.

When they pulled up by the beach, sunset worshippers were spread out at intervals.

"This is a challenging beach to surf, doesn't get too crowded," said Spider, gesturing as though it all belonged to him. "Berawa's further away, and full of Aussies on long weekends."

Spider led the way onto the black sand, carrying a thin printed blanket taken the trunk of the Hummer. He picked a spot without other people within twenty yards and snapped the blanket open so that it shot away from him and then floated down onto the sand with scarcely a wrinkle.

"Smooth," said Rostam and Lucija at the same time, and giggled.

"Fuckin'-A," said Spider, without any apparent irony. Rostam and Lucija each sat on a far side of the blanket, with Spider between them. The sun was in full special effects mode, turning the irregular morass of conjoined clouds a deep orange, and shimmering off the crests of waves impatient to smash themselves into the shore.

"Don't be fooled. Those waves don't look like much from here, but they're plenty big enough when you're out on a board."

"I'll take your word for it," said Rostam. "Never managed to get on a surfboard down at Battery Park. Nor on Lake Michigan."

Lucija laughed, and Rostam felt absurdly gratified.

"We'll get him surfing, won't we Lucy? We've only got Rostam for a coupla days unless I can persuade him to stay. We'll have him doing the handstand scorpion and surfing tubes. He'll never want to go home, huh?"

"Let Rostam make his own decisions," said Luciya. "Not everyone who comes to Bali has to surf."

"Don't go soft on me." Spider's phone rang. "You kids be good. Back in a minute."

Spider sprang up and walked back towards the street.

"Typical David," said Luciya. "We come all this way to see the sun set and he disappears."

Rostam looked up. The orange in the clouds was darkening like sugar in a pan on a hot stove, as the sun slid down to kiss its reflection on the ocean. To his surprise, Rostam felt energized, and even moved.

"This makes me feel like one time I walked into St Patrick's in midtown," he said. "I was cutting school, pretending to be a juvenile delinquent. Can't remember why. No particular reason, I guess. It was the middle of the afternoon, and I had nothing to do. There wasn't a service or anything, and there weren't any tourists. Just a huge, quiet, cold space with stained glass windows and too many crucifixes. I had this sudden sense that God was there. For about a minute I think I might even have believed in Him."

Lucija laughed and Rostam felt he hadn't made a mistake splurging to her.

"That was it, my religious epiphany. Is that what you guys get from the sunsets?"

"Maybe it has a spiritual dimension for some people. I'm not trying to put anyone down. I just think it's a cool thing to see, y'know?"

"Yeah. I think I do," said Rostam, who liked the Croatian woman more all the time. "Lived here a long time?"

"Two and a half years. Things went south with Mirna's dad. We'd been living in London while he tried to make some business things work. Seemed the obvious place to come. I love yoga, I really do, and Bali is Mecca for yogis. I just thought why not move somewhere where I might actually make a living from what I love."

"That's awesome. Inspiring, even."

"Don't get too carried away. There's not much money in it."

"Is that what you're talking to Spider about?"

"David, you mean? He's pitching setting up a new yoga place and putting me in charge. No harm in talking about it."

It sounded like Spider was on an ego trip to Rostam, but it wasn't his place to say so. He wanted to talk about Millie.

"Hey guys, Sara's come along for the party," said Spider, from above them.

Rostam and Luciya each looked up. Spider was standing with a beautiful student age woman wearing a mischievous smile, short, peroxide hair combed in a quiff, Deus ex Machina cut off t-shirt, and yellow bikini bottom.

"Hiya," said the girl in a London accent.

"You missed sunset," said Lucija, managing to sound both matter-of-fact and amused.

"There'll be another one tomorrow," said Spider. "As long as poor Rostam here saw it. The rest of us live here. That's him there - ," he said to Sara, pointing at Rostam, who sat back propping himself up with palms down, fingers spread on the sand and legs crossed before him. "The gorgeous yoga teacher is Lucy."

"Luciya," said Luciya, raising her left hand in greeting.

"We're expected at Wild Air in forty-five. Anyone fancy a dip first?"

"The infinity pool at Wild Air is awesome," stated Sara in a bored drawl.

"*That's* what I'm talkin' about," said Spider. "And the food ain't too shabby. You're a fan, right, Lucy?"

"Never been," said Luciya.

"You're kidding," said Spider. "You live in Ubud and you've never been to Wild Air. We fix that tonight."

He put his arm over Sara's shoulder and led the way back towards the car. It looked wrong to Rostam. There was only a decade between the two in age, but Spider had the degenerate air that habitually settles on single American men who settle in Asia, while the English girl looked like she belonged, if not in a classroom, then not as if she should be thousands of miles from her parents. Rostam stood up and offered his hand to Lucija, who thanked him and pulled on it to help her up.

"Your friend is a disappointment," she said to Rostam, sounding neither angry nor especially let down. "I thought this evening was about meeting his old friend from America and talking business."

"That's more than he told me. I have work to do."

"Then neither of us is going to get what we wanted."

Lucija bent over effortlessly and picked up the blanket, shaking it before rapidly folding it over and over and over, so that with three swift gestures the large expanse of cloth was compressed into a neat A4 sized package.

"But no need to complain," she continued, as they set off in the wake of Spider and Sara. "From what I hear this restaurant is something special."

Chapter Thirty-Seven

What the hell am I doing here? Rostam asked himself half a dozen times on the way from the beach back up the hill to the restaurant in Ubud. Spider squeezed Sara into the front of the Hummer along with himself and the driver, leaving Rostam and Lucija in the enormous passenger area. He felt embarrassed at association with his old friend, just another foreign degenerate living the life of a rock'n'roll aristocrat in Asia where he could get away with it.

"Are you going to settle here?" asked Lucija, pulling him out from the revolving washing-machine of his thoughts.

"Don't think so. Just popping in to see an old friend. I'm nowhere near as rich as him, and I have more obligations." He laughed. "Said out loud that doesn't sound too good, does it?"

"I don't know. Some clever person said too much peace of mind leads to premature old age."

"Isn't that what yoga and wellness is all about, peace of mind?"

It was Lucija's turn to laugh. "You're making fun."

Rostam spread his hands and opened his eyes wide in the universal sign language to show he was saying nothing of the sort.

"Just because we sit in lotus position doesn't mean we're idiots. I was a schoolgirl when my country fell to pieces. I saw terrible things. Terrible. You can't even imagine, because you can't put yourself in the mind of a small child when their real world is a horror film. But yoga and sunsets are the real world too. If I can support myself and my daughter and keep that in my life, why wouldn't I do it?"

Rostam nodded. "I never expected to hear the wisest words of my life from a yoga instructor on the beach. We should high-five."

Luciya giggled and extended her open palm. It was the first moment since the explosion that Rostam felt a sense of lightness, before he settled back in his seat and saw that Spider was now French kissing the young Englishwoman. His good mood evaporated. There wasn't going to be much sense coming out of his friend for the rest of the evening. He should have stayed home and worked on the puzzle.

The approach to the restaurant heightened the mood. The driver took a different route back up the wooded hills and turned up a sharply steeper drive, past a signpost so discreet a casual observer would miss it. Headlights picked out a long series of trees, each sprinkled with solar lights, before entering a copse. Within it stood a miniature Gothic chateau manufactured from dark wood and glass. Four slender conical roofs surrounded by delicate wooden crenelations towered above the surrounding forest. A narrow moat reflected warm candlelight around the building. Their driver stopped the car to wait for a drawbridge to be lowered to allow them to cross. It was painted with a welcoming green dragon, whose tail seemed to wrap around his own body, like the leaves of an unripe banana.

"Bugger me sideways," said Sara in the front seat in her mockney accent. Nobody had anything to add.

Once inside the courtyard a phalanx of serving staff materialised, bowing towards both back doors and the passenger door.

"They know not to bother bowing to the chauffeur," said Lucija with wry amusement, as she, Rostam, Sara, and Spider all climbed down.

"What do you think, man?" Spider addressed his question only to Rostam, though he was holding Sara by the hand. "A-maz-ing, eh?"

"Not too shabby."

"Don't try to play it cool. Chicago has got nothing to compete with this. London neither." The car was turning around. "Kemet's got another couple of people to pick up and join us. Aperitif?"

Rostam looked at Lucija and found she was already staring back at him. *Why do I think she needs protecting from Spider? She'd be in a better position to look after me.*

The two of them followed Spider and Sara into the hotel. The lobby had a vertiginous high ceiling, draped with brightly coloured decorated cloth undulating gently, either with air conditioning or air jets placed to create that effect of standing under a benevolent lightly clouded sky. Generic Euro techno beats played quietly. Fat scented candles burned in tall black metal stands all around the walls, while warm coloured LEDs spread yellows, oranges and hazel green around the ceiling.

Spider was gesticulating with his left hand as he pointed out features to Sara, who showed no sign of resenting the presence of his right hand on her shoulder. Fragments of his monologue floated back to Rostam.

'Best food on the island...Can't escape tourist trash anywhere...Great vegan options babe..."

"I thought *babe* went out with *sweet cheeks* and *honeybunch*," he said to Lucija.

"Money can generally call you whatever it likes. Who's going to argue?"

Rostam wanted to disagree but checked himself. He was here as Spider's friend.

The pair of maître d's, one male, one female, equally beautiful and impossible to age, at least to a tourist like Rostam, stopped walking at the same time, spun around and gestured to a side room.

"My private room, baby. We're having a celebration," Spider shouted as he led the group in. An oval tabletop of polished walnut stood a foot off the ground, with a recessed seating area cut out below it. Rostam copied Spider, Sara and Luciya in kicking off his shoes. One by one they slipped into the seating area, Spider on the far side next to Sara.

"You sit across from me, Lucy, we got business to discuss. Waiter! Cristal. Vintage. Two bottles."

"And oolong tea if you have it, please," added Lucija.

"My apologies, sensei!" called out Spider, with performative sorrow. "But you'll make an exception tonight, won't you?"

"That sounds like a command more than a question," said Luciya.

"Because tonight is a special night. First of all, we have my very good friend Rostam visiting for the first time. A Bali virgin!"

Sara raised her hands and hooted, somehow managing the very English trick of sounding simultaneously sincere and sarcastic.

"And today has seen the successful launch of yet another Spider creation: the Vegan Coin. Zero emissions. Elegant blockchain. No animal products anywhere close to the digital supply chain. Pre-released on the metaverse last week and into general circulation today."

Spider was now speaking directly to Rostam.

"I'm embarrassed," said Rostam. "I've had a lot going on. Forgot to track it."

"I'm here to tell you it's not too late. Two million coins in issue as of this afternoon. Each one worth 1/100th of an ether, so we can keep the kids involved."

Rostam did a quick calculation.

"You've created a $60mm currency overnight?"

"Not overnight bro. These things take planning. Just wait: Vegan Coin is gonna be the next big thing. For us it has already happened. It's paying for supper for sure."

Champagne had arrived more quickly than the tea and they each had a full glass in front of them. Rostam raised his first.

"To Spider - a man of many talents."

"To Vegan Coin!" added Sara.

Spider drank his glass down in one go and a hovering waiter immediately refilled it. Rostam noticed that Lucija raised her glass to her lips without swallowing any alcohol. She quietly thanked the waiter who brought her tea. Rostam was tempted to join her off the booze. He didn't want to get dragged into Spider's weird mood. But the first mouthful of fizzy wine felt good, he was a long way from home and the pressures of the past week were a pulsating fiery fist around his intestines. Rostam raised his glass and offered it in a 'cheers' to Luciya, who played along, chinking it with her small brown clay dish of oolong.

"When did you go vegan?" he asked Spider. "What happened to T-bones at Sparks and Peter Luger's?"

"Different sky, different guy. You do enough yoga and before you know it you just don't want to put animal products in your body. Right, Lucy?"

"He's right. It's no hardship. Balinese cooking is very vegan friendly."

"I'll do better at the eating than the stretching," said Rostam.

Rostam felt a gentle kick on his shin and looked up, surprised. Sara was giving him one of what he already recognised as a trademark mischievous grin.

"Don't worry, Rostam, we're not all goody two-shoes. There's a Maccie Ds in Kuta, where the Aussies throw beer cans at each other and fall off their surf-boards. I'll take you there sometime."

It was ridiculous. Sara was effectively a sexualised child of legal age, but somehow she made the offer of a trip to MacDonald's feel like a promise of erotic adventure. Rostam felt partly enticed but mostly disgusted with himself, and more so with his friend for entertaining it.

"It's all to share," said Luciya in explanation, as food started to arrive on platters.

"Apart from my black truffle ravioli bro," interjected Spider. "Anyone who tries to nab that's gonna lose a hand."

"Civilized people share food in Bali," said Lucija.

Rostam looked down. No chopsticks, but a fork and spoon. Organic tomato roulade, watermelon carpaccio, crispy seared silken tofu, caramelized cauliflower. Black miso. Fresh curry leafy cepe mushrooms.

Spider was making a show of talking yoga studio business with Lucija, who had all the facts and figures in her head. The second bottle of Cristal was upended in its bucket and Spider sounded a little drunk.

"So, what's the status of you and Spider?" Rostam asked Sara. He felt obliged to speak, despite her seeming perfectly content eating in silence.

She laughed. "You mean like relationship status? What do we say on our social media profiles?"

"Sure."

"We're just friends. Spider's a generous guy, you know?"

"You been on the island a long time?"

"Few months. Asia bums either end up here or Thailand. I've done the rest of SouthEast Asia - this is my favourite. Done the tour?"

"I've been to Japan a few times on business. Always Tokyo. Hong Kong and Singapore a couple of times each. None of the fun places."

"That sucks. At least you're here now. The eternal present."

Rostam looked more closely at Sara.

"I can never tell when you're being ironic."

"You mean in an Alanis Morrisette way?"

"She got it wrong in the song."

"So why should I be easier to understand than Alanis bloody Morrisette?"

Rostam smiled in defeat. He was starting to feel a bit drunk too but still grasped he shouldn't underestimate this girl.

The wooden slid open and two women walked in.

"Aulia! Dewi!", shouted Spider, clumsily clambering out from beneath the table. Both women gave a cheerful, shrill response and went over to throw their arms around their host, who kissed each flush on the lips. "Sara, you know the girls already."

Sara raised a nonchalant hand.

"Hiya."

"This is Lucy."

Lucija raised a hand too.

Rostam felt he should get up.

"And this is Rostam, one of my very best friends in the world. He's come all the way from Chicago. He's rich, single and a long way from home." Rostam extended a hand to each woman to make the conversation more adult. Each giggled as they placed small, immaculately manicured paws into his, which looked clumsy and outsized in comparison.

"Dewi, you sit here with Lucy and me. You go that end, Aulia."

The newcomers settled down to sit at either end of the oval table. More champagne appeared along with fresh plates and courses, which were blending into one another for Rostam.

Sara had gone back into her default mode of self-possessed silence. Rostam envied her. Whenever he sat without speaking at a social event he felt like a spare part. This girl made him feel like he had to perform for her. That was followed by a feeling of discomfort that she felt no need to make Aulia feel welcome.

"You're Balinese?" he asked, not knowing how else to begin.

"I come from Jakarta. Not too far. About twenty-four hours in a car."

"I've never been. Very different to here?"

"Oh yes. Bali is much nicer. We all love Bali."

Sara leaned in.

"There are quite a few women from Jakarta here. Isn't that true?"

Aulia tittered as though the English girl had said something incredibly witty.

"Many Jakarta girls here, it's true. You like it?"

Rostam waited for Sara to respond but then realized the question was directed at him.

"I only arrived this morning. But sure, it's lovely. What's not to like?"

"Your friend very generous," said Aulia.

"You know him well?"

"We had dinner couple times. Dewi know him better. They good friends I think."

Rostam looked at Sara to see if this was news to her. *Should have known better. She couldn't care less.* He drained another glass and wondered if it was already too late to slow down.

"I have an early start tomorrow, so I'll say thank you and goodnight."

Lucija was addressing the whole table, but Rostam felt he had somehow let her down.

"No need to get up."

Spider waved goodbye from his seat but Rostam staggered up, feeling the effects of wine and jetlag mixed into a somnolent cocktail. He kissed Lucija gently on each cheek.

"Lovely to meet you. Sorry I couldn't keep up with all the yoga moves."

"You weren't as bad as you think."

"I heard the women at yoga all go for guys who can rock the difficult moves."

"And I suppose you still believe in Santa Claus and the Tooth Fairy too? Take care of yourself, Rostam. I'd ask you to keep an eye on your friend but he can look after himself at this point."

Rostam and Lucija looked down to see Spider whispering something in Dewi's ear which was making her laugh, while extending his left hand towards Sara, who was ignoring it for now, but looked suggestible.

With Lucija gone the volume in the room went up. Rostam shuffled over to sit opposite Spider and Aulia slid into his former seat. More champagne. Rostam tried to see if the Indonesian girls were keeping pace with himself and Spider but gave up. Sara was holding her own. When the waiters came in with pineapple sorbet, caramelized soybeans and kaffir lime chocolate shell desserts, Spider demanded shots.

"I want Baby Guinness," said Sara, biting her lower lip.

"You can order that when it's your party, baby. We want tequila. Rey Sol Anejo. Bring in the bottle so we know you're not passing off with the cheap shit."

Rostam looked at the waiter to see if he took offence, but he seemed unperturbed. *This is like being back in investment banking. And not in a good way.*

There was an edge of anticipation in the room. Even Sara seemed to perk up. The waiter returned with an unusual bottle, a brown glass circular body embossed with a smiling faced sun and fins protruding all the way around for rays. Five shot glasses were filled to the brim and distributed to each diner with precision.

"It's like they're pouring liquid uranium."

"At fifteen hundred bucks a bottle U-235 would be cheaper," yelled Spider.

Spider lifted his glass.

"To VeganCoin!"

"Shouldn't we sip it if it's so expensive?" asked Rostam.

"Live in the moment, man."

Everyone downed their shots.

"You can leave the bottle, pal," Spider said to the waiter, who bowed backwards out of the room, Rostam assumed to tell the owner of their success in shifting an overpriced bottle of liquor. As soon as he left Spider produced an old school silver cigarette case from his trouser pocket, depressed the thumbnail catch which protruded halfway down the seam, and put both hands together to cradle as it sprang open. Inside was a silver tube, old-school razor blade and plastic baggie filled with white powder, which Spider began to rank into lines.

Rostam leaned in.

"I thought this was very, very illegal over here?"

"Bali is a civilized island my friend. You know the definition of civilization, right?"

Rostam shrugged.

"Civilization is when there's one rule for the masses and another for people like us. Drug busts are for Australian peasants who come over here and try to score down in Kuta."

Spider bent down and swiftly inhaled two lines. He passed the straw to Sara, who crawled out of the seating and knelt next to him. She breathed in her line and remained behind Spider, hands on his shoulders, while Dewi and Aulia took their turns. Rostam went last, with some reluctance.

Immediately it hit his sinuses, Rostam's eyes watered and a feeling of great clarity and excitement flooded his brain. It was good stuff. All his questions had been answered, he just couldn't remember what any of them were.

"I haven't done this in years, man," he said, after crawling round and dropping back into his seat. "Not since Celia was born. Not since Millie was pregnant in fact. Damn!"

"Welcome back bro."

Spider was refilling their shot glasses, considerably more clumsily than the waiter had done. He passed them around, spilling more tequila in the process. "Good times!"

The pressure of the week built up steam that needed to come out. Rostam had come to ask for Spider's help, after all.

"You know what I really think, Spider?"

His friend leaned in so Rostam could whisper in his ear.

"I think bitcoin is corrupt beyond repair. I'm going to try to track down Satoshi and see if it can be fixed."

Said out loud it seemed impossible, but Spider looked as though he'd taken it at face value.

"Forget it, man," said Rostam, already regretting his openness. "Good times!"

Everyone repeated the phrase and swallowed their drinks. Rostam wondered how long it would be before the desire for the next line would overwhelm the good feeling that was still ricocheting around his brain.

"Ladies. Gentleman. I'm gonna suggest we carry on this party at home."

Spider closed his silver case with more care than he'd expended on the tequila and stumbled out of the seat, knocking Sara off balance as he did so. She gave a deeper laugh than Rostam had heard from her before and executed a perfect backwards roll before springing to her feet.

"Bravo!" said Rostam, and was rewarded with a curtsey from the English woman.

Spider led the party back to their Hummer, with an arm around Sara to one side and Dewi to the other. Aulia walked close to Rostam. *This is stupid. It's practically ruder not to put an arm around this woman than to do it. And she's a complete stranger.* Rostam couldn't tell if it was that realization or the drugs ebbing away that made him feel like a fool, so he stuck his hands in his pockets. *At least she'll meet one American man who doesn't think he can order her like a pizza.*

Chapter Thirty-Eight

The drive back to Spider's only took ten minutes but that was enough for Rostam's mood to darken. This time all the passengers were thrown together in the back, with Spider again placing himself between Sara and Dewi.

"This heap got Bluetooth?" Spider shouted as soon as he was inside, fiddling with his cell. The Beastie Boys' *Hey Ladies* blasted out. At least he retained that much of an NYC sense of humour.

Rostam leaned against the window on his side, tried to pick out sights in the limpid darkness, but could only see his own reflection. He didn't think much of it. He had to sniff to stop a cocaine nose-drip. Ahmad was still dead, collateral damage in a fight that belonged to neither of them.

He needed to get back and see if his plan could work. Was he crazy to load so much on a potential meeting with a man who probably didn't exist in Tokyo? If he couldn't crack the puzzle he'd never get the chance to find out.

Aulia seemed to get the message. She sat more in the middle of the seat than the opposite end, but the foot of stitched black leather between them seemed a romantic DMZ to Rostam.

Invisible helpers had turned Spider's house back into an immaculate multi-story bachelor pad while they were out. It was midnight, which made it Monday lunchtime in New York, but Rostam didn't want to initiate any long-distance conversations when he was half in the bag.

"Everyone to the screen room," yelled Spider. The three women all knew their own way there.

"Sara, get the girls and yourself whatever you like. Bourbon for my bro and me."

Spider threw his arm around Rostam as they followed down the stairs.

"This is the life, eh? We do what we want here. Nobody is watching. No one to tell us what to do. We've found paradise."

As he said this, Rostam's attention was caught by a liquid drop that spooled out of Spider's right nostril and dropped halfway down his chest. Spider followed his eyes and gave a mighty inhalation while swiping at his nose with the back of his hand.

"Spoils the effect, huh? There's a solution to that."

Downstairs Spider picked up a tablet and reconfigured the screens so that he had Bloomberg on the one largest on the left-hand side, with multiple other screens showing repeated footage of models walking down catwalks. The models' facial expressions were all the same, as were their physiques. The only differences were skin colour and the dresses themselves.

Spider grabbed a small circular mirror with a white wooden border and upended his cigarette case over it, which left a small mound of powder in the middle. He cut three lines, snorted two himself, offered the silver straw to Rostam, who demurred, and then passed the entire caboodle to Sara. Rostam smiled at the alacrity with which the Englishwoman went about marshalling the remaining powder into order.

So, there is something Little Miss Too-Cool-for-School cares about after all.

"Sit next to me, bro. We got matters to discuss," said Spider to him.

Spider pulled on a phone headset and connected to the tablet. He began a short series of self-congratulatory calls. Once or twice, he elbowed Rostam to let him know he was speaking to a shared acquaintance, but Rostam had too much to work out to be interested in gossip. *Crypto community* was a phrase Rostam and Spider both hated but it is what made up Rostam's listener base. Mostly speculators in it for a quick buck. Spider had been one of the few true believers early on, which is how he'd managed to get so rich so fast. Rostam himself was constrained by Loeb's rules on personal investment, and the caution that comes with marriage and a child. If Dread was right, and Theo McNamara was using bitcoin to fund murders and fix elections, did that make the crypto ecosystem no better than fiat currency?

Rostam grabbed the Bloomberg controller to see what had been going on during his travels. It wasn't hard to find Vegan Coin. VEG@N was the ticker. Nice. Created at 1% of ether that very morning. Had traded as high as 2%. Now fallen back to 0.5%. How many high school dreams had been inflated and then punctured by that? Rostam looked at Spider, chuckling and guffawing into his plastic headset as he and his counterparts reinforced how smart they are to one another.

Sara had disappeared. The two Indonesian women were each sitting back on their heels, backs perfectly straight, faces composed and smiling. No sign of their nostrils twitching. Each had a glass of white wine by their side, but neither was drinking. They looked perfectly happy to be there. But there was no way they could be content. Spider had paid no attention to any of the women since handing over his tray to Sara. Rostam kept hearing him use the word DISTRIBUTION on the phone. *Must ask him what he means.*

A general sense of unease receded as the rising flow of bourbon in his bloodstream overpowered the ebbing impact of cocaine. *I shouldn't be so judgemental. Everyone here is an adult pursuing happiness in their own way.* But was that true? Spider spraying money around while young women frolicked in the moisture he threw off didn't sit well.

"Without distribution, we'd be like Satoshi," said Spider. "Sitting on a huge pile with nobody to sell it to."

"He could sell his bitcoin tomorrow if he wanted," said Rostam.

"Ok, bad example. He can because of what Bitcoin has become. But he's still the biggest owner. Things are moving on fast. Bitcoin will soon be like email or Facebook - a legacy medium." Spider gestured at the screens. "This is the future. We're busy defining the nature of reality while chumps in New York are reliving history over and over again. I could use someone like you alongside me."

"I thought you were trying to help me, not hire me," said Rostam, trying to sound friendly.

"Everything is a battle for power between the powers that be and the powers that *would* be. Legacy finance used to be the power in the room. That's why they sucked in the smart guys, like you and me." Spider reached across and clapped Rostam on the shoulder. "Governments too. Remember when working at the State Department was a job for ambitious people?"

"Sure. They're not all chumps you know."

"Yes, they are. Yes they *are*, Rostam. Open your eyes."

"This is the kind of conspirasphere crap I blow up on the podcast."

Spider laughed so hard he pushed his Bluetooth keyboard away and turned to face Rostam for the first time since he entered the room.

"It's a great show. I listen to every episode."

Rostam was too angry to take the compliment.

"What if the freedom fighters we used to admire are becoming the next set of oppressors?"

"Government power is the enemy," said Spider. "We want people to start thinking for themselves, get to a place where people don't think it's normal to have their communication spied on. Their shopping spied on. Every transaction they choose to make has a slice taken out, so governments have even more to spend keeping people down."

Sara walked back into the room with a bottle of Old Rip Van Winkle bourbon and came over to top them up. She reached down to kiss Spider, but he brushed her off.

"I'm just talking to Rostam, honey."

Spider turned around to Rostam and put a hand on each of his shoulders.

"The dream is alive, man."

Rostam nodded. Spider kept staring until Rostam was uncomfortable.

"Lecture over," said Spider. "Doll, bring us another line over here."

Sara nodded from where she knelt on the floor, topping up herself and the two Indonesians.

"Don't you worry you might forget why we started this?" asked Rostam.

Spider inhaled two more lines, tossed his head back and breathed in again while pressing his index finger at the tip of his nose, so as not to waste any grains.

"Sometimes my enemy's enemy is my friend, right?"

And sometimes they're just bad news.

"Enough business talk. Have you made a decision?"

Spider gestured towards the three women. "Sara's gonna stick with me but the other two are floating voters."

"I'm tired. I'm gonna leave you to it and sleep for about forty-eight hours."

"You're kidding, right? You're free of that bitch Millie now. That's why I sorted this all out for tonight. Get it out of your system."

Rostam stood up.

"Don't be rude about Millie. She's still the mother of my daughter. You used to like her a lot."

"That was then," said Spider, looking away.

Rostam wished the women good night as he walked past. They looked surprised but hardly disappointed.

Chapter Thirty-Nine

Wednesday January 19

Rostam spent the rest of the night focussed on the puzzle. He'd looked at dozens of polygons on the screen before he recognized the provenance of the C++ code. It all came from Satoshi's White Paper, where Bitcoin was first invented. Zadi had told the truth, about the puzzle, at least.

Every time he was distracted, thoughts of Millie, stuck on the West Side, and Dana, bereaved in Brentford, sloshed around Rostam's brain like bright flashing light bulbs below transparent thin cotton. Their lights shone through and kept his mind moving, around the rotating puzzle, searching for the way in.

Dawn was breaking outside when he gave in to exhaustion. He was no closer to a solution.

It was only a handful of hours later when he opened his eyes. One press on the fingerprint outline by his bed and the window turned from black velvet to transparent glass. Not too late to call Millie, but she rejected the call on the first ring. An SMS arrived: *Can't speak. Celia doesn't want to go to sleep. Wish she was happier here.* Rostam sent a reply full of loving emojis. *Who knew our feelings would turn into cartoons as soon as we were given the chance to use them to communicate?*

An SMS from Hanratty. *Any news, old boy?*

Carl Force messaged the iPhone. *Feel free to update me anytime. Clock is ticking.*

Nothing from Dread, but an email from his Mom. Enigmatic as ever.

Rostam kuchaloo, if you're stuck, just ask.

Rostam smiled. At least some things remained constant. No man ever ceased to be a baby in the eyes of an Iranian mother.

He looked up the puzzle and started playing again. It took another hour to realise he needed to use a prime number-based algorithm to get in. It was full of mashups of the original code: quotations, tributes, criticisms.

After hours of effort, he was inside. The euphoria of solving the puzzle almost wiped out his grief, if only for a moment. Rostam found the line of code which referenced Alistair Darling, the British chancellor expanding quantitative easing at the time Satoshi launched Bitcoin. He put it through a simple prime number multiplier and typed out his message.

Hi Satoshi. My name is Rostam James. Look me up. I'm coming to Japan and want to speak to you. You will be interested in what I have to say.

He sent the message and sat back.

There goes nothing.

Upstairs there was a fresh breeze in the screen room. Rostam looked towards the waterfall and saw Spider lifting dumbbells, looking towards the water. It looked like he was suspended in air.

"You have a balcony out there?"

Spider didn't turn around but grunted through another couple of repetitions.

"Flushing last night out of the system."

Rostam stepped out of the room to join him on the glass platform stretching two metres over the sheer drop down the cliff face.

"It doesn't make you dizzy?"

"Never look down. That's my motto. Gotta keep climbing higher in everything you do."

Rostam stuck out his lower lip and nodded, as though he was thinking over this gem.

"Have you eaten? I can fix breakfast."

"I've got someone for that. Fresh oatmeal on the stove downstairs." Another couple of reps with a performative grunt. "Soy milk ok?"

"I'd expect nothing else from a yogi. I guess last night's cocaine and bourbon were vegan, huh?"

"Get fucked, choirboy," grunted Spider amiably. Rostam laughed - maybe this guy was still ok after all. "Sorry if I was a bit rough last night," said Spider. "Been away from civilization too long. Forgive me."

Rostam said nothing.

"Pretty please?"

Spider beamed a smile that took Rostam back ten years.

"Ok, man. Just don't mention my ex-wife again, ok?"

Spider completed a final, slow-motion repetition with his weights, sweat dripping down into the clipped black beard that filled out the hollows of his cheeks.

"You got it. Talent, my friend, is always in short supply. That's why I want you. I'm gonna grab a shower. Oatmeal's on the hob downstairs. Back in ten."

Spider slapped his shoulder as he passed, and Rostam took his place on the balcony. A pair of Macaque monkeys played tag in the treetops at his eye level about two hundred meters ahead, next to the waterfall. An earlier rain shower left the air more clear and less humid than usual, and the sun was just the right side of warmth compared to heat. Was this really so bad? The problems of Chicago and London suddenly felt a long way away. There was no sign of the women from the night before, and Spider sober and at least pretending to be apologetic was less aggravating.

Rostam went down to the kitchen to make coffee. If he wasn't careful Spider would try to palm him off with green tea. When he returned to the balcony, he walked into a flight of scarlet butterflies. Each had a single yellow vein through the wing. The flutter of wings on his skin made him feel cleansed, like the butterflies had taken his sloughed-off skin with them. He didn't notice Spider had joined him until hearing the clunk and scratch of a lighter and the scent of burning paper and a potent, sweet strain of weed climbed into his nostrils.

Spider was holding a bulbous joint between thumb and index finger of his left hand, watching its spindly end flare up and settle into a glow, before offering it to Rostam.

"What were you saying about contacting Satoshi?" said Spider, as Rostam took his second puff before handing it back.

"I thought about it again. Ridiculous idea."

As soon as he spoke Rostam wondered why he'd lied but was immediately glad he did. Spider snorted.

"Knew you were kidding. Because what we need to do is keep getting Bitcoin higher. Soon they'll run out of new supply, and then people like us will be kings."

Rostam coughed out a pair of raspy barks. He could hear in four dimensions, so that birdsong, cascading water, and his own breath were all running on different frequencies. A sudden wave of paranoia burrowed up his spine and into his brain. Spider wasn't thinking about things the same way as him at all. Best to misdirect.

"My compliments to your weed guy," said Rostam. "This stuff is magic."

"Better than what they sell in these new dispensaries back home?"

"Hard to say. Maybe the environment." Rostam nodded towards the waterfall. "You got the complete package here."

"So why don't you stay, bro? No reason you can't do the podcast from here. I'll get you back on the inside. We can build an empire in paradise."

Rostam closed his eyes and looked hard. An old trick his Mom taught him. *What you see when your eyes are closed is what really matters.* Celia's pearl-white milk teeth. Ahmad cross legged in his Brentford study. Theo McNamara, Tina Waspell and Bahman Zadi lined up like a series of gremlins destabilising and destroying everything he worked for. The look on Spider's face as he kept repeated his favourite word: distribution, distribution, distribution.

Rostam opened his eyes as he felt Spider reach across his right shoulder with the lit joint between his fingers and bent his elbow so he could insert the rolled cardboard filter between Rostam's lips. He could smell Spider's skin care product.

Rostam shrugged Spider off him.

"It's ok. The paranoia will be gone in a minute," said Spider. "Just think about it. Ideas and energy are what matters. The world's full of money. The rich world's overcapitalised and the problem is just gonna keep building, until there's a purge, like World War Three or the rise of global communism. Or Mother Nature shuts up shop and all this turns against us. Whatever. In the meantime, the music is playing and we've gotta keep dancing."

"What can I do for you?"

"You've got listeners. You know people. You're smart and I trust you. You wanna do something to give Celia a chance of a better life? Do it from here. Ain't nowhere better than Paradise."

Rostam passed the joint back. Spider hadn't lied about the effects. Euphoria was rising in his brain stem and had eclipsed unease. Rostam blinked and the image of Celia reappeared, sticking to his retina even after he was looking again towards the waterfall.

"Give me something practical. Where would we start?"

"A podcast about VeganCoin wouldn't be a bad idea. You could work wonders with that shit. Trust!"

Rostam laughed, partly at Spider's enthusiasm and partly to change the tone. Spider had always been good at corralling people into making decisions.

"Can I borrow your Vespa? Could do with getting down the beach and clearing my head."

"Sure thing. Keys are by the front door. Your eyes will get you in and out the front door. Don't forget to wear a helmet. The police will have a hundred bucks off you in a heartbeat if they spot you."

Rostam walked up the stairs to the front door shaking his head. Watch out for the cops to save a hundred bucks, and don't worry about the death sentence they might give you for drugs. This was a screwed-up world.

Chapter Forty

Riding solo was fun. Rostam looked down at his knees, shockingly white compared to anyone else he'd seen, local or foreign, poking out of Rip Curl surfer shorts. He didn't even feel self-conscious about travelling without a t-shirt. He meant to head to Keramas but took a wrong turn coming through Ubud and turned right for a long descent to Berawa. Roads were tarmacked, but running into packed mud and gravel, before turning to thin sand just before the beach.

A squat single-storey wooden shack sold water in plastic bottles and glass bottles of Bintang Beer, while a long-limbed boy of nine or ten chopped open coconuts with an outsized dull-bladed cleaver for ten thousand rupiah each. Rostam shuffled through a loose pack of local currency before finding the correct banknotes. Berawa beach had more yellow sand and fewer waves than Keramas. Fewer surfers on the sea and more tattooed Westerners playing volleyball, admiring one another's tans, or sleeping.

The beach bar wasn't doing much business. Nobody sat at the matted wooden bench facing out to sea under an awning of coconut leaves. Rostam settled in the corner with his coconut and his thoughts. The only drinkers in the bar were two older male Brits, heavily bearded and with paunches that marked them down by the high standards of the Bali beach population. Both had the complexion of men who woke up two drinks ahead of the next fella.

I bet they'd like to stay here and join the crypto elite. Rostam looked at them again. They looked like they'd accept an invitation anywhere if it came with an open bar-tab.

His cell buzzed in his pocket. The message was a series of meaningless punctuation and arrived with the icon of a famous female porn star, gazing out of the shower, with open lips and lustrous eyes suggesting the water pressure alone had her on the brink of orgasm.

Dread has the sense of humour of an eleven-year-old boy.

Rostam's fingers stabbed their way through the Tor protocol and found the number Dread wanted him to use. Dread's preoccupation with avoiding electronic traces meant he had a pouch full of unused sim cards which he thumbed through in the rare moments his fingers weren't occupied with a cigarette. Number found, Rostam gazed at his phone screen.

"I don't need to ask where you're at," he said.

"Wish you were here too."

"Take a look."

Rostam lifted his cell and spun it around, so Dread would get the panorama of volleyballing Australians on the beach in between the bar and the sea.

"Nice if you like that kinda thing, I guess. You haven't got time for it."

Rostam straighted on his stool.

"What's up?"

"I've scanned all major donations to senators who have spoken publicly on the SEC regulator. The money all comes from the same SuperPAC. Can't prove it's your man but any sane bookmaker would have stopped taking bets long ago."

Rostam looked around the beach, like Theo might be visible.

"Their candidate is Aalen," continued Dread. "Once he's in, they're done. You'll be even more of a loose end than you are already."

The heat of the sun disappeared as Rostam thought about what this would mean. He didn't want to think it could be true.

"You're dragging me into your world where everything is a double triple quadruple bluff?"

Dread turned the remains of his cigarette around between his fingers and jammed it deliberately into the ashtray beside his cell camera three times.

"This is your world now, boy. It's a game for sure, but one where you don't get another life once you're dead. This is one hit and you're out. And Spider's not the solo player he pretends to be. This is for the big boys. Maybe you should find out who he's working for."

Rostam looked up from his cell and towards the sea, just a few hundred yards ahead of him. Nobody had entered the bar. The two older Brits were still enjoying their argument with no solution.

"It stopped being a game when they killed Ahmad. That's all I know."

Dread stared out of the screen.

"I'm sorry for your loss, Rostam, truly I am. I'll keep looking out over here but I'm not optimistic. Your boy Spider is too traceable for his own good, but if I find another nugget about McNamara it'll be because he wants me to. That bastard keeps his good works visible, and hides the rest. The iceberg that took down the Titanic was nothing compared to him."

Dread disappeared from the screen and the sounds of the beach reasserted themselves. Normal life had never seemed so remote. There was no breeze. It was punitively hot even under the awning. Sips of coconut water felt more like part-payments of the vig of dehydration than repayments of capital.

Other people didn't have problems like this. A young couple walked onto the beach and turned right, passing close to Rostam. Attractive, young, tanned Westerners. The man was tall and skinny, with homemade tattoos like handwritten graffiti all over his torso and arms, and seventies-style denim jean shorts cut off just below the crotch. His girlfriend had short blonde hair and a Cleveland Cavaliers basketball top that hung down to her knees. Rostam was about to look away, not wanting to be some guy checking out the talent, when the blonde girl looked over at the bar.

"Hey, Rostam!"

It was Sara. She stood on tiptoe to whisper something to her friend and padded over across the hot sand.

"Fancy seeing you here," she giggled, placing each elbow on the other side of the bar and resting her chin on it. "Have a sip on your coconut? Fuckin' parched out here."

Rostam passed her the straw. Sara kept eye contact with him as she sucked in the juice.

"Didn't expect to see me again so soon, huh?"

She passed him back the straw.

"We're a fair way from Ubud."

"I like this beach. There's a few of us here."

"Is he your - ?"

Rostam tossed his head towards where Sara's pal had wandered. He realized he wasn't sure what word he was looking for.

"Pete? He's one of the gang. We keep meeting up in different parts of Asia."

"He didn't miss you last night?"

"Hey, Rostam, that's not cool. We're all free agents here, right?"

Rostam felt bad and clumsy.

"I didn't mean to...oh damn it, it's not my day for saying things right."

"Never mind. We've all been there. How's Spider this morning? Bright and breezy I bet."

"Pretty much. He's all business today. Thought I'd come out here to clear my head."

"How's that working out for you?"

Sara smiled at him and Rostam realized, with surprise, that he liked the girl.

"Can't complain. If you don't mind me asking, just how well do you know Spider? He and I used to be close but it's a different life out here."

Sara looked at him closely. She had bright eyes of light blue, filled with a challenging optimism.

"Takes months to adjust. I know Spider fine. We've hooked up half a dozen times. Maybe less. Not more. I don't know him very well and he doesn't know me at all. And you know what? There's no need for either of us to get to know much more. I bet we wouldn't even if we kept hanging out for another year. And that isn't going to happen. I'll be on my way somewhere else in a week or so. So, you don't need to worry about any of us, Rostam. Not me, not Spider, not even Pete, who gets himself well taken care of."

"I didn't know I looked like the caring type."

Sara laughed.

"Wanna know what I've learned from all these people who come out to Southeast Asia to find themselves? Most of them have nothing to discover. And the biggest joke is that the ones who do know themselves can't do anything about it, no way, no how. If you ask me,

Rostam, you look like a nurse running around a ward full of patients, hoping you can keep them all safe and well. Want my advice?"

"Sure."

"Stop worrying about other people. Your pal Spider thinks he's having a fine old time, and so are those of us who choose to help him have it."

Pete padded up the beach towards them.

"Hey Sara, have a go at those baby waves. Jem reckons he's gonna stick to the board this time."

"Now that I have got to see," called Sara over her shoulder. "Take care of yourself, Rostam. Leave everyone else to take care of themselves too."

Sara jumped up and gave Rostam a quick kiss on the lips before turning with a wave to follow Peter across the dunes.

Rostam turned around to climb down from his stool and saw the two bearded Brits staring at him in exaggerated envy.

"Alright for some, mate, innit," said the one closer to him, with a beery laugh, before turning back to his pal.

Maybe it is. But for who?

His decision was made. Time to tell Spider and get after Satoshi.

Chapter Forty-One

When he got back to the house it was immaculate, and empty. No note. No sign of where Spider might be. Rostam checked for messages. An SMS from an unknown number.

HI DARLING ROSTAM. TOKYO. FRIDAY 10AM. 17-GON.

Darling Rostam?

Rostam walked to the window and stared at the waterfall.

Darling? 17-gon. A heptadecagon. Seventeen-sided shape. SSS. Darling.

He stared at the mist rising as water pounded off the invisible rock-face until the exhilaration of solving a monster puzzle sent endorphins rushing through his system. *Darling* was an allusion to his line of code. His Hail Mary had been answered. Satoshi had replied. Or somebody had.

Rostam was impatient to be gone. He scoured the house to make sure Spider wasn't sleeping somewhere. The screen room was going full blast: Asian time CNBC flipping over to European hours on the big screen. Rostam recognised the London anchor as someone he'd seen stumbling out of the toilets in Nobu on 57th Street years earlier, rubbing the side of his nose. Matthew Aalen was to be the featured interview when the US woke up. **SEC CHAIR FOR CRYPTO AGE** was the strap line running across the screen.

His own room had been cleaned while he was out. Yesterday's underwear was now clean and folded on the otherwise bare chest of drawers by the door. His laptop stood open on the desk looking over the waterfall, plugged into the low voltage plug socket beneath. Rostam tapped in his six-digit code and found himself face to face with Spider's image, who had taken a profile photograph of himself very close to the camera, mouth open with tongue hanging out, tip of nose pressed backwards with his own index finger, eyes crazy and wide. Rostam fought down a feeling of violation. This was sophomore privacy stuff. Spider was telling him to take his own electronic security more seriously. Or was it a false clue? Mmybe Spider had been thoroughly through everything, and left the joke as a distraction.

There was a 22:00 flight to Tokyo via Changi that night. *What can I tell Spider?* Rostam looked at the crazy eyes leering out at him from his own computer screen. You can't trust this guy any more.

Flight booked, he felt unencumbered, lighter on his feet. He took a shower and packed. The sun was low in the sky when at last message arrived from Spider. This way he could say goodbye.

Chapter Forty-Two

The yoga class hadn't quite finished when Rostam pulled up in a haze of dust and gravel on Spider's Vespa. He walked up the slope. Spider was in his usual place in the middle row, but there was no Lucija. The Yogi facing Rostam was a skeletal, deeply tanned Western man with long chains of beads hanging from his neck towards his navel. Rostam didn't recognise any of the other students. Amazing how a collection of strangers each pursuing their own individuality all end up looking the same.

After the valedictory Namaste, Spider was the last to turn around. His bow had been the deepest, making a point of placing both hands palm down on the ground. Spider seemed unsurprised to find Rostam waiting for him halfway down the slope.

"Wanna head for the beach?" said Spider.

"No time. I've decided to fly to Japan tonight."

Spider sighed.

"Chasing your Satoshi dream? Thought we were gonna work together."

"I have no choice."

"You shoulda listened to me then and you should listen to me now. Look at this place."

Spider gestured widely around them, and pointed at a pair of young American females sharing a scooter ride together.

"Not bad, huh?"

Rostam didn't speak.

"Those two happen to be lesbians, but you take my point. Bali's practically self-governing already. Part of Indonesia in name only. We wanna do the same for the rest of the world. America's got the world pussy whipped with the US dollar, dude. We're shipping out arms to the poor oppressed, just like the West sending weapons to Ukraine. Help them fight for themselves."

Spider raised his hands to put one on each of Rostam's shoulders. Their eyes were locked. Rostam's attention was elsewhere and eventually Spider saw it.

"Ok dude, damn it to hell. It's all good. Let's get ourselves back home and stuck into what we've got left of that tequila. Put this behind us."

Rostam felt relief rising within him.

"I'm sorry, man. Wish I could be more help."

"Never complain. Never explain. You've forgotten that rule, huh?"

Spider reached out with fist clenched. Then Rostam got it and extended his own. Spider bumped their knuckles together, harder than strictly necessary, and fell back dramatically with fingers extended and a loud "Ka-Boom".

"Race you home."

Spider was straight onto an outsized red Ducati motorbike. It wasn't going to be much of a race, but when Rostam got back, there was no sign of his host.

Two hours passed before Spider arrived. Rostam's packed bag was by the front door. He was starving. The kitchen contained nothing but cold drinks, and he didn't feel like getting ahead of the drunkenness rabbit, guessing that Spider would set a fast pace on his return. Rostam called Millie and had a few minutes of smiling at the camera and trying to keep Celia's attention. She looked happy to see her Dad but confused as to why he couldn't reach out from the screen and hug her.

"Bumped into some pals," slurred Spider as he almost fell into Rostam's arms walking down the stairs into the screen room. "They wanted to come back here but I thought it better Mano E Mano, knowwhatimean?"

"Sure, Spider," said Rostam, smiling and embracing his old friend.

"Forgot chow. Bit drunk now. Wanna eat?"

"I'd eat one of the monkeys from the forest if I could catch one. I'll have to be gone in an hour."

"Monkeys, huh? Thas funny. Gonna brew us opium tea. Tried it?"

"Never. Don't fancy it before a flight."

"It's da bomb. You'll sleep like the dead, wake up feeling a million dollars."

Spider went into the bathroom in the corner of the room and relieved himself noisily. He hadn't shut the door.

When he emerged Spider threw his cell at Rostam.

"Go-Jek is the app. Choose us some food."

Spider disappeared downstairs before Rostam had a chance to complain. By the time he'd figured out the app his host was back. He carried a black ebony tray with the meticulous carefulness of the very drunk. Two ochre pots, flaring outwards like martini glasses, emitted tendrils of steam into the air.

Spider inhaled noisily.

"Opium tea. Love the smell. Love everything about it. Just what you need."

Spider stumbled as he spoke, and the ochre pot on the end of the tray closest to Rostam slipped back towards him. His face showed alarm.

"That's your one. Weak. 'Cos you're not used to it."

Spider pushed that pot back towards Rostam and handed it over. Rostam took it and sank down to sit cross-legged at the mat. CNBC had now switched over to the US opening bell. Spider sat down next to him.

"Same old faces talkin' the same old cheese," he said. He stood up and looked around the room for the remote. "Damn thing. Must be next door." Spider stumbled down the stair. The two ochre pots stood steaming on the rattan mat. Rostam looked at them and took a sniff. He expected a heavy, poppy-flavoured scent but found the smell strongly of liquorice instead. His own smelled even more strongly than Spider's. He hated aniseed. Rostam swapped the cups.

Spider returned with the tablet and switched the television over to Sports Centre. Three men bursting out of their suits were talking about the Dallas Cowboys back line with the same fervour and mannerisms their colleagues on CNBC had just been using on the Morning Bell. Spider raised his pot.

"Bottoms up old pal."

He drank his tea in one draught, and Rostam took a small sip.

"Don't leave me hanging."

"What effect am I gonna get from this?" asked Rostam, after draining his cup as demanded.

"Shudda asked before you drank it," said Spider, tapping his nose sententiously. He laughed as Rostam's face changed. "No man, you're gonna be fine. It'll just make you feel lightheaded and giggly, like weed back in the day. Yours is weak too. Not good to overdose a beginner. Be like me. Professional unwinder, man."

Spider lay back on the mat and straightened his legs before him. His eyes were closed.

"Lay back with me. Close your eyes and tell me what you can see. You've got time."

Rostam checked his watch. He did have an hour. He lay back and did as he was asked. He could feel nothing at all, other than the unwanted bitter aftertaste of aniseed.

"This has hit me hard, man," said Spider. "Shouldn't have had so much to drink."

He tried to prop himself up on his elbow to look at Rostam, but slipped back down.

Spider started talking again, slowly and with a slur, his Albertan drawl more noticeable.

"We need to talk." He pointed at Rostam. "I've solved your problems. Your man Theo - he isn't responsible for any of this."

Rostam looked across. Spider's eyes were closed but his mouth was still moving. He sounded drugged out of his mind.

"Say again," said Rostam, scarcely hoping for a reply.

"Theo McNamara, man. He's a big fan of yours. Going to send someone over to make sure you're ok. You don't wanna go against him. He kills people. You go, he might kill me."

Spider chuckled, but it spluttered out into a series of coughs. Rostam heard Spider's breathing slowing and stretching out and looked across. His friend had fallen asleep. Rostam felt as though there had been a loud explosion inside his head. Everything Spider had been doing now made sense. Rostam wanted to slap him awake.

When did you start working for McNamara? Why didn't you tell me?

The doorbell rang. Rostam's head was spinning. Easier to take delivery than leave it. A delivery man in lurid green sleeveless GoJek uniform stood outside with a large, steaming paper bag of noodles. He thanked the rider, shut the door behind him and picked up Spider's cell. An SMS with no contact details flashed up on the screen.

CARL IS ON HIS WAY.

Spider had been taking orders all along.

In the screen room Spider was now curled up in a foetal ball. His breathing was shallow and drool was spooling from the corner of his mouth onto the floor.

Rostam stood over his friend's unconscious body and thought hard. If Rostam had drunk the opium tea made for him, he might have been in that state when Carl Force arrived. A wave of fury flushed through him, mostly directed at Spider, but with plenty left over for himself. This would be the last time he put trust in someone who hadn't earned it.

He had to get away from the house.

Rostam stepped over his former friend's sleeping body, and skipped up the stairs to the front door, electronics and passport in a knapsack in one hand. He could be at the airport before Theo's killer arrived.

Spider deserved whatever happened when they found he had gone.

Chapter Forty-Three

Friday January 21

TOKYO

The glowing soft-focus red of the Sony alarm-radio read 09:25. Rostam felt he'd read every minute since first trying to sleep at 02:00. A flashing light on the phone acted as a metronome, winking between two and three times per minute. Rostam had had ample time to calculate the ratio.

The sterile, antiseptic smell of his expensive Tokyo hotel room had become the whole of reality. He pressed a button and drapes hummed as they rolled themselves into a tight drum, letting in thin daylight.

Half an hour left to prepare.

Rostam was confident he'd read the clue right, but this was his one shot. He'd logged onto the C++ site over and over, and found the seventeen-sided pink shape nestled into one of the many crenelations on the rotating virtual-Lego 3D shape. When he selected it, the same line of code he had used as the key to his own message ran across the screen on ticker tape. No point staring at it now.

He showered, dressed, drank a can of chilled black coffee from the minibar. Sat back down.

Still seven minutes to go.

He couldn't sit still and walked to the window, as struck by the difference in Japan to the rest of the world as on his previous visit, a decade before. The cyberpunk aesthetic which filled Tokyo had changed, an alternative vision of the present, when it had been the future. The rest of the world ended up somewhere else. Japan stuck to its own path.

His window faced south, the view lit by a weak January sun, showing a mass of pale grey roofs stretching to the horizon. Shiba Park behind the tower was the only green space, excluding potted plants deposited like neglected prayers on top of apartment blocks.

10:00.

Rostam clicked on the 17-gon. The puzzle screen went dark. Rostam was staring at his reflection in the black mirror of the screen.

Had he got it wrong?

A pinprick of light appeared in the middle of the screen, and rapidly expanded into an image of the Guido Fawkes Anarchist mask. Rostam instinctively leaned back as the face filled the screen: mocking thin-lipped smile, rosy cheeks, pencil mustachio. The mouth started to move.

"Welcome to Japan, Rostam. We're pleased you reached out. James Hanratty has tracked you to Tokyo. When he contacts you, tell him to accompany you to Geronimo's bar for a meeting at six. Make sure he leaves the hotel with you by foot at 5.45 precisely. Your journey will take you across Roppongi Crossing." A cartoon hand in white gloves raised an index finger to the mask's lips. "And remember to shush. No need to mention that we've spoken."

The face faded and the laptop's normal generic screensaver came back on.

Rostam pressed the red flashing button and James Hanratty's deep voice erupted from little, black-meshed speakers around the room.

"I heard you were in Tokyo and want to make you an offer. Oak Bar. 5pm."

Rostam took a deep breath. He'd assumed Theo would track him down. It was almost a relief to have it confirmed.

Rostam texted Millie a request for her to call. She rang immediately.

"Calling to cry about life in Paradise?"

"Turns out the problem with paradise wasn't a snake after all. It was Spider. I'm calling from the Grand Hyatt in Tokyo. I don't think this trip is going to be a wasted. Satoshi has made contact."

Rostam left a pause, waiting for Millie's congratulations.

She said nothing.

"Millie? What aren't you telling me?"

"I don't want to worry you but - "

"But what?"

Rostam was standing up, nerves stretched to their limit, stomach muscles clenched.

"A stranger tried to get to me while I was grocery shopping. He knew all about us."

Rostam swore.

"Don't worry," said Millie. "I'm fine. Celia and your Mom too."

Rostam wanted to scream, but kept his voice low.

"What happened?"

Millie didn't try to keep the satisfaction out of her voice.

"I left him in a puddle on the floor. He won't be crossing his legs in a hurry, that's for sure."

Rostam made a fist, like he was celebrating a winning basket.

"It has made me think," continued Millie. "How do you know you've picked the right side? These people are ruthless."

A crushing sense of guilt fell on Rostam as though from a leak in the ceiling.

"Rostam?" asked Millie.

"Yeah. I'm here. Just listening."

"My view has changed. You don't have to do this. Come back to the States. This stuff is officially not your problem."

Rostam realized his breath was shuddering. He shook his head to clear his mind.

"Theo and his gang are bad people, Millie. They killed Ahmad. They had you fired. Spider went running to them and they bought him. We have to stop them before they finish us."

Millie kissed her teeth.

"Always the same. You'd make a mule look open-minded. Whatever happened to stopping digging when you're in a hole?"

"This is our only shot, Millie."

"So you say."

Silence dragged out. Rostam thought about telling her about Hanratty, but Millie didn't sound in the mood.

"Is Celia ok?" he asked.

"You know our girl. There's no such thing as too much attention."

Rostam closed his eyes and pictured Millie. The silence started to stretch. Rostam wanted to get off the phone before he said something he might regret.

"I've gotta go," he said. "Whatever happens next, straight after I'm coming to New York. We'll get this fixed. Together."

"I know."

The line went dead.

Rostam looked out at Friday morning Tokyo and tried to picture Thursday evening in Manhattan. Millie was some woman. Beating down an assailant in the supermarket...who else did he know who could have done that? No wonder she'd turned more cautious. Could she be right?

Even as he asked the question, Rostam knew he had to press on. He was so close. The Guido Fawkes message must have come from Satoshi. The boldness and simplicity of the approach; casually overriding security; so anonymous Rostam felt he could identify him immediately. There was even a sense of kinship. Puzzle solving. Satoshi was obviously a computer scientist, but Rostam would bet his first love was mathematics.

Adrenaline had him primed for action, but it was only ten o'clock. Nothing to do until six. Rostam scrapped the gym plan. The only way to work this off was to go outside and into the city. He stuck on a playlist of DJ Hype to get jungle vibes going and hit the shower. The appearance of Satoshi had filled him with excitement. If the inventor of Bitcoin had the same ideals he'd jump at Rostam's plan. His heart fell. Who was to say Satoshi still felt the same way?

Rostam walked into the shower, stomach fizzing with a cocktail of anxiety and hope.

Chapter Forty-Four

Hanratty slipped onto the stool next to Rostam.

"Delighted we have this chance to straighten things out." The Englishman rapped his knuckles on the polished surface of the bar. "I approve of the weekend beginning at five o'clock."

"You've come a long way without an invitation," said Rostam.

"Don't be mean. We're not all free agents you know."

Hanratty looked around. The Oak Bar was a huge wooden oval that stretched the diameter of the room. Tables ranked into a gloomy distance before them, full of snackers: masculine bunches of businesspeople, outnumbered by young couples saluting the beginning of the weekend with wine and canapes.

Hanratty looked like an Englishman who had gone abroad by mistake: purple corduroy trousers, scuffed brown brogues, checked reddish shirt, collar sprouting out of a thick navy sweater, and chequered sports jacket, all squares of different shades and varying length lines, a Modigliani with no sense of proportion.

"You've been here before?" he asked.

Rostam nodded.

"Three month stay, early in my career. Roppongi was our playground."

Rostam raised his finger, and a handsome, tall, young Japanese barman wearing a skin-tight white shirt and severe expression walked over.

"Hibiki on the rocks for me," said Hanratty. "I've had this drink in mind since the moment I learned I was coming to Japan."

Rostam raised two fingers and the barman swept into action. Hanratty leaned in.

"Don't worry about Spider. Theo is concerned that communication has been unclear. He wants to make sure you understand everything is copacetic. The deal you and he agreed in Chicago stands."

Their glasses arrived: large frosted receptacles of golden liquid, containing a globule of ice, dimpled like a golf ball, but twice as large. Hanratty took his first sip and barked in appreciation. Rostam kept quiet.

"Have you thought any more about terms?" asked Hanratty.

Rostam's brain fizzed with the desire to get rid of him. *They must not be sure about exactly what I know, or I'd be dead already. Spider will have told them about Satoshi.*

"I've got no problem with the terms," said Rostam.

He looked around the Oak Bar. The deeply black-skinned maître-d was getting into his stride by the door. The man was powerfully built, round faced and full chested, as though he had too much blood inside his body, straining to get out. It gave his perpetual smile of welcome extra force, so drinkers just did what he told them. Two Western women were waiting for him to distribute them around the bar. One with long dark hair, the other a short blonde bob; both wore tight dresses and tighter smiles.

"Don't take us for fools," said Hanratty, his smile looking more forced. "We know why you're here."

Rostam took a sip. The ice globule looked unchanged, but enough of the surface had eroded into Hibiki that the whisky was cold and refreshing. It acted as a mental stimulant, rewiring the electrodes of Rostam's brain. The serious-faced barman spun round from serving two florid-faced American bond traders on the far side of the oval, and deposited a pair of ramekins before them. Large wasabi coated peanuts in one; the other held tiny salt-encrusted crabs, like miniaturized copies of the real thing. Hanratty immediately picked up a crab and dropped it into his mouth, crunching the shell and pincers with relish. The alternation from friendly relations to threats had Rostam off balance.

"Salty crab and Hibiki, the snifter of champions!"

To Rostam's surprise the barman responded to this salutation and went about pouring them a second pair of whiskies. Rostam took a long look at the bowl of miniature crabs and chose a wasabi peanut instead.

"How much do you know about what Theo has been up to?" asked Rostam.

"Enough to know he's unbeatable."

"The Emperor Hirohito approach," said Rostam standing up.

Hanratty laughed with gratifying intensity. A spray of iced whisky with specks of unswallowed crab dropped across the polished bar surface.

Rostam checked his watch.

"I have someone to meet. Since you're here, you can come with me."

The bar continued to attract customers. There were now no empty bar stools.

The Englishman seemed happy at the bar. Rostam felt a surge of anxiety. What was he going to do if Hanratty declined to follow?

"I'll put this on my bill," said Hanratty, rather grandly, as he stood up and pushed back his stool.

Rostam led Hanratty out the back of the bar. The back way led straight to an elevator. The moment they left the bar and automatic glass doors swished closed behind them, they entered a silent vacuum, the early evening optimistic chatter of the bar shut in behind them while they were still seventeen floors above street level. Rostam was grateful for the pair of whiskies. He expected Hanratty to fill the silence with small talk, but the Englishman seemed absorbed in his own thoughts as they rode down.

The streets were filling up. The sky was grey rather than dark, but strong streetlights, riotous neon shopfronts and car headlights kept Roppongi Dori bright. The only dark patches were underneath steel bridges, crisscrossing the sky above them, heavy with traffic. Worker bees walked singly west while Rostam and Hanratty moved with early evening thrill seekers, a blend of Japanese and gaijin, mostly in groups, and seldom blended together. The closer they got to Roppongi Crossing the more unsettled Rostam became. He fought the desire to look around for trackers. Hanratty asked no questions and Rostam was left to wonder what would happen when they arrived.

"Spider filled us in," said Hanratty, his voice dripping with avuncular concern. "Frankly, I'm worried for you. Theo is a big supporter of yours. Things haven't worked out as he hoped, but that doesn't mean you should give up."

A pair of young Japanese businessmen walked past them in tight fitting suits, one pushing at the other and making him stumble in a cackle of high-pitched laughter.

"Their lunch must have been fun," said Hanratty, indulgently. "What would you say to a call with Theo now, to put your mind at rest?"

"How do you do it, James?" asked Rostam, unable to keep quiet. "Have you got so used to the half-truths you can't tell the difference?"

"I'm not sure that's the right question," said Hanratty. "Ask yourself what Millie wants instead."

They walked through a glowering shadow beneath an elevated motorway and arrived at Roppongi Crossing. Above, gigantic digital advertising hoardings filled the air with laser beans, fired by DoCo-Mo-branded dancers. Cars queued in every direction. A yellow taxi pulled over just past the lights, a pair of young salarymen passengers scrambling out and joining the crowd waiting to cross.

A mass of early evening pedestrians surrounded Rostam and Hanratty. Rostam heard conversations in Japanese and French, while two tall black men overtook them shouting at one another in American English. A Japanese teenager dressed all in purple carried an 80s style boombox on his shoulder and turned up high BPM J-pop. The advertising billboard had the time: 17:58. Was he going to miss Satoshi's deadline?

Hanging above the middle of the road was an oblong light box with a pedestrian image overlaid across a red backdrop. It turned green, and walkers from all sides of the crossing set out. Hanratty placed his hand on Rostam's arm and leaned in to say something. Rostom stepped onto the road.

Someone bumped into Rostam's side. An unseen person forced him sideways.

"What the -" exclaimed Hanratty. The pair of salarymen were either side of Hanratty. The taxi from earlier was still idling, both back doors open. Hanratty was struggling against the two men, but they efficiently pushed him into the back, behind the driver's seat. The taller of the two gestured to Rostam.

"Get in."

Rostam had no time to think. He climbed into the back seat.

The taxi pulled away.

"What the hell are is happening?" said Hanratty, his friendly demeanour vanished like youth. "Do you think you're a tough guy?"

Rostam shrugged, hoping it looked like he knew what was going on.

"You wanted to come along for the ride."

"You're a fool," said Hanratty. "One of those people who can't get out of his own way."

His tone was less casual than his words.

The taxi indicated right and shot into a narrow side street. Rostam looked for identifying characteristics. Just a series of white lit little restaurants. It could be any side street in central Tokyo. Hanratty was trying to look at his cell, but as the taxi swung left into the next turning, he dropped it, and bent down to start searching the floor.

The car turned again and Hanratty swore as his head hit the door handle.

They came to an abrupt halt.

"What is the meaning of this?" demanded Hanratty, looking at Rostam.

Rostam was looking at the driver.

Hanratty turned to see what he was looking at. The driver had turned in his seat. He held a pistol in his hand.

Hanratty opened his mouth. He didn't have time to scream before the driver squeezed his finger. The pistol made a small, apologetic cough. Rostam felt his face splatter with warm liquid.

The far door opened and Hanratty slumped out of it, like a sack of sodden wool. His purple corduroys and brown brogues were the last of him to leave as his corpse was dragged outside. One of the salarymen leaned in and reached out a hand to Rostam. There was something white in it.

"Wet wipes, Mr James."

Rostam didn't move.

"For your face," the young man explained. "You have an appointment to keep."

The door swung shut and the taxi pulled away. Rostam looked at the driver's white gloves and dabbed at his own face. His fingers came away sticky. Rostam took out one wipe from the packet he'd been given and started dabbing away. He needed a second, then took a pinch of several. When the car stopped, seemingly only a moment later, he had the remains of the pack scrunched between his two hands and was scrubbing his face furiously.

His door opened and the noise of Friday night pedestrian traffic flooded the car.

The driver turned around. He was a nondescript taxi driver, not far off sixty years old, with a tired, disinterested expression. There was no sign of the pistol.

"Midtown Tower. Apartment 420. Forty second floor."

Rostam stepped out of the car, feeling he was moving at glacial speed. His legs felt empty, his trousers rubbing against the skin. The anger he had felt for Hanratty had transformed into something else.

The taxi melted into traffic.

Chapter Forty-Five

Rostam was full of questions but there was nobody to ask. His blood pumped with such adrenaline, walking through the lobby felt like quicksilver passing through a still life. He pressed *42* onto a digital keypad and the elevator doors arrived. Rostam looked around to see if anyone was following them. Nobody followed him into the lift.

The doors opened into a small lobby with just one door. As Rostam approached, it opened inwards without a click or whirr.

The main reception room of the apartment was enormous, with minimal furniture to fill the space. Beyond the far wall, all glass, was a bewildering expanse of electric lights outside festooned across buildings, highways, bridges and cables, extending to the horizon.

There was nobody to be seen.

Rostam counted three separate airplanes flying in different directions and altitudes, flashing lights on their undercarriages like temporary escapees from the mass of neon below them. A single, colossal black television screen placed flush into the wall to their left, long white sofa across the room in parallel. Four electric guitars huddled, each on its own stand, next to a second sofa facing the window. Behind him came a man's voice.

"Hello, Rostam."

The speaker was a small, smiling, floppy-haired Japanese man, in a shiny, silvery-grey suit.

"My name is Jiro."

Jiro made a small bow, and smiled, showing irregular white teeth.

"Not what you expected?"

Rostam put his hands to his forehead and covered his eyes for a moment before replying.

"I didn't know what to expect."

Jiro pushed his flimsy, steel glasses back up his nose.

"You want to meet Satoshi, I'm the person who can set it up," he said.

Jiro sighed and ran the fingers of both hands through his hair, so that it lost its shape and hung loose. It made him look younger. Vulnerable. He sat down at the other end of the sofa facing the window and waited for Rostam to join him.

"If you're worried about Hanratty, don't be," said the man. "It's down to us to protect Satoshi from the bad and the dangerous. The Englishman and his friends are both."

Rostam shook his head slightly.

"I've been to his family home."

"Is that what he told you?" said Jiro. "He rented it for the weekend you were in the UK."

Rostam could feel his pulse coursing through his veins. Was he still covered in blood?

"You can shower here," said Jiro. "I apologise for the bloodshed. Hanratty left us no choice."

"Does Satoshi know you murder to protect him?" asked Rostam.

"Absolutely not," said Jiro. "You can tell him if you like. Decide when you meet." He smiled again. "I have neglected to congratulate you on solving our puzzle. You're not quite the first outsider to do it, but you're the one we like the best."

"Who is this *we* you refer to?" asked Rostam. "Do you work for Satoshi? Is Satoshi a collective?"

Jiro sighed.

"Satoshi is very much one man. He is removed from the world you and I live in. We help keep him safe."

He took off his glasses and rubbed the lenses with the corner of his shirt. Without looking up, Jiro asked, "Do you mean Satoshi any harm?"

Rostam's anger was reignited like a flash fire.

"I haven't caused anyone harm, except my own family. I came to help Satoshi but now I see the kind of company he keeps, I'm changing my mind."

Jiro leaned forward.

"I get it. You're confused."

Rostam walked towards the door.

"I've had it. I'm on the first plane back to the States."

He had his hand on the exit button when Jiro spoke up.

"If you do that, you'll miss your only chance with Satoshi Nakamoto."

Jiro sat back and crossed his legs. The name floated in the air before expanding like a smoke ring to fill the room.

"You can't go home before you do what you came for."

The sense of satisfaction that comes from solving part of a puzzle diluted the bile filtering through Rostam's blood.

"Why is Satoshi making an exception for me?" he asked.

"We protect Satoshi, but we don't speak for him. The meeting is set for tomorrow. The question is whether you still want to take it."

Rostam stood up and stretched, hands above his head. His back popped somewhere in between his shoulder blades. Suddenly he felt very tired. He walked up to the window and watched his transparent reflection grow. By the time he could touch the glass his internal organs were composed of night-time Tokyo lights.

He wanted to say no, walk out, and get on the first plane to New York. That was where Celia was. But he had to take the opportunity to pitch his plan to Satoshi. He couldn't keep Celia safe if Theo and Waspell held all the cards. He still didn't know who all the enemies were. He took one deep breath, then another, and with it, through fear and anger, came the siren of anticipation:

This is still my chance to meet Satoshi.

His mind was made up.

"Okay. When and where?"

Jiro exhaled and stood up.

"Good. Not just because it's my job to get you there, but because it's the right thing to do for you. The meeting is tomorrow. Can't tell you exactly where. To say Satoshi is keen on anonymity is the understatement of the century."

Rostam snorted.

"You want me to attend a meeting with someone I don't know, at an undisclosed place and time?"

"Satoshi sets the rules. You wanna meet him, you have to play by them."

Rostam shrugged.

'I've got a sleeping pill for you," continued Jiro. "No biggie. Like Valium, but more of a sure thing. No hang-over. You'll be out between eight and twelve hours. When you wake up, you'll be in the right place."

Rostam was still looking through himself at the world outside.

"It's your choice to take the pill or not. Satoshi wants you to come of your own free will, or not at all. Secrecy is his only condition."

Rostam tilted his head back and spoke to the enamel white ceiling.

"I've never taken a sleeping pill. Always had a strict rule about mind-altering drugs. Recreational only. The medicine doctors dish out to put life in soft-focus is what does real damage."

"First time for anything. I felt the same first time round, and I got one tip. Go to the bathroom first."

Jiro paused, and, as he realized the implications of what he had said, Rostam began to laugh. The horror of Hanratty's assassination found release. In moments the two of them were giggling together.

"I need to change," said Rostam, once the laughing fit settled down.

"Of course. The bathroom is through there. There's a change of clothes for you too."

Now the decision was made, Rostam moved fast. He walked into the oddly domestic bathroom, with Jiro's toothbrush and shaving paraphernalia scattered about. He closed his eyes under the shower head, not wanting to see if the water sluicing off him was dyed by Hanratty's blood. He relieved himself and washed his hands, then splashed tepid Tokyo water on his face. His reflection spoke to him, or at least he could see his own lips moving in the mirror.

Are you really going to do this?

Rostam thought of his frozen crypto wallet. Millie and Celia stuck at his Mom's apartment. The bullying expression on Theo's face when he knew he had Rostam trapped. Tina Waspell, and the moral certainty which went with waterboarding. Zadi. Ahmad, dead in London. Spider passed out on his own opium tea. The furious look on Hanratty's face when he dropped his mask of politeness.

Who am I trying to kid? Of course, I'm in.

He washed his hands and walked back into the fantasy room.

"Dose me up."

Jiro got up without a word, padded out of the room and came back with a small glass of water and a pink capsule.

"Sit down to take it," advised Jiro.

Rostam sat down on the sofa, placed the pill on his tongue, and swallowed.

Chapter Forty-Six

Saturday January 22

White.

White ceiling. White walls. White sheets.

What time is it?

Rostam raised his left arm. No watch on his wrist.

No clock on the wall. There was nothing in the room beyond the futon mattress beneath him.

Three walls entirely blank. The fourth, a closed sliding door. Four panels, divided into four squares on each horizontal and eight vertical, constructed of unvarnished pine. Before having time to think further, Rostam was absorbed in the pattern.

Thirty-two squares per door, one hundred twenty-eight in total. 128. Refactorable. Can't be expressed as the sum of any number of distinct squares.

The door slid open, and his train of thought decoupled. An elderly Japanese woman took one step into the room and bowed deeply. Rostam found himself wondering at her flexibility and shook his head to clear away the dregs of tranquiliser.

"Sorry to disturb, Mr James-san. Master in the drawing room when you ready. You need anything?"

"You speak good English," said Rostam, gathering his thoughts. "Better than my Japanese."

The woman continued to regard him, without response. Rostam became conscious he was wearing only boxers.

"Are my clothes...?"

"Clothes next room. Bathroom too."

Rostam nodded thanks and the woman retreated behind the sliding doors. Her profile shrank backwards, giving Rostam the sense that he was in one of an infinite number of paper rooms. He stood up and shook his head gently to test for any anaesthetic hangover.

No residue. Jiro told the truth, about that at least.

The air smelled clean, natural, warm. Different to the atmosphere in his hotel room. And it was silent. Why? Rostam stood still to figure it out.

I'm not in the city.

Every building and street in Tokyo had an undercurrent of air conditioning, electric hum, neon fizz, street noise, ambient white noise. Air freshener inside and car fumes outside. Not here.

He slid the door, noiseless in its wooden groove, and found a neatly folded pile of loungewear on the floor. Fresh boxers, baggy white cotton jogging pants, white fitted cotton t-shirt and thin cream, logo-less sweater. No socks or shoes. No sign of the clothes he had been wearing in Jiro's Midtown apartment.

Rostam thought he had burnt out the synapses that registered surprise. Then he slid open the door to the bathroom. An enormous wooden tub stood on circular casters. Multiple layers of slats combined around the rim like a drystone wall.

Tall wooden barrels stood on a table on either side of the bath, each with a spout protruding from the bottom eighth over the tub. Hanging low above the tub were a pair of unpainted grips, suspended on a thick string. By the side, a cream ceramic jug, filled with clear, gloopy liquid. Rostam knelt down and sniffed. No fragrance. He dipped his finger: liquid soap. He shed the clothes he had only just put on and tried to fold them as neatly as they had been left.

He reached across the bath and pulled the first grip. After a nervy ten seconds steaming water came down the spout and began to fill the bath. He released the grip and shortly thereafter the flow stopped. Feeling he had passed a minor test, Rostam filled his bath and got in.

I'm completely at Satoshi's mercy here. If it is him. How am I going to talk him into crashing his creation?

Rostam submerged his head beneath the water.

I can't force him to do anything.

He came up, shook his head, and as moisture left his open eyes his plan of action became clear.

The elderly hostess was waiting when he walked out of the dressing room. Rostam followed, surprised at her speed. They turned left into another corridor. No artwork, no functional decoration, until they approached a more substantial door of dark wood. The woman gestured to a pair of ankle-high woollen knitted boots with stiff sewn-on leather soles, and a knee length cream cashmere outer garment, half overcoat, half dressing gown. Nothing had a logo name, or label of any kind.

"What about you?" asked Rostam.

The old lady wore a stiffly starched white kimono and cloth sandals. She shook her head slightly in response. Rostam put on the boots and coat, expecting them to be too small. They fit perfectly.

Outside the house was a wide wood-chip path flanked by three-meter-high trees, with thick brown trunks and spindly branches, bare of leaves. A cherry-tree avenue. It reminded Rostam of the trees by Lake Michigan. Cold enough for him to be grateful for the coat, but the memory of deep Chicago freeze was enough to make Japan in January seem warm.

The old lady set off at an even faster pace, and he had to stride to catch up. At the far end of the avenue stood a single-story wooden building with decking around the ground floor separating it from a lawn with ankle length grass. The only decoration was a small Shinto shrine by the front door. The woman opened the door, stood to one side, and bowed. Rostam wanted to urge her to go in first, then decided the greater courtesy was to do as he was bid. Rostam walked into the building and the door closed behind him.

Two men stood in the middle of the room. One Japanese, forty-ish, smaller than average, thick horn-rimmed glasses, black haircut in such a severe crew cut his scalp was visible. The other a tall, elderly, cadaverous, white-skinned man. Both wore clothes identical to Rostam. Rostam looked from one to the other, not sure who to address. The Japanese man bowed slightly, and Rostam instinctively responded with a bow of his own. The older man stepped forward and bowed.

"Satoshi-san doesn't like to speak English - he fears misunderstandings, so keeps me around to translate. My name is David. How are you bearing up, Rostam?"

Chapter Forty-Seven

David's voice was English. If James Hanratty sounded like the butler in Downton Abbey, this man had the received pronunciation of the Earl himself. His eyes were twinkling blue and, while his smile was restrained, laughter lines creased his face, as though Jackson Pollock had thrown them on. Satoshi's face was immobile, as though he were aggrieved to be wasting time.

"Please tell Satoshi-san I'm grateful to see him," said Rostam.

David spoke rapid Japanese. Satoshi grunted in reply.

"I always figured he was American," said Rostam.

The elderly Englishman smiled and shook his head.

"Satoshi-san is a cryptographer. Doesn't like to set easy puzzles."

A light went on inside Rostam's brain.

"Did you translate the White Paper for him?"

"It was Satoshi's work, but yes, I translated it."

The old man chuckled.

"So that's where the Anglicisms came from? The references to the British government."

"I suppose so. With hindsight we should have made the language more anonymous. Are you hungry?"

Rostam realized that underneath his sense of shock, he was ravenous.

"I don't even know what time it is."

The laughter lines in David's face fell away.

"I apologize. It's Saturday lunchtime. You were unconscious twelve hours. At your age the anaesthetic shouldn't have unpleasant side effects, but you must be starving." He spoke Japanese to Satoshi, who nodded. "Come this way."

Satoshi led the way through an open door into a dining room. A wooden table with three chairs stood in the middle of the room, with chopsticks, a thick black clay spoon and glass of water. The table was set out for two. A tiny brass bell stood in the middle.

"Breakfast. I thought since you would be eating your first meal at this hour, I would do the same," said David. "Satoshi-san doesn't like to eat in company."

David pulled out a chair for Satoshi, who sat next to him. Rostam sat down opposite.

David picked up the brass bell and rang it gently. Moments later the old lady walked in with a tray which looked too heavy for her and placed it in front of Rostam.

"Arigato gazaimas, Yuriko-san," said David.

"Thanks," added Rostam. "And also for looking after me this morning."

Yuriko showed no acknowledgement of either of them, and returned with an identical tray for David. She poured green tea for Satoshi.

Silence stretched out once she left the room. Satoshi stared at Rostam, squinted through the glasses, but said nothing. Rostam was so full of questions he didn't know where to start, so looked down at his tray.

"You must have made a positive impression on Yuriko. She's pushed the boat out this morning," said David. "Steamed rice, miso soup, grilled mackerel – a personal quirk – can't stand salmon for breakfast – tsukemono pickles, nori dried seaweed, kobachi vegetables. And this -," David pointed to the largest bowl of steaming porridge – "congee, with a sprinkling of nutmeg."

It took Rostam a moment to realize the translator was nervous.

"Congee is really Chinese, no?" he asked.

"Quite right," nodded David, in pedagogical style. "The Japanese don't like to acknowledge it. Something my own country and Japan have in common. Island nations that believe in their own exceptionalism."

David translated for his colleague. Satoshi raised his eyebrows and rubbed his scalp vigorously.

Rostam snapped apart his chopsticks, mixed pickled vegetables into steamed rice, and took a mouthful, grateful it didn't spill.

David sipped at his congee. Satoshi spat out a stream of rapid Japanese, volume halfway between speaking and shouting, looking straight into Rostam's eyes. It was disconcerting to maintain eye contact with Satoshi while waiting for David to translate.

"Tell us about yourself. He wants to know who you really are."

Rostam took a mouthful of grilled mackerel and sipped miso to wash it down.

"There can't be much he doesn't know."

"Reading someone's profile and meeting them in the flesh, is as different as staring at the moon through a telescope and walking on it. Take us on a walk on the unique planet that is Rostam James. Where did you grow up?"

"Manhattan. West Side, not far north of the Village. Mom's a high school math teacher. Rent controlled apartment, before you ask how a high school teacher can afford that address."

Satoshi asked no questions as Rostam talked but nodded as David translated after long intervals. Rostam was impressed at how much the translator could recall and then interpret. David ate very slowly and listened with attention. Rostam grew into his task. He had gone through schooldays, his missing father, university, meeting Ahmad in London. At that point he paused, and Satoshi made a remark in Japanese.

"We heard about poor Ahmad. Let's come back to him."

This was the only comment David made until Rostam got as far as leaving Loeb to set up his podcasting business. Rostam had, to his surprise, eaten everything on his tray. David had tried something of everything but hadn't eaten much.

"An old man's appetite," he said. "Does me good to see someone young and healthy enjoy their food."

"Does Satoshi-san want to know why I'm here?"

David interpreted and Satoshi replied in a loud, aggressive staccato. David sat up straighter. No trace of a smile remained on his face.

"Another fortune hunter."

"He doesn't really believe that. He'd never have met me."

David translated and Satoshi sneered a reply, once again rubbing his scalp vigorously.

"No, he wouldn't. Convince him you haven't wasted his time."

Rostam made sure he addressed his reply directly to Satoshi, maintaining eye contact while he took two deep breaths through his nose. For all the politeness of his reception, he felt that the older man might walk out at any moment.

"Satoshi-san, when you wrote your White Paper, you worried about the four horsemen of the infocalypse, right? Drug dealers, terrorists, money-launderers, paedophiles."

David translated. Satoshi said nothing.

"They polluted the dark web alright," continued Rostam, "but they're not what's ruined bitcoin. Government and NGO actors have corrupted the whole system."

Now he had said it, the silence seemed to turn up in volume. All Rostam could hear was the rushing of blood in his ears. Was Satoshi going to throw him out? The old man wasn't saying anything.

"Your silence tells me you know I'm right."

David translated, and Satoshi snapped back in rapid Japanese.

"Don't be impertinent," snapped David. "Silence tells you Satoshi-san is thinking. That's all."

Rostam felt a stab of anxiety but kept quiet.

Satoshi spoke Japanese, while looking directly at Rostam.

"What do you want, Rostam?" translated David.

Rostam couldn't see the point in hiding.

"Theodore McNamara threatened my daughter. Persecuted her Mom. They killed my best friend. They're organizing a ramp in prices to further their own political games. I know I can help you. And I think you can help me."

He snapped his mouth closed, aware his voice had risen in volume. Satoshi took his time to respond, eyebrows contracted. More head rubbing.

"What do you want from Satoshi-san?"

Rostam took a deep breath.

"He has to come public. Show the world who he is, and what he wanted to achieve. We need to destroy Bitcoin publicly and build something better."

David translated this into Japanese. Satoshi glared at Rostam but said nothing. It took all of Rostam's self-possession to keep his mouth closed. Was the old man going to throw him out? Finally, Satoshi grunted a reply, and David translated.

"You're demanding a lot. Let us walk while you bring us up to speed on more recent events."

Rostam stood up.

"We'll show you the grounds," continued David. "Leave your tray. We don't want to offend Yuriko."

Chapter Forty-Eight

A coat rack stood by the back door, with three capacious, cream hooded parkas hanging on pegs.

"You'll excuse me. I feel the cold more than you two younger men. It's five degrees lower out here than in the city," said David with a grimace of apology, as he shrugged on one of the coats.

David opened the door and waited for Satoshi and Rostam to walk out before him. The house stood on a hilltop. Down the slope a flock of screeching black jays took off from the branches of a painted maple tree. The slope fell rapidly away past a copse of spruce trees, broken up with a handful of aristocratic oak and birch interlopers. The far side of the valley was green with massed conifers, rising three hilltops, the highest below their sightline.

"Satoshi-san isn't keen on neighbours," said Rostam, gesturing around.

David translated, and, to Rostam's surprise, Satoshi laughed, and spoke rapidly.

"Satoshi-san says it's embarrassing to admit, but I will," said David. "An industrialist owned a summer house on top of that mountain on the right-hand side when he first arrived. After his death the family seldom visited. Satoshi-san made them an offer, bought it, and had the place dismantled."

Rostam peered at the hilltop.

"You'd never guess there had been a house there."

"Thank you."

Silence descended along with a thin mist of cold rain. David took several long inhalations through his nose before raising his hood.

"We get the most amazing wildlife. Wild boars are a risk in the spring. Brown bears too. The two species are as bad tempered as each other - I'd advise you to avoid both."

Rostam saw David was looking at him for a reaction and decided to make him try harder.

"Once Yuriko found a family of macaques frolicking in the dining room. I was tempted to tell her to make them feel at home, but better sense prevailed."

Rostam rewarded him with a chuckle.

"Monkeys and brown bears aren't what I think of first about Japan."

"Of course not. Foreigners, even the educated ones, think Japan is all anime and manga. Neon and concrete. Overcrowded subways and plastic packaging. Women dressing like schoolgirls and men with digital girlfriends."

David spoke to Satoshi who coughed out a rasping, uncomfortable laugh.

"Let's go this way," said David. "There's something Satoshi-san would like to show you."

A broad, winding wood-chip pathway led down the slope past the copse. Scents of wet grass and moist leaves filled their nostrils. Rostam started to worry his host had lost his train of thought, when Satoshi suddenly rattled out a string of Japanese. David halted and spoke.

"The question Satoshi-san is pondering is: why should he help you?"

The old man kicked softly at the exposed root of an oak tree, pale against the rich, black soil. He stared at the root, as though embarrassed to make such a direct challenge. Satoshi himself glared directly at Rostam.

"Satoshi-san, nobody has heard from you since 2010," said Rostam. "You created a world changing concept. You made the cypherpunk dream a reality. I get that you don't want to be a celebrity, but you've gone too far. Half the conspirasphere compares Satoshi to Christ, or Prometheus. A Chosen One who sacrificed himself for our sins. We've only just met, but I don't think you want that."

David translated. Satoshi snorted and resumed walking.

"Your White Paper is the closest thing I've ever had to a Bible," said Rostam, leaning in front of the older men in his excitement. "Privacy in tech is necessary for freedom against government oppression and tyranny. I believe it. You led the way to use computer science and math to solve economic and political problems." Rostam realized his voice had risen, and his pace was picking up. He took a breath while David translated. "It was a great plan. Visionary. But it isn't working. What's happening to me will happen to millions more. A tool for freedom being turned into a weapon of oppression. Let's fix it together."

He paused. No point trying to force the issue. He found himself holding his breath waiting for Satoshi's response. The Japanese man spoke in the longest passage yet.

"The world is full of false narratives," translated David once Satoshi had stopped speaking. "What we particularly like about your broadcasts is how you dismantle them. You are someone who is not only unwilling to be talked into believing nonsense but helps educate the credulous." David looked across at Rostam and touched his arm.

Drizzle kept falling and their parka hoods were pulled forward. There was something monastic about the recessed oval of the old man's face. "I also admire that characteristic of yours. Few can be bothered to shine a light into the cesspool of conspiracy. It only aggravates the maggots."

"Maggots don't like the spotlight."

"And yet here you find yourself the victim of a conspiracy."

David laughed softly.

"I suppose that's right. I'd find it funny, if the joke wasn't at my expense."

David translated, and Satoshi asked another question.

"Satoshi-san wonders how much you are motivated by hatred of Theo McNamara. He doesn't intend to be your or anyone else's means of retribution. How does he know you mean what you say?"

"Beats me," said Rostam. "Has he got a better option?"

"There's always another choice." David stopped so abruptly that Rostam had to turn around to look back up at him. "Do you worry you're just a part of the puzzle?"

"Only masochists think of themselves as pawns."

David translated, and Satoshi-san grew agitated. He took off his horn-rimmed spectacles and rubbed them with the corner of his parka while David repeated his comments in English.

"We are all just pawns, Rostam. Some have more agency than others, but nobody is their own master." David coughed. "Think of the primes. Each prime is part of a greater pattern. None of us knows how it works. Just think of a prime, shining brightly in the heavens, proud of its uniqueness. Then think of us, looking at it. We know each prime follows simple rules, and we know their relation to one another, but the most powerful supercomputer can't predict the next in the sequence. We are no more free than those primes. Ah, we're almost t here."

Rostam jerked his head around. The parka hood restricted his peripheral vision. All he could see were massed conifers.

"What am I looking for?"

Satoshi shouted and pointed to a spot on the right.

"Don't worry, I'll find it," said David. "Here we are."

David stepped off the path and between two trees. Satoshi stood next to Rostam. On the floor lay a discarded piece of rope.

"Can you tug on that? Easier for you to crouch down to the ground than me. The privileges of age mostly come with hefty price tags, like popping knees."

Rostam knelt down and felt the texture of the coarse, hairy long grass. The rope was sodden with rain but looked new and barely gave when he squeezed it in his hand. He pulled on it and felt resistance.

"Perhaps a little harder."

Rostam put both hands on the rope and pulled hard. The resistance broke and he staggered backwards, almost bumping into his host.

A circle opened in the grass, one meter in diameter. Rostam peered in and saw that a quartet of metal plates, artificial grass attached to the surface, hanging from hinges. A shallow set of steps descended before them with soft artificial light from bulbs set into the stone.

"I'll lead the way."

David stepped in, and Satoshi followed him. Rostam pushed the hood back over his hair, getting his hand wet in the process, and looked around. There was nothing to see but rain and more trees. He had seen no person other than Satoshi, David, and Yuriko since waking in the white room, and he didn't know where he was. *So what?* He followed the old men down the stairs.

Chapter Forty-Nine

The steps were sandstone, dry and firm. Their woollen boots made no sound, but the echoes of heavy breathing became louder the lower they went. After a dozen steps Rostam turned a corner and found Satoshi and David waiting for him.

"Ready?" David asked.

Before Rostam could respond the older man clapped his hands, twice. Bright overhead lights came on without a flicker and Rostam saw they stood in a circular, stone-walled room at least one hundred meters across. The walls were blank.

Rostam looked up. He could no longer hear the rain, nor see daylight through the open trapdoor above.

David continued to breathe heavily, as though the descent from his house had used up more energy than he expected, but he wore a beatific smile. Satoshi was lying on his back on the ground, once again rubbing his scalp.

"I hope you won't mind helping me lie down," said David.

"Are you ok?" asked Rostam.

"Oh, I'm fine. Better than fine. I'm good. To get full value from Satoshi's shrine we'll need to lie on the floor in the middle."

David walked into the middle of the chamber, marked on the floor with a lightly traced yellow disc. When he reached the disc, he turned around and held out both hands. Rostam took them in his own. The skin on David's hands was translucent with age, the blue veins standing out from the inside of his wrists too brightly coloured for the rest of him. Rostam's own hands looked offensively healthy in comparison. With a sigh, David let Rostam take his weight and slid down onto his back. Rostam braced himself for the tension before realizing David weighed very little.

"Thank you, my friend. Come on - you next."

Rostam knelt down beside David, and then spun around so that they were lying next to one another, with Satoshi on the far side.

"Like a set of knights in an old European mausoleum," chuckled David. "Isn't it beautiful?"

Rostam saw that David's eyes were fixed on the ceiling. He looked up himself. It was covered in numbers. Arabic notation, painted in a faux-kanji calligraphy. All integers but in no sort of discernible order. Satoshi spoke and David translated.

"As a child I counted obsessively. Bottle tops. Cards. Flies in the larder. Now I like to lie here when it is time to get away from the world and think things through. Nothing works better than numbers. Perhaps you find the same?"

"Uh-huh."

"Even when we don't understand the pattern, we can trust that it is there. None of the messiness of human affairs."

"Satoshi-san had this place built?"

"He did. I helped a little. A mathematical dojo. What do you think?"

"I'm not sure what to think."

"Take in one or two of the numbers above us and let it work on you. Everything will become clear."

Rostam allowed himself to sink into concentration. The stone of the floor felt warm, almost malleable. Questions swarmed into mental focus and then away again, like goldfish taking turns at the front of the bowl. Physical sensations isolated themselves: a tick in his left calf muscle; an itching scalp; a kind of warmth where his tailbone connected with the ground. Numbers. Numbers.

1,171

3

131,071

443

7

1

1,012,573

David's breath was too loud. Or was it his own? A sudden sensation of drowsiness. It would be terrible to fall asleep. Was it expected guests would doze? Focus. Pick one number. Just one number. 15,559. Is that a prime?

Yes!

Rostam's Mom and he had made a game of this. At university Ahmad and the other number theorists liked to throw four and occasionally five-digit primes at one another. For number theorists it was the equivalent of on-the-spot times table tests for primary school kids. Rostam didn't have to start doing calculations. What's next? 3559? Prime. Next. 887. Prime. 15,639. *15,639?*

"They're not all primes," said Rostam.

"Congratulations," said David with warmth. "I was timing you. You were quick."

Rostam felt slighted to have been examined, but also pleased he had passed.

"So, they're mostly prime, but not entirely. What gives?"

"What do you think, Rostam?"

Now he was engaged in the task Rostam kept looking for non-primes. 2,143. 40,487. 181. 10,027!

"Like religious art, where they include a deliberate flaw? Perfection is only for God."

"Very good. In Japanese art it's called *wabi sabi.*"

Rostam looked across at his host. The old man was still staring at the ceiling. He spoke gently in Japanese, and Satoshi-san rose to his feet and climbed back up the stairs.

Rostam realized he had passed the test.

"You are Satoshi Nakamoto, aren't you, David?" he said.

It made sense. A man as obsessed with privacy as Satoshi would prefer to have an impersonator.

David continued speaking as though he hadn't been asked a question.

"I gave a lot of thought to this design," said the Englishman. "For a long time, I had a Fibonacci spiral of uncommon beauty. But I realized one might as well stare at a leaf, or a snowflake, or a fingerprint. Any one of the countless examples of mathematical beauty in the natural world. Perfection is not the point. The world's monetary system isn't a perfect, natural system of order that exists outside of mankind. It's a reflexive, flawed system. What I have done is to improve it, not perfect it."

"So that's why you have this ceiling. Beautiful but flawed."

"On a good day I take solace from this fact. We cannot understand the pattern of the primes, but we can spot the mistakes. With patience and intelligence, we can spot the ringers. Ah."

This last syllable was elongated as David exhaled. It ricocheted around the circular hall.

"I flatter myself that this is like the whispering gallery in St Paul's Cathedral. I doubt you know it."

Rostam said nothing.

"An architectural curiosity. And a flawed comparison, as the geometry of this chamber is quite different. The great curse of the artistic education, or what you call the liberal arts, is the understanding of the world through metaphor. Understanding things for what they resemble, rather than what they are in themselves. I think that is what draws you to the battle against conspiracy. Am I correct?"

"I guess. I call it false narrativization." Rostam laughed, and the sound echoed back around them "Also it brings in listeners."

"Touché. Rostam - I've brought you here to ask a favour. But first, you'll have to help me up. My mural has done its work."

Rostam scrambled to his feet and extended his hands down to the old man. Again, he was amazed at the meagreness of the old man's sparrow-light body.

"Who was the Japanese man?"

"A valued colleague. I don't enjoy meeting new people, and he helps me decide whether conversations are worth extending. I hope you'll forgive the subterfuge."

Rostam shrugged.

"So, you really are Satoshi Nakamoto. It's hard to accept I've found you."

"At this point I'm not sure the reality can fit the myth but yes, I wrote Satoshi's White Paper." David sighed, as though having confessed to a sin. "You go first up the stairs," he continued. "It'll take me considerably longer."

The rain had stopped by the time Rostam poked his head out of the trapdoor, the air cold and clean against his skin. He had thoroughly dried out underground. The sound of David's slow footsteps coming up the stairs became fractionally louder with each step.

"My exercise for the day," said David, who had emerged behind him while Rostam looked up at the sky. "There's a sensor which will automatically close the trapdoor once it knows there is nobody inside. I keep the rope outside for its aesthetic appeal. Come this way. There's something else I'd like to show you."

Chapter Fifty

The path diverged past the trapdoor. David took a right around the hill, maintaining the same gradient down the slope. The old man had a jerky, irregular gait after the exertions of the steps. Rostam slowed his own pace so they could walk side-by-side.

Now the rain had stopped, the two men pushed back their hoods. The older man's profile was frail, turkey jowls bulging below his neck, Adam's apple precariously prominent, each breath loud, and often wet, as though there was too much saliva in his mouth. Theo McNamara seemed more physically vital, but the two men must be of similar ag e.

"Do you feel more Japanese than British yet?" asked Rostam.

"So, you've spotted I'm not a native of these islands?"

Both men burst into laughter at this: David as though it were the funniest joke he had ever heard, and Rostam in relief at the change in mood.

"Hardly seems fair," spluttered David when the first jags had subsided. "I speak the language. I eat the food. I'm more committed to restoring temples of the Kamakura era than most indigenous specialists. In the past I built a reputation in the analogue world. Nothing to what my digital reputation will be. Yet no-one could ever mistake me for a local. It's why I need Jiro, Yuriko and my other colleagues to keep me safe."

The path turned upwards, and the older man placed his hand on Rostam's forearm. Above their heads came the misaligned honking of a flock of geese. Both men stopped and looked up. The birds were just ten yards above their heads.

"Greater white-fronted geese. One of the glories of this time of the year. We're heading to the same place as them."

The path resumed its decline and David took his hand back. "I'm getting on. Old age is like spinning plates. No matter how much you worry about them falling out of the air, how much attention you pay and the extra skills you develop to keep an extra dish in the air; no matter how stylish each parabola becomes and the oohs and aahs from the crowd; sooner or later it crashes around you."

The trees began to widen out around them, and the sound of splashing became audible.

"Here we are. Our friends the geese beat us to it."

A small lake became visible, hollowed into a depression in the hillside. A dozen geese paddled in the middle, honking to scare off competition and show themselves rulers of the water. They had grey-brown wings and feathers, and white backsides. An elaborately carved and polished wooden bench stood halfway along the bank.

"Let's sit here."

Rostam shivered as they sat down at either end of the bench.

"You're not too cold?" asked the old man.

"It's atavistic. I feel like I should be cold."

The ground was packed earth, firm despite the rain. One small grey squirrel chased another along an oak tree branch trailing down towards the lake. The leader jumped and landed just beyond Rostam's outstretched feet.

"We're far enough away from civilization that they haven't learned to fear humans. Dangerously naive." David pointed at the water. "The fish don't have the brain power to be scared. Sweetfish, black bass, rock catfish. Yuriko lets friends fish here from time to time and serves them up. I'm no blood sports fiend, but I enjoy eating fish from my own lake."

Now Rostam felt confident enough to return to his mission.

"What do you say, David? Will you work with me, or am I on my own?"

David unfolded one leg before him and stretched out before answering.

"I know Theodore McNamara." The old man exhaled, as though feeling he had finally put a card on the table. "Theo and I were partners at General Semi back in the day, as your generation likes to put it. We were friends as well."

Rostam sent a mental message to Dread: *Close, but no cigar. You found Theo McNamara in the files, but you missed Satoshi Nakamoto himself.*

David stopped speaking and cleared his throat. Rostam thought he sounded almost upset.

"We were both part of Tim May's gang in the 80s, tech guys sitting around the Valley trying to make our predictions come true. We theorized about mass electronic communication, and what it might do for freedom." He sighed. "That was a long time ago. It was Theo who engineered the sale of our business to the Pentagon. I was opposed to handing over our technology to the government. Theo was always very competitive. I suppose we all are competitive people. But Theo went to the dark side. Money alone wasn't enough. He wanted power."

"So, he had nothing to do with the beginning of bitcoin?"

"Nothing. Theo isn't one of my team of sixty-four, but it didn't take him long to buy two of the weaker players. I couldn't get it going on my own. I needed allies. It was my greatest fear - that the sixty-four would leak secrets. That's why I put an extranonce into the mining puzzles."

Rostam gasped.

"You embedded extranonces? You can follow who has mined the coins?"

David smiled at the pond. "And more. I can trace ownership straight to Theo McNamara. That's how I know just how much bitcoin Theo controls right now. He's made himself a very rich man, and he keeps buying."

"What do you think he'll do with it, once he gets the price high enough?"

'People like Theo want power above all. He'll use his billions to buy influence." David's voice had risen.

"You've still got your million coins though, right?" said Rostam.

"Why would I sell them?" snapped the old man. "I wanted to build a financial system that allows freedom. Freedom from governments, but also from the electronic mafia. Someone like Theo would only ever want a system that placed himself and his buddies at the top." David placed his hand lightly on Rostam's shoulder. "At the beginning you were just a Hail-Mary shot to fire at Zadi for Theo. That will all change now. Now he knows you're onto him, you're in danger."

"What do you mean?"

"He'll know the hard-liners missed their target. Zadi is back in Tehran already. He's no political slouch. If anyone can talk round the Supreme Leader, he might. Theo will panic knowing Zadi will sell him out. Your best defence is to make him think you have information he needs. Otherwise, he'll have you killed, or just as likely, shop you to the authorities. He'll have no problem manufacturing evidence. I'd suggest you get back as fast as you can."

"Why are you telling me this?"

"Because some of Theo's energy - perhaps most of it - comes from his resentment of what I've accomplished. Do you know many old people, Rostam?"

Rostam thought it over. "Not really. My Mom's not elderly and I've never known my grandparents."

"You'll find the very old can be grouped into four, unequal segments." David raised a hand and held it with the thumb hidden, so Rostam could see four digits raised against the water of the pond. The old man began to count them off. "First, there's the perpetually ill and depressed. Call it old-school old age. Second, hedonists. They can make it a long way, though it's the low-key pleasure seekers who make it to the final innings. Golf and third marriages in their eighties, that kind of thing." He snapped back another finger, leaving two. "Thirdly, the happy ones. I'll tell you, unpopular though it is, many of the happy ones are religious. All that mumbo jumbo seems to pay off in the end." The index finger was the only one left extended. "But I'm sorry to tell you there's the fourth group, the disappointed ones. Envy is their biggest common feature. That sin lasts longer than lechery or gluttony. About as long as its close cousin, greed. Those people with more wrinkles on their face than hairs on their heads who feel like life cheated them, and it's normally because other people they know did better in some way. More money, more sex, better children, better health, more prizes. Could be anything. Envy can get anyone." David retracted the outstretched index finger, so that for a moment his hand was clenched into a fist. "Theo is eating his liver with self-loathing that he didn't change the face of the financial landscape.

"And he is dangerous. This is a high stakes game. If he loses, his best case is to escape the country. He'll kill again and again before he lets that happen. I can't protect you from that, Rostam, so whatever you do, it better be fast."

Rostam had a last attempt.

"He talked about the need for countries to find themselves through conflict. I don't know what he's planning, but it doesn't sound good."

"I know. You're in a tight spot. So am I. I didn't create bitcoin for Theo McNamara to buy influence, any more than for it to be a Ponzi scheme to defraud the world's teenagers of their pocket-money."

"Good luck with that," said Rostam.

David sighed. "This takes me back to the cypherpunk days of the eighties. We were seeking communication that could be encrypted and kept away from the prying eyes of government. Email protocol has been perverted so that it is now easier than any time in recorded history for the powers that be to monitor everyone. Electronic communication is a snooper's paradise. Just think what Walsingham or SAVAK or the Stasi would have done with it. The Berlin Wall would never have fallen in a world of electronic communication. Now authorities want the same to happen to electronic money. You have seen how the brute force of government power treats free and guiltless citizens, such as yourself, and the mother of your child."

"What about your anonymity?"

"Nobody is anonymous, Rostam. Not even me."

Rostam kept looking at the lake. A carp broke the surface and immediately dived back down. It was time to ask Satoshi to commit.

"Will you go public with me?" asked Rostam.

David snorted, as though impatient.

"Absolutely not. If information is power, what I've told you should do the job. I can arrange for you to get back to the USA whenever you like."

Rostam's heart fell. Without Satoshi's word, nothing would change.

"And if I say no?" he bluffed. "What if I just disappear?"

David chuckled, a surprisingly high and youthful sound. "I've listened to your show, Rostam, and now I've spent time with you. If I thought you were going to say no, I would never have brought you here."

The lake stretched out several hundred meters across from the bench. From the far side came an echoing honk as geese took off and flew in formation directly above the two men. Rostam and David both tilted their heads back to see them pass.

"There's our cue," said David. "Let's walk back to the house."

Chapter Fifty-One

David left him in the lobby.

"We old men need our rest. Yuriko will connect you to Jiro when you've decided what you want to do."

His voice was quiet and wet, as though his tongue could no longer keep up with his thoughts.

"I've made my decision," said Rostam. "I need to get to New York."

David's eyelids were halfway closed. It seemed an effort for him to re-engage.

"Very good. Jiro will arrange it. Good luck, young man."

David turned around and shuffled through a white wall. He pressed an open palm against a hidden switch and a door opened before him. It closed silently behind him, leaving Rostam alone. He didn't want to stand around waiting for Yuriko. This was a chance to explore. Now he looked closely he could make out the dimensions of the door that had swallowed David.

Seven doors lay off the lobby, discernible only by thin outlines against enamel-coloured walls. David had taken one to the right. Rostam walked to the most central and placed his palm approximately where David had done in relation to his portal.

It worked.

The door slid open, and Rostam walked down a featureless corridor which led to a viewing gallery: high ceiling, three low sofas and a long window stretching right the way across the wall. A house built for thinking. Rostam was looking across the valley, above the trees which concealed the underground numbers room, towards the hilltop where the industrialist's summer house had stood. Rostam kept probing at plans in his mind, looking for flaws, calculating probabilities. Could he pull this off without more from Satoshi? He had no choice. His Mom's advice from childhood surfaced within: *hope for the best, expect the worst*.

He heard a cough. Yuriko brought a tablet with Jiro's face filling the screen. The moment Rostam accepted the tablet she turned and left the room, as though scared to overhear the beginning of a conversation.

"Hi Rostam, did Satoshi meet your expectations?"

Rostam thought it over.

"Yes and no. It's a miracle to have met him.'

"He is a deeply private man."

Rostam nodded.

Staring at Jiro's face in close-up filled Rostam with frustration.

"He is the real deal, but he's lost his desire to make the world a better place," said Rostam.

"Couldn't be more real. He's a visionary. He literally wrote the code."

"He's old. And he's tired."

"I know that, and so does he. You think you ended up there by accident? He needs someone young and energetic to take things to the next level. David's an idealist. He didn't realize how screwed up things would get so soon. And he's British and lives in Japan. He knows he needs help."

"That makes two of us. You know about the extranonces, the trail? If Satoshi gave them to me, I'd have everything I need."

Jiro nodded.

"I was counting on David to tell you about that. I knew he'd like you."

"I need that information in verifiable format."

"That's David's call. Don't blame me."

Rostam found himself drawn by the contrast between Jiro's compassionate dark brown eyes, parsimonious mailbox mouth and the passion of his words.

"I need to get to New York. I don't know who is looking out for me, or whether I'm gonna get picked up at the airport. Can you fix that?"

Jiro's mouth broke into a smile.

"Ask me a difficult one. That is no problem at all."

"Any idea about how much trouble I'm in back there?"

"There's no evidence of a major search or even an alert at the airports. We can get you into the country no problem. The American economy is built on illegal imports of people and drugs. That's why they make security so intimidating at JFK - compensation for the Swiss cheese borders everywhere else."

"I'm not taking another of your sedatives."

"Really?"

Rostam nodded.

"Give me half an hour."

Jiro's face disappeared from the screen. Rostam lent back into the sofa, closed his eyes, and was woken by Jiro talking to him again.

"Yuriko will bring your clothes. A car will arrive soon. The driver speaks only Japanese. You won't be able to see out of the windows. Other than that it's just a normal limo. He'll take you to a private airport where there's a plane waiting to fly you to New York."

"See you, maybe," said Rostam.

"Don't give up hope," continued Jiro. "I'm here for whatever you need. You have an open line of communication, which makes you unique."

Everything took place just as Jiro had said. In five minutes, Rostam was dressed in his old clothes. His Razer Edge laptop and Nokia phone were restored to him. Yuriko escorted him to the front door where he found an electric Nissan President limousine. When he got into the back a screen rose to block his view of the windscreen. The back windows were blacked out. Twenty-four hours later he was in his Mom's Manhattan apartment.

Chapter Fifty-Two

Monday January 24

Manhattan

Home still smelled of home, even when there was nobody there. Rostam thought he could remember an apartment before this one: skylight swimming with rain; the hum of a huge cathode ray television set; peeling yellow linoleum kitchen floor covered in thin print ethnic rugs, but his Mom had never indulged the belief.

There was no porter at the building, though an Irishman, already fantastically aged in the noughties, had a ground floor room in return for which he was expected to replace communal light bulbs, unblock plumbing, and tell residents to call someone else for anything else. Rostam buzzed him to get through the mullioned glass front door. As a youth when he forgot his keys he waited to slip through behind adults. Tailgate homecomings.

"Hiya, Fionn. Just visiting Mom. How are you?"

The Irishman didn't look closely at Rostam, nor did he answer his greeting. The left side of Fionn's face had frozen beneath its irregular white bristle since Rostam last saw him and he smelled of urine, dabbed with cleaning products. As soon as Rostam got through the door, Fionn turned around, outsized slippers as awkward as flippers, and shambled back to his own room. It felt like a bad omen.

West 21st Street was where he had grown up. People envied him his Greenwich Village youth, and when they said so, Rostam knew what they meant, why they were right, and also wrong. Everything is atomised when you look closely enough. The West Village was a cool place to grow up if you were a clever, curious kid whose Mom was always working and gave you a lot of freedom. It didn't make him part of the jet-set.

The building was a multi-layered anachronism. 1920s Art Deco lettering too dilapidated to reach retro chic; four storeys, which made it stumpy compared to neighbours; rent-controlled so the owner never spent a cent without the threat of an injunction; a collection of winners of the rent-controlled zip code lottery who felt disgruntled and out of place, as the city kept regrowing its skin and they remained the same, but older.

Rostam's Mom had always loved it.

Your grandfather's house in Tehran was too quiet. I don't wanna be stuck behind a gate. I wanna be like a rat. Get out, do my business, back behind the wainscot. Nothing for anyone to take from us. Nothing else we need.

She'd kept the dull brass combination lock installed around the time Rostam had been studying for SATs. Every other apartment had a Yale lock. She updated the code daily. Rostam looked at it and tried to remember the date. January 31. European style: 3101. Round up to nearest prime.

Getting his brain to work through the encrusted layers of exhaustion was like trying to drink water out of a frozen bottle. His finger itched with the desire to use his phone to cheat, while a lifetime of admonishments to think for himself kept his cell in his pocket.

3109? 3109!

Number nine on the lock remained depressed, before slowly emerging with the reward of a click.

The dark wooden apartment floor was covered in Persian rugs in every direction: left to the galley kitchen, right into his Mom's room, the living room and straight onto his old bedroom, which must be where Millie and Celia had been sleeping. The smells of Persian food filled the empty apartment, the zesty scent of raisins, cumin, turmeric, slow cooked chicken, and omnipresent matzah bread. Rostam had grown up with his Mom's sayings and *In this country only the Jews know how to bake bread* was a favourite.

He kicked his Adidas creps onto the pile of footwear inside the apartment door, and walked into his old room. The bed took up most of the space. Rostam smiled to see that Millie had left it neatly made up. His Mom had never cared about neatness. *Was that a tiny part of Millie's appeal? Don't they say boys always compare women to their mothers?* Celia's gonk lay on the pillow, a grey knitted elephant with an abbreviated trunk and sunflowers for eyes. Rostam grabbed it and rammed it into his nostrils, as though he could absorb the spirit of his daughter along with the cotton of the toy. Toddler smells, traces of poop and sick and crumbs and ice cream and fruit juice. *Would these smells from another child be repulsive?* Rostam didn't care.

The television set in the corner of the living room defaulted to Netflix. The first *keep viewing* choice: Monsta Math Club. *Trust Mom. Between her and Millie the poor girl will never get a break.* He switched to CNBC. **CRYPTO RALLY LIFTS ALL BOATS** was the headline at the bottom of the screen. Rostam turned off the TV.

He cracked open a window to recycle the stuffy indoor air. Snow began to fall as he peered out of the window into the gymnasium operating on the first floor of the new block opposite. A forbiddingly handsome couple were running towards him on treadmills, both unsmiling, as if aggravated by their lack of progress. The bobbing of their heads made him seasick. From street level came a desultory car horn. A black SUV honking the UPS truck dropping large flat brown boxes to the trendy bike shop that had opened next door the previous year. Rostam took another gulp of cold air - *too cold, give me brain freeze* - and pushed the window closed.

Rostam checked his watch. Three hours before Mom returns from work. He wanted to find Millie and Celia, but had to prepare. *Whoever acts first will win. If Theo gets to me before I get things in motion, we're dead.*

He walked over to the workstation his mother kept in the corner of the living room, took his Razer Edge out of his bag, attached himself to his Mom's WiFi network and messaged Dread.

Chapter Fifty-Three

Rostam was so busy he didn't hear the combination lock click.

"Salaaaaam Rostam-*kuchuloo*," bellowed his Mom from the hallway. "It takes all this drama to drag you back home to see your Mother?"

It was not such a large apartment that it took more than a moment for them to meet in the living room doorway. Rostam spread his arms and clasped her to him, her outsized acetate spectacle frames bumping into his cheek, grey-black mass of frizzy hair scratching his face and filling his nose. Impossible to break down how much of the aroma of Mom came from perfume, shampoo, the industrial antiseptic soap to which she was addicted, or just *Mommy smells,* the inimitable collection of characteristics that made Mom, Mom. She was barely above five foot in height but was a powerful woman, in body, spirit and mind, and returned his hug with passion.

"I know what we're going to do about your situation," she said once she had released him, and Rostam straightened back up. His Mom stood exactly where he had put her down, staring straight up at him with barely an inch separating them. *Personal space doesn't exist in Iranian families.*

"You're not gonna ask if I've eaten, or I'm alright, or any of that good parent stuff?"

"Now that you're a father and on the run from the law you want I should baby you?"

Thirty years teaching high school math in Lower Harlem had done nothing to erode Mom's Tehrani accent and idiomatic English.

"Why didn't you teach me to speak Farsi growing up?"

"Now you want it? It's too late to get sentimental. English is the world language, Rostam-jun. You wanna learn Persian, be my guest. I sent you to school. You didn't turn out so bad. Get over it!"

She dropped both shoulders and dropped her luggage, a crammed tote bag full of marking on one side, and one that was nominally a handbag on the other. They were indistinguishable from one another to Rostam.

"Sit, sit, you big baby. I'll bring tea. Then we'll sort out your mess. Ridiculous child."

The bustling of his Mom down the corridor to the kitchen sounded like one of Satoshi's wild boars had made the journey from rural Honshu to Manhattan.

"I bought an electric samovar on internet," came a shout from the kitchen. "So much easier."

"What happened to the old brass one?"

"Gave it to the parents of an Afghani kid at school. His family managed to get into the country God knows how. Told them they should go to California where it's sunny and people speak Farsi. They ain't got nothing. Samovar's a start."

Clattering of glasses and sugar bowls echo down the hall.

"You started Celia drinking tea yet?"

"Don't be stupid. That girl's an angel. Her Mom's not so bad either. You're an idiot, Rostam. Did I tell you that already?"

"Thanks, Mom. I intuited it."

"Anyway, Millie doesn't like tea. Must own shares in Starbucks. The prices! I tell her she can make better coffee here for half the price, but does she listen?"

"She-does-not," mouthed Rostam in synchrony with his Mom. "You're getting predictable in your old age, you know that, Mom?"

"I'll predictable-you-now-in-a-minute! You should listen to your mother instead of making fun."

She reappeared coming down the corridor carrying a tray with a single sugar bowl and then everything in pairs: teaspoons, nectarines, mini-cucumbers, side plates, knives, and large glasses of black tea. Rostam took the tray and placed it on a glass-topped side table.

"Thank you, Jun-am," said his Mom, and burst into tears. Her face collapsed in on itself and her shoulders shook. An avalanche had taken place inside her body.

"Ignore me," she choked out through the tears. "It's too much. I thought you might be dead, or in prison, or just disappeared."

"Hey Mom, it's gonna be ok. I've got a plan," said Rostam, taking her back in his arms. This time she was prepared to be clasped tight to him.

"How did this all happen to us?"

"It's not our fault. I just got dragged into things."

"I don't mean that. I mean the divorce. She's a good woman, Rostam."

"I know it. Things are complicated. Can we deal with one thing at a time?"

"Time!" spluttered his Mom, pulling herself out of his arms and cuffing him, as though blaming him for wasting it. "Time is what we don't have." Lilac eye shadow rubbed with mascara as she rubbed her eyes. "Don't stare at your mother. I put on make-up for myself and nobody else."

Rostam sat down, head bowed. He knew better than to argue.

"You better tell me what trouble you're in. Start at the beginning and omit nothing."

Mother and son giggled together. That was the exhortation with which she greeted Rostam every day when he got back from high school. He had made a sport of concealing as much as possible in the face of the daily demands for reports. The highlight had been when he claimed to have missed an entire day of school after being headed off at the pass.

"It all started when someone offered me a deal that was too good to be true."

It took two full samovars before he got to the end. Rostam wondered which part of the story would grab her attention first. He didn't have to wait long.

"So, Bahman Zadi is an important man now."

"I liked him."

"You're not a child anymore. Of course, you liked him. He wanted you to like him. The question is *why did he want you to like him?*"

Rostam shook his head and reflected that this wasn't the first time his Mom had made him think things through clearly.

"He thought I could get to Satoshi."

Mom pointed at Rostam.

"Maybe he needed your help."

"Some help I've been," said Rostam.

"Perhaps you need help yourself," said Maryam, looking deep into her son's eyes. "You remember Hosein. Little man. Gray skin. Smoked cigarette after cigarette. Slight lisp. Terrible at backgammon."

"Of course. He used to bring pizza."

"The very same. If it weren't for you, I'd be worried about him. He's been working on a big story, got himself into trouble."

"What story?" asked Rostam, not really interested.

"Wouldn't say. Something political. He had a writing partner but she killed herself and now the Times don't wanna know. Could it be the same thing?"

"Maybe later. Time for plan A first."

Maryam wiped her nose.

"Have it your way. Now where is that ex-wife of yours?"

The sun had set long since outside. Rostam stood up and stretched. The tips of his fingers touched the ceiling.

"Remember how proud I was when I could do that for the first time?"

"You don't know how pleased I was myself. Your grandfather was a tall man. I was desperate for you to be the same."

"You never said."

"Only idiots care about winning the biological lottery. So sue me."

A phone rang out, loud and abrasive in the small apartment. Rostam's Mom had never been prepared to give up on a landline. She picked it up.

"Allo. Millie-*junam*. He's here."

Rostam picked up the phone.

"Millie. Where are you? Everything ok?"

"Everything's fine. I just can't believe you're here. I've got Celia with me. Wanna come for a walk? We're at the Mercer playground."

"Sure." Rostam was about to hang up. "Isn't it late and cold for a trip to the swings?"

"You think I need a man to tell me that?"

Rostam looked in his Mom's liquid brown eyes, lids and lashes caked with comedy make-up. "I guess not. Find you by the statue?"

"Bring coffee."

Rostam hung up the Bakelite handset which let out half a ring, like the bark of an old dog disturbed by the fire.

"Thought she'd bring Celia back here."

"You're a fool, Rostam. The poor woman loses her career because of you, who already cost her a marriage. She's been shacked up with her ex-husband's Mom while we try to put things back in order. You expect her to waltz in here and play happy families?"

Rostam felt stupid. Not an unfamiliar sensation with his mother.

"I guess I did."

"Get out of your own head and start seeing things from other people's perspective for a change. And ask her how she's doing. She had a sniff of a job offer the other day, but she's told me nothing."

Rostam felt flustered, as though he were going on a first date.

"I haven't showered since landing."

"Your daughter is going to care about your personal hygiene at this point?"

"I didn't bring her a present."

"Who? Your daughter or your former wife?"

Rostam looked back at her, confused.

"Get out of here. You've still got that ridiculous trench coat hanging in the cupboard. And take a scarf. It's freezing out."

Rostam grabbed his thrift-store Second World War greatcoat. It had the musty old person smell of a piece of clothing that has hung in darkness for a long time. No longer broad enough in the shoulders for him. The first scarf he could find was purple, thick pearled and hairy. He wrapped it around his neck multiple times, like a New England undergraduate.

Rostam went down the stairs rather than waiting for the wheezing accordion of an elevator, taking two at a time. As he entered the mirrored hallway of his Mom's building he smiled at his own reflection, an adult man in a teenage coat and Mom's scarf. What a sight. Before leaving he held the front door open for a hugely fat man trying to squeeze his way in, clutching a brown paper Wholefoods bag. The thought ran through his head like ticker tape: *it's good to be back with people I can trust.*

Chapter Fifty-Four

Rostam walked east along W 21st St across Fifth Avenue before turning down Broadway. He wrapped his Mom's scarf around his face against the biting New York cold.

Every store had an association. Paragon Sports where he'd out-cooled himself as a teen and spent six months of saved allowances on Kobe Bryant Adidas sneakers that were too tight and gave him blisters. The Dr Marten shop where he'd bought Millie a pair of splash-painted limited-edition boots on an early trip to meet his Mom. Barnes and Noble at the top of Union Square for tourists who didn't know they'd prefer The Strand down a block.

The desire to see Celia exploded, like an airbag had been triggered inside his chest. He kept walking into clouds of his own breath in the cold air, making his scarf hot and wet before it froze, and his face dripping with moisture. The usual Manhattan morass of Uber Priuses, yellow taxicabs, FedEx and UPS vans, branded delivery trucks and private cars for refuseniks who hadn't got the memo. Past Morandi, their New York date night restaurant on Waverley Place. *Need coffee for Millie.* Ah:

ARTISANAL SMALL BATCH COFFEE SHACK

$10 for an oat milk latte from an ageing hipster, with a neat goatee and untidy belly protruding from a leather barista apron.

Stop panicking. Almost there. Slow down and catch a breath.

Rostam sped up instead. The playground was on the far side of the park. It was dark and the painted black metal gates were locked. No matter. Just across the railing from the statue of the soldier stood Millie, playing hopscotch with Celia on the paving stones.

"Somebody ordered coffee?"

Millie spun around and smiled.

"About time."

"DADDY!" shrieked Celia, abandoning her mother and running straight into Rostam's legs. He picked her up and brought her round, flushed face up to his own, pulling it into his own and shaking his head so they could do their standard nose-rub kiss. Millie plucked her coffee from his hands.

"Turncoat!" said Millie with reproach to their daughter. "She wouldn't leave me alone for a second all day and now look. I'm being chop-livered by my own daughter."

"I dunno who is sharing more snot, Celia or me. C'mon Millie - get involved. Team hug."

Millie leaned into his side and put her arms around both. She pecked a chaste kiss onto Rostam's cheek.

"Welcome back, asshole."

"Feels like a long time since wiener night in Chicago. What did I miss?"

Milie biffed him gently on the nose.

"Don't push it."

Celia was squirming to be put down. Restored to the sidewalk, she started to run in figures of eight through her parents' legs.

"I haven't felt this happy since...I don't know when I last felt this happy," said Rostam to Millie.

"Well as long as you're ok," said Millie, "I guess we can all relax."

"Gadan!" demanded Celia.

"So, she still has her own word for ice-cream."

Rostam reached down to put a hand beneath each of Celia's arms, swung her up and around, before placing her on his shoulders. He crouched down so that she could fist-bump her mother.

"Must be someone who'll sell us ice cream on a freezing January night. This is New York. If we wanted a deep-fried rat with mustard, someone would sell it us."

Without discussion they turned around to walk up Mercer St and though the NYU buildings thronged around Washington Square.

"How have things been?" asked Rostam.

"I'm not gonna lie. It's been tough. Those bastards did a thorough job. Threw me out of Loeb like a criminal. I'm grateful your Mom took us in. I didn't wanna be around Chicago and have to keep explaining myself to everyone I met."

"Celia seems happy."

The little girl was squealing with delight, while squirming so much on his shoulders Rostam knew he'd wake up with mild neck pain in the morning.

"Why not? She's got her mother available twenty-fours a day and Grandma thinks sugar is the only food group for three-year-olds. This is better than a vacation for Celia."

"And you?"

"I'll be back in the game soon enough."

"Mom said," said Rostam. "What's the new gig?"

"Carmen called with something, but I don't wanna jinx it," said Millie, looking at the ground. "I'm not prepared to let them take away everything I've worked for. That's what's keeping me going."

"*That's* what'll keep us going." Rostam pointed to a hot-dog stand at the entrance to Washington Square. "Two dogs," he said to the vendor. "One real, one vegetarian. Ketchup and mustard on both. Double mustard on the meat one. Ice cream in a cone."

"Your Mom usually cooks," said Millie. "I haven't had a hot dog since we got here. She won't mind?"

"I can eat two dinners if that's what it takes to keep her happy."

Rostam fished around in his back pocket for a bill to pay but Millie flashed her Wells Fargo debit card at the machine in the van.

"Still solvent enough to pay for treats. You wanna fill me in on what's been going on?"

They sauntered a diagonal through the park in its liminal phase, when daytime tourists, bag-people and winos faded away, replaced by criss-crossing commuters, before the vulnerable hustlers of nighttime staked out their turf later in the evening. Rostam recapped what he had told his Mom as they walked slowly up Sixth Avenue. Now he had Celia on his shoulders, the sense of urgency had diminished.

Millie was a more interactive listener than his Mom. Devastated to hear about Ahmad. Distraught for Dana and the girls. Happy to hear about the fate of Hanratty. Disgusted by Spider. Cynical and full of questions about David/Satoshi. Sixth Avenue was widening into the Avenue of the Americas as he got to the end of his tale, and they turned into W 21st. Celia was becoming heavier, like a bean bag filling up with moisture, and was starting to rest her chin on Rostam's crown in a way which told him she would soon be asleep.

"So, what's the plan?" asked Millie.

"Under development. I've got ideas. Want to discuss it with you and Mom together."

"I've got one too. Let's take it upstairs."

Chapter Fifty-Five

Maryam had not been idle. The smells coming from the kitchen floated into the corridor outside her front door.

"I'm regretting that hot dog already," whispered Rostam while they waited for the door to open.

"There's already one baby around here," whispered Millie, poking him below his rib cage.

"I've baked flounder and aubergine and mushroom in cumin and turmeric, all inside saffron rice. You'd better not been snacking out there," said Maryam as they walked inside.

"Gadan!" demanded a revived Celia.

"No ice cream for you until after supper," said Millie.

Rostam's Mom glared at them. "This isn't fair. It's for the grandmother to hand out treats. With your generation it's the likes of me who still must maintain discipline. Come on people. Into the living room with you."

The television was switched on and Celia sat cross legged before the 1951 *Alice in Wonderland*. Rostam and Millie sat at either end of the sofa. Mom made repeated trips into the room until everyone had a bowl of steaming saffron rice and a glass of New York City tap water.

A bowl of natural yogurt stood on the coffee table in the middle of the room.

"So now you three have had time to catch up, what we gonna do?" demanded Mom.

Rostam swallowed a mouthful of rice and put his three-quarters full bowl down on the carpet.

"Theo's plan is to take control of regulation. Let's speak to the regulators first."

Millie coughed.

"How do you know you haven't got this all upside down? Why do we have to fight McNamara at all? It's not like he's done anything that bad that we know of for sure."

Millie raised an index finger to stop Rostam shouting her down.

"No, you listen to me," she continued. "You can't prove he's got anything to do with Ahmad's death. Sure, he blocked your bitcoin account. Tell him about Satoshi and he'll turn it back on, most likely. You're here in the room with Celia and your Mom." Millie shrugged. "I get the knight in shining armour vibe, but what's really going on here?"

Millie sat back on her chair, eyes flickering between Rostam and Maryam.

"What do you say, Rostam-*jun*?" asked his mother.

"I'd love to agree," said Rostam. "Make a call to Theo McNamara and walk away from the whole thing. But it's too late for that. McNamara's looking to buy power. He's already rigging financial markets. Next stop the whole country." Millie snorted. "Just look at what he's done to us already. You're pretty quick to forgive Cantillon and his mob at Loeb. They're all part of the same conspiracy. These guys broke into your apartment while Celia was asleep. They attacked you in Wholefoods."

"I'm moving on," said Millie. "Losers fight yesterday's battles. You sound like Dread, or one of the conspiracy crazies you used to laugh at."

Rostam smiled.

"You have a point. The problem with a conspiracy theory is, once you know it's true, you have to act. And I know this is true."

Maryam clinked her spoon against her bowl twice, like the toaster at a wedding.

"What about Hosein Dardbash, Rostam? This story of his could help. You wanna talk to him? He can see you tonight."

"I don't want to get a journalist involved, not even an old family friend," said Rostam. Maryam looked at him over her spectacles. "Ok, ok. I'll see him if it makes you happy." He turned back to Millie. "Look, if I thought I could make this go away - no harm, no foul - I'd do it. But that offer isn't on the table, and it's not gonna be. We must fight with what we have."

"So, what's that, hotshot?" said Millie.

"Dread and I will do an episode where we talk through the whole thing. I'm just waiting on the hope of more hard evidence I can post simultaneously. But first I need a favour from you. Are you still friends with Betty Dai?"

"Betty, my sorority sister who worked in compliance at Loeb? She's now five years into life at the New York Fed. Working on crypto regulation. Constant battle with the other agencies over who is gonna take it over." Millie took a sip of water. "She'd love to hear about Satoshi and the Iranians. Give her a head start over her oppo."

"Let's give her a shot."

"But does she have the clout to help you?" demanded Mom. "No point us handing over everything so Rostam can consider her gratitude from the inside of a Max Security Prison."

"How senior is Betty?" Rostam asked.

"On the up," said Millie, "and ambitious. Give her something worth having and she'll have the boss straight into the room."

Rostam sat back, trying to work it through.

"See if we can meet with her tomorrow."

Maryam coughed.

"Look at the television kids - you might learn something.".

Celia was lisping along with the Carpenter and the Walrus. Her enunciation was poor, but timing spot on.

"You see that? The carpenter spots the oysters, builds the shack and prepares the meal."

As Rostam and Millie caught up, the animated carpenter on the screen waltzes out of the kitchen with a tray of bread and butter and sauce of peppercorn and mustard seeds and other seasonings. On the table all he can see is the menu. He crawls across the tabletop to peer over it, finds nothing but a dozen empty oyster shells.

"That idiot carpenter can chase the walrus all day and all night, but the oysters have gone."

Millie shrugged.

"You lost me, Maryam. This is a kids' film."

Rostam and his Mom tutted in synchrony. Mom looked at Rostam.

"This film isn't just for kids. This is mathematics in cartoon form. This is all Mom would let me watch half the time."

"Explains a lot," muttered Millie.

"Listen to this," said Maryam.

Alice was explaining to Tweedledum and Tweedledee that their story had a very good moral, if one happened to be an oyster.

"What she's asking is, who are we in this situation? I've been thrown around the world like an oyster. You too. All these bad guys think they're gonna eat us. They think they get to be the walrus. We need them all to be carpenters."

"I ain't no oyster," said Millie.

"That's my girl!" said Maryam, leaning in to kiss her on both cheeks.

"I appreciate the love. But I'll be happier when I'm back behind a desk."

"And what about you, my boy? What good is this mad Englishman Satoshi in Japan going to do for you?"

"He changed the world, Mom."

"Sounds like a fruitcake," said Maryam.

"I don't get what Satoshi wants," added Millie.

"He's living his nightmare. Built a magical system and now it's turning rotten," said Rostam. "Maybe he just decides to stay hidden. It's a head scratcher and he figures that maybe I can help him."

"Easy for him to say. He's not taking any risks," said Maryam.

"Looked at another way this is the battle of his whole life. All we can do is play the cards we've been dealt."

Celia got up from her spot in front of the TV and came over to sit in his lap.

"Let's give this gorgeous child a bath. Gotta be my turn to read stories. I've got an episode to put together and a plan for tomorrow."

Millie held up her phone.

"Betty says yes. We see her at her office tomorrow at 10."

Chapter Fifty-Six

Rostam was just patting Celia dry when his Mom called him into the hallway.

"You need to go now."

Maryam stood up and placed a hand on each of Rostam's shoulders. She had to reach up high, but still had the physical force to press down hard.

"You must talk to Hosein, *junam*."

Even under extreme pressure Rostam felt his Mom was mocking him. Light sparkled in her liquid brown eyes.

"You're sure he can help?"

"I think so. But he's paranoid about who's listening."

"Don't blame him. I don't want to talk over an electronic network."

"He said you'd say that. He's in Union Square.

Rostam looked at his mother.

"Why do I get the sense you're enjoying this, Mom?"

"Because I believe in you, *kuchuloo*. And I know you'll get this mess sorted out. Just remember to aim high. These people are treating you and your family like skittles. You have power in this situation. You just have to work out how to use it."

'Union Square is full of crazies at dusk. I walk up to all of them and say 'salaam'?'

"It isn't full of well-dressed Iranian guys close to sixty. You've been all around the world chasing trouble, now you can't find a man in the square just down the street?"

Maryam was becoming frenetic. It was always a fine line between her extremes of mockery and nerves. Rostam reached out and drew her in for a hug.

"Mom, you know how much we appreciate this?"

"There's nothing else I can do *jun-am*. I wish there were."

"Sorry to cause all this trouble."

"If I didn't like trouble, I'd never have had a kid. Children are like math. You solve one problem, and it takes you to the next. That's how it goes. You go solve your problem."

Rostam looked at his daughter sitting on Millie's knee in the bathroom. He sank to his heels and kissed her on her brown-hair, smelling of sweet apples and soap, warm to his lips. There was no acknowledgement from her at all.

"You go. We got this," said Mom, as she plumped down onto the sofa with a pile of marking.

It was cold outside. Rostam regretted not bringing the scarf as the heavy glass doors of his Mom's apartment building clicked shut behind him. Streets once again full of early evening traffic, the desert days of deep lockdown behind them. W 21st had always been a tony neighbourhood. It hadn't needed to transform, like the areas near Rostam's old school. Trader Joe's. Artisanal coffee. Lululemon kit. Every cuisine in the world delivered to-go to feed the skyscraper armies of Avenue of the Americas. He turned south of the too-period-to-age Flatiron and down Broadway towards Union Square.

It was half-past six as he slowed his pace to enter the square, a nexus of darkness in the otherwise brilliantly illuminated city. A handful of commuters strode purposefully in various directions, and there was no congregation of the homeless tonight. He began a counterclockwise circuit of the path around the small square. A bench on the east side had three middle-aged black male cigarette smokers conducting a high-volume argument which had the familiar sound of friendship about it. Rostam envied them having each other to hang with.

Nobody else was visible by the time he'd reached the southern apex of the square. George Washington stood there, looking south, remembering the flight of the British from New York in 1783. The effort of looking for Hosein sharpened Rostam's vision. He had never consciously examined the statue before. Washington's statue had four flaring fluorescent lights around it, making the grass centre of the park even darker. As he looked up, trying to see if the sculptor had made Washington's face meaningful, or just another proto superman with granite features, a shape became dimly visible on the grass. A pale hand was raised in the air, immediately followed by a small oval grey face under thin white hair, combed in an outdated side parting, as the man stepped into the light.

Rostam walked around the statue and climbed over the low stone wall behind onto the grass. Hosein's hand was extended again, and they shook.

"Your overcoat and shoes are black," said Rostam. "You could have hidden on that grass all night."

"It isn't any kind of disguise. These are my normal work clothes. I don't make a habit of assignations in the park at night."

Hosein spoke with a heavy Iranian accent in a quiet, aspirated voice.

"It's not just paranoia. I know I'm being watched. The Times won't print what I bring them. My partner Ellen Kelly was killed working on the story, and the police called it suicide." Hosein ran his hand through his wispy, white hair. "Ellen had a great future ahead of her. She deserves revenge." He took a stick of gum out of his pocket. "Nicotine gum. Want one?"

Rostam shook his head.

"I don't suppose you remember me coming to the apartment when you were small" continued Hosein. "You were tiny then. Such a strapping man now."

"I'll be honest with you, Mr Dardbash. All I remember is the pizza."

Hosein was still holding Rostam's hand in a soft, affectionate way while looking up at him in the darkness. He laughed gently.

"You remember the pizza! Of course, your Mom was worried in those days about you being too American. She wouldn't have pizza at home unless I brought it. And she couldn't shut me out or she'd have had nobody to beat at backgammon."

Hosein sighed and patted Rostam's hand before releasing it.

"I could talk about the old days for hours but we're out of time. What do you need?"

"The Alt-Lib SuperPAC. You're the expert on it, right?"

"If anyone is. I follow all the significant donors, but ALSP is the big daddy. Much of their support goes to Vice President Galway and the slate she supports. Then it trickles down a long way. Below congressional elections it funds local elections. Campaigns for Presidential appointments, like the Supreme Court, and the new SEC chair. But also foreign policy special interests. I'm convinced it supports a whole network of far-right libertarian groups, including domestic terrorism. But as soon as I get close to proving something, the chain is cut. I have nothing I can prove 100%. I think when I get there, I'll get disappeared to o."

"My colleague Dread is onto the same story. I can put you together. But neither of you has the missing link."

Hosein reached into his coat breast pocket and brought out a cell. He fired it up and showed the screen to Rostam.

"This guy?"

Rostam leaned in. It was a headshot of Theo McNamara in close profile. There could be no doubt about it.

"That's him. Can you prove he's behind everything?"

"He was a big stink for libertarian causes in the past, and I'm always interested when powerful Americans get involved in Iran," said Hosein. "His immediate aim is to get Galway's candidate chosen for the SEC chair so he can take charge of crypto regulation. Former Loeb executive called Matthew Aalen. Not the President's top pick. Maybe that's why they've spent so much taking control of the grass roots of the party. Take away the President's power to choose."

"You haven't taken this to the law?" asked Rostam.

"It's not illegal to run a super Pac," said Hosein.

"What if I can connect it to Iran, China, extremist libertarian groups here in the USA. Would that make a difference?"

"It might. Depends on how far their influence has already gotten."

"Their power comes from money, right?"

"You got it."

They were strolling to and forth on the dark, moist grass of Union Square. It was now half past seven and Rostam was thoroughly cold. His shoes were soaked through. Nobody had walked up to ask for cash, the time, or a light. It started to feel to Rostam that he had always been on that piece of grass, walking in tight, small circles, telling his tale. *Can this guy really help me?* Hosein seemed too small, too foreign, too insubstantial a person. A fresh plume of cigarette smoke was blown across them from the friends on the bench.

"I miss cigarettes," said Hosein, breathing in hard through his nose.

"Mom said you were always smoking."

"Had to stop for work. I wouldn't let the doctors bully me but once they outlawed it in offices it was a simple choice. Can't concentrate if you have to go outside for ten minutes of every hour. I miss it like hell. Too old to find another bad habit I like." Hosein took in a deep breath. "What next?"

Rostam took a deep breath. "You need hard evidence to print your story. Get me as much detail on the ALSP as you can, and I'll try to find it. We have a chance of blowing them up. A small chance, but still."

Hosein stopped moving.

"If you achieve that, Rostam, you'd be doing the world a great service."

"Can you give me something I can read?"

"I need a day to knock it into shape. Maybe this time tomorrow."

Hosein turned on his heel to make another circuit of the Square and left Rostam with the illusion of privacy. All the way back to W21st he threw around what he knew about Theo McNamara from Satoshi, Dread and Hosein. Even when it was proven, it might not stop him.

Chapter Fifty-Seven

Tuesday January 25

Rostam had slept in some unusual places over the past week, but nowhere as uncomfortable as his Mom's sofa. He woke up at five o'clock with a crick in his neck and a sense of excitement. Sounds of early morning deliveries at street level barely made it through the thick glass of the windows. Celia coughed next door where she was sleeping with Millie. His Mom's sonorous tenor snores were comforting.

He padded through to the kitchen and packed a moka pot with ground coffee. His Mom liked to pretend coffee was a filthy American habit, but the pot saw as much use as her samovar. The sounds of the apartment block heating system were enough to conceal the hissing of gas and spluttering of thick, black coffee. Rostam opened the aluminium lid and bent over to breathe in the vapor.

In the living room he fired up the Razer Edge and logged back into Tor. *Is Jiro gonna get back in time for this meeting with Betty at the Fed?* He found the message waiting for him when a hand pressed his shoulder.

"How are you feeling about today?"

His mother wore a green towelling robe, hair piled above her head in a messy ball.

"Working on it now," said Rostam. "You were right about Hosein. About both things. He is in danger, and he might be able to help."

"He messaged. Told me he'd give me something for you at work this morning. Come to me after this meeting. You're confident about that?"

"Everything's gonna be fine. I'm digging up the last of the ammo we'll need for Millie's pal at the Fed. Once they know I'm not turning up at a gunfight with a lemon in my hand, everything will be ok."

His Mom had always been able to spot when Rostam was bending the truth, but this time she just bent down to kiss him on the cheek.

"You'll knock 'em dead. You always do."

"What are you doing up this time of the morning anyway?"

"At my age you need less sleep," said Maryam. "There's a crèche next to the school. I'll take Celia there this morning so Millie can go with you."

"Childcare in Manhattan. A pearl beyond price."

"Gotta be some benefit to teaching there so long. Lisa who runs the crèche was a student of mine. Any coffee in the pot?"

Rostam nodded and turned back his laptop to open Jiro's message.

Still waiting. Sorry.

"Damn."

"Not the news you wanted?"

A spurt of inner defiance overwhelmed Rostam's disappointment.

"Nothing we can't handle."

Chapter Fifty-Eight

A bright, thin sunshine shone on the sidewalk as Rostam and Millie left the building.

"Ten minutes to the Federal Reserve building," said Millie. "I've built in time for coffee, obviously."

"You're looking good, Millie."

"Why thank you, kind sir." Millie smiled up at him. "I'm glad I brought a suit with me. No such qualms for you."

"Don't think I've worn a suit since the training programme. It'd feel weird now, like putting on a Cubs uniform to go to the ballpark."

"You never liked office life."

A turquoise Prius flashed its lights and pulled over next to them. Rostam opened the door for Millie to get in first, then ran into the street to get in behind the driver. A Poland Spring van honked him for his trouble.

"Anything I need to know ahead of this meeting?" asked Millie. "Or am I just the introduction?"

"You're much more than that. The way I see it we're doing your pal Betty a huge favour. We could go anywhere with this. In their worst nightmares we'd be in a video clip on the Daily Beast telling the world about what's happened. Or we could have picked a different agency. She'll know the value of what we're bringing her."

"I always liked her. Stupid move leaving Loeb for the Fed but whatever."

"The bull market in regulation only keeps rising," said Rostam. "Maybe she's smarter than we think."

Millie smiled with one side of her mouth.

"Betty's the only one of us in employment," she said.

The driver passed the Whitney and headed south on West St, the Hudson twinkling in the sunlight. Millie was stabbing at her phone. LinkedIn.

"I'm not sure about this meeting."

It's gonna be fine, Rostam thought and almost said, before stopping himself. Millie took life too seriously for platitudes.

The car spurted from one intersection to the next.

"Why is it that cab rides in New York always make me feel a bit sick?" said Millie.

"You've gotta let go and let the karma of the city take over," said Rostam with a smile.

"What happened to you in Bali? In a minute you're gonna tell me you've started doing yoga."

There's a story there, thought Rostam, as the car pulled left away from the river and into TriBeCa. *But I've told her too much about Spider already.*

"Remember our trip to the Fed?" asked Rostam.

"All that sticks in my mind is the pile of gold bars in the basement. Looked like papier-mâché models from a film set."

"Most of it Iranian, right? The finders-keepers' school of diplomacy."

"Funny to think of it as a proper place of work," said Millie. "Betty's office is on the thirteenth floor. She has a view of Wall St from there."

"Graveyard at one end. River at the other."

"And a collection of thieves in between."

The car reached Liberty Street and took a dangerous loop around a flat-bed truck, with a crane extended into the sky for a pair of skyscraper window washers. Rostam tried to pull the same trick of running around the back, but Millie had gotten herself out before he arrived. The stones of the building looked warm in the sunlight, but it was still freezing on the sidewalk.

"We've still got fifteen minutes," said Millie. "There's a Starbucks round the corner on Fulton St."

"My caffeine levels are dangerously low," said Rostam. "Nobody'll take us seriously if our teeth aren't chattering by the time we walk in."

"Shut up and buy me coffee, ex-husband."

Rostam extended an arm for Millie to lead the way. It felt good to be back.

Chapter Fifty-Nine

Their mood changed as they walked round the corner of Liberty Street back to the Fed. Ugly twisted yellow metal corkscrews erupted out of the tarmac to deter car bombers. Millie became snappy when Rostam attempted to lighten the conversation.

"I guess security will be as bad as an airport," said Rostam.

"It'll be worse," said Millie. "You've got your passport, right? The real American one?"

Rostam patted his back pocket to make sure it was still there. They were walking by a series of small brutal bollards which provided the sidewalk with additional protection. The proscenium arch of the entrance was topped with Old Glory, hanging limp in the absence of wind. Millie walked slightly faster, making him extend his usual stride.

"Game face on," she muttered, and elbowed Rostam, as though he might have forgotten. "We've got a meeting with Betty Dai in regulation at ten," she told the pair of security guards standing outside, scarves wrapped around their throats, badged black MA1 jackets, showing off a handgun on one hip, baton on the other.

"ID inside," was their only reply, as Millie started to take her passport out of her Karen Millen clutch. The heavy revolving door bundled them straight up the next rank of guards, standing beside a conveyor belt and scanner. Millie put her hand out for Rostam's passport and showed both, while Rostam went about the familiar tasks of taking off his belt and shoes to go along with what he had in his pockets into the tray. Rostam flashed back to Chicago Executive Airport. He found himself scanning the staff at the other side of the X-ray machine to see if he could spot a giant albino in Homeland Security uniform. Everything looked normal, but he no longer believed normality existed.

The elevators to the thirteenth floor were ornate and old fashioned, with large circular buttons of soft brass, and no option to close doors faster.

"I hate that," said Millie when the doors closed leaving the two of them alone. "Only thing worse than slow moving pedestrians is having to hang around waiting for the lift doors to close."

"Glad you haven't lost the habit of making waspish small talk."

Millie looked up with serious eyes.

"Sorry, Millie. I meant I agree with you."

"Stop talking and think. This is your last chance to pull out. We might not get a second one."

The doors opened at the twelfth floor before he could reply, but he knew Millie was right.

An unsmiling male receptionist met them as the doors opened.

"Millie and Rostam James? Ms Dai will see you in the conference room."

The corridors had the same grand-but-poorly-maintained feel as the rest of the building. Rostam sensed dust silting up his nostrils. Everybody they passed was formally but sloppily dressed. *Did government employees not get the memo of death of the necktie?* It was so quiet whispering would feel disrespectful.

The conference room had a polished wooden table down the middle, blank television screen in place of a whiteboard at one end, and natural lighting through small windows all the way along the far side. There appeared to be an expansive green lawn immediately outside the windows.

"Water? Coffee?" barked the receptionist, as though offering alternative punishments rather than refreshments. They shook their heads. "Ms Dai will be here shortly."

Rostam wandered over to the windows to see how the lawn came to be. To his surprise the windows could be opened, letting in sharp, cold air.

"What are you doing?" asked Millie.

"Just trying to ... oh I get it. That's just a foot or two of artificial grass outside. Perspective makes it look like it stretches right the way across the street."

"So what?"

"I'm glad the custodians of our financial well-being understand the importance of a good visual illusion."

There was a quick rap on the door, and Betty walked in.

"Millie. So good to see you."

Mille went over and air-kissed her old colleague.

"And Rostam. We're putting the gang back together, huh?"

Rostam had always found Betty intimidating. She had been a ferocious, hard-to-impress worker on the training programme. She and Millie had been more natural allies as dedicated career women than Rostam. As he shook her hand he found it hard to reconcile the earlier, hardcore Betty with the smiling woman shaking his hand and briefly meeting his eye.

"It's all gossip around here this morning," said Betty. "Decision on the new SEC head is expected on Friday. Rumour going around there might be a change of Fed governor too."

"What have you been working on, Betty?" asked Rostam.

Millie and Rostam went around to sit on the window side of the table, in the middle, while Betty took a seat opposite.

"A lot of crypto stuff, as it happens. I was glad when you got in touch - I could do with learning. There's been a rush of these bridge heists - I've spent half the weekend on the phone to Vietnam."

A spark flickered in the recesses of Rostam's brain. *Vietnam?* "The Axie Infinity game? Oh yeah - you mean the hackers getting into between the Ronin and Ethereum chains over the bridge?"

"That's the one." Betty nodded at him. Rostam felt some relief at establishing credentials early. "I mean, nobody really cares, because the victims are gamers who signed their lives away when they clicked 'accept' on the smart contract going into the game."

"Come again?" asked Millie.

"Axie Infinity is another game where players earn in-game currency points," said Rostam. "They can convert them to Ethereum and hence into fiat currency, but to do that they have to transfer their Ethereum from one blockchain to another. The thieves were lurking in the breach."

"Correct," said Betty. "We don't have too big a problem because all the crypto within the game is contained in a smart contract. The gamers don't own their crypto, because they don't have the key. The game has the key. So, they can't complain too much if someone steals it." Betty rapped her knuckles on the table. "It is still theft though. And if we don't learn how to fix these things now as parts of games, where will we be down the road?"

"History will repeat farce as tragedy, or something like that," said Rostam.

"That's why I'm on it. But what about you? Millie says you have something to tell me. I'm honoured but maybe you should first explain: why me?"

Rostam felt Millie looking at him from the side.

"Betty, what we have to tell you is frightening. This relentless crypto rise. It isn't just market forces. There is a collection of libertarians in this country and forces outside who are ramping crypto to replace the US dollar, and disassemble our financial infrastructure while they're at it."

Betty looked at Millie and raised her eyebrows. Rostam leaned in on the table. "It's market manipulation for sure, and it might count as treachery too. If the Fed and the SEC don't stop this, you'll find the power taken away from you from above."

Betty was shaking her head.

"You know me," continued Rostam. "I decided to come to you first because we're going to need protection and the Fed should be able to organize it. What do you say?"

Betty's face gave nothing away.

"I'm not interested in gossip, not about you but also not from you," she said. "There are stories going around. I don't care. But if you want protection from my organization, you're going to have to be very persuasive indeed. I'm not asking for a medal here but not everybody in this building would take a meeting with people who are under suspicion."

Millie's gonna hate that, thought Rostam but she was nodding at Betty and radiating empathy across the conference table. Then he felt his credibility kicked out from under him.

"Just hear Rostam out, that's all we ask," said Millie. "Nobody expects you to put yourself and your organization at any risk just for the sake of a couple of old friends. Rostam's been under a lot of pressure."

Suddenly all the nervous energy that had been troubling Millie transferred itself to Rostam. He felt a strong tremor rise through his chest to his jaw and shook his head slightly.

"I didn't bring a presentation because - "

The door opened again, and Rostam paused. Betty looked over her shoulder.

"This room is blocked out for the next hour."

"We won't need an hour, honey," came a woman's voice with a slow Tennessee twang.

Tina Waspell walked into the room. Behind her came two uniformed NYPD officers, one male, one female. Rostam's stomach folded in on itself, and he felt an instinctive fear of being cast back into the frozen water of their last meeting. A corrective wash of adrenaline gave him the spirit to call her out.

"No albino guard to back you up this time?"

"Hi, Rostam. Fancy bumping into you. I don't need my own security when New York's finest have got my back."

Betty stood.

"What is the meaning - "

"Sit down, honey" said Waspell, handing over a badge for Betty to inspect. "I have jurisdiction. Officers, that's the one we're looking for."

Waspell was pointing across the table, but not at Rostam.

The pair of cops walked around the table from either side, as though concerned Millie might make a break for the border.

"What do you want with me?" asked Millie, shaking her head.

"Amelia James, we are arresting you on suspicion of money laundering," said the first cop to reach her. He was a physically unassuming man, drooping greying mustache, large paunch and short stature, accentuated by a stoop.

"That's bullshit." Millie's voice was calm, but her face already inflamed. "I'm here for a meeting."

The female cop already had a pair of handcuffs out of her holster and held them up for Millie to see.

"I'm gonna put this on you now," said the cop. "If you fight it'll only make the cuffs tighter."

"You're threatening me?" said Millie.

"I'm not threatening nothin', but I am gonna put these cuffs on you, one way or the other."

Rostam stared at Waspell, who didn't bother to conceal the growing smirk on her face.

"What do you think you're doing, Tina?"

"Tina? You know this bitch?" shouted Millie.

"We've met before," said Waspell. "Rostam's been a busy boy in the week since we first met."

Betty was still on her feet, looking from Waspell by the door to Millie, who now had her hands cuffed behind her.

"I don't understand what's happening. Who are you people?" asked Betty.

"My name is Tina Waspell. I don't know who you think these two are, but you can bet your bottom dollar that whoever that is exactly who they're not. Take a piece of advice from a woman who's got a few years on you: don't stand up for losers."

The cops had now marched Millie the long way around the conference table, past Betty and Tina, and were waiting by the doors.

"Take her to the elevators. I'll be with you in a moment. I just need to have a quick word with Rostam. Betty, you can stay if you'd like."

Rostam wanted to chase down Millie's bodyguards but decided it would be counterproductive.

Betty was on her feet, caught between conflicting desires and the frustration of sudden powerlessness.

"I'm gonna speak to our security before anything else happens," said Betty, on her feet and looking confused. "You can wait for me, whoever you are."

Tina Waspell had already walked to the head of the table, opposite the television screen, and sat down.

"Nice view you have here. Your head of security, O'Malley, worked for us before he took this retirement job. You'll find him just outside."

If it is possible to pirouette with murderous intent, that is what Betty did before leaving. Tina Waspell's smirk was the loudest thing left in the room.

"The view is an optical illusion," said Rostam. "Take a walk on that lawn if you don't believe me."

"I'd make some people happy if I turned into the largest roadkill on Liberty Street in a century," said Tina, smoothing her skirt over her knee. "But I'm not in the happy-making industry. My business is the security of this country, Rostam."

"Is that why you keep railroading the civil liberties of citizens?"

Waspell rolled her eyes. "We don't have long before Betty comes back in here. Anything you'd like to ask me?"

"Why have you arrested Millie? You must know she's not involved in money laundering. Or anything else for that matter."

"Unlike her ex-husband."

"If you had any proof against me, you'd have thrown away the key long ago. You haven't, because there isn't any. So, unless you're planning to start manufacturing evidence, get off our case."

"You talk tough for a man with very few cards to play."

"If I hold so few cards, why am I a free man?"

Waspell inhaled so hard her cheeks hollowed out and she widened her eyes.

"Free - is that what you think you are? Did you choose to go to London? To Indonesia? To Japan? Did you lock yourself out of your crypto wallet? Did you get Millie thrown out of her industry and into handcuffs? If that's freedom, I'm gonna campaign to have it rebranded."

"Now I'm getting lectures from a renegade."

Waspell let that sit a minute.

"I let you go the last time because I wanted to know who you were going to meet and what was going to happen."

Rostam opened his mouth.

"Shush, Rostam. Listen. What I need from you is the evidence to lock up Theo McNamara. Help me with that and your problems go away. This is what I propose. You have forty-eight hours to come back to me. I'm keeping Millie safe and sound until then, but you won't hear from her. The sooner you come back and persuade me, the sooner she'll be back home with Celia."

"And what if you don't like what I bring you?"

"Make sure I do and you won't need to worry."

Silence stretched out. Rostam tried to subtract rage from his thought process. He'd got all the way back to Millie's side just for Tina Waspell to separate them again. Conflicting thoughts rolled around his brain, roiled by resentment of this woman. It wasn't the memory of the terrifying ice bath, or even Millie's arrest, though both were bad enough on their own. What was least tolerable was her projection of confidence and cleverness. *You think everything is gonna fall into your lap, courtesy of bullying Rostam James.*

"Do I get to ask a question?"

"I'll answer any question you have, so long as I want to answer it."

"Why should I believe you?"

Waspell laughed, a surprisingly deep and likeable sound.

"You're not impressed by my back door access to anywhere you go?"

"A cardboard business card isn't exactly an RSA key."

"I'll tell you what, Rostam. Ask your friend Betty."

"She doesn't know you at all."

"She didn't. Wait for her here. You've got forty-eight hours. Call me or lose me forever, sweetheart."

Tina Waspell stood up and for a moment Rostam feared she was going to blow him a kiss.

A moment after she left, Betty came back in.

"What the hell, Rostam?"

"I don't think I've heard you swear before."

"I haven't had a former colleague and present friend arrested in front of my eyes before."

"Can you tell me anything about the people who turned up?" asked Rostam. You were gone a while."

"Only that they are clued into the top of this place. O'Malley is the head of security and he told me that Waspell woman can do what she likes. IRS."

Rostam's brain flashed red. *IRS? So that's her angle.*

"O'Malley's an important guy himself," continued Betty, not sure what what had just happened - "she was being shitty calling this a retirement job. O'Malley reports directly to the governor and the governor gives Waspell carte blanche."

Betty was slumped in her chair. She looked completely different to the poised career woman who had greeted them earlier.

"I'm sorry, Betty," said Ramon. "I hoped we'd be doing you a solid coming to you."

"You're going to need evidence for that story of yours. Maybe just focus on getting Millie out."

"Millie isn't guilty of anything and Waspell knows it. She's just leverage being used against me."

"And what have you done?"

"Honestly, nothing illegal. But I'll tell you one thing. Waspell is not going to get away with all of this. I've gotta get going Betty. None of this should blow back on you. I'll make you one promise. If I can get this fixed, I'll make sure you're filled in as soon as possible."

"Thanks Rostam. And good luck," said Betty, but in a voice so quiet he had to imagine it as much as hear it.

Chapter Sixty

The big hand on the gigantic stone ornamental clock across Liberty St hadn't reached 11 when Rostam stepped onto the sidewalk. The atmosphere in the corridors on the way out was electric compared to the way in. An arrest on the premises! Gala day at the office.

Millie's arrest struck deep. Rostam tried not to visualise what might be happening. He failed. Millie in a holding cell with felons from the streets. Millie in a windowless cell in solitary. Millie refusing to answer repeated questions from Waspell's minions. Millie submerged in cold water.

Rostam snapped out of it. If Waspell wanted him tracked she could have it done. But why would she bother? She had him on an invisible string now. Best to stick to first principles. There was a CVS next to Starbucks on Fulton St. He headed there to buy a burner.

The memory of the walk in the other direction, less than ninety minutes before, mocked him, as he barged past pedestrians, muffled against the cold in their winter coats. What problems were weighing them down? Everyone in Manhattan seemed miserable, apart from two middle aged black women swapping life stories, laughing loudly waiting for a green light on the crossing of Nassau and John. Rostam resented everyone, even the laughing women. An entrepreneur was still roasting chestnuts on his hotdog stand, a month too late for Christmas. That aroma on a cold day was the smell of Rostam's Manhattan infancy. Today the cloud of nutty vapor nauseated him as he pushed the door of the CVS.

Prepaid cells in blister packs stood on a rotating rack, between cut-price plastic sunglasses and low-octane sex toys. He grabbed a prepaid iPhone and paid the $299 before sales tax with McNamara's credit card.

Rostam checked his watch. Wednesday just started in Tokyo. Hard luck Jiro. Having a photographic memory for phone numbers came in handy on the run. He typed in the fifteen digits he needed and started walking North. The phone rang and rang and then went to Japanese voicemail.

He's probably asleep. Wake up, Jiro. WAKE UP!

The cell in Rostam's hand blurted out the Apple signature ringtone. The number began 81.

"Jiro?"

"Who is this?"

A quiet, distant, mumble.

"Rostam. Jiro?"

"Rostam?" A series of rasping coughs. "I figured this would be you. What's up?"

"Satoshi needs to make up his mind if he wants to stop Theo McNamara."

"What would you like from him?"

"Connections between McNamara, Loeb, Iran. Anything that links him to political contributions. A journalist here has been working on the story. With Satoshi's extranonce trail, it could solve everything. With that I can get things moving. Without it, I don't want to think about it."

"Send me the story and I'll do what I can."

"This time over-promise, then over-deliver."

Jiro chuckled.

"Sure, Rostam. You following markets?"

"I've been busy."

"There's a digital smash going on. Everything down, apart from the dollar backed stablecoins. Not a good time for the speculators. Speaking of which, your pal Spider was found dead this morning. Someone ran his scooter off the road."

Rostam didn't have time to feel sad.

"Spare a thought for the widows and orphans Spider has been manipulating," he said.

Rostam hung up. His Mom made a virtue of not carrying her cell at work. Rostam had grown up with it. *I can't tell the kids to keep their fingers off their idiot screens if I'm always on it.* Would she have made an exception for this? Had Hosein got to her already? They had to meet in person but getting a teacher out of a New York public school during the day was harder than jumping the queue for the Staten Island Ferry. He typed in an SMS.

I'LL BE OUTSIDE SCHOOL AT LUNCH.

He dived into Fulton St subway station and caught the A train.

Chapter Sixty-One

Maryam James had taught math at the same high school since dropping out of her PhD programme. The kids there were smart, poor, and trouble. If they couldn't see why something was going to work for them, they couldn't see the point.

Staff turnover was high. The school attracted a lot of ambitious young teachers who figured they could keep the kids under control, only to leave defeated: some almost straight away, some after toughing out an academic year or two, like servicemen boasting of dangerous overseas tours. Those that stayed were often the thickest skinned, which was good for discipline, but not necessarily the quality of teaching.

Maryam managed to achieve the near impossible, distant enough from the kids to keep discipline, without the carapace of indifference which deprived students of due care and attention. She had made an exception for Rostam. He was the best math student in her class by a mile and she never gave him a single break in class. It was tough on him, but she'd explained: *You got three years in this place. I'm here for the rest of my life. I've gotta be tough on you or I'm finished.* Fourteen years after graduating high school, Rostam had mostly forgiven her.

The school building was in the higher reaches of the Upper West Side: dappled grey bricks, cream doorways, and window frames on the corner of Convert Avenue. In Europe it would be unremarkable. In Manhattan it looked like a medieval castle.

The school bell was ringing for lunch period as Rostam approached. Nothing on his phone from Mom. He leaned against the tall grey post which did triple duty: dangling traffic lights across the intersection, pedestrian lights on the sidewalk and street signs across from the school and kicked the toes of his creps against its base. It didn't make him any less cold but helped with frustration.

Five minutes passed. Then ten. Rostam's hope turned sour and repeated on him, leaving a sour taste at the back of his throat. He checked his cell yet again.

"Stop staring at the idiot screen!" snapped his Mom.

Rostam jumped.

"How did you get over here so fast? There was nobody outside a second ago."

"Spend less time in cyberspace, more time in reality and you'll get better at noticing."

Teenage Rostam hoped his Mom would become less pedagogical as she grew older. Adult Rostam had reconciled.

"Love you too, Mom."

"How did it go?"

"Disaster."

Rostam recapped the events of the morning. His Mom listened without asking a single question.

"You don't seem surprised."

"*Junam*, I grew up in Iran under the Shah. I've lived in a foreign country for forty years. I don't expect authorities to behave well."

"Of course. No-one does."

Mom put her hand on his arm.

"Oh, Rostam, it's different for you. You *think* you don't trust the authorities, but deep down you suspect they're probably ok. That's alright: I take it as a compliment. You've grown up in a world that makes sense, under authorities that didn't seek to actively destroy you. I didn't. It's the difference between thinking something is true and knowing it. I've met too many people like your Tina Waspell to be shocked."

Rostam wasn't going to debate the point.

"So, what can I do to help, *junam*?"

"I need the evidence against McNamara and Loeb. Did Hosein bring you the files?"

Maryam fished a USB stick out of her coat pocket. "You must have made a good impression on him. He tells me this is the biggest story he ever had. And the most dangerous. Don't let him down."

"I'll do my best." A thought struck Rostam. "What job did Millie go for?"

"She didn't say, jun-am. Is it important now?"

"Maybe. Where's Celia?"

"The nursery's across the street. Don't fret. I'll bring her home. See you at four."

"I've barely seen her for the past fortnight."

"You've been globetrotting, and the job's not done."

"All I need now is to think. Celia is great for the brain cells.Am I gonna need ID to get access over there?"

Maryam grabbed her son's jacket in her fist and pulled, so that he had to bend over smartly to avoid it ripping. When he reached her, she kissed him hard on both cheeks.

"I knew you'd pull a stunt like this *kuchaloo* so I told them not to be surprised if you turned up. It's over there."

She physically turned Rostam around and pointed at a sign twenty yards past the intersection.

"Hamilton Heights Preschool. They put them down for a nap around midday so don't be surprised if she's grouchy."

"Thanks, Mom. See you back home."

There was a bench of chipped, black-painted steel on the sidewalk. Rostam sat down, hunched against the cold, and plugged Hosein's USB stick into his laptop. Scrolling through were page after page of donations to elections and causes. Bulletpoint by bulletpoint, Hosein showed how a web of optically unconnected SuperPACs were all funding similar causes, and how Theodore McNamara was at the heart of them, but without the hard evidence to prove it. The Vice President featured heavily. Lobbying around the new SEC chair. Any number of local elections, congressional seats, even two gubernatorial races. Rostam forgot about the cold as he kept reading. In aggregate this added up to a well-funded campaign to change both financial regulation and the political climate of the USA. With hard evidence, it was dynamite. Without, just a colossal lawsuit. Rostam connected his laptop to the burner signal and emailed everything over Tor to Jiro. He sent an accompanying text:

IF THIS DOESN'T PERSUADE SATOSHI TO STEP IN, HE CAN CONCEDE DEFEAT TO HIS OLD PAL THEO RIGHT NOW.

Nothing to do but wait. Rostam walked across to Celia's nursery.

Chapter Sixty-Two

The entrance to the crèche was covered in colourful artwork and warnings. DON'T MAKE CHILDREN BREATHE YOUR SMOKE and CARE FOR OUR STAFF - THEY CARE FOR YOUR KIDS, interspersed with splashes of paint on pieces of card and artists' signatures, written on by carers, in the bottom right-hand corner of each. *Every child a Rembrandt*, thought Rostam, before admitting to himself he thought every scribble Celia did was fantastic.

The intercom at the door had multiple buttons, one for each age group, but with the rooms defined by characters from kids' movies. Rostam had to choose between Cheshire Cat, Shrek, Dorothy and Pumba.

"I'm here for Celia James," he said into a one-way video screen, wondering what his face must look like as he crowded the intercom. "I'm her Dad. My Mom dropped her off with you this morning."

The intercom crackled back at him with the occasional distant children's shrieks in the background. He was about to try again when an impotently hostile voice spoke:

"I've got your name here, Mr James. Just wait, we'll bring Celia to you."

There were signs saying NO PHONES but Rostam decided to catch up on Jiro's market update over the cellular network anyway. He inputted his fourteen-digit key - a nonsense series of punctuation unless you knew that each comma, apostrophe, ampersand and the rest denoted a prime number between 100 and 1000 in a cryptogram Rostam had devised as a Christmas present for his Mom in his teenage prodigy years. How long would it take Theo to track down a new cell number? *No matter - speed is the fourth dimension of cryptography. This will all be over one way or the other before they hack into this cell.*

He'd only just finished when the rattle of chains preceded the door being pushed open. Celia was in the arms of a smiling, large, brown haired woman with Sian on her name tag and rainbow-coloured socks on her feet.

"I need ID before I can pass her over, Mr James," she said, a total absence of apology in her body language.

"Daddy!" screamed Celia, squirming in Lisa's arms in her desperation to break free.

Rostam put his hand into his breast pocket and felt two passports nestled together. *FFS. What is she gonna think if she sees me shuffling passports from two different countries?* Rather than hesitate he pulled out one at random and showed her the ID page.

"Thanks," she said, and placed Celia on the ground. Rostam took back the passport in his right hand after sweeping his daughter off the ground. "She slept for half an hour at naptime."

"I'll tell her a few Dad jokes. That'll send her back to sleep soon enough."

Sian stared at Rostam blankly.

He reached under Celia's arms and lifted her smoothly up to sit on his shoulders.

"I guess we'll go to see if that playground in the top left-hand corner of Central Park is still there, huh?" he said to his daughter, happily burbling away, and pulling at his hair.

Rostam looked over to Sian to see if she could confirm but the carer had silently closed the door and disappeared.

"It's just you and me, kid," he continued, hoping he wouldn't be able to say the same by the end of the day, and headed south on Convert Avenue to the playground.

The storefronts were higher class than they had been when Rostam went to school, but this part of the city was never going to be a second Park Avenue. Tailors, launderettes, coffee shops, accountancy firms, ambulance chasing lawyers, a cannabis dispensary, grocers, and liquor stores. Reflected in the window he could see Celia, beaming away and rocking from side to side.

Waiting for the green light to cross into the Park, Rostam marshalled his thoughts. Dread promised to come back to him by six pm that evening. He'd see what Mom could dig up when she got back from school at five. The unanswerable question was Japan. Would Satoshi come through? Something told him that Tina would positively enjoy keeping Millie in custody overnight. Hee needed to get her out today, which meant finding a plan B.

The playground was quiet. Temperature was barely above zero, and it was termtime. An ancient Chinese grandmother and a trio of Hispanic nannies were the only other adults, their charges on baby swings and a one storey plastic climbing frame at the other end of the playground. An undersized peloton of Central Park's frustrated distance cyclists whistled past. It seemed crazy anyone had the peace of mind to do something as pointless as ride round and round the Park.

"This surface was hard tarmac in my day," Rostam said to Celia, after depositing her on the spongy playground floor surfacing and following her to a large inverted teacup of moulded fuschia plastic.

"Daddy push!" commanded Celia, waiting for him to tip her inside.

The teacup rotated more quickly than he liked.

"It makes me dizzy looking at you," he said, but the moment he grabbed the rim to slow it down Celia complained.

"Faster! Faster!"

"Whatever you say," said Rostam.

"Faster Daddy! You've got no time to waste," said a Southern, male voice just behind him. Rostam whirled around as fast as his daughter.

Carl Force's bright blue eyes looked back at him.

Chapter Sixty-Three

"It's good to see you with your daughter," said Force. "So many divorced men end up alone. How's Millie doing?"

Rostam looked around the playground. Force was the only new arrival. In the cold white Manhattan January sunlight, he looked even more wolfish, and his tan more fake.

"I'd ask how you knew I was here but - "

" - but you've learned not to ask stupid questions. Good for you. You haven't been keeping me in touch with your movements." Force tut-tutted. "Bad boy."

Rostam took another look around the park. There were surely too many people for Celia to be in danger.

"Daddy. Push!" Celia's momentum had slowed until her yellow rubber boots protruded from the teapot either side of Rostam. Her features contracted into a tiny handful of squiggles.

"You should get to it, Rostam. This little lady is used to quality service."

Don't talk about my daughter, you psycho, thought Rostam.

He was glad he hadn't said it out loud. Force would be more comfortable in the register of obscenities and threats. Best to keep the conversation polite. He leaned down, kissed Celia on the forehead, and gave her a whirl. The moment she started to move her features expanded back to their normal positions.

"Glad to see you've changed your boots, Carl. What do you want from me?"

"What you found out on your travels."

"You first. Tell me what you know already, so we can both save time, and I can go back to playing with my child."

"You sound hostile, Rostam."

"Of course I'm fuc-." Rostam looked at his daughter - *can she hear me swear while she's whirling around like suds revolving around the sinkhole?* "You've forgotten Ahmad Jamalzhad."

Rostam leaned down to slow the momentum of the upended teacup. Surely the girl had had enough?

"Faster Daddy faster!" came the command, as soon as it came to a halt. He spun the cup counterclockwise.

"I can see you've been waiting a while to get that out of your system. Here's something you should forget. Your little Asian tour. Spider, and your Japanese friends. Don't try to recycle anything you think you learned over there."

"Tell me. Was Spider part of your organization?"

Force laughed. "Oh - you're already talking about Spider in the past tense?"

The teacup had come to a half again and this time Celia wasn't demanding another push. Her arms were held out and Rostam leaned down to scoop her up. For a sweet moment she clutched his head tight to her and he felt moisture welling up behind his eyes. *I'm not crying in front of this jerk.* It was only a moment of sentimentality.

"Daddy. Swings."

"Ok honey. Just give Daddy a moment to talk to his friend, ok?"

Rostam levered his daughter around so that she could sling her legs around his neck. For whatever reason, this made him feel he had the upper hand on Force.

"What is it exactly you want from me?"

"Two things. First tell us what Zadi had to say."

"He told me patriotism is the last refuge of a scoundrel. You're not the only customer for what I've got to sell."

Rostam shook his head, getting his thoughts in order.

"I'm not saying I'm not going to help you. I even want to, if only to get back a bit of peace. I need to pull a few things together first and my priority is sitting on my shoulders right now, staring longingly at those swings over there. Grandma looks like she's about had enough of the baby swing, and a vacancy on one of those is worth a pair of front row tickets at the Knicks. So, with the greatest of respect, Carl, you can back off and let me come back to you in my own sweet time."

Force stuck his hands in his pockets, leaned back and laughed at the sky.

"I wasn't gonna do this but - oh well." He pulled a cell out of his pocket and hit call. "There's someone who wants to talk to you."

Rostam took the cell. He didn't need to guess who was on the phone.

"Hi, Theo."

"Hello to you too," came the old man's voice out of the earpiece, with a cigarette-cured chuckle. "If Carl has called, you must have decided to cause problems."

Rostam said nothing, keeping an eye on his daughter running around the roundabout. "I hear you've visited my old British friend in Japan. If you think anything he could do would make any difference, you're too late. You should be smart, like your ex-wife, and ask me for a job instead."

Rostam took a second to grasp what he had heard.

McNamara chuckled.

"Do you need me to repeat myself?" he asked.

"What?" said Rostam.

"Millie was very happy to tell us all about your conversations with Satoshi. And now she's been arrested. Still, I'm sure you can bail her out when the time comes. I'd tell you to be more careful next time, but I don't think there's going to be one for you."

The line went dead, but Rostam kept the cell to his ear while he thought things through. Then he threw it high in the air in an arc over Carl Force's head.

"Catch, Carl," he said, "we're done here." he said. Rostam smiled to see the tough guy almost trip as he turned on his heel. Celia ran past and Rostam swept her into his arms and walked towards the swings. There were three in a row: one for older kids, one like the bucket seat of a miniature racing car, and only the one at the end with a safety cage for smallies. Could what Theo had said about Millie be true? Rostam had to take comfort in the fact that Theo was a confirmed liar.

As he lowered a delighted Celia into the safety cage, he saw Force had already disappeared. *One down, lots more to go.*

Rostam liked to joke with his Mom that Celia's appetite for being pushed on the swing reminded him of Goldbach's conjecture. Nobody can prove there isn't an even number greater than two that isn't the sum of two primes for the simple reason that there is always a higher even number. Just so, Rostam would tell Maryam, the maximum number of acceptable pushes on the swing had not yet been calculated because it had never yet been reached.

Breathing in the cold January air of Central Park, keeping warm by using alternate hands to push his three-year-old. Shades of the past fortnight passed before his imagination. Who did he need to worry about the most? McNamara knew Tina Waspell had picked up Millie, but Tina claimed to be after Theo. And why hadn't Millie told him who she had gone to work for? Nausea started to swell within Rostam's stomach, like soluble aspirin fizzing in a glass. Is that why she'd asked so many questions about Spider and Satoshi - to pass it on?

A blowsy older white woman with masses of black frizzy hair pushed a grumpy faced five-year-old in a buggy up to the racing car seat. She nodded at Rostam as she hauled in the boy.

"You are too old for this," she said to her child. "These swings are for babies like this one. You're twice her size. How old is she, mister?"

Rostam shook his head.

"Three. Four next September."

"Ya hear that ya rascal? You'll be six before this one's three. And here's me pushing you like a pudding."

Rostam smiled noncommittally and returned to his thoughts. What if Jiro came back with nothing?

"Higher, Daddy! Higher!"

"This is as high as it gets honey. If I push you any harder, you'll go over the top."

"Higher! Higher!"

"They build these swings special so that can't happen," said the dark-haired woman, pointing at the bolts on the supporting bar.

He switched to pushing Celia just with his left hand, while navigating the iPhone screen with his right. Jiro had replied.

SATOSHI IS IN. FILES TO FOLLOW.

A sense of triumph flooded Rostam's system and settled his stomach. Millie can't have known who was offering her the job.

Let's find out what Mom's got on the SuperPACs and we've got the ball game.

He checked his watch.

"Hey Celia, you swing monster. You wanna long walk down 8th on Daddy's shoulders or do we take the subway?"

"Shoulders! Shoulders!"

"Ask a stupid question," said the woman to his left.

"You can say that again, sister."

"Ask a stupid question."

Rostam took a quick look as he laughed. That'd teach him to take people for granted. He hooked Celia out of the swing and launched her up onto his shoulders.

"Hey ho hey ho, it's back to home we go."

Chapter Sixty-Four

"How did it go, Mom?"

Rostam found Maryam drinking tea on the sofa in the living room. She gently tossed the remote control at him.

"You gonna keep my granddaughter happy, or what?"

Rostam found *Sesame Street* and had a moment of relief when he saw Celia's face relax into the absorption.

"Gadun?" she demanded.

"Hang on, little one."

Rostam turned back to Maryam.

"You first," she said. More developments since I saw you outside school?"

"McNamara sent his goon to warn me off. They think they've won. He knows about Millie. Claims she wanted to work with him."

"You what?" Maryam's lips compressed and her eyes seemed suddenly double their normal size.

"Doesn't want Satoshi spilling his secrets. He sounded confident. Whatever he's trying to pull, he thinks he's there."

"Is he right?"

"It depends on timing. The first thing I need to do is get Millie out. Find out what she thinks is going on. Then we'll see who's winning."

"No way that woman is working with McNamara," said Maryam with absolute certainty.

Rostam picked through his pockets, struggling to remove Waspell's business card from his inside pocket without spilling the rest of its contents: his collection of plastic, from English pre-paid debit card to Theo's limitless AmEx; passports; a cigarette lighter he hadn't had the opportunity to use for days. He found the card and rang.

A male voice picked up on the fifth ring.

"What?"

"I want to speak to Tina Waspell."

"Who does?"

"Rostam. Rostam James."

Scuffle, scratch, amplified plastic noises.

Is this a power-play? Or is someone keeping an eye on Waspell? If she goes quiet on me now, who do I go to for Millie?

The certainty of a meeting was picked apart to reveal the chasm of endless possibilities beneath, each one better suited to Waspell than Rostam.

Keep calm. These people are bullies. Don't let them smell fear on you.

Sharp footsteps. A hand adjusting position over the mouthpiece. Indistinct, angry, staccato chat. Hand peeled away. Clear.

"Hello, Rostam. Fancy you calling so soon."

Don't let her rile you.

"I've got what you need. I want Millie back. Where do we meet?"

"The Federal building on Hudson Square. Millie and I are having an interesting conversation, and we're not quite finished. When will I see you?"

Rostam checked the time.

"Half an hour. Call it 8.30."

"I'll have someone meet you at the front desk."

Chapter Sixty-Five

The taxicab smelled of spicy food, overlaid with an aerosol that blended pine air freshener and baby sick. As it jerked its way down W 15th and then turned left into 7th, Rostam's emotions slopped around his body like water inside an open glass.

He had walked past the Federal Homeland Building on Varick Street a thousand times growing up without giving it a thought. Three featureless floors in a long, flat building: the Federal Government's utilitarian architect flipping the bird to the Manhattan skyline. Only cement blocks scattered about the sidewalk to dissuade car bombers suggested anything interesting about the building. The decor was that of a hospital in a state with zero income tax. *What would I have thought of Tina Waspell if she walked past me in the street on her lunch break? Nothing at all - she looks like Martha Stewart would if her hairdresser went on strike.*

There were no pedestrians. The buzz of Greenwich Village even on a Monday night never felt more elsewhere to Rostam. Few offices above them had lights on. One NYPD cop stood by the front door, wrapped up in a navy parka, bored as hell and carrying a semi-automatic weapon. The ground floor was lit inside. It struck Rostam that once he walked in there, there was nobody with the power to come and get him out. He'd just have to make sure he got through to Waspell. The guard showed no signs of interest as Rostam walked up.

"I guess we missed normal business hours. You guys close at five?"

"On the dot."

"I gotta appointment inside. 8.30pm. Tina Waspell," said Rostam to the silent cop. "Any problem with me going in?"

"No problem, for me. They'll search you inside."

Rostam grabbed the aluminium handle of the glass fronted door and pulled hard. There was a sucking sound, as though the air didn't want to be disturbed. Brown linoleum curled up a couple of inches before where the door began.

"I guess I'll see you on the way out," said Rostam to the cop as they entered.

"Sure."

The cop interrupted his laconic gum chewing to spit on the ground. Rostam was running through the pitch he was going to make to Tina Waspell. The door slammed shut behind him with a jerk, as though the building had sucked it in.

"Hello, Mr James," came a high-pitched, amused man's voice. "Hands out wide like a good boy." Rostam turned around. Towering over him stood Tina's smiling albino.

"For a big guy you're good at popping up unexpectedly," said Rostam. "You think I'm trying to smuggle weapons into a Federal building?"

"No harm in keeping things business-like," replied the albino, patting Rostam down thoroughly, but without aggression. "I'm not gonna put you through the metal detector. The machines they've got here are for show."

"You don't wanna apologize for what happened last time we met?"

"Nah. I don't remember nothing. After you, lover boy," said the albino, gesturing forwards. "Second floor." The guard walked up to the low turnstile, just above knee height, that government employees had to negotiate every day on their way into the office and waved a plastic card at it. The squeak of their shoes along the linoleum floor reminded Rostam of high school: hall-passes, massed lockers, smell of cleaning products and body odour, low-level apprehension blended with gallons of boredom.

"We're the only people in the building, looks like," said Rostam, not expecting a reply.

"Nobody joins the government because they want to work the night shift. Overtime's for shit," replied the albino, with a smile but no laugh.

"Is Millie James upstairs?"

The guard didn't reply but pressed the elevator button. It arrived with a muted *ding* which only made the corridor seem more deserted. The back panel of the elevator showed they made an odd couple in the dull mirrored back panel: tall, slender Rostam looked short and skinny next to the mass of the guard, almost a foot taller and a hundred pounds heavier.

Rostam enumerated the strategies Waspell was deploying to strengthen her position: kidnapping Millie, her mysterious knowledge of his whereabouts, the deserted Federal building, reusing a guard he knew positively enjoyed hurting his victims. She was the supreme example of someone who tried to load every dice in her favour. The living antithesis to math, a world where everyone must play by the rules. Still, his plan should work, so long as she was chasing Theo.

"Turn right and straight to the end. Corner office."

The guard waited for Rostam to precede him out of the elevator. The silence of the building coalesced into a whirlpool of furious hissing in Rostam's ears.

Is Millie gonna be there? What if Waspell just refuses to let her go? What if she just takes the information and keeps us both?

He felt defenceless, out of his depth, befuddled. He passed his reflection in the glass of an office door, was surprised to see an optimistic, calm expression on his own face, and they were in the room.

It had windows over Varick and King Streets, the view segmented by ugly wide brimmed plastic blinds. A short conference table stood in the middle of the room, with four chairs on casters either side. There was a smell of stale coffee and polish.

Tina Waspell sat on her own on the far side of the table. She did not stand up or offer to shake hands.

"You moved fast. What do you have for me?"

Rostam sat down across from her. The guard stayed outside the door.

"Where's Millie?"

"She's in the building. This is show and tell. You first."

"You want Theo McNamara, right?"

Tina recrossed her legs.

"We have different understandings of show and tell," she said.

"Come on, Tina. You thought I was working for McNamara, and you waterboarded me over it. Then you find out I'm his victim, and you decide to threaten the mother of my child to make me cough up info. If it weren't so messed up, it would be funny. Have you asked yourself why your bosses are so keen for you to nail the old man?"

"Stop posturing, Rostam."

Tina had her full Tennessee headmistress voice on. She revelled in the asymmetry of power. The kind of person for whom other people's pain was ammunition. Someone who would find it amusing to leave a hose running in her garden in drought season as her neighbours' lawn burned.

"You don't understand how big McNamara's plans are, but I'll tell you what. Give me Millie, and twenty-four hours, and I'll hand him over to you gift-wrapped."

Tina said nothing, but kept staring. It was an effective interrogation technique. Despite everything, Rostam felt a desire to impress her.

"A taster. Theo was working with Zadi. The two of them met in Davos along with representatives from China. I have photographs of them together, and you can use electronic surveillance to prove it."

"Good." Waspell nodded. "You've done good. That is something. But tell me - why did Theo try to blow him up?"

Rostam coughed, a gentle, retiring sound, like an audience member at a recital between movements, who doesn't need to clear his throat but thinks it would be rash to pass up the opportunity entirely.

"Theo and his allies thought they were being smart, recruiting the Revolutionary Guards to join them in their support of crypto. McNamara worked on the principle that his enemy's enemy must be his friend. He was half right. There are strong voices within the Iranian leadership who want to use crypto to destroy the power of the US dollar...but not Zadi. He just wanted to use crypto as leverage to get the US back into the joint plan with Iran. He wanted to build bridges, not blow them up. Once McNamara realized this he spread word in Tehran about what Zadi was up to, and it was the hardliners who used that as their excuse to try assassination."

Waspell leaned forward. It was the first time she'd forgotten to play it cool.

"You can prove this?"

Rostam carried on as though he hadn't been interrupted.

"That's not all. Cantillon and two others at the top of Loeb are working with McNamara, and so are the heads of two other investment banks. The libertarian influence runs deep. I'll soon have blockchain transaction evidence about what they've been up to. It'll stand up in front of a criminal jury. Or a court martial. So maybe now would be a good time to let Millie go."

Waspell raised a hand and ran her fingers through her hair, paused, and then repeated the action. A strand remained out of place, hanging by her large rectangular grown spectacles. She looked less composed than at any time Rostam had seen her before.

"Why do you ask about my superiors?"

"McNamara is ramping bitcoin and funnelling the profits into Alt-Lib SuperPAC. You've never heard of ALSP, but it's changing your world. His big project is to replace the head of the SEC and take charge of crypto, and then the Fed. But he won't leave the heads of the security agencies intact. You're being used as a pawn, Special Investigator Waspell. Your boss is using you as a shield. Bring down McNamara and he or she will be pleased. Lose, and you'll carry the can."

Tina Waspell looked as though if she gargled and spat, poisoned darts would fly out of her mouth. Rostam widened his eyes.

"You're IRS, right? You need to see the financial trail. It's lucky I'm being so nice to you. Bring me Millie now, and I'll get you what you need. If we get going, she might see her daughter before bedtime."

Rostam watched the woman across the table think through her options. Tina Waspell would make a good poker player. Only the strand of hair betrayed her.

"I owe you an apology, Rostam. I came on strong because I assumed you were part of McNamara's organization. You've proved me wrong."

She reached out a hand. Rostam looked at it but didn't shake.

"You're an end justifies the means kind of person," he said. "I have no time for that."

Tina took back her hand.

"You seem very confident your ex-wife is playing on your team. She didn't have much to say for herself."

Rostam smiled back at her. After Theo and Carl, he wasn't about to discuss Millie with this woman.

"We have a deal?" he said.

Tina nodded. She stood and walked around the table to the door, where she whispered to her guard.

"Rostam. Today you are her get-out-of-jail free card. Wait downstairs. Millie will be brought to you."

Tina's Tennessee accent became pinched and exaggerated as she spoke with the frustration of a venomous child, desperate to poke mice at the back of the cage, who finds her pointed stick is too short.

Rostam stood up, leaving all his tension behind him like a scarf dropping to the floor. Without speaking another word, he walked back to the elevator.

Chapter Sixty-Six

Rostam hadn't had time to think of the future since Lake Shore Drive, and it was still hard to imagine one, squeaking down the musty, institutional brown corridor decorated only by Homeland Security fliers, posters and notice boards.

This is where hopes of the land of the free come to die, he thought with the intensity brought when hard anger meets fear. There was no sign of the albino guard. *Where would they keep Millie?* Different scenarios of nightmare outcomes flickered through his head like images on a kineograph.

Nobody was visible on the ground floor, not even a security guard. Only the NYPD officer left on the doorstep outside, whose image wobbled through the door as he shuffled his feet. Distant hum of traffic - a reminder of normal life carrying on elsewhere. Occasional pedestrians talking on the sidewalk. Inside squeaks, the lapping and sucking of water in slowly cooling radiators, noises only noticeable because they interrupt silence. The bell of an elevator arriving.

Rostam spun around to see Millie walking towards him from the elevator bank: steps rapid, face pale, clothes immaculate, no handbag. He strode towards her and opened his arms. She came in for a hug. The smell of her Chanel perfume and brand of shampoo was as familiar to him as toasted bagel. She pushed away before he had time to say what was on his mind.

"Those bastards are gonna pay for this. Let's get out of here."

The cop guarding the front door jumped slightly as Rostam and Millie bundled onto the step.

"Woah. You guys done?"

There was no sign of him reaching for his gun, or even for the walkie-talkie hissing and grumbling on his left shoulder. He looked like someone on a dull assignment whose significance he didn't know, hoping for the sound of the going-home bell. Rostam sensed Millie was about to verbally unload and grabbed her hand to stop it.

"All done here. The others shouldn't be long. Night, officer," he said, pulling Millie behind him.

They turned left on Varick Street heading towards Seventh Avenue.

"Are you ok? Should we grab food? Coffee?"

"Get me back to Celia right now." The fury radiated off Millie in waves. 'I've been locked in a room with that Waspell woman all day." Millie stopped walking and began to cry. Not soft tears of sorrow, but hard, angry rage. Rostam knew better than to try to offer comfort. "Just tell me we're gonna get even for all this. I can't believe it. Marched out of Betty's office like a criminal. Didn't arrest me, just took me down the precinct, took away my shit, left me in a holding cell for hours then delivered me to that place. Nobody answered any questions. I was a non-person. And for what?"

They had come to a halt opposite Shake Shack on Carmine at the beginning of Seventh Avenue. The only traffic was a pair of cabs approaching on their way north. The light on the first was off, and Rostam saw a Wall Streeter in the back seat staring at her phone as she was spirited back uptown to home. The second had its number lit up. Rostam stuck his hand in the air and it pulled over.

"Let's get back to Celia. We're better to talk on the way."

In the anonymity of the back of the cab Millie breathed more normally but sat wound up tight, legs crossed, straight back, the posture of a woman ready to leap into action. *Is this the right time to tell her we're pulling things together?*

"What did you tell that bitch to get her to let me go?" Millie turned away to look out of the window. When she spoke each word was distinct, quiet, full of venom.

"The information she needs to lock up Theo. I guess she spent her time trying to tie you to me?"

Millie snorted.

"You can be so arrogant, Rostam. You think this is all about you. The only thing you're good at is picking the wrong side."

Rostam winced. An innocent person incarcerated for the day was entitled to lash out. Millie tapped away at her phone.

Rostam spotted Waverley Place as they pushed north. The desire to say *remember our date nights there* was so strong he shut his eyes. It wasn't what Millie wanted to hear.

"Remember our date nights there?" said Millie, looking out of her window. Her right hand was pressed open, palm down, on the back seat. Rostam placed his hand on hers.

"I was just thinking that myself."

"We were different people back then," said Millie, retracting her hand. "Celia is at home with Maryam?"

"Mom took her to nursery. I picked her up. We hit the playground at the top of the park. Then guess what? Theo's killer Carl Force turned up."

"Poor Daddy."

"You may well laugh. Celia and I got the better of him."

"So, you've been playing happy families while I was locked up?"

"Happier family now you're back."

They were passing twentieth street. Rostam rapped on the Perspex screen.

"Driver, drop us here."

He held the door open for Millie and held her hand to help her over a slush puddle outside Momoya, the Japanese restaurant they'd been to often when visiting Rostam's Mom from Chicago.

"You know what I kept thinking while I was in that room?" asked Millie.

"How much you missed us?"

Millie ignored the hint.

"She kept on and on about McNamara, and money laundering, and why wouldn't I tell Loeb the truth, and why was I helping Rostam James, my knight in shining armour, who'd walked out on a decent career to be a digital warrior."

"We can talk this over later," said Rostam. "It's been a traumatic day."

"Fuck you, Rostam. What I kept thinking was, why did I put up with you in the first place? McNamara's gonna end up on top. In fact, he's already won."

They were outside the apartment block. Rostam's emotions moved from sympathy and relief to something darker.

"What do you mean?"

He remembered what McNamara had said on the phone. The look on Tina Waspell's face at the end.

"You know McNamara is a killer, right? He killed Ahmad. He's killed Spider. He probably killed Hosein's partner, Ellen. And that's just the people we know of. Has he got to you, Millie?"

Millie stared him in the eye.

"You lost the right to ask me questions when you moved out of the apartment. Go upstairs to your Mommy. I've got a call to make."

Chapter Sixty-Seven

Maryam met him at the door to the apartment, Celia wrapped around her neck like an animated comforter.

"Where's Millie, *junam*?" asked Maryam. "Everything ok?"

Rostam picked up Celia and turned her around, her chin resting on his shoulder, their cheeks pressed together. He kept his voice level.

"Everything isn't ok. Something happened in there. I'm trying to figure it out. It sounds like McNamara got to Millie somehow."

Maryam coughed out a laugh from deep in her belly. "Millie? Never. Strong like a lion, that woman. Here she is."

"Mommy!" screamed the little girl and scrambled down her grandmother like a pixie-marine on manoeuvres. Millie swept her up for a wordless embrace.

"You ok, my darling?' asked Maryam.

Millie looked over her daughter's shoulder to look first at Maryam, then Rostam, then back again.

"I'm fine, but this visit has come to an end. Sorry, Maryam. Ask your son what he's been doing. A car is coming for Celia and me. I'll let you know when you can see her next."

Millie walked into the apartment carrying her daughter.

Maryam turned to Rostam.

"What's happened here, *junam*?"

"I think I know, but there's nothing we can do about it right now. We don't want a shouting match in front of Celia. Let Millie go."

Rostam looked up at the ceiling of the corridor, and imagined he could see the moving parts of his brain projected onto the peeling cream paint. Did Hosein have enough evidence to make his story compelling?

Rostam only realized he was on his own still thinking in the hall when Millie marched past him, Celia holding her hand, refusing to leave without kissing Daddy goodbye.

"See you soon, lovely daughter," Rostam whispered in Celia's ear, and he breathed in another lungful of her sweet-smelling hair. "You're gonna have a lovely time with Mommy."

Celia squeezed her arms tight around his neck. Rostam looked over at Millie.

"You're sure you know where you're going, and who it's for?"

Millie narrowed her eyes.

"I know what I'm doing."

It was clear to Rostam now.

"You'd do better to leave Celia here."

"No chance."

"Don't make long term plans based on Theo McNamara."

In answer Millie extended her arms for Rostam to hand over their daughter. Rostam thought about everything McNamara could offer: the autonomous cars, private jet, St James's apartment, unlimited spending power. He was standing outside his Mom's rent-controlled apartment with nothing but a theory he hadn't had the chance to explain. There was no choice but to let Millie go.

He found Maryam slumped on the sofa, choking out tears, face obscured by thick, greying hair. As he stretched an arm around her shoulders, he felt her rigid torso. He put a hand over the taut muscle fibres either side of her neck and began to massage. It took several minutes for the tears to stop.

"I don't understand," said Maryam eventually. "I thought you and Millie were gonna get back together, start again. Now what?"

"I know, Mom," said Rostam, realising he had to hide his own devastation from his mother. "I'm sorry too. The fairy tale is off, but that doesn't mean we've lost. Let me turn on the TV."

CNBC was running a panel discussion on crypto regulation. VP candidate Matthew Aalen was being put forward for Senate confirmation on Friday.

"We know he's gonna be pro the crypto industry," said one talking head. "Prices stopped falling today when the President confirmed Aalen was his choice. Is the stage set for a rebound?"

Rostam hit the mute button. Maryam had come back in with small glasses of black sugary tea.

"Mom, I asked Hosein to pull his story together. Can you get him over here?"

"He doesn't like using his phone anymore. I could go over to his apartment."

"Take a cab and bring him back here when you can. It's a long shot, but with his help we can deal with this."

Maryam finished her tea, kissed him on the top of his head and disappeared into the hall.

It's not too late, thought Rostam, as he fired up his Razor Edge laptop. Midnight in New York. Hosein had had time to get his evidence in order. Jiro would be back from lunch in Tokyo, Dread perched at his end of the bar at Dick's in Chicago. *Time to go on the offensive.*

Chapter Sixty-Eight

Wednesday January 26

It was six-thirty on Wednesday morning before Rostam and Hosein finished going through evidence on ALSP.

"I'm not surprised you've been frozen out on this," said Rostam. "If McNamara knew what you had here, you'd be dead."

"I haven't told my editor the bulk of it," said Hosein. "No point. She won't publish without hard evidence. Ellen Kelly had found the missing link, but her killer stole her laptop. Once we have evidence the story will be too powerful to keep quiet."

"And if we can supply it, when will it get out? We need this public before the Senate hearing on Friday. We can always publish online, but it'll be a much bigger stink coming from the Times."

"You get me proof and I'll get it in the paper."

Chapter Sixty-Nine

"What do you have?" asked Jiro over the video conference.

"The whole network. Theo McNamara to Cantillon at Loeb to Iran to domestic terror groups to a hundred important political local elections. They've been firing money at every problem, and the biggest comes on Friday. That's when they're having their SEC chair confirmed and take control of financial regulation. Crypto has been their way to take over."

"You've seen price action the past few days."

"It's everywhere."

"Satoshi wants to talk. He's going to make a public statement and he'll do it with you."

Rostam felt a jolt of excitement through his exhaustion.

"It won't be enough without the files."

"I'm sending them to you now. You should be able to figure it out but, if not, I can help."

Rostam looked across at Hosein and mouthed, "How long?"

Hosein held up both hands with fingers outstretched, thought about it, shrugged, and whispered "maybe more".

"Ok Jiro, here's the deal. We need twelve hours here to get everything into publishable form. Best for me to have it straight here before I talk to David. Thursday will be the day."

Rostam texted Millie. "Tell McNamara I want to talk. He wins."

The reply was immediate.

WHAT DO YOU WANT FROM HIM?

"I have some questions of my own."

Twenty minutes later the reply came through.

STRAWBERRY FIELDS. MIDDAY.

Chapter Seventy

Thursday January 27

It was a bright, cold, windy Thursday when Rostam climbed out of the subway at 66 St-Lincoln Centre at 11:45. He pulled down his Cubs beanie, thrust his hands into the pockets of his Canada Goose parka, and went through plans as he walked down sixty-sixth street towards Central Park West.

Rostam crossed at sixty-ninth street and entered Central Park. It was as quiet as the park was ever likely to be during daytime. He checked his watch. 11:58. *Was Mcnamara going to show?* An older Japanese couple holding hands were the only visitors to the Imagine Mosaic: the man with wispy grey hair blown out of place by the wind, his wife with hair dyed purple, like her cool grandkids in Shibuya. They both wore Uniqlo navy padded overcoats, identical electric pink Dr Marten boots and were the same height. *There's no eccentric like a Japanese eccentric,* thought Rostam, his mind snatching at the chance to focus on something that was of zero importance to him. When he joined them at the mosaic, the Japanese man spoke to him.

"Imagine there's no countries. It's easy if you try."

Rostam was trying to remember the next line of the song when he saw Theodore McNamara walking up from West Drive on the other side of the mosaic. Adrenaline flooded his body.

"Cool idea. Not so practical at passport control," he said to the couple, who rewarded him with a high-pitched, identical giggle, before wandering off towards the Dakota, still hand-in-hand.

Rostam stood by the Imagine logo at the centre of the black and white disc and watched McNamara approach, a Giacometti mobile, all bristling steel-grey hair, long cashmere overcoat and mirrored shades.

"Thanks for coming, Theo," said Rostam.

"I should be thanking you." McNamara looked over his shoulder. "Our mutual friend Carl is here."

"Hi Rostam," came Carl Force's Arkansas drawl. Rostam didn't turn around.

"Still in town, Carl?" said Rostam, and was pleased to hear his voice was steady. "Check away."

Force patted him down.

"There's nothing I've got in my pockets to scare you," said Rostam. "We good to talk?"

The old man nodded.

"Tell me, Mr McNamara, why did you really choose me to go to London?"

McNamara pushed his sunnies back up the ridge of his nose.

"Don't want to hurt your pride, but we figured you were well placed to beat Zadi out of cover. And we were right. Afterwards you took me by surprise. Didn't expect you to keep going."

Rostam looked hard at McNamara and saw nothing but his own reflection in the old man's mirrored sunglasses.

"What did you offer Millie, once you realized threatening her wasn't going to work?"

"An opportunity. She's a simple woman. She wants to be a big crypto player, and I gave her the chance. You'd let her down so badly it made it an easy decision." McNamara cleared his throat. "I hate a sneak though, don't you? She turns on you, who knows who she'll turn on next?"

Rostam felt sick.

"What have you done to Millie? Where is she?"

"What do you care? You're divorced." McNamara reached into his pocket and took his time shaking loose a fresh Marlboro. "I'd say you lose, Rostam, but from what I've seen of you, you decided to start losing a long time ago, and have stuck to it."

A ringtone came from behind them.

"Is that your emergency phone, Carl?" asked Rostam, without turning around.

"Never mind," said McNamara. "I wanna hear what the great Satoshi said to you in Japan. He's been waiting a long time."

"Boss," called out Carl.

"Hold it, Carl," said Theo. "Come on, Rostam, we don't have long for this."

"Carl has the answer you're looking for," said Rostam. "I've been speaking to Satoshi about you. We did it on camera. Posted just now."

McNamara showed no reaction, so Rostam continued.

"Also, Hosein Dardbash's research on your SuperPAC and all the activities you've been funding. Finally got it past his editor. The Times has just made that the above-the-online-fold story."

McNamara said nothing.

"And we've just posted the extranonce files on our podcast site. Blockchain connecting you to all that activity. Thought the Senate researchers might want time to go over it before they interview your candidate for the SEC tomorrow."

McNamara took off his sunglasses and polished them with a cotton handkerchief.

"Rostam, you disappoint me. You think you're going to change anything by releasing a bit of information. Did you learn nothing from Edward Snowdon, and the Panama Papers debacle? What happened to the people they tried to embarrass? Sweet Fanny Adams."

"Boss," called out Carl Force.

McNamara was too busy imprinting his personality on Rostam through his stare.

"It's all over, Theo," said Rostam. "The crypto crash is just getting started. Satoshi's going to keep selling until there's nothing left. He's shown us everywhere you've spread your dirty money, and it isn't pretty viewing."

"I'm not a politician, said Theo. "I don't embarrass easy."

"Boss," called Carl Force again. "Look around."

McNamara pulled his gaze away from Rostam. A dozen armed police were approaching from all around, like the digits of a clock converging on the centre. Tina Waspell was approaching from Rostam's three o'clock, a badge held out before her.

"What do you all want?" demanded Theodore McNamara, his voice low, controlled, faintly exasperated.

"I'm Special Investigator Tina Waspell of the Inland Revenue Service," declared Tina, her Tennessee accent coming across strong. "Theodore McNamara, I'm arresting you on multiple counts of tax evasion."

Behind him came a cry and the sound of struggle.

Rostam turned. Tina's attention was on McNamara, but behind him Carl Force had tried to break through two cops at nine o'clock.

Now he was squirming on the ground, with one sprawled across his back, while the other fished out handcuffs.

"I've heard of you, Tina," said McNamara, with great forced calm. "You have no idea who you're accusing."

"I have every idea, Mr McNamara. We have your payroll data, and it doesn't look good for you, nor for most of your employees."

"You're arresting me for tax fraud?"

"Yes, I am. Given your financial assets it wasn't hard to persuade a New York City judge that you're a material flight risk."

Rostam felt a shocking silence grow. He looked around. The police circle was sufficiently wide to keep curious tourists away. Carl Force had stopped struggling and lay cuffed on the ground. McNamara was staring directly at Rostam. A moment passed, and the old man removed his sunglasses. In the thin bright sunshine of a New York February the lines around his eyes were frail, papery, vulnerable.

"You've put your faith in the Deep State," said Theo. "All that freedom talk your kind spout was so much bullshit."

McNamara spat at the ground, but he didn't have enough saliva to make an impression. He looked feeble and old.

"Where's Millie?" demanded Rostam.

"Why are you asking me about your ex-wife?" said McNamara.

"Tell me where she is, you old bastard."

"She's got nothing to do with me. You wanted to take care of your family, you've gone about it all wrong," McNamara called after him, as the police parted to allow Rostam to leave.

Chapter Seventy-One

Rostam sprinted to the edge of the park to W 73rd knowing there would be no taxis on Central Park West. He started speed walking north, looking over his shoulder for cabs, while pulling his cell out his pocket. He called Millie. No answer. Maryam didn't pick up either. A cab pulled over just as he was shouting into her voicemail.

"Mom, get over to the nursery right away and see if Celia is ok."

He threw himself into the back seat and bashed his knee against the miniature screen advertising Manhattan tourist attractions.

"Convent Avenue," he shouted to the driver, before realizing he hadn't hung up. Why hadn't he asked Millie where she was going the night before? What if she hadn't taken Celia to kindergarten?

Traffic on a winter Thursday heading north was terrible. At the third red light Rostam tried Maryam again but got nowhere. It occurred to him to try the nursery, but now he was only seven minutes away. What if Millie had kept Celia with her? Rostam remembered the look on Carl Force's face when he had surprised them at the playground, and then his look when kicking the drunk to pieces on the London Underground. His stomach twisted with horror.

He texted Millie.

ARE YOU OK? WHERE ARE YOU? PLEASE CALL.

The cab arrived across the road from Celia's nursery. Rostam stuffed a twenty-dollar bill into the plastic tray and bolted across the road. It seemed incredible that the street was quiet, and that klaxons weren't going off everywhere to announce an emergency.

He hit the buzzer, and couldn't stop himself doing it again and again, until a furious woman's voice came down the intercom.

"What is your problem?"

"Celia James," Rostam shouted. "I'm her father. Is she ok?"

The intercom stopped crackling. Whoever had answered must be checking. Rostam started to kick the doorstep in front of him in impotent frustration. The bolted door before him might as well have been a castle wall. The intercom came alive.

"Who is this?"

"Rostam James. This is an emergency. I need to know if she is there and safe."

"Hold on."

It went dead again.

The door opened and a cleaner came out. Rostam pushed past him and dashed up the stairs directly by the door. At the top was a safety door with a large green button to press for access. Rostam pressed the button and ran straight into an enormous security officer, who kicked his feet from under him and threw Rostam to the floor. He landed before he had time to breathe, and the shock of the last remaining air in his lungs being expelled overwhelmed the pain from cracking his nose against the floor.

"Sir, you have no business invading this kindergarten," said the security guard in a reasonable tone, kneeling on Rostam's back.

A door down the corridor opened and three infants ran into the corridor.

"Daddy!" cried the smallest one and ran towards him.

"Thank God," said Rostam, as Celia started to stroke his hair. "It's ok, officer. You can get off me now. Everything's ok."

"I'll be the judge of that," said a high, threatening voice. Rostam looked up and saw a thin, pale woman with reading glasses hanging on a chain around her neck. "I'm Lisa and this is my kindergarten. What is going on?"

Rostam was so relieved to see Celia he couldn't stop smiling.

"My daughter's mother dropped her off this morning. It's a family emergency. We need to contact her. Do you have information on where she might be?"

Lisa looked at Celia, still stroking her father's hair, and nodded at the security guard, who clambered off Rostam.

The intercom crackled again.

"It's Celia's grandmother asking for her," came a shout down the corridor.

"You're Maryam's son?" asked Lisa, as Rostam scrambled to his feet.

"Yeah. Sorry about the confusion. Please tell me Celia's Mom's address."

Maryam walked through the door, to see Rostam holding a squirming Celia in his arms, and a smile from Lisa.

"Maryam, your son almost got himself into serious trouble here."

"He's always been trouble."

"Mom, we need to know where Millie is," said Rostam. "McNamara is under arrest, but I didn't like what he was saying. She will have given her new address when she dropped Celia off this morning. They're not gonna tell me."

Maryam looked at her son, and then at Lisa.

"He's telling the truth, Lisa. He's not going to cause any more trouble."

Lisa looked up at the ceiling and made up her mind.

"Everyone at the kindergarten knows where Celia's Mom is staying. We were joking about it. The Plaza Athenee, she told us this morning. Very smart we said, but she was in too much of a hurry to - ."

"It's on the upper East Side. I'm on it."

Rostam handed Celia over to her grandmother and sprinted down the stairs. This time there was a taxi outside. Rostam called the hotel, his hand shaking with the stop-start of the cab and adrenaline. Knowing Celia was safe was half the battle.

"Plaza Athenee, how can I help you?"

"Put me through to Millie James's room."

He was put straight through, but the line just rang until the receptionist jacked back in and asked if he wanted to leave a message.

Rostam said no and hung up. Millie might be at an office, but he had no way of knowing. McNamara's organization would either be being scooped up by Tina Waspell's officers, or on the run. If they had a Manhattan office space it would now be deserted, but would any of the stragglers have told Millie what was going on? They'd only just recruited her, and it sounded from McNamara's comments like they had very little use for her. *What had they offered*? Rostam wondered. If they'd asked her to take control of a crypto portfolio, she'd have found it hard to resist. Rostam thought of Spider, dead by the side of the road in Bali. Another individual who thought he was making his own decisions, when he was really a pawn in the hands of the real players.

The cab stopped at temporary road signs on the bridge crossing the lake in Central Park. Rostam stuffed money through the grille and jumped out, spotting winter tourists in Central Park Zoo to his right as he sprinted across the bridge and towards the east side of the park.

The sidewalk was broad enough to run easily through pedestrians and up to the black and gilt art deco frontage of the hotel. Rostam made himself walk fifty meters before he arrived, in the hope of not appearing in a mess for the second time within an hour. He was still breathing heavily and had a sheen of sweat across his forehead that replenished itself every time he wiped it away the cuff of his sweater.

He took a series of deep breaths as he approached the front desk. The woman at the counter wore the demure, felt tweed of the Plaza Athenee, and spoke with a German accent.

"My wife is staying here - Millie James."

"Yes, sir."

"Can you call and let her know I'm here please."

"Certainly, sir."

The woman looked away from Rostam as she called. After thirty seconds she hung up.

"I'm afraid she doesn't seem to be there, sir."

"She might be unwell. Ask housekeeping or security to go and check."

The woman looked to her left to check with a colleague.

Rostam leaned over the desk.

"Look, I'm not asking you to give me her room number or send me up there. I'm asking you to make sure one of your guests is ok. Can you do that for me please? Ask your manager - they'll tell you it's fine."

The young woman disappeared into a backroom. Rostam tasted blood and realized he had bitten his own tongue. Full of nervous energy, he walked to the entrance to the bar. It was still early in the afternoon. There were no drinkers in there, only a clean-shaven young barman discreetly looking at his phone screen behind a row of mixers. Above the fireplace was a huge TV screen with CNN on silent.

NEWSFLASH: read the perpetual rolling bar at the bottom of the screen.

SATOSHI NAKAMOTO UNVEILS HIMSELF

It hadn't taken Tina Waspell's team long to spread the good news.

VICE PRESIDENT GALWAY NAMED IN BLOCKCHAIN EXPOSE

MATTHEW AALEN WITHDRAWS CANDIDACY FOR SEC CHAIR AMID RUMOURS OF IRS INVESTIGATION

The Press Secretary at the White House was busy telling reporters absolutely nothing in a live recording.

CRYPTO COLLAPSE ACCELERATING took its turn, with the screen a sea of red. How long before they found a photograph of Satoshi from when he was known as David Taylor?

Rostam wasn't interested in the news. He walked back to the front desk, where a pair of French men were at station, looking at him with the unfriendly expression of hospitality industry professionals towards someone who wasn't on their approved list. The German woman walked out of the backroom and spotted him. She flushed and looked down at the ground. Rostam rushed up to the desk.

"Miss, did you get through?"

She came over and dropped her voice.

"I'm very sorry, sir. You were right. The door had a do not disturb sign so housekeeping hadn't been in."

Rostam's vision went black. He shook his head.

"What room number?"

The woman looked back at him, unsure.

"What number?" he repeated.

"201," she muttered. "The hotel manager is already there."

Rostam sprints towards the stairs on the right of the lobby, wide maroon carpets with gilt runners up the sides. The stairs fold back on themselves, so there are three short flights between each storey, and for a sickening second Rostam thinks he's gone too far, but there is the placard reading "2", and he's bundled through the suction-pad door and at the end of a corridor at room number 213, and at the end of the corridor is a huddle of people whispering, a cadaverous woman in housekeeping uniform sobbing into her apron, and a security officer looking into the room is saying "Don't often get women like this, normally it's guys,", and Rostam has burst past them into the room, and there is Millie, in her Bloomingdale lilac suit, one shoe fallen off, lying in a parody of the recovery position, eyes open, pool of vomit down her chin and onto the carpet, and the security guard tackles him from behind, and Rostam is saying "It's ok I'm her husband," but he isn't her husband and it isn't ok.

Chapter Seventy-Two

Saturday February 5

Rostam turned off the Zoom Video Preview. He couldn't look at himself.

He willed his leg to stop jumping with adrenaline, acid at the bottom of his stomach telling him to despair. A familiar, unwelcome inner voice telling him it would be worse if his call was answered.

This was the first day since Millie died Rostam hadn't divided entirely between interviews at government agencies and caring for Celia. She was at nursery: the advice was to maintain routine where possible. He had two hours before he had to report there for a session with the paediatric grief counsellor.

He hadn't had the alone time to begin to confront his grief, and he was trying to call someone who had known the same pain for twice as long.

He wanted her to answer.

He didn't want her to answer.

Dana appeared on the screen. The echo of a smile flashed across her lips. Rouge and lipstick only accentuated her pale-as-milk complexion.

"Hiya, Rostam."

Another attempt at a smile.

"Where are you?" asked Rostam.

"West Cork, with my parents. I had to get the girls out of the house. Goldsmiths gave me leave of absence."

"How are Fatimeh and Esmerelda?"

Dana opened her mouth and closed it again. Rostam showed his open palm in apology.

"Stupid question. How are you?"

Dana leaned toward the camera. Rostam could see her make-up had been roughly applied. She was doing what she could to cover up.

"I'll be honest with you," she said. "Every day is a little bit worse."

"I'm so sorry - " began Rostam. He stopped mid-sentence when he saw Dana gently shaking her head.

"Apologies help nobody," she said, "and, anyway, it's not your fault you were Ahmad's best friend."

"Neither of us had any better offers."

Rostam wanted to swallow the words as soon as they were spoken but was overtaken by tears. His entire body shook. He raised a forearm to shield his eyes. When he lowered it again the wool sleeve was coated in tears and snot.

Dana was looking at him, dry-eyed.

"Was Millie just another piece of collateral damage?" she asked.

Rostam cleared the catarrh from the base of his throat.

"Different, not that it helps. Millie was killed because she could have made a good witness. Ahmad was just in the wrong place. Both would be alive today if I hadn't involved them."

Rostam leaned towards the screen. He couldn't read Dana' expression. He waited for her to speak.

"Don't indulge yourself, Rostam," she said. "Nobody thinks you got Ahmad or Millie killed on purpose." She left a pause. "But they would both be alive without you. There's nothing you can do to make any of it better."

Rostam had nowhere to hide. He felt Dana's pixelated eyes, reconstituted on his screen three thousand miles away, burning into his own. He wanted to put his hands across his face.

"Have you spoken to the British police?" she asked.

"I wanted us to talk first," he said. "I've been grilled by NYPD, the FBI and the IRS all week. They compete with each other, and left the British at the back of the queue, but they'll get to me soon."

"They think it was an extraterritorial strike," said Dana. "You're not a suspect. Though they're not mad about you leaving the country so fast."

"I'll tell them everything,' said Rostam.

"How's Celia?"

"Confused, mostly," said Rostam. "Two weeks ago she was living with Millie in Chicago. Now she's at a preschool in Manhattan, living with Maryam and me. We've told her. I don't think she understands." The tears started again. "I'm not sure if I do either."

He used his dry sleeve to wipe his eyes. When the blur had gone, there were tears coursing down Dana's cheeks.

"We're all getting used to things, one day at a time," she said. "What else is there to do?"

"Do you want to be kept in touch with the investigation here?" asked Rostam. "The media attention is incredible."

"Not interested," said Dana. "Maybe one day in the future you can tell me all about it, but not now."

Rostam nodded.

"Anyway," she said, "I said I'd join Mammy and the girls outside. They're out walking the dog. Best recommendation I can make. You should get one."

Rostam thought of how Maryam would react to having an animal in her apartment.

"I'll ask the boss," he said.

"See you, Rostam. Keep your chin up."

"You too," he said, but Dana had ended the call.

Chapter Seventy-Three

Monday February 14

Live podcast transcript

CRYPTO CONSPIRACY CHICAGO

DREAD: So you are famous now, Rostam. Famous for being wrong.

(Dread laughs. It turns into a cough. Sound of Zippo being sparked and an aggressive, long inhalation. Dread coughs some more.)

Rostam: How do you figure that? We're at eleven million listeners right now, and climbing as we speak.

DREAD: I told you there were dark forces attacking the dollar. You told me - and I quote, dear listeners, 'conspiracy theories are for crazies and children'. Who's crazy now?

Rostam: Ok. So the libertarian right and some of the banking industry got together to use crypto to take control of the financial system. You weren't entirely wrong.

DREAD: Just like JP Morgan using the financial crash of 1907 to bulldoze the Federal Reserve through Congress, Christmas 1913.

Rostam: You know what they say, history doesn't repeat, but it rhymes.

DREAD: What we really want to know, Rostam, is how you convinced Satoshi Nakamoto himself to crash bitcoin. You - one of the biggest fans of bitcoin IN THE WORLD. How did you do it?

Rostam: I didn't do anything. Satoshi decided for himself. This is going to be hard for you to accept, Dread - and listeners, a lot of you too - but Satoshi really is a good man, as well as a brilliant one. You don't believe me, go back and read his White Paper. He never cashed in any of his million coins. They were worth twenty billion US dollars at their peak.

DREAD: What's he gonna do with what he raised selling it all the way down?

Rostam: I doubt he'll tell us but - you ask me - I'd imagine there are some good causes who will come into funds. I'd guess math grants and Japan heritage, but it isn't my money.

DREAD: What changed his mind?

Rostam: Bitcoin was supposed to free individuals from the control of governments, like how the cypherpunks thought email would allow us all to communicate freely. You know what happened to that?

DREAD: Damn FBI can read every thought we have now.

Rostam: That's right. And as soon as bitcoin became valuable, dark forces started to take control. Satoshi saw it happen, tried to work out how to fix it, and decided he couldn't allow his creation to turn rotten.

DREAD: So that's it? Game over for the crypto crew?

Rostam: No way. This will go down as the first, exciting chapter. Someone will come up with a better Crypto 2.0. I'm working with a team who're onto it already.

DREAD: And what's gonna happen to the bad guys this time round?

Rostam: We'll leave that to the courts to decide.

DREAD: We've reached the top of the hour, and just edged over twelve million listeners.

Rostam: This whole episode of the podcast - like all previous, and all to come - can be downloaded from the website, or wherever you get your podcasts. From Dread and me, it's over and out. Just remember everyone - do your own research.

Rostam pushed the red record button. Dread stubbed out his cigarette, and lit another.

"You sure that thing is off? I'm always paranoid, man," said Dread.

"You're right to be paranoid, about this at least. It's off."

"What's gonna happen to McNamara?"

Rostam tilted back his chair. "Defendants with influence and money often get off, right? But I think the IRS has him pretty good on the tax stuff. And the investigation in his SuperPac will go on a long time. The staff have pretty much gone."

"And the bankers?"

"Top brass at Loeb has already changed. Cantillon won't be working in mainstream banking again. Nor will the heads of two of the other firms. They really lost their heads. Working in regulated industries. They must have thought nothing could be traced. Money, man - it can really mess with the head."

"The Iranian connection?"

"Zadi is back in Tehran. He escaped London no problem. They're a nest of vipers over there, just like here. Maybe the hard liners get the better of him, or maybe he'll be able to show the Supreme Leader just how many of them were in league with McNamara from all the data Satoshi gave us."

Dread blew a long plume of smoke into the dark room of their recording studio.

"Anything gonna be proved about Millie?"

A long pause.

"I don't think so. No evidence for the police to use. And - before you start complaining - the police did their job. Young mothers don't kill themselves in fancy hotel suites. But even if they find the killer, they'll never track it back to McNamara."

"Your little girl?"

"She's got her grandma and me. Three-year-olds aren't big on telling you their feelings. God knows what griefs she'll be telling her therapist about later. I can't help but feel it's my fault, you know. Millie only got dragged into it because of me, no matter what she said."

"It's your grief, man. I'm not gonna argue with you. You gonna rebuild your life over in New York?"

"Time for a fresh start. Celia and my Mom are in a love affair only a criminal would break up. And we ain't gonna run out of conspiracies to explode anytime soon."

Dread leaned over to clink coffee cups with Rostam.

"True dat, my man."

THE END

Afterwords

Bitcoin is a remarkable work of imagination - an attempt to remake the world's financial system, without intermediaries. So remarkable, in fact, one might compare it to a religious concept and, in keeping with the early days of many religions, it has attracted a series of manias and perversions.

This novel is a work of fiction, but all the background information on Bitcoin is accurate. I'm not going to list the main sources, because they are largely blue chip investment firms who would not like their research used in fiction, but the names of individuals who have been particularly helpful are listed in the acknowledgements.

The FT journalist Jemima Kelly has been a source of good sense in an extraordinary sector. I also listened to many podcasts on both crypto and conspiracies, though Rostam and Dread's show is the only one I know which explicitly takes on both subjects at the same time. I'm not going to list the podcasts, simply because I don't want to increase the quantity of disinformation in the world.

The sorry morality tale of Sam Bankman-Fried and BTX played out in real time while I was writing this novel. Indeed, at a time when BTX was valued at above $30bn, Spider had a conference call with a character loosely based on Bankman-Fried. Sadly for all concerned, reality has caught up with BTX, and I therefore took it out of the book. Enthusiasts of the intersection between crypto and theft will recognise that Betty Dai's Axie Infinity bridge heist took place in March 2022, which is an anachronism, as the events in novel take place between January 11 and February 14 of that year. Oops.

Much time has been spent attempting to identify the *real* Satoshi Nakamoto. I am sorry to say I don't know who he, she or they are...but the quality of coding and Anglicisms in the White Paper make an elderly English technologist a plausible, if entirely imaginary, candidate.

Satoshi's White Paper did appear on Halloween 2008, and it included quotations from the UK newspaper The Guardian, in which the then Chancellor of the Exchequer, Alastair Darling, explained quantitative easing in very simple terms. To my knowledge, no other major financial figure in modern history has made public the magical nature of money in quite such a fashion. It can be no coincidence that it was as people realised the illusory (one might say 'fictional') properties of money that an alternative system was created.

There are several non-fiction books about this subject - all too current for me to wade into criticism here - but it seems to me a subject well suited to story telling. The crucial plot point of Satoshi embedding extranonces to track the activity of the Bitcoin 64 is taken from an Cornell academic report, 'Cooperation among an anonymous group protected Bitcoin during failures of decentralization'. I have taken considerable liberties with this report, which has a number of authors: Alyssa Blackburn, Christoph Huber, Yossi Eliaz, Muhammad S. Shamim, David Weisz, Goutham Seshadri, Kevin Kim, Shengqi Hang, Erez Lieberman Aiden. I hope they will forgive the latitude taken for the purposes of this novel.

While the spirit of 'The Hunt for Satoshi' is quite different to the following books of sci-fi/speculative fiction, I owe a debt to Neal Stephenson's 'Cryptonomicon', William Gibson's 'Pattern Recognition' and especially Vernor Vinge's 'True Names'. The latter was packaged with a collection of relevant essays with an introduction by Hari Kunzru in 2016. For anyone interested in the origins and philosophy of crypto, I'd suggest starting with those essays.

Rostam and Satoshi were both mathematicians before they were cryptologists. The books I most enjoyed reading while putting myself inside their heads were Piers Bizony's 'Atom', Apostolos Doxiadis' 'Logicomix' and 'Uncle Petros and the Goldbach Conjecture' (fellow fans will notice Goldbach's Conjecture making a cameo appearance in this novel), 'The Man Who Loved Only Numbers' by Paul Hoffman, 'The Music of the Primes' by Marcus du Sautoy, and the peerless 'A Mathematician's Apology' by GH Hardy. The amazing Maryam Mirzakhani features in the novel as the hero of both Rostam and his Mom, Maryam. The best resource about her life and work (for those of us who can't aspire to understand her work itself) is the documentary 'Secrets of the Surface'.

There are more speakers of American than British English in this novel (as well as Japanese, Balinese, Canadian, Irish and Iranian). Nevertheless, home bias made me decide on English spellings. I hope it isn't too jarring. If it is, please let me know.

The Iranians Maryam, Zadi and Hosein use a variety of common Farsi vocabulary - *junam* (my dear), *kuchaloo* (darling), *taarof* (a system of etiquette), *bori-kalor* (well done).

If a novel can be said to have a point, this one's is to tell the story of Rostam and Millie. However if, after reading the book, you'd like to debate any of the issues within it, please sign up for Arlo's reader club on arlofoxauthor.com. I promise to respond.

Acknowledgements

Arlo Fox lives in the UK with his wife and four children. This novel is dedicated to his wife.

Arlo would love to hear from you.

Please join his readers' club at www.arlofoxauthor.com.

Reviews power book sales. Whether you loved this story, hated it, or would have liked a different ending, please tell people about it on Amazon and/or Goodreads.

Like Tom, the AI powering Rostam's autonomous car journey to Lake Shore Drive, I have so many people to thank it would make an Oscar winner blush. Then again, if shame was a dominant characteristic, I'd never have published a novel.

Special thanks go to #teamsatoshi: cover designer Deb Thompson www.debthompsondesign.com, website designer Nick Dockerty ht tps://improve-seo.co.uk/, and my editor, Jennifer Robinson.

The following people have helped by reading extracts, entire former drafts, offering guidance, research on Bitcoin, or just been stand-up friends. Seeing a novel go through twelve drafts and innumerable tweaks is an exhausting spectator sport. More words have been discarded than made it to this final edit, and some of the people on this list were prepared to read most of them. Thanks to all.

Russell Allen, Bill Bailey, Julija Boulton, Huw Bowen, Paul Budd, Afonso Campos, Liz Chettur, Alisa Cromer, Andy Conway, Mary Durndell, Bex Eastwell, James Flint, Richard Gati, Liz Good, Chris Keogh, Patrick Kincaid, Paul Krake, Tony Lindsell, Roxana Marie, Breda Murphy, Jill Owen, Kristen Pedroja, Jennifer Robinson, Hilary Scott, Mansoor Sheikh, Robert Smithson, Oscar Stainton, Andrew Stead, Deborah Thompson, Lindsay Virgilio, James Vogl, Ben Waller, Matthew Wigington, Peter Wigington, Sarah Wigington, Christopher Y ates.

Printed in Great Britain
by Amazon

33748932R00218